THE DRAGON PORTAL SERIES

FACETS OF POWER

BOOK 3

JAMIE A. WATERS

Cover Art: Deranged Doctor Design
Editor: Novel Nurse Editing

ISBN: 978-1-949524-23-9 (Hardback Edition)
ISBN: 978-1-949524-22-2 (Paperback Edition)
ISBN: 978-1-949524-20-8 (eBook Edition)

Library of Congress Control Number: 2020903204
First Edition *October 2020

ACKNOWLEDGMENTS

I want to say thank you to the people who helped make this book possible.

To Jenn, Adrienne, Meg, and all the other wonderful and inspiring writers who are part of Writer's Retreat, I'd like to say a huge thank you for all the countless hours of writing sprints, Zoom and Discord chats, and kick-in-the-butt motivation pep talks. Let's face it; 2020 has sucked some major donkey nuts but you guys have helped keep me sane. You rock!

Jenn, I can't tell you how much I appreciate you reading the earliest versions of this book and giving me so much encouragement. You've been my cheerleader and confidant for the past year, and I can't tell you how much I value your friendship. You've got one of the best hearts of anyone I've ever met. Don't ever lose that special spark.

I'd also like to say a HUGE thank you to my wonderful and amazing sister, Tracy, who not only reads several versions of my books and tells me who to kill off (*snicker*), but also acts as my compass in life. Without you, I never would have found my way to the person I am today. I feel blessed to not only have you as a sister but also as my best friend. I love you to pieces, Tracy. Thank you for supporting me on this journey and for everything you do.

Mom, I don't even have words to express my gratitude for everything you've done. Not only do you attend every single one of my signing events, but you also read countless versions of my books and help make them so much better. Your feedback is invaluable, and you're so amazingly supportive. I mean, how many moms call you up and critique your latest sex scene? LOL One day soon, we're going on another trip together for more writing "inspiration"... and maybe more of that Italian wine. ;)

I also have to thank my amazing editors, Angie and Janna. You guys have taught me so much. I'd also like to say a huge thank you to the incredibly talented artists at Deranged Doctor Design. I've been working with you for several years now, and I'm constantly blown away by how you can capture the essence of my characters the way you do. You're true wizards.

But the biggest amount of gratitude goes to YOU, my readers. You're the reason why I write. Several months ago, I started having carpal tunnel pain in my wrists and had to push back the release date of this book by a month. I was worried about making people angry, but the outpouring of love, support, and understanding I received was overwhelming. Thank you so much for your emails and Facebook messages. I can't tell you how touched I was by all your comments. I read every single one (and tried to respond to as many as possible), and even went through a box of tissues in the process. You guys are truly amazing, and I feel so fortunate to have such incredible people reading my stories.

Thank you from the bottom of my heart! This story is for you.

THE DRAGON PORTAL SERIES

FACETS OF POWER

To Kill a Fae
By Blood and Magic
Facets of Power
Shadows and Twilight
Dance of Wings
Forest of Secrets

Chapter One

"Land ho!"

The lookout's shout reverberated throughout the ship. Sabine's hands tightened on the railing, and she turned to stare out across the poisoned sea. The wind whipped her hair away from her face, carrying a hint of the burnt metallic scent of corrupted magic. It had been growing stronger the farther south they traveled. She tried to ignore it, just as she'd been doing for the past two weeks.

She'd wanted to visit the home of the dwarves ever since she'd been a child, but not in these conditions. The merfolk's warning to avoid the southern lands still weighed heavily in her mind. No one knew what was killing those who traveled south, but the lack of sea creatures and birds was troubling. If their mission to seal the Dragon Portal wasn't critical, Sabine would have agreed to heed the merfolk's warning.

The ship changed headings, moving through the water toward their destination. Malek, the charismatic dragon who masqueraded as a ship captain, called instructions to his crew in preparation for making landfall. She instinctively turned to watch him, captivated by the way sunlight danced upon his golden skin and how it contrasted with his dark hair. She paused, aware she was staring but not willing to look away just yet. Gods. He was beautiful.

Malek moved across the deck with a quiet strength and grace, every gesture reinforcing his competency and command. Even now, she had to stop herself from going to his side. She'd been drawn to him and the power contained within him since almost the first moment they met, but this incessant need seemed to grow with every moment they spent together.

Sabine's heart thudded in her chest, and she forced herself to turn back toward the sea. Even through their shared bond, she could sense Malek intimately. It was rather unnerving and more than a little distracting. Pushing aside her unease, she decided it would be better to focus on their imminent arrival to the dwarven city. At least that should be safer than fantasizing about a dragon shapeshifter. They were the sworn enemy of her people, no matter how much she'd already grown to care about him.

In the distance and rapidly approaching, she caught sight of the mountainous landscape that was their intended destination. The tips of the mountains' peaks disappeared into the cloud cover, but the true heart of the dwarven city was nestled within the mountain. She'd heard there were ways into Razadon other than this remote peninsula, but no one except the dwarves had hope of finding the hidden entrances.

"Well, little one, it looks like we'll be in Razadon before nightfall," Bane said and leaned against the railing beside her.

Sabine smiled up at her demon protector before turning back toward the sea. "It's been a long time coming."

"That it has," Bane said in agreement, placing his clawed hand over hers and squeezing it gently. He siphoned off a trace of her magic, infusing her power with his own. It was enough to cement his ties to the surface for the time being. Without her acting as an anchor to keep him above ground, Bane would be forced back into the demonic underworld.

"You must be cautious, little one," Bane warned in a low voice. "The moment you step foot on land, any sign of weakness will be used against you. To survive whatever your family has planned, you need allies. The dwarves may help tip the balance in your favor, but you must force them to treat you as the power you intend to be."

"We're here to ensure the Dragon Portal remains sealed, not to play political games," she reminded him with a frown. "My family will have to wait. We have other priorities."

"*My* priority happens to be keeping you alive. It should be yours as well."

She arched her brow, somewhat surprised he was so dismissive of the warnings they'd received about problems in the southern lands. "Has the stench of corrupted magic blinded more than your nose?"

Bane snorted. "No more than the dragon has blinded you to the precariousness of your situation. You've been spending your days making eyes at him, instead of making plans to solidify your throne. Your family still wants you dead." He paused, his expression turning to one of cold calculation. "You claimed you weren't interested in whoring yourself for the dragon's alliance, but it's proven an effective tactic. Do you intend to have him burn the Silver Forest around your homeland to the ground? I'm sure he would, especially if you take him to your bed again."

Her back went ramrod straight at the insult, and her magic flared to the surface. She glared at Bane, barely resisting the urge to wipe away his smug expression. "How dare you—"

She paused when Bane's lips twitched in amusement. He

looked rather pleased with himself. She narrowed her eyes at him and scowled. Demons could be incredibly infuriating. Sometimes Bane tried to rile her up just to get a reaction. He'd taught her a great deal of self-control, but it was still annoying.

"I hate it when you do that," she muttered and turned back toward the sea. She focused on her breathing, using a mental exercise to calm her magic. "I know what's at stake, and I'll deal with my family soon enough. We have more critical matters to focus on right now."

Bane chuckled. "Indeed, but you need to get used to hearing such things. Others will make the same comments or worse, and you need to be prepared. The queen of the Unseelie does not apologize for her actions nor explain her choice in bedmates. Do not allow your doubts or affection for the dragon deter you from your true purpose. You *must* embrace your birthright, Sabine. The time for hiding is in the past."

Sabine swallowed her misgivings, knowing her demon protector was right. She straightened her shoulders and gave Bane a curt nod. The dwarves, like the demons, were one of the original races and most closely allied with the Unseelie Fae. If she had any hope in formalizing an agreement with them, she needed to give the impression she was approaching them from a position of power and not of desperation.

Rika, the human seer Sabine had agreed to look after, ran across the ship toward them. Her dark braided hair flew behind her, the style a testament to Blossom's influence. The pixie was leading the girl's charge, a near constant companion to the teenager since they'd left Karga. Sabine had caught the two of them laughing and conspiring among themselves on more than one occasion.

Bane frowned in disapproval. "That flying bug is teaching

the girl some bad habits. I caught Rika distracting the crew earlier, while Blossom hid worms in the sailors' bunks. You should consider separating them before the pixie gets your seer into trouble."

Sabine's mouth quirked in a smile, not terribly surprised by the news. "Don't let Blossom hear you calling her a bug again, or you'll be the target of their next prank. Besides, don't think I haven't noticed you've grown rather fond of both of them. You'll keep them out of the worst trouble."

Bane harrumphed but didn't dispute her words. Although Rika had initially been wary of the demon, she'd quickly taken to him and begun seeking him out at every opportunity. Bane might not ever admit it, but he seemed to enjoy her company too. It hadn't taken long for Rika to become a welcome addition to their makeshift family.

"We're almost there!" Blossom shouted and landed on Sabine's shoulder. "Rika's going to help me look for plants, and Esme's gonna build a drying rack for us. Then we can bring even more plants with us when we leave!"

Rika grinned and nodded. "Esme's helping Levin organize crates in the hold right now so we can take them ashore to trade with the dwarves. She was teaching me about some of the dried herbs she has and what they're used for. She promised to show me how to make some of her teas."

Bane grimaced. "I would suggest you have someone else show you how to craft teas, little seer. Or just gargle some seawater instead. It might taste better."

Sabine jabbed her elbow into Bane's side. He narrowed his eyes at her, but she simply smiled up at him. Esmelle was a talented part-dryad witch, but her creations were hit or miss. The witch might be well versed in an herb's medicinal effects, but she failed to grasp the subtle nuances of complementary flavors.

Unfortunately, Bane hadn't forgotten the last time he'd tried one of her experiments. He'd spat it out and accused Esmelle of trying to poison him, which had resulted in the witch throwing the entire teapot at his horned head before storming off. Not for the first time, Sabine had needed to wade in and smooth things over between them. Although, she secretly agreed with Bane; that particular brew had been one of Esmelle's worst.

"Oh, look! The dwarves made those, didn't they?" Rika leaned over the railing to point out what appeared to be large monuments far in the distance.

Sabine smiled at the seer's enthusiasm, pleased Rika was adjusting to leaving her home behind. She was still melancholy at times, but Rika's natural optimism usually won out. Being around the cheerful pixie had helped, and Blossom relished having a new friend who embraced her brand of mischief.

Looking in the direction Rika indicated, Sabine could make out the shape of tall stone obelisks, which served as markers for traveling ships. They were still too far away to make out any details, but it was clear they weren't natural.

"I believe so," Sabine said. "Malek mentioned they help identify the location of the docks for any approaching ships. I've heard the dwarves infuse magic into the stone, similar to the way the Fae use their forests to enhance their power."

Bane leaned against the railing again. "The dwarves prefer using crystals. The stone won't hold a magical charge nearly as long. If we were approaching at night, you'd see each of those stones topped with a crystal that can glow as brightly as the sun. That mountain would also be lit up like a beacon. They have crystal windows embedded in the stone that reflects the light from their lanterns inside their homes."

Rika's eyes widened. "Have you been to Razadon before, Bane?"

"A few times, little seer," he admitted, scanning the beach

with a frown. "Never by this entrance though. My brethren use the underground tunnels."

Something in Bane's voice caught Sabine's attention, and she studied her demon protector carefully. His shoulders had tensed, and the corded muscles of his arms were rigid. His amber eyes hadn't shifted to silver, but his midnight-toned skin pulsed with a bluish glow, a sign he was performing magic. She looked in the direction he was staring, but she couldn't tell what had caught his attention.

Placing her hand on Bane's arm to supplement his power, Sabine asked, "What is it?"

He absently covered her hand with his and accepted her magical offering, but he didn't tear his gaze away from the mountain peninsula. "I expected more of a dwarven presence at the docks. I don't sense any living creatures in that direction."

Sabine's smile faded. She leaned forward and scanned the coastline, but they were too far away to make out any details. She trusted Bane's abilities, but she desperately hoped he was wrong. The dwarves wouldn't have retreated into their mountain home unless things were dire.

The sky over the mountain range had changed from the deep blue of daytime to an eerie greenish color. Lightning flashed in the distance, almost directly over the mountain range.

Sabine frowned, her heart pounding in her chest. Something wasn't right. The goddess's symbol on her wrist warmed, almost in warning. Sabine glanced down, and her eyes widened. The chalice mark was alternating between flashing silver and gold, the magical glow breaking through her strongest glamour. She touched it, and lightning streaked across the sky again. It was resonating with the approaching storm.

Bane looked at her wrist. "What in the underworld? You're not doing that, are you?"

"Bad magic," Blossom shrieked, fluttering her wings in agitation. "It's bad magic, Sabine! The goddess said her gift's been corrupted. She's really angry."

Bane frowned at Blossom. "Speak, bug. What did the goddess say? Her exact words. Now."

Blossom crossed her arms over her chest and glared at Bane. "You're not the boss of me, and I'm *not* a bug. Take it back or I'll dust you!"

Sabine muttered a curse under her breath. Great. The gauntlet had been thrown. The demon would have worms in his bunk before nightfall, or even worse. But he was right about needing to know exactly what Lachlina had said. Blossom was the only one who could communicate directly with the renegade goddess in her makeshift prison.

"Blossom, what did the goddess—" Sabine stated, faltering at the sight of Bane's eyes shifting to silver and the sound of his low, throaty growl. *Damn.* She didn't need him to lose control on top of everything else.

"Bane?" Sabine asked in a soft voice, continuing to focus on the demon and mentally willing Bane to get control of himself. Allowing her power to build, she placed her hand on his arm and studied him carefully for any sign he was preparing to attack. There were too many humans around, and many of them were already wary of the magical passengers aboard the ship.

Rika worried her bottom lip but remain silent, her eyes darting back and forth between Bane and Sabine. It spoke to Rika's level of trust that she hadn't run away from an angry demon and a power-infused Fae.

Blossom's eyes widened, and her dust shifted to red. "He's gonna try to eat me, Sabine!"

"Blossom, stop," Sabine ordered, not tearing her gaze away from Bane. "He won't eat you."

"Maybe not, but I'll pluck the bug's wings off her body if she doesn't start talking," Bane said with a growl, gripping the railing tightly enough Sabine was surprised it remained intact. At least his eyes had shifted back to their normal amber color, a sign he was back in control. Sabine relaxed a fraction and released his arm.

Determined to stop this situation from escalating any further, Sabine said, "Enough. Both of you. We don't have time for this."

Without waiting for a response, she lifted her hand and sent a soft wave of reassuring magic over Blossom. Bane huffed with impatience, but Sabine ignored him. Until Blossom was able to focus on their questions and her dust was no longer tinged in red, they wouldn't be able to get any information out of the pixie.

"He won't hurt you, Blossom, but you need to stop provoking him. Now tell us what Lachlina said."

Blossom hesitated only for a moment. "The goddess wants you to stop whoever's doing bad magic. She says if you don't, you're not protecting the land like you agreed. We have to get to shore right away, or she'll use your bonds with Malek and Bane to stop them herself. Sabine, you can't let her hurt people again!"

Sabine froze, a sick feeling creeping in her stomach. After Lachlina had slaughtered dozens of human hunters using Sabine's power, Sabine had managed to elicit an agreement with the renegade goddess not to use the bonds she'd forged with Bane and Malek. If Lachlina set her mind to it, she could use them to kill thousands. If Sabine had a chance to stop it from happening, she needed to do whatever was necessary. Lachlina didn't make idle threats.

Sabine turned toward Rika and ordered, "Rika, run and join Esmelle and Levin in the hold. Tell Esme to put up her strongest warding to protect everyone down there. Don't come out until I tell you it's safe."

Rika's eyes widened, and she nodded. She turned on her heel and fled toward the ladder on the far side of the deck.

Blossom fluttered her wings against Sabine's neck and said, "I can help too, Sabine! What should I do?"

The wind changed directions and brought with it a biting cold and an even stronger stench of corrupted magic. The green tinge in the sky was spreading rapidly outward, chasing away the memory of the pleasant day. They only had minutes until whatever was happening overcame the ship. No matter what, they needed to protect the humans on board from Lachlina's threat and the impending storm. Malek, Bane, and Blossom should be safe enough, thanks to their shared bond with Sabine, but everyone else was in danger. Humans didn't have the same resistance to foreign magic.

"Use our bond. Share my power with Esme to fuel the ward and then find me," Sabine said, gesturing for Blossom to take flight. The pixie launched into the air, leaving a stream of glittering pixie dust as she chased after Rika.

Sabine ran across the deck to where Malek was standing. She could only see him in profile, but his expression was pensive as he stared up at the sky. He turned at her approach, and his eyes warmed when he spotted her. His gaze roamed over her features, his smile fading almost immediately.

Malek took a step toward her and asked, "Is it the storm?"

"Yes," she said quickly, gesturing toward the approaching clouds. "It's not natural, but it's unlike any magic I've seen before. The goddess says it's been corrupted. We have to somehow get to land and stop whoever's doing this, or Lachlina is threatening to use our combined power to do it herself. I don't know if we can keep your crew safe if she uses our bond, Malek. You have to get them down in the hold and away from us. Esme's creating a ward to protect them."

He looked in the direction of the storm again, his jaw tightening in silent fury. He pressed his hand gently against her midsection and turned her back toward Bane. "Do not allow anything to happen to her."

Without waiting for a response, Malek leaned over the railing to the deck below and shouted, "Lower the sails and get below deck. All of you! Now!"

As Malek continued issuing instructions, Bane grabbed Sabine's arm and said, "If this goes bad, I'm locking you in your cabin. I don't trust that storm, and I damned well don't trust *her*."

"You and me both," Sabine agreed, pulling away from him and taking a step toward the railing. The crew was rushing around, hastening to obey Malek's orders. She ignored them, her attention on the sky overhead. In between where the natural blue sky met the eerie greenish glowing cloud, there was a silver lining with flashes of gold. It was similar to the pulsing colors of the chalice on her skin.

"What do you see, little one?"

"Jagged edges," she murmured, surprised by the cloud cover. They appeared almost sharp, cutting into the blue of the sky. She absently touched her wrist, feeling the chalice mark pulse slightly out of sync with the flashes of color in the sky.

She tilted her head and took a deep breath, trying to determine what her instincts were telling her. There was a hint of both Fae and merfolk magic in the air, but also something else too. It was lacking somehow, crude in its design and inelegant compared to her magic.

She shivered, her breath creating patchy fog in the air. The temperature was rapidly dropping. Bane wrapped his arm around her, his body heat warding against the worst of the chill. A light dusting of snow began to fall, and her eyes widened. It shouldn't be possible. Summer was nearly upon them. Neither the dwarves nor the merfolk had such power. Other races had a bastardized version of the ability to manipulate the weather, but she hadn't thought they could create winter. Only a Fae from one of the royal lines had the power to completely change the seasons, and such magic had a terrible cost.

Sabine held out her hand and caught a snowflake on her palm. It was cold to the touch, but it looked different somehow. Wrong. Her eyes narrowed as she studied it. "It's snow and something else. What is that?"

"Ash?" Bane frowned, leaning closer to look at it. "No. It looks like a piece of a dwarven crystal, frozen over with magic." He lifted his head to stare upward. "There must be millions of pieces. What the hell are they doing under that mountain?"

The crystals were falling heavier now. She turned and saw them coating the deck of the ship with what appeared to be an icy mixture of sleet and shattered crystals. Not even the freezing chill could ward against the stench of tainted magic. If anything, it had become stronger with the appearance of the falling crystals.

She turned to warn Malek, but most of the crew had already disappeared from the deck. Only a few were still rushing to secure their workstations before retreating to the hold. She took a step toward Malek but halted abruptly at a strangled cry from above. One of the men fell from the rigging, and his body hit the deck with a sickening thud.

Sabine gasped in horror as the man's body spasmed. It

was Eshon, one of Malek's most skilled riggers. She'd seen him scamper up the ropes in the most vicious of storms without losing his footing. It had to be the tainted snowfall. Nothing else could have made him fall.

She started to go to him, but Bane hauled her against him. He wrapped his arms around her in a protective gesture. She was too startled to even think about protesting. Malek shouted something and ran over to check on his fallen sailor. From the twisted angles of Eshon's jerking limbs, it didn't look good.

Sabine managed a shaky breath and whispered, "Bane?"

"No, little one. His mind is mostly gone. His body will linger in pain an hour or two more, but no longer. With your permission, I will end it."

She squeezed her eyes shut, wishing there had been some shred of hope. "Release him."

Bane's arms tightened around her. He lifted his hand, curling his fingers into a fist. He yanked hard at an invisible line, and the man's body went still. Sabine sensed the man's ebbing life force surround Bane before the demon absorbed it. There was an undeniable beauty in the mercy Bane had shown Eshon, but few would ever see the demon as anything other than a killer.

Malek lifted his head to meet Bane's eyes and gave him a curt nod. It wasn't exactly gratitude, but there was respectful understanding despite their differences. Underneath, it was impossible to miss the regret on Malek's features. He took his duties as captain seriously, and the loss of any of his crew hit him hard.

She swallowed, watching as Malek and Gardine, one of Malek's other crewmen, lifted Eshon's body and carried it to the side of the ship. Eshon would be given to the sea in the time-honored tradition of most sailors, but it wasn't an easy thing to witness. Bane continued to hold her tightly against him, his body trembling slightly. It always took Bane a few minutes to regain control of his instincts whenever he claimed a life in such a manner. Sabine relaxed against him, telling him without words she would stay with him to keep him centered.

Falling snow and shattered crystals continued to coat the ship in a heavy blanket. Malek surrendered Eshon's body to the waves and then turned to face her. Through their metaphysical connection, she could sense his pain and sense of loss. She held his eyes, and he headed directly for her as though drawn by some invisible force.

Taken aback by the fierce hunger in his predatory gaze, Sabine asked, "Malek?"

"*Mine*," he snarled and yanked her away from Bane.

She stiffened, shocked by his declaration. "I am *not* yo—"

Malek thrust his hand in her hair, lowered his head, and kissed her as though she were the air he needed to survive. She gasped, and he swept in, claiming her with his mouth and surrounding her with his heated draconic magic. The chill was swept away, and despite her intentions, her body softened against his. Some part of her knew this behavior wasn't normal, but she wasn't quite sure how to extricate herself without harming him. Dragons were possessive, but Malek had always respected her boundaries before.

Bane hissed and then launched himself at Malek, shoving Sabine aside and into the railing. A sharp pain lanced through her side at the impact, and she winced.

The dragon shapeshifter and demon rolled across the deck, lashing out at one another with dizzying speed and ferocity. They moved in a blur, far too fast to ever be confused with being human. Gardine froze in shock at the display, but Sabine couldn't pay the crewman any attention.

The two fighting idiots were going to kill each other while the storm was nearly upon them.

"Enough!" she shouted, infusing her voice with enough power to send a shockwave through the air. Bane and Malek slid along the deck from the force of her power but continued fighting. They swiped at each other, their fists pummeling with purpose as their magic built in a frenzied display. Something wasn't right. Bane always responded to her magic, but he had brushed it off as though it were of no consequence. Such a thing had never happened before.

She stared at her hands and released her glamour. If she needed to engage her full power to stop them without killing them, she couldn't afford to be shackled by the restraints of her illusion magic. But without Bane or Malek to shield her, her family would know her location as soon as she performed major magic. She had no illusions about her inability to outrun the Wild Hunt a third time.

Malek's skin began to glow, a sign he was about to shift into dragon form. Her eyes widened. She had to stop him before his weight capsized the ship and killed them all. They were officially out of options. She'd have to take the chance they could make it to Razadon before the Wild Hunt made their appearance.

She grabbed Gardine's arm and yelled, "Get to the hold and under the warding. Now!"

Her voice broke through his shock, and he turned in that direction. Green lightning flashed in the sky, striking the sea near the ship. Gardine staggered and fell to the ground with a sickening thud. Like Eshon, he began twitching violently. She stared in horror at his fallen body and then up at the storm.

Blossom came barreling out of the hold, flinging glittering red pixie dust in every direction. She screamed, "It's the storm, Sabine! It's claimed Malek and Bane! The goddess says to use your bond to break the magic over them."

Sabine didn't respond, having already come to that realization. May the gods protect all of them.

She withdrew her knife and sliced it across her palm, the pain sharp and biting. Her blood dripped upon the deck, and she used the power from her sacrifice to fuel her magic. The wind whipped around her wildly, stealing her breath from the icy chill.

"By blood and magic, I command the elements to attend me," she shouted to the heavens. The silver markings etched on her skin glowed with a strange light, syncing with the flashes of lightning in the sky. Whatever had fueled this strange storm had originally been the magic of the Fae but was twisted somehow, almost beyond recognition.

The snowfall became even heavier, shifting to a mixture of icy rain as her power warred against the foreign magic. The temperature was still dropping, making it difficult to take a full breath. Ice formed along the railings, but even the deepening chill didn't stop Malek and Bane from their battle. Blossom had zipped over to hover near them, shouting at them to stop. They ignored the tiny pixie and crashed against the center mast. Nearby crates toppled over, spilling their contents across the deck.

Raw magic, dark and sensual, swirled around her as she tapped into the power at her command. She lifted her head and closed her eyes, reaching outward with her awareness. The thin bonds connecting her to Malek and Bane visualized in her mind's eye, but they had frozen and turned brittle from the magical cold. Even her connection with Blossom had been affected. The corrupted magic threatened to fracture her link to her allies, separating her from those she trusted.

No. This could not and would not be. These bonds were

hers to command, and she refused to allow them to fracture unless *she* willed it.

Sabine opened her eyes and thrust out her hands, unleashing a tremendous blast of magic. It ripped through their bonds, shattering the ice clinging to them and infusing them with heat and power. The force ricocheted through Malek, Bane, and even Blossom. Malek and Bane were thrust apart and slid across the deck to the front of the ship. Blossom squeaked and landed facedown on a nearby crate, her wings twitching.

Sabine rushed to the pixie and scooped her up, checking for any damage to her sensitive and fragile wings. "Blossom? Are you all right?"

Blossom rolled over with a silly grin on her face and flung out her hand. "Wheee! That was even better than drinking from the magic spring. Let's do that again, Sabine!"

Sabine let out a relieved breath and slipped the pixie into her pocket. It would take her a little while to recover, but at least Blossom hadn't been hurt. Picking her way carefully across the frozen deck, she approached Bane and Malek. They were both regaining their bearings, but the effects from their battle was evident. Malek's shirt had been sliced to ribbons from Bane's claws, and Bane's dark blood dripped down the side of his face. Malek had a particularly colorful bruise forming on his jaw, but he appeared mostly unharmed.

Bane climbed to his feet. He leaned heavily against the icy railing for a moment and then staggered toward her. He wrapped his arms around her and siphoned off some of her power with his touch. His body relaxed as he stabilized himself. "Did I hurt you when I pushed you away from me, little one?"

"I'll be fine," she said, the pain in her side a minor annoyance compared to his injuries.

Sabine lifted her hand and wiped away some of the blood dripping down the side of his face, using her touch to send another wave of magic over him. For anyone else, his blood was poison, but she was immune to its effects. His injury knit itself together, one of the benefits from Bane's particular type of power. It was difficult to kill a demon, and his ties to Sabine gave his already remarkable power a significant boost.

Bane slid his hand under her shirt and pressed against her injured side where she'd hit the railing.

She grabbed his wrist and shook her head. "Healing me isn't necessary. Conserve your power until we're safe."

Bane frowned but didn't argue, a sign he was still out of sorts.

Malek ran his hand over his hair and then shook his head as though trying to clear it. "What in the name of the underworld was *that*? I didn't… shit, Sabine. I'm sorry. I didn't hurt you, did I?"

Sabine turned toward Malek, who was leaning against the railing. She scanned him up and down, but he appeared less impacted than Bane. The conflicted expression on his face worried her. She closed the distance between them, unwilling to let him think she was upset with him.

"No, you didn't hurt me," she said softly, looking up at him. "The corrupted magic was affecting our bond. I had to flood you with power to clear it. Are *you* all right?"

Malek didn't answer right away. His gaze fell on Gardine's body, and a flash of regret crossed his face.

Her heart went out to him. "Malek? Talk to me."

He scrubbed his hands over his face. "The rage. It wasn't normal. I almost shifted. I could have killed everyone on board if you hadn't stopped me. Dammit. What the hell is going on? I haven't lost control like that since I was a child."

Sabine frowned and shook her head. "I don't know, but

we need to get to land right away. Everyone on board the ship is in danger. I'm not sure why I'm not being affected, but it might have something to do with the goddess marking me."

Malek's expression turned thoughtful. "Does Blossom know why you're immune?"

Sabine gestured to her pocket where the pixie was snoring loudly. "She passed out, so I can't ask. I had to flood all my connections with power, and Blossom was affected too. We need to get inside the mountain right away. I wasn't shielded when I used major magic. My family knows where I am."

Bane growled and flexed his clawed hands. "The cowards won't come themselves. They'll hide behind assassins or the Wild Hunt."

Sabine met his silvered gaze and shivered, both from the cold and the fear that rushed through her. "Yes, but the Wild Hunt can't pursue us into Razadon. As long as we're not under the open sky, we should be somewhat safe. I'm hoping the dwarves will honor their agreement with the Unseelie and provide us with sanctuary until we can figure out what to do. We need to get to shore."

Bane lifted his gaze upward to the masts overhead. "The riggers need to remain under Esme's ward. If this magic is affecting all of us, the humans or anyone not bonded to Sabine won't be able to help us navigate. Whatever we're doing, we need to do it quickly."

Sabine's teeth chattered. The freezing temperature was becoming unbearable. "Can you fly with the ship, Malek?"

Malek encased her in his arms, and she leaned against him. The warmth from his body helped alleviate the worst of the chill. "It's too heavy. You may have stopped whatever's affecting us temporarily, but I feel it at the edge of my awareness, trying to creep inside my mind. My magic is keeping it at bay, but if I have to tap into my full power for the strength needed to fly with the ship, I'll risk losing control completely."

The goddess's mark on Sabine's wrist warmed. She stared at it, instinctively understanding what Lachlina was trying to tell her. It was risky, but they didn't have much of a choice.

Sabine swallowed and managed to say, "I might have an idea, but it's going to be dangerous."

Chapter Two

"What are you thinking?" Bane asked, glancing at her glowing wrist.

Sabine opened her mouth to tell them her plan, but a sickening creak and groan resounded through the ship. She staggered, but Malek caught her before she could fall. The ship shuddered, giving the impression it was moments away from breaking apart.

"Ice!" Bane called, looking over the side of the ship. "Dammit! It's all around us. We need to stop the storm."

"I don't have enough stored power." Sabine pointed toward the mountainous range in the distance. "We have to get to shore so I can tap into the magic of the land. It's the only way."

Malek's jaw clenched. "I know you don't like it, but I'll fly with you to shore so you can stop the storm, Sabine. Even if I lose control, my dragon instincts won't allow any harm to come to you."

Sabine hesitated. Everyone on the ship would die if the temperature continued to plummet. Sabine pressed her hand against Malek's chest and urged, "That'll take too long. We can't leave everyone on board and risk them freezing to death. I can use the merfolk's power to control the waves. It should take us closer to land, even without the sails."

Malek's gaze flew back to her, and his eyes widened. "It might be our only chance to get the crew to safety. I'll clear the ice from the front of the ship while you power the ocean."

Bane gave him a curt nod and grabbed the wheel of the ship. "We've got this. Go!"

Sabine wrapped her arms around Bane, holding on tightly while Malek prepared to shift. Malek raced to the front of the ship, a brilliant white light exploding around him. The ship dipped forward from his weight and then tilted back precariously. A moment later, Malek was airborne, a striking creature whipping through the snowfall. Flames shot out in front of him, piercing the cloak of the storm as he flew overhead.

"He's the most beautiful thing I've ever seen," Sabine whispered, awestruck by the sheer power in his movements. His wings spanned the length of the entire ship several times over, and his tail whipped through the air as he soared overhead.

"He'll make a decent pair of dragonskin boots. I'll give him that much," Bane said with a smirk. "Are you ready?"

Sabine nodded, turned toward the dwarven mountain range, and closed her eyes. Lifting her hands, she reached for the merfolk's unfamiliar magic buried within her. She'd been gifted the essence after saving one of the merfolk who had been imprisoned in an abandoned Fae city.

Reaching for her newly acquired power, she allowed the seawater to fill her from within. It clamored for release, wanting to be set free upon the world. It was wild and chaotic, wholly foreign and alluring like an icy temptress.

She gathered the seawater in her mind, struggling to breathe under its weight. Carefully and with painstakingly slow progress, she pushed the waves forward, urging the ship onward toward land. Her control was awkward and clumsy, her efforts similar to those of a child learning how to walk. She struggled to wrest control of it while the waves crashed against her psyche.

"We're moving!" Bane shouted, but Sabine couldn't afford to respond. The magic was slippery and unwieldy, and any miscalculation could have disastrous effects. The call of the ocean beat against her temples, eager to obey and also to claim her for itself. She'd never fully understood the beauty and unmistakable power of the ocean until now.

A cold chill wrapped around her, the foreign and alien power singing to the darkest parts of her soul. Her head throbbed as she focused on the scent and feel of the ocean, the salt spray, and the chill of the waves. The ship shuddered when she whipped the waves to an even greater frenzy, propelling the ship forward.

"Faster! More power!"

She opened her eyes at the demand in Bane's voice. The ocean was freezing faster than Malek could destroy the ice. He was still soaring overhead, circling back around to breathe more dragonfire in front of the ship. It wasn't enough. Ice had completely coated the railings and deck of the ship. Sabine could even feel Esmelle's wards beginning to falter, threatening to endanger the crew's lives.

Sabine tossed back her silvery hair and shed her reservations. The merfolk's power surged to the surface inside her, and she allowed the seawater to rise to even greater heights. It clamored for release, demanding to be set free upon the world.

Sabine spread her hands, the wind whipping wildly around her. The salt spray from the ocean coated her skin, encouraging her to join its watery depths. She channeled even more of the merfolk's magic, the lure of the sea dancing along her skin like a thousand promises. She opened her mouth and a wordless song filled the air, a blend of both Fae and merfolk power. The ship cut through the waves like a knife, streaking through the sea on a wave of pure magic.

Overhead, Malek sent out large bursts of fire blasts, breaking the ice formations around the ship. Sabine continued to channel the wild power of the sea, the crash of the waves beating against the ship and her mental shields. The call of the ocean was hypnotizing, and it would be so easy to lose herself in its depths. She closed her eyes, listening to its song blend with her own. She was one with the primal power of the waves.

She inhaled sharply, the press of the wind also fueling her Fae magic. Her skin glowed with flashes of silver and gold streaking down its etched markings. For the first time in her life, she felt as though she were becoming whole somehow. It was almost as though she'd acquired a small piece of the fabric making up the tapestry of the universe. She drew upon even more power, trying to determine exactly what she was feeling and where the other threads of power had scattered.

"Pull back, Sabine!" Bane shouted. "It's too much."

Sabine's eyes flew open. They were approaching land too fast. She could make out the details of the obelisks on land, directing them to the docking location. She struggled to wrest control of the merfolk's power, trying to separate it from her natural abilities. The etchings on her skin continued to pulse with flickering gold and silver. She needed more time.

Sabine clutched her head, the merfolk power still holding a claim over her. She'd bound herself too tightly to the power surging within her. The urge to fling herself beneath the waves was overwhelming. Unlike the merfolk, she'd never survive in their underwater kingdom, but she needed to return the excess power to the sea before she drowned everyone. There was only one way to save the crew and herself, but it would be a near thing.

"Keep Blossom safe," Sabine ordered, shoving the sleeping pixie in Bane's pocket.

Bane looked up with surprise. "What are you—"

Sabine shook her head. There wasn't time to explain. "I have to return the power!" she yelled and raced to the edge of the ship. Without waiting for his response, she dove overboard.

The icy shock of the waves slammed into her, stealing her thoughts and slicing into her skin like knives. Sabine stretched out her hands, the silk of the water surrounding her and cradling her in its chilled embrace. She quickly wove her magic around herself, creating a mental net to store the excess merfolk power she'd summoned.

Drawing upon Malek's draconic power and Bane's volcanic embrace, she reinforced her webbing and sent the merfolk's magic outward in a heated blast. It was enough to shove her backward, slicing through the water.

Sabine broke the surface with a gasp. The magical explosion worked. The ship was safe, but now she had a new problem. She kicked in the water to keep herself afloat, but her clothing was heavy and waterlogged. At least the water was warmer than the outside air, but she didn't think it would last long with the storm still overhead.

She wasn't a very strong swimmer. She'd grown up playing in the rivers and lakes around Faerie, but she'd never even seen the ocean until she moved to Akros. Even there she'd only touched the water a handful of times. Unfortunately, that decision was now plaguing her. It looked like she was going to need to swim to shore or drown in the attempt. She hoped the merfolk's power would make it a little easier to stay afloat.

Sabine took another deep breath and prepared to go

below the waves to remove her water-logged clothing. Fire lit up the sky overhead, and she stared up at the glorious dragon above her. His golden serpentine eyes focused on her, and he swept downward.

Her eyes widened and she kicked her legs, trying to swim in the opposite direction. No. He couldn't be thinking—

Malek's claws extended and he dove downward, then plucked her out of the sea like a fish too close to the surface. A terrified scream ripped from her throat as she was swept into the air. Acting on primal instinct, she slammed her power against him. His flying faltered, and they started to drop. Sabine screamed in terror. He managed to right himself before they plummeted into the sea, but it was a near thing.

Shaking in fear, Sabine tried to calm her rapid breathing. A strange heated bubble surrounded her, and even the noise from his flapping wings had quieted. Her heart pounded in her chest, but she didn't blast him again. She didn't want to hurt him. Not really. The logical side of her knew he didn't intend her any harm, but it didn't do much to offset the irrational fear gripping her.

"Where are you going?" Sabine shouted, knowing she was probably just wasting her breath. As far as she knew, Malek couldn't communicate with her while he was in dragon form.

He continued to soar through the air, riding the wind currents. She hoped he was simply taking her to land. She could continue to expend pointless energy trying to fight against him or trust the man she'd come to know. Eventually, curiosity won out and she relaxed in his hold.

Frozen and shattered crystals continued to fall in front of them in heavy sheets. It obscured visibility, but she could still catch glimpses of the world below them. The ocean was impossibly blue, shifting to a lighter green the closer they came to shore.

It was... incredible.

Seeing the world from the clouds was unlike anything she could have imagined. Everything appeared so much smaller, and even the ship in the distance was almost toylike. She would have thought she'd be uncomfortable up in the air, but Malek had obviously considered that and encased her in some sort of protective cocoon.

Sabine pressed her hand against the ward-like creation, marveling at how it was crafted. It was magic but unlike anything she'd ever seen before. The cold wasn't affecting her, nor the wind. Malek had tucked her close enough to his body for her to see individual scales on his underbelly, while his claws cradled her gently. A shimmer around his claws caught her attention, and she leaned in closer.

Her eyes widened in surprise. A different sort of ward surrounded his claws. She pressed her fingers against one, and they sank into the spongy, jellylike coating before springing back. Even without touching them, she could see his claws were razor-sharp, but he'd obviously made an effort to protect her from harm—both from the elements and himself.

The realization caused the last of her fear to melt away, leaving her strangely disconcerted. Sabine sighed, knowing she needed to decide how to handle Malek. The care and tenderness he kept displaying toward her softened her resistances, but she couldn't allow her feelings for him to grow stronger. No matter how much she might be drawn to him, they could never have a future together. It would only be that much harder when she would be forced to let him go.

The dwarven home was now within sight, but the beach was coated with a combination of snow and sand. Malek started his descent, and her stomach lurched from the sharp decline. She held her breath as the ground rushed to meet them.

"Malek!" she screamed, terrified they were going to crash.

A brilliant white light enveloped her, and she was airborne a moment later. Malek's arms wrapped around her, and they landed against the ground with a solid *oomph.*

"Sorry about that," Malek whispered in her ear, holding her tightly against him. "I didn't hurt you, did I?"

Sabine blinked, trying to take stock of her surroundings. They were on land, but where was anyone's guess. She didn't see the ship or a beach nearby, but she'd watched her friends make landfall while she and Malek were airborne. Oh, gods. She'd actually flown with a dragon. Her head whipped around to focus on Malek. He was studying her with his piercing blue eyes, which were filled with concern.

Malek's brow furrowed, and he sat up with her still in his arms. He cupped her face and searched her expression. "Sabine? Talk to me, sweetheart. Are you all right?"

Her mouth opened and then closed again. Was she all right? She was still freezing, and her waterlogged clothing wasn't helping things, but nothing was broken. At least, she didn't think so. Adrenaline was still coursing through her, and she was having trouble thinking clearly.

She managed to nod. "I think so."

He brushed her wet hair away from her face and trailed his thumb across her cheek. "I think my heart stopped when you hit the water. I'm guessing you're not interested in flying with me again anytime soon."

Sabine frowned and pressed her hand against his chest, feeling his heartbeat beneath her fingertips. No matter how much she trusted Malek, she wasn't sure about the whole flying thing. Perhaps her fear was a weakness, but she'd grown up hearing terrifying tales about dragons who plucked random Fae from the ground. If she were truly meant to fly, the gods would have gifted her with wings.

"I couldn't figure out how to pull back on the merfolk's

power in time," Sabine admitted, scanning the empty valley coated with a light dusting of snow. "Where are we?"

"I wanted to land a distance away from the ship so you could do what was needed without endangering anyone. The ship is right over that rise." He pointed toward a nearby hill. "Can you stop the storm?"

"Yes," she said as Malek helped her stand. Her legs were a little shaky, but Malek put his arm around her waist to steady her.

"Is there anything you need me to do?"

She frowned. "Can you shield me? My family knows my approximate location, but the more I use major magic, the faster they'll be able to pinpoint us. I might need to draw upon your power to disrupt the spell. I'm not sure how they corrupted the magic."

"Of course," Malek replied immediately and then paused. "How long will we have before your family tries to kill you again? It took several days before they located you in Akros."

Sabine hesitated and shrugged. She bent down and quickly removed her wet boots, needing direct contact with the land to fuel her magical working. "I have no idea. When I was hiding in Akros, I'm sure my father had suspected I was still alive. He didn't have confirmation until then. But when I used unshielded power several times in rapid succession, that made it easier for him to affix the tracking spell. He's probably been waiting for me to do something again. We have a few hours at most."

Malek frowned. "We need to get you into Razadon right away."

"Yes, but that will only slow down the Wild Hunt. A clever assassin could still penetrate the city." Pushing aside her fear, she stood and wiggled her toes in the freezing grass until she touched the soil. The corruption was only on the surface here, where the snowy crystals were resting. It was uncomfortable and somewhat slimy.

She shivered, partly from the cold but also from the unnerving sensation of the poisoned magic touching her skin. The sooner they eradicated all traces of it, the better.

Malek placed his warm hand against the back of her neck. He enveloped her in his heated draconic power, which also eliminated the worst of the chill. She gave him a quick smile and pulled out her knife. Taking a steadying breath, she pricked her finger and allowed three drops of blood to fall onto the ground.

Infusing her voice with the power of her ancestors, she called, "By blood and magic, and by my rights to both, I call the elements to attend me!"

The wind swirled around her, chilling her through Malek's protective magic. She called upon the power from the earth beneath her feet, feeling the magic surge within her. It wasn't the same as being able to tap into Faerie directly, but Sabine was a child of the land. This was her domain, and no other race was as powerful as the Fae when they embraced their birthright.

Lightning struck the ground near them, and Sabine tilted her head toward the sky. Snow continued to fall against her skin, but it was warmer than it had been a moment ago.

Weaving Malek's power with hers, she tapped into her Seelie magic and focused on the sunlight. Reaching upward, she broke through the clouds to call down the sun's rays. Her skin warmed, and she embraced the light, allowing it to blanket the area.

Lifting her hands, she used the heat from Malek's magic to direct her intention. The snowfall faltered, then turned to rain and melted away the worst of the ice. Her Seelie magic complemented Malek's power, and the two fused together in an intricate dance. She allowed it to wash over her and

Malek before unleashing it outward in a brilliant display of light and warmth.

The sun shone brightly overhead, and soon the storm was nothing more than a memory. The wind calmed, except for a slight breeze that still contained the distinct metallic scent of corruption.

She paused and tilted her head, breathing in the wrongness. The storm had abated, but something still wasn't right. She lowered her arms and frowned. Nothing in her experience could account for this strange sensation, but her instincts warned her it was dangerous.

"What's wrong?"

Sabine shook her head. "I can't be sure, but the origin of the imbalance is in that direction." She pointed north. "It's not something I can remove without physical contact. Even then, I'm not sure I can do it. I've never felt anything like this before."

Malek frowned. "That's the direction of the entrance to Razadon. There's a path that leads from the beach to a small market and then up the mountain to the home of the dwarves."

"Sabine!"

Sabine turned in the direction of the voice and saw Blossom flying toward her. She let out a sigh of relief at the sight of the pixie. Holding out her hand for Blossom to land, she asked, "Are you all right? Is everyone safe?"

Blossom nodded and grinned. "Yep! Oh, and there are lots of flowers here, Sabine! Lots and lots! I had to make sure you were okay first before I started exploring."

Sabine frowned. "Did the goddess say anything to you about what's happening here?"

Blossom cocked her head for a moment as though listening. "She said you still need to fix it. She's not as mad as she was before, so I guess she's happy you stopped the storm."

Malek took Sabine's other hand in his. "Let's grab our supplies and head up to Razadon. We need to get you inside and out of danger."

Sabine looked up at him and nodded. Between the corruption permeating the air, the goddess threatening to control her bond with Malek and Bane, and the knowledge assassins were hunting her, this entire situation had the potential to go wrong very quickly.

Chapter Three

Malek took the pouch of rare spices Levin offered him and placed them in his bag. The dwarves didn't have easy access to such things, and spices always fetched a hefty price in their marketplace. He considered it for a moment and then motioned toward Levin.

"Hand me the other one too. We can replenish our supply when we head back north. I'm going to want to stop in Vestun to see Eshon's family and deliver the news about his death. As far as I know, Gardine didn't have any family."

"Both he and Gardine were good men," Levin said and offered him the other pouch. "I've been giving it some thought since we left Karga, but losing them cinched it for me. Life's too damn short, and I don't want to wait any longer in telling Sabine and Esme everything. They need to know what we're planning."

Malek's head whipped toward Levin, and he stared at his friend in shock. "What?"

Levin held up his hand. "I know what you're going to say, but it's better if we tell them both now. I've seen the way you look at Sabine. Hell, everyone has, which is probably why that demon looks like he wants to fillet you half the time. But the longer this goes on without telling them the truth, the worse it'll be when it finally comes out. I don't want any more regrets, and I don't think you do either."

Malek yanked the bag shut he'd been hastily packing. Dammit. Levin had a point. Malek had been having similar thoughts over the past month. But if he made one wrong move when it came to Sabine, she'd walk away from him and he'd never see her again. No matter how much he might want to tell her everything, he couldn't take that chance. Not yet.

Darting a quick glance around to make sure Blossom wasn't nearby eavesdropping, Malek said quietly, "I'm not disagreeing, but it's too risky to say anything right now. If I give Sabine any reason to doubt our intentions, she'll never trust me again. You *know* what'll happen to our people if we aren't successful. It's not something I can just spring on Sabine."

Levin crossed his arms over his chest. "If you tell her now, I believe Esme could help us convince her. She doesn't want Sabine to return to Faerie, and I don't think Sabine wants to go back either. Not if the way she looks at you is any indication."

"You're wrong," Malek warned in a low voice, remembering the longing in Sabine's eyes when they'd been in the small pocket of Faerie controlled by the merfolk. "Not only does she miss her home, but Sabine still isn't completely sure about me. Every time I think she's finally starting to let down her guard, she takes another step back. When we were in Karga, I thought I was finally getting closer to her. I almost told her then."

Levin's brow furrowed. "You mentioned you'd gotten

closer to her, but I haven't seen you spend much time with her since we set sail."

"I haven't, but not for lack of trying," Malek muttered, tossing a few more trade items into another bag. "Bane's been whispering in her ear again, and she's back to keeping me at arm's length. I'm planning on telling her everything, but I need to find the right time."

"When will that be? It's been months since we left Akros, Malek."

"I know," he admitted, knowing he needed to tell her his intentions soon. "Are you willing to risk Sabine believing I've been plotting against her? You know she'll disappear, and there's a good chance Esme will go with her. All feelings aside, we *need* Sabine and the artifacts she possesses. We won't get another shot at this."

Levin's jaw worked, and he glanced at Esmelle and Sabine who were standing on the far side of the ship waiting for Malek. They'd come back long enough for Sabine to change out of her wet clothes and quickly pack a bag. Bane was prowling back and forth near the women, stopping only long enough to glare in Malek's direction before resuming his pacing. Levin was right; the demon really did want to kill him. If it weren't for Bane, Malek was sure he would have already broken through Sabine's barriers.

Malek studied Sabine's profile, marveling at her delicate bone structure, her small upturned nose, and those full lips he kept fantasizing about. Her silvery hair was loose around her face and tumbled like shimmering waves of moonlight over her shoulders. She hadn't yet re-applied her glamour, and the effect of the magical etchings on her skin was striking. The crew was giving her a wide berth, but they couldn't hide their furtive and longing glances.

She might appear like every man's walking fantasy, but

the remarkable power within her could easily strike fear into most people's hearts at a moment's notice. As far as Malek was concerned, it had the opposite effect; he wanted nothing more than to steal her away and get lost in her again.

He couldn't get that night they'd spent together out of his head, and Sabine was quickly turning into an obsession. The past two weeks had been full of tossing and turning at night, while the woman he wanted was in a separate cabin, surrounded by a pixie, a dryad witch, and a young seer. Malek grimaced. He was turning into a lovesick idiot if he was jealous of Blossom, Esmelle, and Rika. He needed to get a grip on things.

Malek exhaled slowly and rubbed the back of his neck. "Look, I know you care for the witch. It's killing me not to tell Sabine what's at stake, but our personal feelings come secondary to our purpose here. You know we don't have a choice in this, Levin. Sabine won't put our needs above the lives of her people, not without good reason. We can't risk alienating her right now."

Levin frowned. "Esme already knows there's something I'm not telling her. They're going to find out sooner rather than later. If we control the way the truth comes out, we have more of a chance to convince Sabine to turn against her people—especially if I can get Esme to help us."

Malek nodded, having already considered the same thing. Levin and Esme had become involved during their captivity with the merfolk, and they'd been mostly inseparable since then.

He stared at the crates of supplies they'd brought onto the deck. Their stores were lower than he'd like, and he wasn't sure what was happening in Razadon. He needed to make alternative arrangements in case things didn't work out.

"We have a little over two weeks of rations for the crew before we run into a problem. If we're not back here within a week, you'll need to take the ship and head north for the nearest friendly port. Tell Esme then, and I'll find some time to talk to Sabine. If we survive, I'll leave word with our contacts where we're heading. You'll need to continue to search for the portal's location while I focus on finding the artifacts."

Levin frowned. "We could always keep trying to locate the artifacts without Sabine's help. We only need her when it comes time to activate the portal. If Sabine's life's in danger, the magic around the Sky Cities will prevent anyone from harming her. You could fly there with her until this threat is resolved."

Malek scrubbed his hands over his face, wishing it were that simple. "She was terrified when I pulled her from the sea, Levin. She eventually settled, but I didn't ward against her attack right away. If it weren't for the mark she'd gifted me, I'd be at the bottom of the ocean right now." He gestured to his wrist where Sabine had etched his skin with a triangular design. "Every day, I'm closer to convincing her to trust me. The Fae may want her dead, but she's still loyal to them for some reason. She's the key to all of this, especially with her connections. We need Sabine as our willing ally if we're going to control the portal."

Levin hesitated and then nodded. "All right. I don't necessarily agree with your reasoning, but I'll wait to tell Esme. I'll handle things here while you try to stop this corruption and gain access to Razadon."

Malek let out a sigh of relief. "Look, I get it. It's not easy for me either. I hate deceiving them, even by omission. There's a good chance even if Sabine does agree to help us, she won't forgive me for not telling her everything right away. I don't want to lose her, but I don't have a choice. Neither one of us do."

Levin looked at the two women again. "There's a lot

riding on this, Malek. Assuming we survive, I've been thinking about asking Esme to join me in the Sky Cities once all this is done."

Malek didn't respond. He'd considered the same thing, but he didn't believe Sabine would be willing to travel to the home of dragons. If it weren't for her birthright and perceived responsibilities, things might be different. Even if she did agree, Malek would likely end up fighting other clans for the rest of his life trying to protect her. Sabine and her remarkable power were a prize many of them would covet. Dragons tended to hoard their most precious of treasures to keep them safe, but he doubted Sabine would ever willingly allow him to claim her as such.

With a defeated sigh, Malek grabbed the two bags and slung them over his shoulder. "I think that's all. You have everything you need to keep order here?"

Levin frowned and eyed Malek closely. "I've never seen you look so conflicted." He paused, cocking his head as he considered Malek. "I know you care about Sabine, but exactly how serious are you about her?"

Malek didn't answer right away. He'd been trying to deny it, but it was pointless. The events earlier had proven that. "I've been trying to avoid such complications, but I almost shifted earlier when Bane had her in his arms. I think part of it was that storm, but that's not all. I keep losing control around her, and it's getting worse."

Levin's eyebrows rose. "You're serious? That's one of the first signs of mating. I haven't even had that reaction around Esme yet."

"I know what it means," Malek snapped and narrowed his eyes on his friend. "Do you think I'd admit such a thing otherwise? I've traveled all over this world and met countless women. The one woman I end up falling for is the one person who holds the power to either save our people or damn them for eternity. If I have to lose her in the process of saving them, I'll do it. I'll hate every second of it, but I'll do it."

"Shit," Levin muttered and shook his head. "You're going down the same path as your grandfather. The clans are going to *love* that."

Malek scowled but didn't reply. His grandfather had fallen in love with a Fae captive during the war. His family had been accused of being Fae sympathizers for centuries, a label many in his family had gone out of their way to prove wrong.

Levin reached up to unfasten the warding medallion around his neck and offered it to Malek. "If you're going to keep yourself in check, you'll need this more than me. Besides, if you go into Razadon, it'll help keep your identity secret from the dwarves. Esme should be able to help hide my presence if we run into anyone. Either way, as long as the beach remains empty, I'll be fine."

Malek stared at the warding medallion and gave Levin a curt nod. The necklace Malek wore to hide his identity had been lost back in Karga. He'd eventually need to find a powerful witch who could replace it.

He accepted the offering and fastened it around his neck, the cold metal immediately squelching the flames of his heated draconic power. It served both as a masking effect and as a warning when he was in danger of losing control. It was uncomfortable but a necessary precaution if he was going to pass as being human.

Levin rubbed his chin. "That demon still looks like he wants to kill you."

"Caught that, huh?" Malek muttered, grabbing a few extra weapons to keep on hand. "I should head out. We need to eliminate this latest threat before things get even worse. And I need to figure out a way to convince Sabine not to kill me when she finally learns the truth."

"Good luck," Levin said and shook his head. "I have a feeling you're going to need it."

Chapter Four

Sabine waved farewell to Esmelle before turning away to head up the mountain path where Malek, Rika, and Blossom were waiting for her. Bane had disappeared from the beach a few minutes earlier to scout ahead.

Until they determined what was causing the corruption and put a stop to it, Sabine wasn't willing to risk losing anyone else. Malek hadn't mentioned the two crew members they'd already lost, but there were shadows under his eyes that hadn't been there yesterday.

Everyone not bound to Sabine or under her sworn protection was in danger from either the goddess, the corruption, or both. Although Esmelle would have been safe from Lachlina, thanks to Sabine's protection oath, the redheaded witch hadn't wanted to leave Levin behind.

It was for the best, Sabine decided. When the Wild Hunt made another appearance, everyone was better off staying as far away from her as possible. Part of her had been tempted to leave Rika behind, but a young woman fending for herself among a rough group of sailors had its own potential for disaster.

Malek turned toward Sabine and said, "I'm not sure how long Bane's going to be gone. We should probably start heading away from everyone. I want to get you to safety as soon as possible."

She opened her mouth to agree but stopped when she caught sight of Bane up ahead. His mouth was pinched in a frown, and the demon looked more than a little annoyed.

Sabine walked toward him. "I'm guessing you didn't find anything?"

"Nothing, and that's suspicious in itself," Bane said with disgust. "I only saw a few dwarven statues and some trees along the path up ahead. No dwarves or any living creatures as far as I can tell. Even if we hadn't been nearly shipwrecked by that damn storm, something's definitely not right here. My gut's telling me we should keep sailing or head directly for the underworld to get you out of sight."

Sabine glanced up the mountain path. It seemed unremarkable at first glance, but she'd learned at a young age that appearances could be deceiving. She trusted Bane's instincts, and normally, she'd agree with him about leaving right away.

"We need to stay," she said firmly. "I'm not willing to risk the goddess's wrath. Let's try to find out what's happening with this corruption and whether we can get inside the city. If not, we'll let Esmelle and the crew know and then find the nearest underworld entrance. It's not ideal, but I don't see another option. I need a few minutes to read the land."

Malek didn't look altogether pleased with her words, but he didn't argue. He scanned the horizon, likely searching for any sign of the Wild Hunt making their pursuit.

"Ew, we might go to the underworld?" Blossom asked, landing on Sabine's shoulder. She wrinkled her nose. "Demon magic smells funny. They probably don't have any plants down there either."

"We can find some plants here for you just in case,"

Sabine said, catching another faint whiff of the corrupted magic. The salt from the ocean was interfering with her abilities to tell where it was originating.

Rika smiled at Blossom. "I can help you look for flowers, Blossom. Which ones do you like?"

Blossom trilled happily and flew toward Rika. "My favorites are pink ones, but I like yellow too. Maybe we can find some to braid in your hair. There's a new style I want to try out."

Sabine tuned them out and sent a pulse of power along her markings to better focus her magic on their surroundings. Reaching out with her amplified senses, she tried to determine what they were telling her and where the source of the corruption was.

Bane was right; other than the wind rustling through the plants, no other sounds greeted them. Even the usual noises from birds or small animals in the nearby foliage was absent. The strange odor was stronger and coming from the north, which was a sign they were on the right path. But something was odd about the rotten scent. She inhaled deeply, trying to isolate it and follow the source.

Malek glanced at her. "Can you tell where it's coming from?"

"I think so. The smell is the strongest, so I'm trying to focus on that. It's familiar, but I can't quite place it. I have to try to isolate some of it to properly track it."

Sabine closed her eyes and took another deep breath, trying not to gag. The scent was almost metallic, like the air after a powerful storm, but there was a harsh and bitter undercurrent. The first part of the scent reminded her a little of Fae or merfolk magic when they commanded the elements to generate a storm, but she wasn't sure about the rest.

"Smells like the unholy merging of demon and Fae magic," Bane muttered. "Maybe a few other things tossed in."

Sabine's eyes flew open. "You're right! Demon magic was the sulfur scent I detected. But it's faint and coupled with something else."

"What would possess the dwarves to combine different types of magic?" Malek asked, staring in the direction of the mountain. "I would have thought they'd know better. And don't forget, combining magic was the reason the treeheart went crazy back in Atlantia."

"Fucking dwarves," Bane said with a shrug. "They dabble with all sorts of banked powers. Those crystals of theirs stink when they shatter, no matter what they're mixing. We've had to seal some of our underground tunnels because they make lousy neighbors."

Malek frowned. "You mentioned the snow was from shattered power crystals. Is there any way to tell the purpose?"

Bane scowled. "Hell if I know why the shorties do anything. They make decent weapons and brew, but that's about it. Beyond that, they're focused on politics, drinking games, and whatever they're cooking up in their crystal caverns. It might have been an experiment gone wrong."

Blossom sniffed a nearby flower. She gagged and then waved her hands in front of her nose to clear the air. "Icky. A dwarf was here not too long ago. It doesn't smell right when they use their crystals near the plants."

Sabine threw a surprised look at Blossom but then quickly covered it. She hadn't been aware Blossom could smell someone manipulating magic. Many Fae had the ability to see colors associated with the different types of magic and even hear music, but she hadn't realized pixies shared that talent.

Rika bit her lip. "My grandmother used to say the dwarves treated magic like another form of currency. They would buy and sell powers they needed to earn more coin."

Malek chuckled. "That's a pretty apt description. If there's another race more focused on earning money, I haven't met them. I believe that's why the dwarves have managed to build such a profitable trading empire." He turned to stare at the empty beach behind them. "That's one of the things that makes their absence strange. That beach should have been littered with trading tents and kiosks. Something significant must have happened for them to retreat."

"Which way, Sabine?" Bane asked, turning toward her again. "I can smell it but can't tell the direction."

Sabine frowned and focused on the scent again, incorporating the similarities of the magic she recognized to locate the source of the power. It was still an active working, but she wasn't sure of the intent. At least she had a general idea of the direction they needed to travel.

Sabine rubbed her nose, wishing she could erase the memory of the smell. "As far as I can tell, if we follow along on the northernmost path, we'll be heading in the right direction. I'll know more once we get closer."

Bane nodded and started prowling up the well-worn path away from the beach. Rika ran up to walk beside him while Sabine and Malek followed. The winding path sloped upward, but it wasn't too difficult of a climb. They passed a few stone benches sprinkled amid the foliage, making it obvious this way was frequently traveled. If it hadn't been for the threat of the Wild Hunt descending upon them, it would have been a pleasant hike.

"I wish I could have seen you fly, Sabine," Blossom said, zipping around in the air and pausing only long enough to inspect the plants growing along the path.

Sabine glanced at Malek and gave him a small smile. "It was quite an experience."

Malek chuckled and pressed his hand against Sabine's lower back. "I'm hoping to eventually convince you again."

"Over my dead body," Bane growled without bothering to turn around.

"That can be arranged," Malek called in a neutral voice and then winked at Sabine.

She sighed and remained quiet, not wanting to mediate another argument. It was sometimes a little unnerving how Bane was always cognizant of her every move. Almost every time Malek had tried to get her alone on the ship, Bane had suddenly appeared. She couldn't completely fault him though. They needed to avoid her Seelie magic growing any stronger, and Malek always seemed to bring it to the forefront.

Rika slowed her footsteps and looked over her shoulder at Sabine. "Did I miss something?"

Sabine managed a smile and shook her head. "Bane has *very* good hearing. You'll find most non-human races have enhanced senses of some sort. You should always expect someone to be listening."

"Aww, Sabine," Blossom complained, fluttering to another plant. "You're making my job harder. I don't want people to know I'm listening. Then they never tell their secrets."

Sabine's smile became genuine, and she winked at the pixie. Blossom loved a challenge, especially when it added a bit of excitement. Blossom grinned at her before sniffing a purple flower.

Rika peered up at Bane, her eyes wide. "Really? What other enhanced senses do you have?"

Bane grunted and didn't respond. Instead, he continued marching up the path.

Blossom flew to Rika and handed her the flower. "Nope. Won't happen. Demons never tell people their strengths and weaknesses."

Rika frowned. "Why not?"

Blossom landed on Rika's shoulder and shrugged. "They

don't want to give their enemies any advantage. My brother said demons get beat up in the underworld if they're weak or puny. Is that true, Bane? Did you get beat up a lot?"

"Shut up, bug, before you get stepped on," Bane muttered and then stopped at an archway, sweeping his gaze over the area.

Sabine slowed her footsteps at the sight of a large clearing with several large stone obelisks erected around the area. Carvings decorated the stonework, and colorful mosaic tiles had been inlaid into the ground. A rainbow of colors peeked up through crystalline blue dust, offering a hint of the life usually present. Aside from the dust, it reminded her of some of the plazas at home with the swirling colorful designs.

"If I were as big as a dragon, I'd step on demons all day," Blossom said and landed on Sabine's shoulder. She placed a flower in Sabine's hair and then flew over to investigate more flowers. Bane grunted and prowled around the clearing, studying the ground.

"The tiles are so pretty," Rika said, following in Bane's footsteps. "It's a shame they're all covered up with this blue stuff. What do you think happened here?"

"Someone's been shattering crystals," Bane said, kneeling and sniffing at the small blue fragments they'd been walking over. "Watch where you step. I don't believe they're active, but some of the edges are sharp."

"The ones we saw on the ship were clear or white." Sabine frowned, taking a closer look at the small fragments they'd been walking over. They were mostly mixed in with the dirt and tilework, but it was obvious a great number of crystals had been broken in this area.

Malek frowned and said, "I thought crystals were blue only before they were infused with power."

"Normally, yes," Bane said, continuing to study the patterns. "They can also revert back to blue once they've expelled the magic they contain. Based on the number of fragments, I'm guessing a handful of large crystals were broken in this area, or dozens of smaller ones. For what purpose, I can't say."

Turning her gaze upward, Sabine walked to the large monoliths towering into the air, fascinated by their construction. She'd never seen anything quite like them before. In addition to the large stone obelisks, there were also unusual stone arches facing each of the four directions. Each was intricately carved with both pictures and words etched in the ancient language of the gods.

Sabine ran her hands along the stonework, both awestruck and captivated by images she'd only seen described in books. Unlike the abandoned desert stones outside of Karga, these had been created by master artisans and lovingly tended over the centuries.

"Can you read them?" Malek asked, staring up at them.

"Yes," Sabine said quietly, a pang of sadness filling her as she scanned over the list of names. "They're burial stones honoring those who were lost during the Dragon War."

Malek slowly turned in her direction, his expression pained. "They're all names of dwarves who were killed by my people?"

Sabine shook her head, knowing her next words would hurt him far more. "No. These are the names of the dwarves who were lost. Their bodies were never recovered. The dwarves believe their essence is still trapped above ground somewhere, and these stones were built here to call them home."

"So many names," Malek murmured, sweeping his gaze over the plaza and the thousands of names etched into the stones. His jaw hardened, and his eyes filled with determination. "If there was any doubt about the need to ensure the portal doesn't open again, this would have tipped the balance. Sabine, we *must* find a way into their city and acquire their artifact."

She nodded and reached over to place her hand on his arm. "I know, and we will. We won't allow anything like this to happen again. But first, we need to stop the corruption and protect the rest of your crew. I'd hoped to have seen someone by now who could tell us what happened here."

Malek frowned. "I've been here before, but I've never seen it like this. This is where the main trading hub is usually set up. The dwarves rarely allow traders into the city and only with special permission. I've been inside twice, but most of my business was conducted here. This area should be filled with tents and kiosks, but it doesn't look like anyone's been here in weeks."

"The dragon's right," Bane said, studying the ground where the tile ended. "The shattered crystals could be masking something, but I can't detect any recent footsteps other than ours. I still don't sense any living creatures in the area."

"Stinky magic," Blossom said, pinching her nose and fanning the air in front of her. "I bet everyone left because they dumped toxic magic on the flowers. I wouldn't want to stick around either."

"I might be able to find out what happened." Sabine released Malek and knelt, then placed her fingers against the mosaic tiles on the ground. Since she wasn't a dwarf, her ability to read their energy in the stones was limited, but it might tell them something. At the very least, she could connect with the land energy and hear the echoes of their song.

She closed her eyes, trying to concentrate and listen. A low hum sounded in her ears as though listening to someone speaking on the other side of a door. She strained to listen, catching a flash of color in the corner of her mind. It had the resonance of the speaker's aura, and she reached outward trying to grasp ahold of it. Emotions whipped through her thoughts, fuzzy and opaque like the memory of a dream.

"I hear you," Sabine murmured, sliding deeper into the speaker's song. "Turmoil. Anger. Fear—"

"You will not fall into their memories! You are *mine*!" Bane roared as he grabbed her wrist and yanked her upright. She gasped, shocked by his reaction. His eyes were pure silver, and his midnight-colored skin glowed blue from barely contained power. With a snarl, he pulled her close and extended his claws, his threat clear if anyone dared to approach.

Blossom squeaked and dove into the nearby underbrush. Rika scrambled backward to the edge of the plaza, hiding behind one of the obelisks. Malek started to move toward Sabine, but she held up her hand to stop him.

If Malek pulled her away, they would have a repeat of what had happened back on the ship. At least she was connected to the land and could draw upon some of its strength.

Sabine moved even closer to Bane and held his gaze. Showing fear to a demon was one of the worst things she could do, no matter how she was feeling. Drawing upon every acting skill she possessed, she tossed her hair back and narrowed her eyes on the enraged demon.

"I do *not* belong to you," she reminded him sharply.

Pressing her hand against his chest, Sabine sent a sharp lash of power into him. His back bowed, but his eyes didn't shift back to their normal amber color. Instead, his gaze became even more predatory. He snarled at her, showing a hint of his teeth. Sabine froze. This wasn't good. Physically, she couldn't hope to match him in strength, and Malek might kill him if she couldn't bring Bane back to awareness. She could scarcely afford to unleash a power display when she still needed to end the corruption, but she wasn't willing to lose Bane either.

She grabbed the mark on Bane's wrist, digging her nails into him until she pierced his skin. Demons understood pain, and it might be the only way to reach him. His poisoned blood trickled over her hand, and she forced more magic into his wound.

Her skin glowed, each of the marks on her skin flaring with power. Bane staggered, his grip on her loosening. She took another step toward him, using her magic like the edge of a knife to cut away his defiance.

Infusing her words with the magic of her ancestors, she said, "You are *mine*, Bane'umbra, son of Kal'thorz. First bound, first blood. You *will* obey me. Now, kneel!"

Bane dropped to his knees in front of her, breathing heavily as though prepared to lash out at her. Pulling out her knife, she sliced it across her palm. With her other hand, she gripped one of his horns and jerked Bane's head back. She thrust out her bleeding hand, and he grabbed it and drank deeply of her offering as though it were a lifeline. She needed to be more careful. Too many blood sacrifices in rapid succession would weaken her too much.

After a long time, Bane's shoulders relaxed, and his eyes reverted to their normal amber color. He released her and took a ragged breath. His expression was stricken, the realization of how close he'd come to the jagged edge filling his gaze.

Sabine lowered herself to the ground in front of him, putting them back on even footing. She wrapped her arms around Bane, catching sight of Malek's frown out of the corner of her eye. She shook her head a fraction, not willing to explain just yet. Instead, she focused on Bane and her desire to cement his ties to the surface. Intent was a large part of magic. This was part of their pact, and she would not be forsworn.

She enveloped him in her power once again, and he shuddered. Bane pulled her close and ran a hand over her hair to siphon off even more of her magic. She was nearly lightheaded from the loss by the time he stopped. She couldn't remember the last time he'd taken so much from her.

When she felt his body relax, Sabine leaned back to search for any sign he was still in danger of losing control. Bane rarely succumbed to his instincts without good reason. He'd always been much more even-tempered compared to his brother, Dax. Whatever corruption was plaguing the area was hitting Bane harder than the rest of them. She wasn't sure which was more dangerous, an angry goddess or an enraged demon. Either way, people usually ended up dead.

Rika took a hesitant step toward them and asked, "Is Bane okay?"

"For now," Sabine said, still focused on Bane's breathing and body language. "The corruption is affecting all of us. Once we stop it, we should be fine."

Bane slowly rose to his feet and helped her stand, not tearing his gaze from her. He took her injured hand and ran his claws over it, sealing the wound with a trace of his power. "You have given me enough, little one. I will not take more from you."

Sabine wasn't completely convinced he'd taken enough, but she wouldn't challenge him in front of the others. If they were alone it might be different, but insinuating a demon was weaker than they appeared was a grave insult. Besides, she needed to conserve her remaining strength.

When she didn't comment, Bane turned away to scan the area once again.

Malek moved to stand beside her and pressed his hand against her lower back. "Are you all right?"

"Yes," she said quietly, still troubled by Bane's behavior. She could sense the weakness within him through their bond. Something wasn't right, but she couldn't push him. Sometimes his pride grated on her nerves.

Bane scowled at Malek before focusing on her again. "How close are we to the source?"

Sabine hesitated and then closed her eyes, reaching out with her senses. The origin of the corruption was still strong, and it coated her skin with a slick metallic slime. She hadn't reapplied her glamour, which made it easier to use her skin markings to burn away the worst of the negative effects. It was requiring a great deal of sustained magic to keep the corruption from overtaking her companions' bonds.

She tilted her head, trying to gauge the distance through the layers of corruption. Now that they were closer, she could sense the distinct threads of power overlapping one another. "I'd say it's less than a twenty-minute walk in the same direction we're traveling. I can't tell much more than that."

Malek frowned. "That's not far from Razadon's main gate."

Bane's jaw clenched. "Those damn dwarves. What the hell are they up to now?" He cocked his head for a moment, and his eyes flashed silver briefly before reverting back. Turning toward Malek, he ordered, "Keep her safe. I need to scout ahead."

Without waiting for a response, Bane stepped off the path and disappeared into the underbrush. Sabine took a step after him but stopped. She couldn't lead Rika into danger when she'd sworn to protect the seer, and Malek wouldn't be willing to sit aside and babysit while Sabine followed the demon.

She clenched her fists, irritated Bane had taken off when he wasn't at full strength. The foolish demon was either trying to prove himself or he'd sensed something that could be dangerous.

Blossom landed on Sabine's shoulder and patted her hair. "He'll be okay, Sabine. You don't need to worry."

"I'd worry about you too, Blossom," Sabine said quietly. "I'd worry about any of you."

Rika approached Sabine, staring in the direction where Bane had disappeared. "Why did he leave? Isn't it better for us all to stay together?"

Sabine didn't answer right away, surprised by how quickly Rika had warmed to a demon. Even after witnessing Bane nearly lose control, Rika still worried about him.

"Bane can sense people's life force, and it's easier if he's away from me," Sabine said, settling on a partial truth. She wouldn't betray Bane by sharing his weakness. "Sometimes my magic interferes with his abilities. He probably caught a hint of something and wants to see if anyone's around who might be responsible for what's occurring here."

Malek arched his brow. "I didn't know your power interferes with his. You weaken him?"

She hesitated. "Not in the way you might be thinking. Our bond allows him to monitor my life force, even when we're a great distance away. It's similar to listening to my heartbeat, or at least that's how he's explained it. When I'm close, it's harder for him to hear the whispers of other people's lives. In all other ways, his proximity to me strengthens his abilities."

Malek touched her mark on his wrist, but he didn't respond. Sabine studied him, sensing he didn't like her answer for some reason. Something was troubling him and had been for a while now. In many ways, Malek was still a mystery to her. She didn't want to pry but hoped he might tell her when he felt comfortable.

"Rika and Blossom, why don't you gather some of the

flowers to take with us? I'm not sure whether the dwarves will have much of a selection inside their mountain. Blossom will need them to sustain her magic."

Rika nodded. "Will any flowers work?"

Blossom pointed at some pink-and-white flowers. "I recognize that kind. Rika, let's grab a few of those and check out the ones on the other side of the plaza. We can stick them in your bag."

Rika walked toward the flowers, and Blossom instructed her how to properly harvest them. Sabine watched them for only a few moments before her gaze gravitated toward where Bane had disappeared.

If he hadn't lost control on the ship and again a few minutes ago, she wouldn't worry quite so much. Bane could take care of himself for the most part, but he was still her responsibility—and her friend. Not to mention, he knew the Wild Hunt could be descending upon them at any moment. The sense of urgency was grating on her.

Malek reached over and tucked Sabine's hair behind her ear, drawing her attention back to the dragon shapeshifter. He trailed his fingers down her cheek, the tenderness in his gaze causing her stomach to flutter in response. The emotions he evoked were both equally thrilling and terrifying. She was definitely falling for him, but she still wasn't sure if that was a good thing.

Malek wrapped his arms around her and lowered his head, then brushed his lips against hers in a whisper of a kiss. She softened against him, unable to resist the promise in his eyes. His touch was gentle as though she were made of the finest crystal and more precious than the finest gems in the dwarven mines.

It would be better to keep her distance from him, but he was quickly becoming her weakness. No one had ever treated her like this, and she wasn't willing to lose it so soon.

But every moment she spent in his presence made her resistance soften that much more.

She pressed her hands against his chest and blinked up at him. "Not that I'm complaining, but what was that for?"

"You needed a distraction, and it's doubtful I'll get a chance to kiss you again any time soon," Malek said, continuing to hold her in his arms. "Once Bane gets back, he and I will go back to giving each other dirty looks. You'll sigh a lot, and Rika and Blossom will get up to their usual antics while we wait for the next disaster to strike. I need to seize the opportunities to kiss you while I can."

Sabine's mouth twitched in a smile, and she arched her brow at him. "We do seem to run from disaster to disaster, don't we?"

"That's an understatement if I've ever heard one," he replied with a grin.

She gave him a teasing smile. "I suppose we'll have to see about finding a few more opportunities for something a bit more fun. After all, the Fae are all about balance."

He chuckled. "In that case, I think we need to find an inn and lock ourselves in for the next few years. I doubt that would balance everything out, but it would be a fantastic start." He kissed her lightly and said, "We'll give Bane five more minutes and then we'll go after him. I know you're worried, but Bane can take care of himself."

"I know," she agreed, her gaze drifting to the spot where he'd disappeared.

Rika walked up to them and held out the flowers she'd collected. "Do you know what these are? Blossom said you had a way of finding out."

Sabine glanced over Rika's shoulder and saw Blossom still investigating the nearby plants. Grateful for the diversion, Sabine lifted one of the long stems from Rika's collection and assessed it. The flower was deep red at the base, shifting to pink in the middle with white at the very tip. The stems and leaves were deep green with a hint of silver in their veins.

She inhaled deeply and unlocked her memories, allowing the familiar scent of home to fill her lungs. At the edge of her awareness, she caught a trace of the corruption, but the flower was doing well to withstand its influence. "Yes. They're called caverias. They're wildflowers, but they don't grow in the northern lands outside of Faerie. They usually prefer the cooler temperatures of the mountains. My people tended them in this place once, most likely before we stepped aside to allow the dwarves to reside here. Our touch can be felt everywhere if you look hard enough."

"Your people once lived here?" Rika asked with wide eyes.

Sabine nodded, trying to ignore the unease filling her at Bane's continued absence. Their shared connection was strangely silent. "Yes. The Fae are the original caretakers of the world. Some of my people were children of the mountains and heralds of the sky. The dwarves, demons, and others came much later. Once the dwarves were born, we offered up our mountain homes to them so they might have a place for themselves. It was our gift to the gods to celebrate the birthright of their newest children."

Malek stared at her. "Wait, you're saying Razadon was a nameday gift?"

Sabine cocked her head and then shrugged. "I've never thought of it quite that way, but I—"

Rage, hot and molten in its intensity, slammed through her. She gasped, doubling over from the sharp fury threatening to overwhelm her. It wasn't her emotion. She'd never experienced such intense rage, so piercing it nearly stole her breath. She struggled to get control over it or at least suppress it enough to think clearly.

Malek's expression became alarmed. "Sabine? What is it? Is it the Wild Hunt?"

"Bane's in trouble," she said in a rush, her pulse pounding in her temples. Bane had never pulled so hard on their bond. Motioning toward Blossom, Sabine ordered, "Keep Rika shielded until it's safe."

Blossom's eyes widened. "You want me to pull power to hide her?"

"Do it," Sabine said, hoping the pixie could boost her magic enough by tapping into the power of the flowers growing nearby.

Without waiting for a response, Sabine sprinted out of the plaza and up the mountain path. Bane needed her. Malek was right on her heels, his boots crunching along the tile path. Sabine raced upward, instinct guiding her as she followed the bond she shared with the demon.

She darted off the walkway and through the overgrown foliage, following the most direct path to get to Bane. Up ahead, she could make out the sounds of battle, a combination of weapons clashing, screams, and the distinct sound of Bane roaring.

Sabine stumbled to a halt on the outskirts of a clearing. Blood. So much blood. And gore. She'd never seen anything like it, not since leaving the Faerie courts where torture had sometimes been used for entertainment. The pressure of corrupted magic was even stronger here, and she could barely breathe under its weight. It was all originating from this clearing somehow. This was the source.

Bane stood over several bodies, many of whom had been eviscerated. One of them was using his arms to crawl away from the demon, but there was no hope for him. Half his body was gone. It was only his contact with the stone that had likely allowed him to survive this long.

"Bane!" she shouted, but he didn't seem to be aware of her

presence. He was in full battle mode, and even his horns had shifted to silver.

More than a dozen dwarves were trying to surround the enraged demon. His skin glowed with a midnight-blue light, interrupted only by the molten blood trailing down his body from the wounds he'd already taken. He gripped one of the dwarves tightly and swiped downward with his clawed hands before tossing the body aside.

She took a step forward, but Malek grabbed her arm. "He'll kill you, Sabine. He's in full battle lust."

"I have to do something to break the corruption's hold on him," she said, searching the clearing for the source. Bile rose in her throat, and she blinked several times, trying to breathe through her mouth. One of the bodies was different than the others and appeared almost to be staged for some unknown purpose. The body had been decapitated and laid out spread-eagle in the center of the clearing, but she couldn't see any sign of the head.

Another dwarf lunged forward, his spear digging into Bane's side. The demon roared again, jumping forward to rip the spear from the dwarf's grasp and grab his assailant.

Sabine's hand tightened on Malek's arm. "The head. Where is it?"

Malek pointed toward a stone table on the far side of the clearing. "There. Are those crystals?"

Sabine's eyes widened in horror. Giant crystals had been shoved into each orifice, and one had even been embedded into the top of the head. The one at the top was pulsing a strange green color, the pattern reminding her of the lightning strikes from the storm.

"I need to get to it," she said, sensing those crystals had something to do with the corruption. She pulled away from Malek and quickly circled the clearing. She didn't want to risk getting into the fray or drawing attention yet. Malek already had his sword in his hand. He took a protective position running alongside her, keeping himself between her and the fighting.

Sabine knelt beside the bench where the head was resting. Pushing aside the wave of nausea that threatened, she breathed through her mouth and tried to focus on the details. The facial features, from what she could see, belonged to a male dwarf. Three glowing crystals had been shoved inside his eyes and mouth, and they swirled with colors—green, blue, and red. Smaller crystals had been set up in a circular pattern around the head with blood coating each of them.

Another scream from the clearing caused her to jump, but she tried to ignore the sounds of battle and focus on the crystals. They were being used as some sort of magical working, which appeared to be crude in its design, even if the magic powering the spell wasn't. She'd never seen such a thing, but the sense of *wrongness* emanating from it was overwhelming. Her knowledge was lacking when it came to these types of crystals, but there had to be a way to break the spell.

"Whatever you're going to do, it needs to happen soon," Malek warned, angling himself in front of her. "Bane's still fending them off, but they've gotten some hits in. I'm not sure how much more he can take."

Sabine gave him a curt nod. Through the bond she shared with Bane, she could sense his growing weakness and the corruption infecting him. The crystals had to be the key. If she removed them, it might be enough to disrupt the spell over the entire area. It should be enough to bring Bane back to awareness. She just hoped pulling them out wouldn't have a backlash effect. Unfortunately, they were out of options.

Taking a steadying breath, she reached for the crystal sticking out of the dwarf's mouth. Searing pain lanced through her. She jerked away with a pained cry, staring at her hand. Her fingers were red and blistered where she'd come into contact with the crystal.

"Dammit," Malek muttered, dropping his bags on the ground. "Let me try to find something we can use to pull them out."

"Mundane objects won't work on this type of magic," she said, determined to stop the corruption no matter the cost. Gritting her teeth, she started to reach again, but Malek grabbed her hand.

"No," he said with a low growl, the ferocity in his gaze surprising her. "I'll do it."

She pulled away from him, ignoring the scream of another dwarf. "It might make it worse. This was created with Fae, merfolk, and demon magic. With my ties to both Seelie and Unseelie magic, I have a chance of overriding it. I don't know what'll happen if you touch it without me acting as a buffer."

Malek stared at the decapitated head and said, "If dragon magic wasn't used, we might be able to use that to our advantage. You have access to my power through our new connection. At least it'll give you immunity from the burning if you open our bond."

Her eyes widened at his suggestion. She had some resistance to demonic magic because of Bane, but Malek's power might help tip the balance. "You might be right. I can override the blood sacrifice with one of our own making. That should allow me to touch the crystals and possibly even fracture what's fueling the spell. I need some of Bane's blood and yours for the working."

Malek grimaced. "Shit. A bit of demon blood coming right up."

Without waiting for a response, he leaped over the bench and darted into the clearing. Sabine gasped, watching as he rolled forward and then sprung to his feet with a dagger drawn. The dwarves had surrounded Bane, jabbing at him with their elongated curved spears to push him back. Another dwarf was placing containment crystals on the ground while they tried to lure Bane toward their trap.

Sabine inhaled sharply and held up her hand, flinging some of the crystals aside with a sharp gust of wind. She didn't want the dwarves to be hurt, but they'd send Bane back to the underworld if they managed to contain him. While he might survive the banishment, she'd promised to do everything within her power to keep him above ground.

Malek used the commotion to dart forward, slicing downward on Bane's arm with his weapon. The demon roared, his eyes glowing silver as he swiped at Malek with his poisoned claws. The dragon shapeshifter kicked out, landing a well-timed hit in Bane's midsection to push the demon back. The dwarf with the crystals was fumbling and trying to set them up again, and Bane turned his attention on the hapless man. The dwarf's eyes widened, and he scrambled back into the group of his companions.

Malek escaped out the side of the clearing and raced back toward her. Breathing heavily, he offered her his knife. She paused, her eyes widening at the sight of the injury on Malek's side. Bane had hurt him. She ignored the proffered knife, grabbed Malek's shirt, and pulled him down toward her. She kissed him hard, using the contact to push her power into him, infusing him with her strength. Through her bond with Bane, she was able to negate the demonic poison. Otherwise, it could weaken or even kill Malek.

She released him, searching his expression for any hint of the madness or confusion that frequently occurred when someone encountered demon blood. "Are you all right?"

"Better now," he murmured, pressing another light kiss against her lips. "What's next?"

She took Malek's knife and pierced her skin with the

blade, allowing Bane's blood to intermingle with hers. If she hadn't been bound to him, this theft of demonic power would never have worked. They still needed to hurry; the potency of Bane's blood wouldn't last long outside of its host.

"Quickly," she urged, handing the knife back to Malek and gesturing for him to cut himself. Her blood would prevent Bane's offering from harming Malek. "Our connection is still too new. It won't be strong enough. We need a blood sacrifice to break the corruption."

Malek cut his palm, and she clasped hands with him. His draconic power slammed into her, but she was better prepared this time. She welcomed his heat into her, finding a balance between the burning sensation she'd experienced when she'd touched the crystal and the fiery inferno Malek represented.

Kicking off her shoes, she used her connection with the land to fuse together the shared might of dragon, demon, and her special blend of Fae and merfolk power. Her skin glowed and she tossed her silvery-white hair back, breathing deeply of the corruption permeating the air. It was an affront to the natural order of things, and it could not be allowed to stand.

She reached outward and grasped the crystal embedded into the dead dwarf's mouth. It was hot, nearly burning her hand, but she pushed aside the discomfort and yanked hard. With a sickening sucking noise, it dislodged. Another wave of nausea rose within her at the sight of the strange gooey substance coating the end of the crystal. She tossed it to the ground, willing the elements to reclaim it.

Lightning struck the ground at her feet, shattering the crystal into dust.

She took another deep breath, the corruption in the air not nearly as choking as it had been. Bracing herself, she reached for the next crystal affixed in his eye socket and then yanked hard until it came out. She tossed it aside and repeated her summoning with the lightning.

Sweat trailed down her face from the heat of Bane's and Malek's blood, but also from that of the crystal. Her strength was beginning to falter from the tremendous expenditure of magic. They likely only had an hour at most before the Wild Hunt was upon them. She hadn't considered shielding herself before she attempted this binding. It wouldn't take much time for them to pinpoint her location.

Malek squeezed her hand and said, "Two more, Sabine. You can do this."

She nodded. With grim determination, she grasped the one in his remaining eye and yanked it clear. After dropping it to the ground, she barely managed to summon the lightning. Her legs were shaking to the point she was in danger of collapsing.

Sabine reached for the last and largest of the crystals on top of the dwarf's head, but it was too unwieldy. Her hands were slick with sweat, and she couldn't get a grip on it. Tears of frustration threatened to fall, and she could feel Bane's weakness through their bond. He was losing too much blood.

Malek moved behind her, wrapping one arm around her waist. "Lean into me, sweetheart. You can do this."

She took a shaky breath, giving him her weight. He held her upright, and she reached forward and used the last of her strength to yank the final crystal free.

Light exploded from the decapitated head, knocking Sabine and Malek backward and shattering the last crystal. She hit the ground with a thud, darkness claiming her.

Chapter Five

Draconic power fueled her from within and surrounded her with its heated embrace. Malek's magic flowed along her skin in a caress, urging her to awaken. He broke their kiss, and Sabine blinked open her eyes to stare into Malek's striking blue ones.

He searched her expression. "Take it slow, sweetheart. You lost consciousness for a minute. Are you all right?"

She didn't answer right away, taking stock of her condition. Her head was throbbing slightly, but the pain was already dissipating. The magic he'd infused into her had restored her quite a bit. So much for keeping her distance from him and his power.

It was impossible to feel regret when he was this close. Unable to resist the pull of him, she trailed her fingers along the strong lines of his jaw. It was tempting to pull him back down and kiss him again, and not just because she could use another power boost.

"Sweetheart? Talk to me," Malek said, running his thumb across her cheek.

"Hi," she whispered, captivated by the tenderness and

concern in his eyes. Once again, he'd come to her rescue and done whatever was necessary to protect her. Her stomach fluttered at the realization she was more than halfway in love with him. At the moment, she was hard-pressed to find a reason not to fall the rest of the way.

His gaze softened, and he tucked some of her hair behind her ear. "I'm guessing breaking the corruption took a lot out of you. You sure you're okay, sweetheart?"

She nodded and sat up, looking around for Bane. He was on the ground in the middle of the clearing, shaking off the effects from the magical explosion. Malek fastened the warding medallion around his neck and stood, helping her to her feet.

The dwarves hadn't appeared to fare much better, but their resistance to some forms of magic was making their recovery a little faster. They grabbed their weapons and started circling Bane, but the demon's eyes had reverted to amber.

Through their bond, Sabine could sense the corruption that had consumed Bane was gone. All that was left were the aftereffects of the carnage and destruction he'd caused. Bane's clawed hands were pressed against the ground, and his entire body trembled as though trying to wrest control of his power. The last time she'd seen him like this was when he was drunk from sipping on the life force of multiple souls.

She started to go to him, but Malek hauled her back. In a low voice, he whispered, "Tread carefully, Sabine. Bane just killed several of their men, and I doubt they're feeling friendly."

"I'm not going to allow them to hurt him."

"I know," Malek agreed, keeping his voice quiet. "I'll do what I can to help, but we need to get you inside their city before the Wild Hunt arrives."

Sabine swallowed, inwardly warring between caution and

concern. She swept her gaze over the grisly scene again, trying to make sense of what had happened. The dwarves were still busy securing Bane and hadn't noticed her and Malek standing off to the side of the clearing. She wasn't sure if these dwarves had been responsible for the corruption or if they'd stumbled upon it like Bane had.

One of them stepped forward and slapped some crystalline restraints on Bane's wrists, but Bane didn't struggle. He was still out of sorts. She needed to infuse him with more power to help bring him back to stasis. For some reason, the corruption had affected him more than anyone else.

A dark-haired dwarf with a curved sword angled his weapon toward Bane. "Yer under arrest by order of the Council of Ten for murdering our brethren and bringing a plague upon our lands. You will come willingly or be executed here and now."

Sabine inhaled sharply, unwilling to allow them to take Bane from her. Rumors of the harshness of dwarven prisons had been a thing of legends for centuries. If they didn't kill him, they'd strip Bane of his powers completely and leave him a soulless husk. It was a fate worse than death. If she had to scatter the dwarves across the clearing and negate any chance for an alliance, so be it. She wouldn't let Bane die.

"Release him," Sabine demanded, infusing her words with a sharp sting of power.

The blood-splattered dwarves spun around to face her, angling themselves to also keep Bane in sight. They were all heavily armored with a myriad of both short- and long-range weapons gripped tightly in their hands. This was no random encounter. They had the look of a dwarven patrol searching for trouble.

One of the other dwarves, a short man with cropped red hair, pointed his spear in Malek and Sabine's direction. "We don't allow anyone to make demands on our mountain, especially when they're consorting with demons. Run back to yer trees, little Fae. Unless you want to lick my boots first."

Sabine narrowed her eyes. Such insults couldn't be allowed to stand if she intended to take her rightful place as queen of the Unseelie. With a wave of power, she whipped the dwarf's weapon out of his hands. It flew beneath the underbrush and she stepped forward, sending a pulse of power along her markings. The fool either had no experience with Royal Fae or he didn't recognize her for who she was. Either way, he would be enlightened or dead by the end of this conversation.

"I am Sabin'theoria of the Unseelie, daughter and heir of Queen Mali'theoria, and great-great-granddaughter of Theoria, first of the Fae and daughter of the goddess Lachlina and the god Vestior."

She took another step toward him, the wind whipping her hair away from her face. She made a fist, wrapping a tight band of power around the dwarf and sending him to his knees. "Your rights to this mountain begin and end with *my* bloodline, dwarf. Someone has befouled this land and tainted the magic of this place. It is only by *my* intervention that this corruption has been purified. Now you add further insult by suggesting I lick your boots and arresting one of my companions?"

The red-haired dwarf cowered in front of her, his eyes wide with fear. "M-m-my apologies, Your Highness. I didn't know."

The other dwarves exchanged wary glances, looking decidedly worried about this newest development. Sabine released her control over the rude dwarf, and he scrambled backward as far away from her as possible. He cast a quick look in the direction where his weapon had disappeared, his hands twitching as though aching to retrieve it.

Sabine might not have enough remaining power to

enforce her threat of reclaiming their mountain home, but she had no intention of backing down, especially not while they held Bane captive. She looked over at Bane, but he was focused on Malek. Some unspoken communication was happening between the two men.

Malek gave him a nod and moved to stand beside her. "I'm sure these dwarves meant no disrespect, Queen Sabine. They likely didn't recognize you."

Sabine arched her brow at Malek, but his expression was carefully blank. Instead, his attention was focused on the dwarves. Sabine paused, studying him closely. He was up to something. He'd never used her title before, especially not with her informal name.

Deciding to play along, she shrugged and said, "Perhaps. However, I won't ignore the insult to this land or the corruption that's been wrought. Who is responsible for this desecration?"

"We ain't done nothin' to the land," a dwarf with a long scar down the side of his face sputtered in protest. "Everyone knows the demons twist magic."

Bane snorted in contempt. "Fool. We steal lives, not play with magic."

"Who you callin' a fool?" the scarred dwarf sneered, jabbing his weapon in Bane's direction and nicking his chest.

Anger ripped through Sabine, and her hands curled into fists. Before she could intervene, Malek stepped forward and held up his hands in a peaceable gesture.

"My name is Captain Malek Rish'dan. The captive you're holding is Bane, a passenger on my ship and ally of Queen Sabine," Malek said, gesturing toward the demon who was still bound. "I'm well acquainted with Hargrim Icemail, one of your trading leaders. If you'll allow us to speak with him or one of your council members, I'm sure we can get this matter cleared up without any more bloodshed."

The dark-haired dwarf who had arrested Bane took a step toward Malek, eyeing him up and down. Like the other dwarves, he was covered in a combination of sweat and blood from the recent battle, but he carried himself with an air of command. The metallic jewelry he wore was more intricate than the others, with colorful crystals embedded into the ornaments. The hand axe at his side was a work of art, with carvings in the handle and decorated with precious gems. If Sabine had to guess, he held a position of leadership among this group.

"Aye, Captain Malek. I've heard of you. Hargrim's spoken well of you." He darted another concerned glance at Sabine. "The name's Volack Greatspear. While I'm not disputing yer lady's claim to the demon, we can't release him to you, even if she decides to strike us down. He killed some of our brethren, and their blood still paints our skin. I can assure you he'll be dealt with in accordance with our laws, but such matters are beyond any of us. We need to turn him over to our council."

Panic rushed through her. Her tightly bound control on her magic faltered, and the markings on her skin glowed when her power flared.

If Bane was imprisoned in Razadon, Sabine wasn't sure she'd be able to free him. It was one thing to handle a few dwarves standing beneath the sky, but she'd be at a disadvantage once Bane was inside their underground city. Demons were a convenient scapegoat whenever something went wrong. They might be neighbors with the dwarves, but the two groups rarely got along.

"A moment," Malek said to the dwarves and stepped in front of her, blocking her view of them. He wrapped his arm around her waist and pulled her close. In a low voice, he urged, "Wait, Sabine. If you use magic against them, they'll bring the full might of Razadon against you. The only thing dwarves love more than a strong drink is a worthy political opponent with the potential to unite the clans. We need to get you inside Razadon and out of the line of fire."

Disbelief filled her. Malek and Bane had something of a contentious relationship, but she hadn't truly believed he wanted Bane killed. She curled her fingers into his shirt and whispered, "You can't be serious. You want me to allow this? They'll kill him, Malek."

"Not immediately," he whispered in her ear, pulling her even closer. "Let's see how this plays out. If Bane wanted you to fight for him, he wouldn't be such a docile captive. He knows what's at risk. Your safety is paramount. We need to get you into the city before the Wild Hunt descends upon us."

She hesitated and then peered around him to study Bane. The demon gave her a barely discernible nod, indicating she should listen to Malek.

It went against everything inside her to back down. She'd promised to protect Bane, and now he was willing to allow himself to be taken into custody? A sharp wave of guilt filled her. The only times Bane had ever abandoned his principles or went against his instincts was when he was determined to protect her. She didn't think she would ever forgive herself if something happened to him.

"I'm asking you to trust me," Malek murmured, running his hand down her back in a gentle caress. "You need to rest and restore your magic. I don't know how much you have left, but I can't give you more without revealing myself. We were lucky the dwarves didn't notice when I roused you. We won't be that fortunate again."

Drat. She hadn't considered that. If the dwarves caught Malek using dragonfire, they'd do everything within their power to kill him. The silent communication between Bane and Malek now made sense. They both had likely realized how weakened she was after breaking through the corruption and were trying to buy some time. Unlike her, both Bane and Malek had firsthand knowledge of the dwarves. She needed to defer to their judgment.

Recognizing the wisdom of Malek's words, she nodded. "You're right. I'll try to buy us some time or at least muddy the political waters until we figure out how to get Bane out of there."

"Good. I have an idea, but I'll need you to keep playing up your birthright. I'm going to pretend to be a simple human ship captain who's managed to catch your eye. For some reason, you actually think I'm charming."

Sabine's mouth twitched. Malek was anything but simple. He winked and released her, stepping aside to face the dwarves once again. They were all watching them, likely wondering about their relationship and what they'd just discussed. Remembering Bane's words aboard the ship about not showing concern for her choices in bedmates, she decided to ignore their curious looks.

If she needed to play up her birthright, her best chance was embracing her mother's memory. For centuries, her mother had cultivated a reputation of ruthless determination. If fate had taken a different turn, her mother would have been the one to step foot on this mountain instead of Sabine. She wouldn't have hesitated in executing each of these dwarves at the first sign of disrespect. Sabine had no intention of doing the same, but these dwarves didn't know that.

Sabine inclined her head, emulating her mother's regal bearing. "Very well. I will allow you to escort my companion to Razadon until I have spoken with your council. Until then, I expect him to remain unharmed."

Relief flashed through Volack's eyes, and he nodded. Good. He didn't want an altercation either, and Malek had offered them a neat alternative without anyone losing face.

"Of course, Your Highness," Volack said with a low bow. He thumped his fist against his chest in a gesture of respect. "You have my word that no harm will come to yer demon until after the council makes their ruling. If you'll follow me, we'll be happy to escort you to Razadon. We'll send others to gather our fallen so their bodies might be returned to the stone."

He motioned for the other dwarves to gather their prisoner. Bane rose to his feet, towering over his dwarven escort. They started to march him toward the mountain path, but Sabine hesitated.

She glanced back in the direction they'd come from, searching for any sign of Rika or Blossom. It might be safer to send Rika back to the ship, but Sabine had made a promise to Rika's grandmother to watch over the seer. "We still need to find Rika and Blossom. They're probably still hiding."

Malek picked up their bags and nodded. "I'll tell Volack we need to collect them. Give me a minute."

While Malek headed over to speak with Volack, Sabine took a few steps away from the clearing and scanned the forest. She didn't see any sign of Blossom or Rika.

She paused, glancing back at the gruesome scene in the clearing. Even having grown up witnessing such things in Faerie, this amount of blood and carnage had shaken her. Rika had been much more sheltered as a child, and Sabine had no intention of shattering what was left of her innocence. With a wave of her hand, Sabine crafted a temporary illusion to hide the bodies from view.

"The others are going ahead, but Volack's going to wait with us," Malek said, gesturing toward the dwarf walking at his side.

The dwarf eyed the pristine clearing with a frown. "Handy trick. Glamour?"

She inclined her head at the dwarf's question. "Indeed. It

will only last a short time. By the time your people arrive to reclaim your fallen companions, it will have faded. Until then, it will remain undisturbed."

"Can you call Blossom or do we need to go back to look for them?" Malek asked, placing his hand against her lower back.

"I'll call her."

Sabine infused her breath with a hint of magic and whistled sharply. Blossom appeared a few moments later, trailing a stream of glittering pixie dust behind her. The pixie's eyes were wild, and the red tinge to her dust indicated she was extremely agitated.

Sabine tensed and held out her hand for Blossom to land. "Where's Rika?"

"It wasn't my fault!"

"Blossom," Sabine warned, growing more concerned by the pixie's reticence. "What happened to Rika? Where is she?"

"I tried to make her look like a butterfly," Blossom said in a rush, pointing at the trees behind her. "I used the magic from the flowers, but it went wonky. You have to fix it, Sabine!"

A sick feeling rose in her stomach. Seers were resistant to many forms of power, and magic didn't always behave around them in a predictable manner. It was one of the reasons her people had hunted down and tried to eradicate seers for centuries.

The dwarf arched his brow at her. "What's the bug talking about?"

"I'm not a bug! I'm a pixie!" Blossom shouted, her wings twitching in agitation. "Can I dust him, Sabine? Pretty please?"

Malek leaned toward the dwarf and whispered loudly, "I'd apologize for insulting her pixie if I were you, Volack. Your people have already issued grave insult to Queen

Sabine today. She's been far more tolerant than most rulers, especially given the circumstances." He glanced at Blossom, and Sabine caught a trace of humor in his eyes. "Trust me, you don't want to be dusted. Pixie dust is anything but pleasant."

Volack considered Malek for a moment. He lowered his head and said, "My apologies, Your Highness. To you as well, Lady Blossom."

Sabine inclined her head, acknowledging his sincerity. She doubted many dwarves had ever seen a pixie. To her knowledge, they didn't travel this far south without a Fae escort.

"He called me Lady Blossom, Sabine. Did you hear him?" Blossom preened, immediately forgetting the previous insult. "Can we make that my official title?"

Sabine blew out a breath. Now she'd never hear the end of that request. "We need to focus on Rika right now. Can you take us to her?"

When Blossom nodded, Sabine motioned for her to lead the way. The pixie took flight and zipped through the trees. Sabine hastened after her, glancing up at the sky for any sign of the Wild Hunt. So far, it was clear, but they were running out of time. She just hoped the treaty was still in force and the Wild Hunt couldn't continue their pursuit once she was within the dwarven mountain.

The pixie stopped at a large tree covered with a light dusting of snow crystals. "Um, you can come out now, Rika. If anyone can fix it, it's Sabine."

Rika took a step away from the tree, her eyes shimmering from unshed tears. Sabine jerked back, gaping in horror at the human girl's altered appearance. Rika appeared mostly unchanged, except for the twitching antennae poking out of her head and giant butterfly wings affixed to her back.

"I'm—I'm hideous!" Rika wailed and burst into tears.

Volack made a strangled cry that sounded a lot like a laugh. "Now that's a bug."

"Shit," Malek said from behind her. "Please tell me that's an illusion."

"Not my fault!" Blossom shrieked, zipping around Rika. "I don't like this place. Bad magic. Really bad magic."

Sabine recovered quickly and walked toward Rika. "You're not hideous, Rika. Just different."

Sabine circled the seer, studying her wings where they'd sprouted from her back. Rika's shirt had torn, and there was a trace of blood on the edge of the material. Sabine frowned. This wasn't good. Blood should never be involved in an illusion.

Rika's wings shimmered midnight blue and black in the sunlight. Under any other circumstances, they would have been beautiful. Sabine reached out to touch one of them, and a light dust of glitter coated her hand when Sabine pulled away. She stared at the residue on her hand in shock. It wasn't an illusion. Rika's wings were real.

Blossom landed on Sabine's shoulder, her wings drooping. "I'm sorry, Rika. Don't be mad at me. I didn't know the magic wouldn't work on you. If anyone can make it better, it's Sabine."

Rika took a shaky breath and wiped away her tears. "Is Blossom right? Can you fix it?"

Sabine hesitated a little too long. When Rika's eyes began to water again, Sabine mentally kicked herself. "It's going to take a little bit of trial and error to figure out how to reverse whatever Blossom did."

Hope shone from Rika's eyes, but Sabine didn't elaborate. She tried to think of a possible solution, but her eyes kept gravitating toward those wings again. Blossom had somehow managed to turn illusion magic into a physical manifestation. Sabine had never seen such a thing before, except in books describing how the Fae had created other races like the Beastpeople. She shared a small bond with Blossom, which allowed the pixie to draw upon power, but Blossom shouldn't be able to do this.

Another dwarf with a long scar on the side of his face came running up to them but skidded to a halt at the sight of Rika. "By the stone's breath! Is that a giant pixie?"

"Pixies don't have antennae, you stupid shorty!" Blossom yelled, her face turning red. "She's part butterfly!"

"Who ya calling shorty, bug?" The scarred dwarf turned back toward Volack and elbowed him. "Did her da have sex with a butterfly?"

Volack shrugged. "I don't know, mate. The tall ones are weird."

Malek muttered a curse and turned toward the dwarves. He spoke a few quiet words to them, gesturing toward Sabine and Rika standing a short distance away.

Rika covered her face with her hands and cried. Sabine put her arm around the girl's shoulder, careful not to injure her fragile wings. "It's all right, Rika. This is temporary. If it bothers you that much, I can temporarily mask it with an illusion."

Rika sniffled and looked up at her. "You really think you can fix it?"

"You have my word I'll do everything within my power to return you to your normal form."

"The Fae can't lie, right?"

"No, we can't," Sabine agreed, not pointing out she hadn't promised she would fix it. It would cost her a considerable amount of magic to maintain an illusion over Rika, but she needed to make it right. She should have taken the time to boost Blossom's power without having the pixie rely on the flowers growing nearby, especially since the magic in the area had been corrupted.

Sabine brushed away Rika's tears and asked, "What do you wish of me, Rika? Do you want me to hide your wings from sight?"

"For what it's worth, I think your wings are very pretty," Malek said and walked toward them. He gave Rika a disarming smile. "Besides, how often can someone say they have wings like a pixie? You'll have some great stories to tell everyone."

Rika's cheeks pinked at Malek's compliment. She worried her lower lip and glanced at Blossom. "I-I guess it might not be too bad to have wings for a while. Do I really look like a pixie?"

"A bit," Sabine replied in agreement, but secretly she thought the twitching antennae were a little bizarre.

Blossom grinned and clapped her hands. "I can teach you all about being a pixie. Maybe we can even have Sabine shrink you so you can get the full experience! I wonder if your wings are just for show or if you can really fly?"

The scarred dwarf cleared his throat. "Uh, Volack? The demon's giving us a bit of trouble, and we promised not to hurt him."

Volack scowled. "What's the problem?"

The scarred dwarf winced. "He says he won't take another step unless his queen accompanies him. We tried to move him along, but he tossed Wospin up into a nearby tree and broke his spear. The demon's threatening to strangle the next dwarf who comes near him unless we bring his queen."

Malek's mouth twitched in a smile. "Effective, isn't he?"

Sabine sighed. It likely wasn't an idle threat. She motioned for Volack to lead the way. "Let's go. We'll figure it out after we get to Razadon."

Chapter Six

"Hey, shorty. Have you ever considered learning how to use that weapon properly? Or were you too busy sucking on your mother's teat to pay attention to your lessons?"

Sabine inhaled sharply at Bane's insult. The dwarf he was addressing didn't appear pleased by the comment either. The tips of the dwarf's ears turned bright red, and he snarled something too low to be overheard. He waved his axe threateningly in the demon's direction, and the other dwarves roared with laughter.

"What is Bane thinking?" Sabine muttered and shook her head.

Malek chuckled and placed his hand against her back, making her skin prickle in awareness. "I wouldn't worry. Dwarves enjoy a good ribbing. Like demons, they admire strength. He's already proven himself to be a capable warrior. The fact that he's willing to keep poking at them even while he's their captive will only make them respect him more."

She arched her brow but didn't argue the point. In some ways, demons and dwarves had more in common than with her people. They all respected strength and power, but the Fae prided themselves on maintaining a cultured dignity. It was one of the traits that had shocked her the most after leaving Faerie and living among the demon brothers.

"Not again!" Rika cried, thrashing her legs and arms in midair. Sabine grabbed Rika's hand and pulled her back to the ground. The seer's wings kept fluttering uncontrollably, and she kept gaining a little too much upward momentum.

"You okay?"

Rika wrinkled her nose. "Yeah. Thank—I mean... That was close."

Sabine smiled, pleased Rika had caught herself before expressing her gratitude. It was happening less often, but she still forgot on occasion. "I won't let you fly away. Perhaps Blossom can give you a bit more advice on how to keep your feet on the ground."

"You'll get the hang of it, Rika," Blossom said with a grin. "Baby pixies fly out of their flowers all the time, but it doesn't take long to learn how to control your wings."

Rika brushed one of her lopsided antennae away from her face. "I'm worried I'm going to end up in the clouds."

"We won't let that happen," Sabine promised, noticing more of the decorative archways on the path. These had glowing white crystals on the top, each swirling with smoky bands of the power contained within them.

Malek leaned in close and whispered, "Keep an eye on the crystals embedded into the archways, particularly the ones as we near the city gates. The purple ones act as an alarm to detect foreign magic. I'm not sure what the other colors do."

She frowned, hoping the alarm wouldn't be a problem for the dragon shapeshifter. "Will Levin's warding necklace hide your identity?"

He hesitated. "I believe so, but the necklace wasn't calibrated exactly for my type of power. It's close enough to

Levin's wyvern magic that it should also mask mine. At least in theory."

"Maybe we should walk in together," she suggested quietly. "They already know about me, and I doubt their crystals will be able to differentiate the types of foreign magic it encounters. Our bond may help negate it."

Malek nodded. "It's worth a try. If anything goes wrong, I should be able to shift and get us out of here. If we head to the Sky Cities, you'd at least be protected from the Wild Hunt."

Sabine's stomach lurched at the thought. She might trust Malek, but the idea of walking into the dragon's den terrified her. There were thousands of dragons in their world, and she was as much their enemy as Malek was to her people.

Blossom landed on Sabine's shoulder. "So what's the plan? Are we going to launch a big escape to free Bane? Are we going to blast their mountain wide open? Are we going to take over the dwarven kingdom and make a big garden out of the rubble?"

Sabine grimaced. "How about we acquire information first and leave the bloodbath as a last resort? I'd like to have Bane freed peacefully if possible."

Blossom saluted her. "Snooping. Got it. I've got lots of flowers, so I'm ready for action."

Sabine glanced at Rika, but she didn't appear to be having any difficulties keeping pace with them. Other than her feet occasionally leaving the ground from the uncontrollable fluttering of her wings, Rika appeared to be adapting quickly to her new appearance. Sabine kept catching Rika trying to get a better look at her multicolored wings. Every time Rika twisted her body, her antennae fell forward and bopped her in the forehead.

Turning back toward Blossom, Sabine asked, "Do you

have any of the flowers you used to change Rika's appearance?"

"Yep. I figured you'd need some of them to reverse it."

Sabine nodded. At least that would make it easier to determine how such an anomaly had occurred. If it was from the corruption, she had a better chance of reversing it. If it happened to be from Rika's seer abilities, Sabine wasn't sure how to help her.

The wind changed, and Sabine's skin prickled in awareness. She turned her gaze upward. The sky was darkening, a sign the Wild Hunt's approach was imminent. Panic rushed through her. They were out of time.

Sabine leaned toward Malek and whispered, "It's the Wild Hunt. We need to hurry. How far away are we from Razadon?"

Malek lifted his head, his eyes narrowing on the sky. He placed his arm around her waist and pulled her closer in a protective gesture. "The main entrance is right over that rise. Another ten minutes at the most."

Blossom squeaked. "They're moving really fast, Sabine. I can feel them."

Sabine gauged the distance and the dark clouds in the other direction. "That's not enough time. We won't make it before the Hunt's upon us."

In a loud voice, Malek called, "Hey, Volack! Can we get a move on? There's trouble approaching."

Volack paused, glancing upward. His eyes widened, and he muttered a curse. "Double time, men! Make haste. That storm has a bad look about it. If it's tied into whatever happened to Badac, we need to get to shelter now!"

They all increased their pace, heading faster up the path. Suddenly, the sun disappeared behind heavy cloud cover and the sky darkened to midnight. A cold wind filled the air, whipping Sabine's hair away from her face and chilling her down to her bones. The ground trembled beneath their feet, and a low peal of thunder rumbled throughout the mountain.

Sabine looked over her shoulder and another flash of silvered lightning lit the sky. Dark hooded figures emerged from the dark clouds, riding atop creatures of nightmare. Silvery tentacles emerged from beneath the riders' cloaks, while the eyes of their mounts glowed red with malice. It was the Wild Hunt, and she'd always believed the next time she saw them would be the last.

"Run!" Malek shouted. "They're nearly upon us!"

The dwarves rushed up the mountain. Sabine grabbed Rika's hand to keep her grounded while they ran. Malek pulled out his sword but kept pace with them while they raced ahead.

Rika stumbled in the darkness, pulling Sabine down with her. Sabine hit the ground, her palms biting into the sharp rocks and stones. Malek pulled both her and Rika to their feet.

"Sabine!" Bane roared, jerking against his captives to reach her. The dwarves shouted obscenities at him, pushing the demon onward.

"Go, Bane!" Sabine yelled, motioning for him to run. Rika was human and couldn't hope to keep pace with them, but Sabine wasn't about to abandon her charge.

"They're here!" Blossom shrieked, clinging to Sabine's neck. "You have to run, Sabine!"

"We won't make it," Rika said, choking on a sob. Sabine grabbed her hand again, but Malek scooped Rika up and threw her over his shoulder.

"Run, Sabine! Dammit, run! I've got her!"

Trusting Malek at his word, Sabine lowered her chin to her chest and ran for her life. Using the glowing crystals affixed to each of the archways as a beacon, she raced up the mountain path. Malek's footsteps pounded on the stone behind her, while the rumble of thunder from the Hunt's mounts became nearly deafening. The riders were nearly upon them, but Sabine couldn't stop. The lightning strikes were coming faster, and Sabine's markings began to flash in resonance.

In the distance, Sabine caught sight of what appeared to be some sort of cave. She flew toward it, following the dwarves as they nimbly darted up the path. As they drew closer, Sabine realized the opening wasn't natural in design. The dwarves had sculpted a stone archway directly into the side of the mountain. Three large crystals were embedded around the entrance, and they flared with a deep red and purple glow in warning.

Sabine raced inside the cave along with the dwarves and Bane. She skidded to a halt right beside a sealed stone door. Malek entered moments after her with Rika still over his shoulder, passing directly beneath the crystalline arch. Sabine lifted her hand to protect them but froze. The crystals hadn't changed. Whatever protective measures had been enabled, Rika had either negated them with her seer ability or Malek's warding necklace had protected him.

Malek lowered Rika to the ground and turned toward Sabine. He cupped her face, his brow furrowed as his eyes roamed over her features. "You're all right?"

Sabine started to answer him, but Rika's gasp broke through her thoughts. A creeping shadow moved toward them like tendrils reaching for its quarry. In the deepest part of the darkness, Sabine caught sight of the Wild Hunt and its riders.

"Activate the barriers!" one of the dwarves shouted. Two of them rushed forward, yanking hard on silver rings embedded into the cavern wall. A second later, the archway glowed an even deeper shade of red, but the light didn't touch the riders outside the cave.

A dark hooded figure approached on his mount, the shadows enveloping him with aching familiarity. The black steed tossed its head, its mane of fire piercing the darkness. The rider gripped the reins with his skeletal hands and turned his mount to the side just outside the cave's entrance.

The rider fixed his glowing red eyes on Sabine, his gaze penetrating down to her soul. It was as though every secret and every thought she'd ever held were laid bare in front of him. A tight band wrapped around her chest, threatening to steal her will. She took a shaky breath, staring into Death's face for the third time in her life.

"The godsforsaken Wild Hunt," one of the dwarves whispered, his eyes wide with terror. "They'll strike us all down."

Rika whimpered while Blossom trembled against Sabine's neck, trying to make herself as small as possible. The smell of fear rose sharply in the cave, nearly choking Sabine with its sickly-sweet stench. Several of the dwarves crumpled to the ground, praying to their ancestors for forgiveness for various transgressions. Only Malek and Bane remained standing, but even they appeared shaken by the sight of the Wild Hunt.

Sabine held the Huntsman's glowing gaze, refusing to succumb to the wave of terror the Hunt evoked. He was the living embodiment of nightmare, a tale of such fearsomeness that few who encountered his sight ever recovered.

The riders would hunt her to the ends of the world to fulfill their pact, no matter what lives they endangered. She wouldn't allow anyone else to be harmed when she was the one they wanted. Sabine straightened her shoulders and took a step toward the Huntsman, prepared to meet her fate. If this was her end, so be it.

"Sabine!" Bane shouted, pulling at his restraints. "Malek, stop her!"

"Don't do it!" Blossom shrieked, yanking on Sabine's hair. "He'll squish you! Malek! Help!"

Malek grabbed her arm, halting her in her tracks. "That archway marks the entrance to Razadon, Sabine. Don't cross the crystal's light or you'll be outside its protection."

"H-He's right," Volack said, the tremor in his voice making it difficult to understand the dwarf. "W-We're within Razadon territory now. They—they shouldn't be able to cross. At least, that's what I've heard."

The Huntsman inclined his head in acknowledgment of Volack's words. Sabine froze, unsure what this meant. How long would the Wild Hunt wait for her to emerge? She couldn't remain trapped in Razadon for the rest of her days.

Volack knelt on the ground and flipped open a small trapdoor with several glowing crystals inside it. He worked quickly to arrange them in some sort of pattern. Sabine could sense a trace of magic coming from whatever he was doing, but it was foreign and unfamiliar power.

Sabine's vision wavered the longer she stared into Death's gaze. There was something about him that tickled the edge of her memory. It was almost as though she could hear a song far off in the distance. It was vaguely familiar, but she couldn't quite place it.

The Huntsman's mount snorted and impatiently pawed at the ground. Sabine pulled back, unaware she'd been reaching toward him. The Huntsman remained immobile, continuing to watch her.

"The Hunstman's mount wants to eat me!" Blossom shrieked, her wings fluttering rapidly and sending pixie dust everywhere. "I'm not cut out for this. Look at me! I'm losing dust. I'm too young to lose my dust. We need to get into the city and away from that thing!"

"Blossom, stay out of sight," Sabine said quietly, not tearing her gaze away from the Huntsman. She wasn't sure the pixie was wrong about the Huntsman's mount. His steed hadn't taken his glowing eyes off Blossom the entire time. Blossom hid underneath Sabine's hair, hugging Sabine's neck even tighter.

Malek frowned. "She's right about one thing. Volack, we need to get inside. Are you almost done unlocking the seals to the city?"

"Aye," Volack said and finished stacking the crystals. He slammed the panel shut and turned toward two of the dwarves standing nearby.

"Close the damn gate, and let's get the door open," Volack ordered, snapping his fingers. "We'll send people out to retrieve the bodies of our men once they're gone. Move it!"

The dwarves jumped to attention and ran to an enormous door, which took up almost the entire back of the cave. Runic symbols had been etched into its design, and Sabine could sense layers of protective magic embedded within it. Beside the door were two large wheels with heavy metal spokes jutting out of them. Both dwarves gripped the spokes tightly while Volack counted down.

"Three, two, one! Now, men!"

The dwarves strained, their faces turning red as they slowly turned the wheels. Deep within the mountain, Sabine could hear a loud clanging noise like chains grating against metal. With a creak and a groan, the heavy gate began to close, cutting off their view of the Wild Hunt. Volack moved closer to the dwarves turning the wheels, shouting encouragements.

Her heart pounded at the intensity in the Huntsman's gaze. It was almost as though he were trying to communicate something to her. In the past, he'd used his mental form of communication to speak. Perhaps the barrier was preventing him from touching her mind.

"Uh oh. What's that?" Blossom asked, tugging on Sabine's hair and pointing toward the growing shadows.

The dark fog surrounding the Wild Hunt was creeping forward, moving up and over the archway as though testing its resistance. Sabine swallowed, mentally willing the dwarves to hurry in closing the gate.

"They can't get through it, can they?" Rika asked, sidling closer to Malek.

"I don't believe so," Malek said, but Sabine heard the uncertainty in his voice. "Razadon is one of the most secure fortresses in the world. No one other than dwarves can open the gate or doorway to their city. It requires two dwarves working the wheels simultaneously."

Rika paled. "We're going to be trapped in here once the gate closes?"

Malek hesitated and then nodded. "It's only for a short time. They can't open the door until the gate is closed. It's another security measure to prevent anyone from accessing the city."

Sabine remained quiet. It might be nearly impossible to enter, but that also meant it would be equally difficult for them to leave. If things fared badly in Razadon, they were going to be trapped. Freeing Bane might be even more challenging than she'd first thought.

Rika darted a glance back at the dwarves. "What's taking so long?"

"They have magical protections in place," Malek said. "The dwarves use their ties to the stone to make the gate and door obey their command. All magic requires concentration, and they're a little distracted."

The gate sealed shut with a loud *clank*. Sabine let out the breath she'd been holding and nearly staggered in relief. Malek immediately wrapped his arm around her waist, and she leaned against him for a moment. At least they were safe for the time being.

Volack turned toward them and said, "We have to wait a bit until we can disable the wards on the door."

Sabine nodded. Being trapped inside their cave wasn't ideal, but it was better than the alternative. Besides, it would give her the opportunity to see to Bane's injuries.

Several of the dwarves opened their packs and pulled out their flasks. Many of them took a seat on the nearby benches or on the floor. Blossom flew off her shoulder, likely to investigate the contents of the packs. If any of them had any honey or sweet treats that might appeal to a pixie, they'd likely end up with a much lighter load.

Sabine walked toward Bane, who was still being guarded by two dwarves. They eyed her warily but didn't try to order her away. The crystal restraints around Bane's wrists swirled with grey-and-white magic of some sort. Sabine wasn't sure what they did, but she suspected they impeded Bane's magical abilities.

She eyed the dwarven guards and said, "I need a moment with my protector."

"Yer not plannin' on freeing him, yeah?"

Sabine narrowed her eyes and didn't respond, refusing to give any such promises. The dwarves exchanged a look, appearing decidedly uncertain.

Volack waved them away and said, "Let her pass."

They grunted and moved aside. Sabine closed the distance between her and Bane, worried by his pallor. She still didn't understand why he'd chosen to surrender. It was too risky to ask him when they were surrounded by people she didn't trust.

In a low voice, she asked, "Can you heal yourself if I give you enough magic?"

Bane gave her a curt nod. "The shackles prevent me from

using my abilities against anyone, but I still retain control over my body."

Sabine nodded and pressed her hand against his arm, sending a strong wave of power over him. She might not possess the ability to heal, but Bane could twist her magic to heal his own injuries. She had little magic to give him, but she wouldn't allow him to enter Razadon as a wounded captive.

His eyes flashed silver for a moment before reverting again. His skin shimmered, and his wounds began knitting themselves back together.

"It's enough, little one," Bane murmured, pulling away from her. He leaned against the wall and closed his eyes. "I must rest before we enter the city."

Sabine nodded in understanding. Fatigue was plaguing the corners of her mind, but she couldn't risk showing any weakness. Her mother had once told her there were ways to recharge Fae magic within the dwarven city, but she wasn't sure where or how. Bane likely needed to center himself as well, focusing on healing his internal injuries with the power she'd provided.

A tickle of magic passed along Sabine's skin, and she absently rubbed her arms. It hadn't felt corrupted, but it was a little too similar to Fae illusion magic.

"Sabine, look!" Rika said, pointing at one of the walls.

Sabine's eyes widened, and she took a step toward Rika. The dwarves had used some sort of glamour to hide the true appearance of this cave. With every second that passed, new wonders emerged from the once mundane walls and bare flooring.

The tiled floor was embedded with a combination of crystals and colorful stones laid out in a design that reflected the phases of the moon. Expansive murals had been carved into the stone walls, detailing the history of the island and the dwarves. Sabine paused to stare at them, awestruck by the intricate details and obvious skill by the artists. One in particular caught her attention, so she approached it, staring at it in wonder.

A woman was seated on a carved wooden throne. Her hand was outstretched, while a glowing crystal floated in midair. Beneath her, dozens of dwarves bowed their heads in subservience.

"It's Lachlina," she whispered, gingerly touching her wrist where the goddess had marked her not once, but twice. The mark warmed in acknowledgment of her words. "She taught the dwarves to infuse their crystals with power."

"The goddess looks like you," Malek said with a frown, studying the mural carefully.

Volack moved closer to the image to study it and then Sabine. "Aye. You've definitely got the look of her. You really are her descendant, eh?"

Sabine nodded as she reached out to touch the mural and moved her fingers along the smooth stonework. With Lachlina's long silvery hair, her resemblance to both herself and her mother was staggering. It was almost as though the artist had captured the essence of her family's line in this image.

One of the other dwarves snorted and spit on the ground. "The gods wanted their pet Fae to look like 'em. The rest of us were experiments or created as amusements. Lachlina was the only one worth a damn."

Sabine lowered her hand and frowned. Lachlina was a rare exception, but Sabine wasn't convinced the goddess had been completely altruistic. "We may appear more like the gods than most, but the Fae were amusements as well. We were simply colorful decorations to be used and abused at their whim."

"At least all the rest of the gods are dead or gone," Volack said, his voice carrying a hint of disgust.

"Good riddance." The other dwarf huffed in agreement and went to speak with one of the others, making it clear the topic had touched upon a nerve.

Sabine remained quiet, deciding it would be best to end the discussion. Her time away from Faerie had shown her how little she truly knew about the world. She was beginning to question the merits of the beliefs dictated to her by the Faerie Elders. Both Malek and her own experiences had shown her things weren't always the way they seemed.

Her knowledge about the dwarves was academic at best, studied through snippets of books or conversations she'd overheard in her youth. She needed to be careful not to offend these people but also maintain a position of power, especially since she desperately needed their help.

Turning away, Sabine moved throughout the chamber, seeing other such murals on the walls and even the ceiling. They all reflected different moments in early dwarven history, prior to the time of the Dragon War.

A loud gong sounded somewhere nearby, and two of the dwarves leaped to their feet. They grabbed the wheels again and turned them. The ground reverberated beneath her feet, and the sound of heavy metal chains moving across the stone resounded through the chamber.

The heavy stone door slowly opened. Volack held up his hand, indicating they should wait while another dwarf slipped through and disappeared from sight. The doorway continued to widen, and Volack finally gestured for them to follow him.

Sabine took a steadying breath, eager for her first glimpse of Razadon and to put more distance between her and the Wild Hunt.

A colorful stone walkway lay before them, while crystal lanterns chased away the shadows. Everywhere she looked, there were more carvings and crystals of different colors.

Each facet captured the light, casting a rainbow across the murals and painting them with a variety of colors.

Her eyes widened at the realization the effect was intentional. They'd specifically designed the placement of each colored crystal so the light would fill different parts of the images. It reminded her of the kaleidoscope Malek had shown her back in Akros.

Blossom landed on Sabine's shoulder and said, "It's almost as pretty as the flowers in Esme's garden."

"It's beautiful," she whispered, trying to memorize every detail.

Malek's hand brushed against hers, a small reminder he was beside her. She darted a quick smile at him, but it quickly faded at the sound of footsteps rushing toward them. Dozens of armed dwarves, both men and women, spilled into the pathway, angling weapons in Bane's direction.

"Kill the demon!" one of the newcomers shouted, his spear jabbing into Bane's midsection. Bane's eyes flashed silver. He jerked away from the weapon and growled at his assailant. Sabine started to take a step forward, but Volack rushed ahead and shouted, "Move aside! The demon's under my protection!"

The metal of Volack's axe caught the light as he swiped it toward the crowd. Most of the dwarves scrambled back, but others were still edging forward. The small group of dwarves who had led them into the city stood by their commander, but they were no match for the sheer number of dwarves making their threatening approach.

One of the advancing newcomers yelled, "Spill the demon's blood! I bet he's the one who murdered Badac Coinbasher!"

Volack's fist struck out and slammed against the accusing dwarf's helmet. He flew backward, crumpling to the ground.

Volack turned to the next one and quickly disabled him as well.

"The demon needs to die!" another shouted, rushing toward Bane who was still bound and unable to defend himself.

"Blossom, stay with Rika," Sabine ordered and pushed forward, unwilling to allow this assault to continue. Malek's sword was already in hand and he moved with her, his weapon clashing against those in their way. The dragon shapeshifter fought with fierce skill, parrying and dodging attacks, hampered only by his desire to avoid causing the dwarves undue harm. Other than Malek and Volack's small party, no one else showed the slightest inclination to stop the dwarves from attacking Bane.

Sabine made it to Bane and reached for the restraints holding him captive. He jerked his bound wrists away from her and warned, "No, they will not forgive such treachery. One of their councilors has already been alerted to our presence."

"You won't survive that long," she argued, trying to be heard over the clash of battle surrounding them. Someone fell to the ground at their feet, groaning as another dwarf slammed into him. It was complete chaos.

"Then buy us some time," he growled, his eyes flashing to silver. She felt a rush of pain through their connection and quickly scanned him up and down. He was hurt. Badly. The dwarf with the spear had managed to pierce open one of the injuries she'd helped her protector seal shut.

Bane's poisoned blood oozed down his side, dripping precariously close to the fallen dwarf. It was a wonder the demon was still standing. He couldn't take much more. Slapping her hand against Bane's injury, Sabine infused her magic into it.

"Heal yourself," she ordered. "I'll figure something out."

Turning toward the angry mob, she gathered her magic within her. A strong wind picked up, and the markings on her skin glowed with a silver light.

Infusing her voice with a sharp lash of power reminiscent of the peal of thunder, she clapped her hands together and shouted, “Enough!”

The magical onslaught was enough to send dwarves flying through the air. They hit the ground, walls, and anything within their path. It wouldn’t stop them for long, especially with her dwindling power supply, but she wasn’t going to let them hurt Bane.

“Volack,” she called, not tearing her gaze away from the mob of angry dwarves. “You *will* get this crowd under control or be forsworn in your promise to me.”

“I’ll do what I can, Your Highness.” Volack put his fingers to his lips and let out an ear-piercing whistle.

The crowd quieted down somewhat, but they were still muttering angry complaints about Bane’s presence.

“This demon is a prisoner being transported to the jail where he will await judgment by the Council of Ten,” Volack shouted, loudly enough to be heard by all the gathered dwarves. “We will do this according to our laws, or I’ll bash every single one of your heads in.”

“The runner said Badac Coinbasher is dead,” one of the dwarves called. “The demon deserves to meet the same end as our Elder.”

Sabine froze, her heart thudding at the woman’s words. The murder of an Elder was one of the most heinous crimes imaginable. She hadn’t thought any of the men Bane had killed in that clearing were Elders, but she couldn’t be sure. If the decapitated dwarf had been their Elder, they might try to blame Bane for his death.

Malek held up his hand. “This demon was a passenger on my ship until a few hours ago. We came directly from my ship to Razadon. Other than your patrol, we didn't encounter anyone else. This demon couldn't have been responsible."

"He could have been working with a partner!"

"Demons don't share," Bane snapped, his gruff voice carrying over the din of the crowd. "The fact that I'm bound is proof enough of my innocence. If I had taken your Elder's life, I would have sipped on his life force and used his power to escape rather than allow myself to be taken captive."

The dwarves murmured at his pronouncement. Understanding dawned, and Sabine darted a quick glance at Bane. That was why he hadn't wanted her to free him. He must have expected to be accused of such.

Another man stepped forward, a dark-haired dwarf whose limited height didn't negate the impression he would be a powerful and formidable opponent. The weighted battleaxe at his side was affixed with glowing crystal points. He even had small magical crystals braided into his beard, which pulsed with a silver light.

"A demon, a human, and a Fae? Sounds like a bad joke," the dwarf sneered, making the crystals catch the light. The effect was strangely distracting with the way his beard lit up when he spoke.

Crystal-Beard waggled his eyebrows at Sabine. "Quite a few markings on yer skin fer such a little girl. Why don't you give us a peek to see how far they go under that skirt, eh?" He grabbed his crotch. "Maybe I'll give you a reward and then let you braid another crystal into my hair."

Sabine stilled, a white-hot fury engulfing her at the insult. Braiding hair among the Fae was only performed by lesser Fae who needed to absorb magic from their more powerful counterparts. The idea of this stranger suggesting she would braid his hair was the equivalent of calling her a goblin whore.

Bane roared, and even with his wrists bound, he managed to slam the dwarf into the ground. He ripped away the dwarf's axe and shoved it against Crystal-Beard's neck. "You are addressing Queen Sabin'theoria of the Unseelie. You *will* show respect, worm."

Sabine stepped around Bane and approached the man on the ground. She withdrew a knife, leaned over him, and snipped one of the crystals off his beard. She held it up to the light, pretended to admire it, and flicked it away. A hushed gasp went through the group.

Sabine tilted her knife to catch the light and warned, "Make such an offer again, and I'll ensure you don't have any hair left to braid."

Several of the dwarves sucked in air. A dwarf's beard was indicative of their placement among their cultural hierarchy, similar to the way her markings indicated she was a member of the royal family. The fact that he'd woven crystals into his beard was surely a sign he had a high social standing within Razadon.

She waved her hand, and Bane released the dwarf.

He climbed to his feet and stroked what remained of his beard. "Our condolences, daughter of Mali'theoria, but we've got something of a problem with you being here."

Sabine arched her brow but didn't respond. He'd made it a point not to call her by her title.

Crystal-Beard tapped his hand on his great-axe, the gesture not overly friendly. "Faerie sent word you've been exiled. Looks like the Unseelie throne is controlled by yer brother, Rhys'Ellesar."

Sabine narrowed her eyes, trying to rein in her temper. Beside her, Bane's entire body vibrated with anger. She held up her hand in a command for him to hold.

"Since when do the dwarves claim to know the inner workings of Faerie and her politics?" Sabine demanded, glaring at him in challenge. "I will address these claims only to your council, and not to underlings who run to see who's knocking at your front door."

Crystal-Beard stared at her for a long time and then burst into laughter. The effect was instantaneous, and the other dwarves lowered their weapons and began to chuckle.

He gave her a flourished bow and grinned. "The name's Thetar Opalmaker. We don't have much tolerance for those Seelie pretenders, but I was curious whether you had the same mettle as yer mum."

Determined to keep her bearing despite the annoying dwarf's provocation, Sabine inclined her head and said, "Well met, Thetar. These are my companions, Bane'umbra, son of Kal'thorz, Captain Malek Rish'dan of Obsidian's Storm, Rika, the Seer of Karga, and the pixie Blossom."

Thetar tensed, staring at Bane with unease. "We've heard of the demon assassin, Your Highness. Interesting choice in companions, but I'm a bit unclear why you've brought one of the exiled demon princes to our city."

Bane snorted. "The demons don't recognize inherited rule like the Fae, dwarf. Like your people, we fight for what we're due and step over the bodies in our way."

Thetar smirked. "Aye, but yer daddy is ruling the underworld all the same. Heard yer brother's back underground, sentenced to the fighting pits for causing some bit of trouble down there. Wouldn't be surprised if he didn't last longer than another week or two."

Sabine forced her body to stay relaxed, but inwardly, her heart was pounding. Thetar could only be referring to Dax. Without her being close to cement his ties to the surface, he would have been forced back underground. Something must have happened if Balkin, her Beastman protector, hadn't been able to keep him out of the underworld.

"Bane is my sworn protector, and he is here at my direction," Sabine said, wanting to curtain the discussion. There were too many prying eyes, and Sabine needed time to gather information.

The crowd had been talking in low whispers during the exchange, but the cadence of their voices changed slightly. The group fanned outward, making way for a stout woman wearing a headdress of gold and glowing crystals. Her blonde hair was parted in the center and hung nearly to her waist in two long thick braids, strewn with golden ribbons and a myriad of crystals. Tiny bells had been attached to the ends of the ribbons, and they jingled as she walked.

"Such nonsense to call me all the way down here simply because Badac lost his head," the woman said, elbowing her way through the group. When someone didn't move out of her way fast enough, she kicked out hard. The dwarf in her way stumbled backward, his eyes widening at the woman's derisive look.

She put her hands on her hips and said, "All of you who don't have business here, get back to work. If anyone remains behind, I'll assume you want to be cleaning up cave troll dung for the next week. Now go!"

The crowd quickly dissipated. Several people stopped to help those with injuries hobble away, leaving only a few curious stragglers behind who started cleaning up broken stones and tiles that had been damaged during the fight.

The newcomer swept her gaze over Bane and Malek before her eyes fell on Sabine. "Well, well. A Royal Fae. Don't that beat all. And a woman at that. Last thing we need are more knuckleheads intent on waving their sticks at each other. I'm sure Thetar's been making a right ass out of himself." She gestured to herself. "The name's Astrid Onyxborn, but most simply call me Astrid. And you are?"

"Sabin'theoria of the Unseelie," Sabine said, electing to

forgo her formal titles in lieu of the woman's more familiar greeting. "My friends call me Sabine."

A crafty smile crept over Astrid's face, and she chuckled. "Interesting. Didn't think most Fae yanked the stick out of their asses long enough to make a simple introduction. Yer mum was a bit of a firecracker too."

Sabine stared at her in surprise. "*The* Astrid? Councilwoman on behalf of the Powerbroker Guild?"

Astrid laughed, a big booming noise that shook the headdress she wore and made the gems dance in the light. "Ah, I see yer mum told you about me. Shame about her death. I was hoping to collect a pretty new power crystal after our next game of taspern. Woman was a shark with magic but had the gods-worst luck at cards." She arched her brow. "Don't suppose you play?"

Thetar and the dwarven guards who had escorted them into the city had become eerily quiet. Bane had also gone still, a warning in his amber eyes. Sabine tilted her head to regard Astrid, deciding the woman was testing her.

From what Sabine could recall from her mother's description, Astrid was a shrewd and calculating woman. Almost everyone knew Sabine's mother had been murdered, and Astrid's callous remark set Sabine even more on guard. Her mother didn't have many friends, but she'd considered Astrid to be one of them.

"I haven't played that particular game, but I've proven to be a quick study," Sabine said with a disarming smile. "As my mother's sole heir, she left me with a number of her gifts—both good and bad. Perhaps we'll see if I inherited her skill at games of chance."

Astrid cackled in delight and slapped her thigh. "Gifts, eh? I heard about some of those gifts. One of them appears to be camped right outside our main gate. Too bad such gifts can't be returned when the packaging doesn't meet yer expectations. Maybe you should visit our market while yer here and shop for a particularly sharp ribbon cutter? I've found it to be an easy way to eliminate such nastiness."

"Indeed," Sabine agreed with a smile. "If you'd like to join me while I browse Razadon's wares in search of such a tool, we can also discuss my potential for losing at cards. Your headdress would be even more astounding with another crystal to adorn it."

"Aye. You'll do, girlie. You'll do." Astrid grinned, showing her bright white teeth. "Well then, since you've decided to come to Razadon to claim yer proper place, we'll let you head on to the Faerie embassy. Dagmar is yer steward, and she's a right good girl. Kin on my mum's side somewhere. Or maybe it was half-aunt's cousin? Could even have been one of our oath-bound servants."

Astrid waved her hand as though it didn't matter, but her eyes fell briefly on Bane before turning back toward Sabine. "Kin's kin, blood or not. No one knows that better than the Fae, eh?"

"I'm so glad you agree," Sabine said and tilted her head in acknowledgment of Astrid's unspoken words. The only way to keep Bane safe would be to claim him publicly as hers.

Turning back toward the demon captive, Sabine ignored his restraints and pressed her hand against Bane's cheek to send another fortifying wave of power over him. His eyes briefly flashed, and even his horns took on a silver sheen as her magic rushed through him. She'd need to rest soon, but it was imperative she kept up with appearances.

"I will see you soon, my protector," she said, loud enough for her voice to carry to those who were lingering nearby. With any luck, rumors about her claim over Bane would circulate throughout Razadon and offer him another layer of protection.

Bane knelt before her, but she caught a gleam of approval

in his eyes before he lowered his horned head. "As you command, My Queen."

Astrid guffawed. "Nicely done, girl. That'll make those buffoons think twice about harming yer guard. The demon will be safe enough until the council decides what to do with him. It'll likely be a day or two for those fools to pull their heads out of their asses and get organized."

Sabine pasted on a pleasant smile and motioned for Bane to rise. His obeisance was unsettling. It was likely grating on him as well, but she'd continue to emphasize their sworn blood bond if it helped them win his freedom. She needed to learn more about the dwarven justice system and fast. Astrid would probably be their best chance of that, especially with her connection to Sabine's mother.

Malek motioned for Rika to stay close, while Blossom flew to Sabine and hid under her loose hair. Blossom patted her neck and whispered, "I don't think I like this place. I don't see any flowers, and it smells like dust and bad cheese."

Sabine made a noncommittal noise. Despite the beauty of Razadon, she wasn't sure she liked it either.

Astrid studied Rika. "Well, don't that beat all. Look at those wings. Is she a giant pixie? Don't know about those antennae though."

"They're something else," Thetar said, cocking his head and studying Rika.

Malek put his arm around Rika and whispered something in her ear. Rika's lower lip trembled slightly, but she nodded and straightened her shoulders.

"I'm actually part butterfly," Rika said, holding her head high.

A rush of pride flowed through Sabine. She gave Rika a nod of approval and then turned back toward Astrid. "Is the Faerie embassy far from here? I'd like to get cleaned up before the next council meeting."

Astrid motioned for Sabine to follow her. "Aye. Yer quarters are right this way. I'll introduce you to Dagmar so you can get settled." She glanced over her shoulder and said, "Thetar, fix yer damn beard while I'm gone. It looks like a cave rat's been chewing on it again."

Chapter Seven

Sabine followed Dagmar down the streets of Razadon, while four more guards trailed behind them. Malek had elected to remain a few steps behind her, presumably to keep a close eye on Rika and Blossom. Astrid had only stayed long enough to introduce their redheaded guide before a messenger had called her away on an urgent council matter.

Dagmar was surprisingly friendly, and she bounced down the street with an enthusiasm Sabine found endearing. None of the stories Sabine had heard about Razadon had done it justice. Everywhere she looked, new marvels begged to be explored.

The air was both cooler and heavier with the faint scent of incense lingering around them. Despite the city being nestled within a remote mountain, everything was brightly lit and bustling with activity. The streets were crowded with people intent on various destinations. Sabine spotted a few ogres, trolls, goblins, and other mixed magical races, but the majority of the denizens were dwarves.

What she hadn't expected was the sheer height or the vast

number of stone buildings nestled within the mountain. Windows overlooking the streets had been carved into the walls and covered with different colored glass. Everywhere she looked was a rainbow of colors and remarkable artistry.

Each building they passed was narrow and tall, with some of them appearing to be dozens of stories in height. Crystal lifts moved groups of people up and down to the different levels, taking them to various winding paths. Sabine leaned over one of the balconies to try to gauge the distance, but it was impossible to see the bottom level of the dwarven city. If the twinkling lights were any indication, the lowest part of Razadon descended nearly to the underworld.

Rika was staring wide-eyed at everything, and even Blossom was silently gaping. It was one of the first times Sabine had seen the pixie rendered speechless.

"Everything's been in an uproar since Badac went missing," Dagmar said, leading them away from the main thoroughfare in Razadon.

Sabine glanced at her, curious about this Badac. "Do you know what happened to him?"

"Nope. He simply disappeared, and none of our crystals could track him anywhere in Razadon. We sent a patrol out to try to locate him, but it looks like they found you instead."

Sabine frowned. That didn't bode well. If the Elder had been the one murdered with those strange crystals, it might explain the strength of the corruption.

Dagmar approached a set of wooden double doors. An image of the Crown of Shadows and Moonlight had been etched into the top of the archway. It was a visual reminder that everyone who passed beneath the doorway was beholden to the Unseelie court and subject to their laws.

Dagmar pushed open the doors and led them inside. A trace of Faerie magic caressed her skin, causing her markings to flare briefly.

"I can't say I've ever been in this part of Razadon," Malek said to Dagmar.

"This wing is private from the rest of the city," Dagmar said. "Except for the guards, you won't see hardly anyone else on this level. This is part of the Faerie court. No one's allowed here unless they've been sworn to serve the Unseelie Fae."

Rika frowned. "If someone's Fae, how can you tell if they're Seelie or Unseelie?"

Sabine smiled at Rika. It was sometimes easy to forget she'd grown up around humans and without much knowledge concerning the magical community. "I suppose it may be a bit harder for a human to tell, but it has to do with our type of magic. Some races and creatures naturally gravitate toward lighter or darker aspects of power."

"A lot of the pixies still follow the Seelie, but that's starting to change," Blossom said.

Sabine nodded. "Yes. It's essentially a choice, but many races like the gnomes, dryads, brownies, and gryphons naturally gravitate toward the lighter magics. They rely on sunlight to help fuel their power."

The rustle of wings beating softly overhead caught Sabine's attention. Large insectoid creatures were perched on the ceiling at regular intervals. Their tails glowed, bathing the hallway with a warm light. The rest of their chitinous bodies were dark brown and blended with the ceiling. If it weren't for the slight hum from their silvery wings fluttering, Sabine probably wouldn't have noticed them.

"What are they doing with their wings?" Rika asked, pointing at the ceiling. Her own wings fluttered, almost as rapidly as those of the insect-like creatures. Malek placed his hand on Rika's shoulder, keeping her firmly on the ground.

"Oh, the tarjin help circulate the air throughout the entire mountain. It would get pretty musty down here if it weren't for them. I guess you don't have much need for them up on the surface, huh?"

Blossom peered up at the ceiling and wrinkled her nose. "Why does Bane always call me a bug? I don't look like anything like those things."

"Maybe he's envious of your wings," Malek said with a wink.

Blossom nodded sagely. "Wing envy. No wonder he's always so grumpy."

Dagmar turned down an even larger and more ornate hallway. Crystal tiles had been affixed into the ground, catching the glow from the tarjin and reflecting it back upon the walls. A few benches were nestled in alcoves, with murals of forests painted on the walls behind them.

"Are the tarjin intelligent creatures?" Sabine asked, wondering if they might be similar to the pixies in their ability to spy on others.

Dagmar shook her head. "Nah. No more than any other bugs. The demons breed them and munch on them as snacks." She made a face and stuck out her tongue. "We barter with them whenever we need more drones hatched to light our hallways."

"Yuck," Blossom said and made a gagging noise. "Demons eat anything."

Dagmar grinned. "My friend's uncle cooks them when they stop glowing. If you want to try them, they serve them in the taverns."

Rika wrinkled her nose. "That doesn't sound very appealingfsup. What do they taste like?"

Malek chuckled. "I've had them before. They're crunchy and a little bit nutty. Not terrible, but not anything I'd like to eat on a regular basis."

Sabine bit back a smile. "I'll have to take your word for it."

"I couldn't believe it when I heard the queen of the

Unseelie decided to visit Razadon," Dagmar said, turning down another brightly lit corridor. "We thought it would be another century before you decided to leave Faerie. My mum warned me even when you did, you might not come here until I was old and wrinkled."

Blossom's eyes widened. "I've never seen a wrinkled dwarf. Pixies don't get wrinkles."

Dagnar cocked her head. "Really? I didn't know that. I've never met a real live pixie until now. We have cave trolls that are a little bigger than you, and I don't think they get wrinkles either. Maybe it's a size thing? The wrinkles would just swallow you guys up." She laughed and slapped her thigh. "Can you imagine the size of the wrinkles on a giant? I bet their wrinkles even have wrinkles."

Rika grinned and shook her head. "I'm not sure I'd be brave enough to get close enough to a giant to find out."

"Very wise of you," Malek replied with a smile. "I don't believe I've ever seen a cave troll. Is that similar to a regular troll?"

Dagmar wrinkled her nose. "Ew, no. Regular trolls are big, stinky, and always creeping around bridges and stuff. Our cave trolls only come up to my knee and hardly ever leave our crystal caverns. They're fuzzy, cuddly, and keep our crystals polished to a shine."

Sabine tilted her head. "I haven't seen one either. They're lesser Fae, correct?"

"Yep, but they're kinda shy around strangers. They like to hide. You might bump into one, especially if you tour the crystal caverns," Dagmar said, turning down a corridor. "The guest suites are down this hall. Yours is the biggest and best of the bunch. We always keep it ready in case any of the royal family and their attendants stop in. I guess it's a good thing we do that, huh?"

Sabine made a small noise of agreement. "Indeed."

"My mum got to meet Queen Mali'theoria once," Dagmar said. "I heard she was really pretty for a tall person, even if she was kinda scary. Then we heard she died, and I thought, well drat. There goes my chance." She winced and darted a quick look at Sabine. "Oh, sorry. Guess that didn't come out right. I didn't make you angry, did I? Mum told me not to make you mad or ramble too much. Sometimes my tongue gets carried away."

Sabine managed a weak smile. "It's all right, Dagmar. I'm not angry."

Dagmar let out a relieved breath and then grinned. "That's good. At least I did something right. I told myself: 'Self, don't mess up. Escorting the new queen is an important job.' Lots of my clanmates wanted to meet you first, but I won the raffle. Mum was supposed to do it, but she broke her leg falling off a lift. I'll be your guide almost the whole time you're here, except when I'm asleep. Or eating. Or during breaks. Then it'll probably be one of my cousins. They're all really nice, even Ostin. He doesn't bathe a lot, so you might want to hold your nose if he gets too close."

They stopped outside a large double door. A stunning forest scene had been lovingly carved into the wood and then painted with rich earthy tones. Birds nested in the branches, and Sabine could make out individual details of each feather. The workmanship and attention to detail was extraordinary.

Dagmar gripped the ornate silver handles and pushed open the heavy doors. The guards fell back, taking their positions outside. Dagmar led the group into the room, stopping only to press her hand against the crystal plate affixed on the wall.

Light flooded the small hallway. Several small benches sat alongside the wall, while a fountain gurgled in the corner. It was a small holding area of some sort, likely for visitors waiting to be announced.

"Okay, Mum says I gotta do this all formal-like." Dagmar cleared her throat, straightened her shoulders, and gestured at the room. "Welcome to the entrance chamber to the royal suite. You may have one guard accompany you into the next room or you can complete the ritual alone." She paused and wrinkled her nose. "Oh, yeah. I forgot to tell you—anyone who waits here will be returned to the surface if you mess up. The guards will take them up there, so you don't have to worry about your people being killed or anything. I heard the demons aren't as nice when you attempt their ritual."

Sabine stilled, a sliver of fear working its way under her skin. She had to force herself not to react. This wasn't good. She hadn't considered the ramifications of invoking her title.

Malek frowned. "What ritual?"

Dagmar blinked up at him with her green eyes. "It's forbidden for anyone to enter these rooms without permission from the Unseelie monarch. The ritual was designed to protect this place and keep it as a haven for the Unseelie. I don't know if it's true, but I heard not even the gods could enter these halls with malicious intent."

"These suites are technically governed by the magic of Faerie," Sabine said, mentally berating herself for not expecting something like this. "They might be located within Razadon, but they're not part of it. The rules and rituals must be observed, or we won't be welcomed. It's been this way ever since the Unseelie split from the Seelie."

Dagmar nodded. "I'll wait for you in the next room while you make your decision. Don't worry about privacy. I've screamed at the top of my lungs in here, and no one can hear you with the doors closed. Pretty neat, huh? It's great if you want to practice singing new songs."

Malek frowned. "What if Sabine decides not to participate in this ritual?"

"Uh, I don't think that's a choice." Dagmar pointed

toward the entrance door where the guards were waiting. "She'll be executed for being a pretender. The only option is to move forward."

Sabine gave Dagmar a curt nod. "I understand."

Dagmar hesitated and then headed for the door. She paused again, looked over her shoulder at them, and said, "I really hope you survive."

Without waiting for a response, the dwarf disappeared into the next room.

Sabine lowered herself onto the bench and rubbed her temples. This was a disaster.

Malek sat beside her and took her hand in his. "Talk to me. How dangerous is this ritual?"

"I don't know much about it," she admitted with a frown. "The Unseelie monarch is supposed to accompany their heir after they've reached their centennial. The heir is given the opportunity to either participate or observe any rituals or tests once they reach their majority."

"Uh oh. You're not old enough for the super-secret forbidden knowledge," Blossom said, landing on her shoulder.

"No, I'm not," Sabine replied in agreement, staring at the swirling mosaic design on the floor. "If the monarch dies before their heir reaches a majority, it falls upon the heir's protector to enlighten them."

"You're talking about Balkin," Malek murmured, his hand tightening over hers.

She nodded.

"Who's Balkin?" Rika whispered to Blossom.

"He's Sabine's Beastman protector," Blossom said, landing on Rika's shoulder. "He's the one who helped Sabine escape from Faerie. He took her to live with Bane and Dax in Akros."

Rika brushed her antennae out of her face and asked, "Is

there a way to reach Balkin? Maybe you can delay doing the ritual until he comes here."

Sabine glanced at Rika. "Balkin lives in a small village outside of Faerie. Even if I could get a message to him, it would take him weeks to arrive. He also needs to be careful not to reveal he's still loyal to me. His family's lives would be in jeopardy if the wrong person found out he's been aiding me all these years."

Blossom fluttered her wings. "I don't know much about rituals, but I can be your guard, Sabine. Maybe I'll be able to help."

Sabine smiled and shook her head. "In spirit, you're one of the bravest and most valiant individuals I've ever known. Unfortunately, these rituals only allow a bodyguard to accompany the participant because their strength is usually depleted by the end of it." She frowned, wishing Bane were with them. "Bane would normally act as my protector. He doesn't have the same level of knowledge as Balkin, but his experiences far outweigh mine. The demons have a similar ritual, and he might have some insight."

Malek ran his thumb over her hand. "I don't know anything about these rituals, but I'm not going to allow you to go alone. I'm going with you."

"No," she said immediately. "It's too dangerous."

Malek arched his brow. "More dangerous than facing the Wild Hunt?"

Sabine shook her head, trying to quell the fear threatening to choke her. Gods. This was a mess. She was having trouble thinking straight. Something wasn't right. This wasn't like her.

Malek frowned, his eyes filled with concern. "You're really worried about this."

She squeezed her eyes shut and nodded. "Even if Balkin were here to instruct me, I'm still decades away from reaching majority. My magic may not be strong enough for the demands of the ritual."

"All the more reason I should go with you."

Sabine hesitated and then nodded. "You can accompany me, Malek, but you can't participate in the ritual. I'll need to do that part of it alone."

"Why? Wouldn't our bond help you?"

She sighed. "This ritual was designed for the *Unseelie* monarch. Your magic calls to my Seelie side and makes it stronger. Not only that, but I have no way of knowing how the ritual will respond to you. We can't let anyone know the truth about you."

"Shit," he muttered, scrubbing his hands over his face. "I can't let you do this if there's a chance you'll be hurt. Do we have any options for getting you out of here?"

She placed her hand on his arm. "I have to do this, Malek. It would have been better if I had been able to prepare, but we don't have a choice. Even if they agree to allow us to leave in peace, I'll forever lose standing among the dwarves. Faerie may even decide to reject my claim to the throne outright if I waver in my resolve. This is also part of the test."

Malek stood and paced the length of the room. "This is unacceptable, Sabine. We're essentially trapped in here. If you leave, the Wild Hunt will try to kill you. If you walk through that door, this ritual might." He paused, his eyes hardening. "I'm done with this. You're going to the Sky Cities. If we leave now, there's a chance I can outrun the Wild Hunt. You'll be safe once you're under the protections of my home."

Sabine blanched. "You can't be serious."

His eyes narrowed. "Are you that afraid of me still? After everything we've been through? I would *never* hurt you!"

She frowned, surprised by his vehemence. "I know that, Malek."

"Dammit, Sabine," he snapped, prowling toward her like a predator who had sighted their prey. "I'm not going to lose the woman I love because of some bizarre dwarven ritual. Why won't you trust me to protect you?"

Sabine's heart melted at his words, even though she couldn't bring herself to say the words back. No matter how deeply she cared for him, her feelings were a liability she couldn't afford. It would destroy something inside her to lose him, but she couldn't allow him more power over her.

She stood and closed the distance between them. Placing her hands against his chest, she asked, "Is that what you think? That I'm afraid of you because you're a dragon?"

"Aren't you?"

Sabine smiled and shook her head. "In the beginning, yes. But I stopped being afraid of you before we ever reached Karga. I still get nervous when I see you in dragon form, but I think anyone would. You're one of the most beautiful and terrifying creatures I've ever seen." She pressed her hand against his cheek. "I know who you are, Malek Rish'dan. I trust you with my life."

He drew her into his arms and held her close. "Then allow me to take you to safety, sweetheart. You don't need to do this."

Sabine softened her body against him, breathing in his masculine scent. The faint hint of burnt leaves that always surrounded him had become strangely comforting. "Running away would be the easy solution in the short term, but I don't belong in the Sky Cities. No matter how much I care for you, I have a duty and responsibility to my people. My actions don't affect just me, but all of the Unseelie."

Malek's arms tightened around her. He closed his eyes and exhaled slowly. When he spoke, there was a strange gruffness in his voice. "I could take you away by force."

A tendril of fear slid through her and took root inside her

heart. Sabine stilled, trying to wrest control of the overwhelming urge to pull away from him. Her dealings with demons had shown her how dangerous it was to flee from a predator—and Malek was the ultimate predator. Sabine knew he wouldn't hurt her, but like the demons, he might try to do what he considered best for her welfare.

Something was wrong. Malek had never threatened her like this before. She swallowed and whispered, "You could try, but it would change everything between us."

He opened his eyes, and Sabine was staggered by the haunted look on his face. It was almost as though he wasn't truly seeing her.

"It would be so easy," he murmured, running his thumb over her cheek. "I could shift and steal you away. You would be mine forever."

She searched his expression and then her eyes drifted down to the warding medallion against his skin. She brushed her fingers against it but pulled them away quickly. It was hot to the touch, almost searing her. Malek had once told her it heated when he was in danger of losing control. This situation didn't warrant such a reaction, unless something else was going on.

Uncertainty filled her. With the demons, she'd always used her magic to force them into submission. She didn't know if pitting her will against Malek's would work or how it would change their relationship. It was too dangerous to risk such a thing right now, especially when they were surrounded by potential enemies lurking outside the door.

Curling her fingers into his shirt, Sabine decided to appeal to him on a more personal level. She pressed her body against his, sending a soft wave of sensual magic over him. He trembled slightly, but his arms relaxed around her.

Infusing her words with a touch of power, Sabine whispered in the language of Faerie, "Don't betray my trust, Malek. Please."

His eyes softened as he gazed down at her, but he didn't answer right away. Instead, he reached up to tuck her hair behind her ear, his touch impossibly gentle and contrasting with his earlier harsh words.

She reached up and touched his medallion again. The heat was dissipating. She hoped that was a good sign.

After a long time, Malek said, "If I can't convince you to leave with me willingly, then I'll be with you every step of the way."

She slumped against him in relief. He kissed her hair and ran his hand down her back in a gentle caress. This was the Malek she'd come to know and care about. Part of her wondered if the time would come when they would actually be at odds. The thought terrified her more than the Wild Hunt pursuing her.

She caught sight of Blossom and Rika still sitting on the bench. Rika's knuckles were white where she gripped the edge of the seat, and her eyes were wide with fear. Blossom had been uncharacteristically quiet during her argument with Malek, but her wings were tinged with red.

Sabine pulled away from Malek and held out her hand for the pixie to land upon it. "Blossom?"

The pixie immediately flew over to her and flopped onto her palm. With a wail, she grabbed Sabine's thumb and cried, "I don't want Malek to take you away, but I don't want you to die either. You're my favorite person in the whole world, Sabine!"

"Blossom," Sabine said, trying to figure out the best way to diffuse the situation. Before she could say anything, Rika jumped off the bench and launched herself in Sabine's direction. Rika threw her arms around Sabine, her entire body quaking in a sob. Sabine floundered for a moment and then returned the hug with one arm, careful not to damage Rika's wings.

"What's all this?" Sabine asked, her shirt getting soaked by Rika's tears. "You're going to be fine, Rika. You too, Blossom."

Rika hiccupped and gripped her even tighter. "I'm not worried about me. I don't want anything to happen to you!"

Blossom continued to sob in Sabine's outstretched palm, leaving a smear of red pixie dust on her skin.

Sabine blew out a breath in exasperation and glanced at Malek. "A little help here?"

Malek's mouth twitched. "Apparently, I'm not the only one unhappy about this."

Sabine stared at him in disbelief. First Malek had threatened to abduct her, and now a seer was clinging to her like she was a beacon in the storm. Their reactions were completely out of character. Well, maybe not for Blossom. The pixie could get herself worked up over a bee leaving pollen footprints on a flower petal.

"I have every intention of surviving this trial. I may not know specifics, but I know the magic of Faerie," Sabine said, still troubled by everyone's behavior. She hadn't been immune either. Ever since she stepped foot into this room, her fear had been nearly overwhelming.

She paused. If Faerie wanted to test her mettle, she wouldn't be given any official warning. Faerie played by her own rules, and the magic adjusted itself as it saw fit.

Malek frowned. "What's wrong?"

"I believe our emotions are being manipulated," Sabine said, extricating herself from Rika's grip. She gently eased a sobbing Blossom onto Malek's hand and walked the length of the chamber. Tilting her head, she closed her eyes and read the pulse of the room.

"Clever and incredibly subtle," Sabine murmured, holding out her hand to better assess the intricate layers of magic woven throughout the space. "It's a test to gauge my determination and resolve. Bane often reminds me how emotions can be a weakness. It would appear Faerie decided to exploit my feelings and manipulate yours too."

Malek arched his brow. "Are you sure? I've never made it a secret about my desire to keep you out of harm's way."

She nodded. "No, but you've never threatened to steal me away without my consent. I've been in far more danger before, and you've never reacted this way. You didn't even back down when your medallion heated. I believe the magic is simply amplifying your emotions."

Blossom cried even harder, beating her tiny fists against Malek's hand.

Malek looked at Blossom, his frown deepening. "You might be right. It was almost as though my inhibitions were lowered." He winced. "Shit. I was ready to abduct you and hide you away from the world."

Sabine kissed his cheek. "But you didn't."

He gave her a pained expression. "It's still a tempting thought."

Rika sniffled and wiped away her tears. "I don't understand. You're saying this isn't real?"

Sabine gave Rika a small smile. "Not completely. I believe you're worried about me, but not quite as much as you believe. Focus on yourself and allow your seer abilities to shine through. You'll be able to break through the illusion with your will."

Rika closed her eyes for a moment. Sabine could see traces of magic sliding off the seer's skin like rain. Rika opened her eyes, her expression filled with wonder. "You were right. I'm still worried about you, but I don't feel as hopeless and lost."

Malek angled his head in Blossom's direction. The pixie was crying so hard, her entire body was shaking. Glittering red smears of pixie dust coated his palm, dripping from Blossom's tears and wings. "Do you want to try to tell her it's an illusion?"

"It won't do much good," Sabine admitted with a sigh. "When pixies get this worked up, they usually keep going until they pass out. She won't respond to words, only magic. I'd normally let her just cry it out, but we need her."

Sabine withdrew her knife and cut a small lock of her silvery-white hair. She dangled it over Blossom, accompanying the gesture with a soft wave of magic. Blossom froze. The pixie lifted her head, her eyes widening at the sight of the hair. She sat up and snatched the offering out of Sabine's hand.

"So much magic," Blossom whispered, clutching the hair tightly against her chest. "It's so pretty. So sparkly. So soft." She rubbed it against her cheek and trilled softly. "Is it really all for me?"

Sabine bit back a smile. "Yes, but I need you and Rika to stay here while I handle the rest of the ritual. If there's a problem, you'll need to use that magic to send a message to Balkin."

Blossom eagerly nodded, her dust already turning back to its normal golden color. She flew to Rika's shoulder, still cuddling the lock of hair against her cheek. Blossom would likely have it braided and worn as jewelry by the time Sabine stepped into the next room.

Sabine turned toward the door leading to Dagmar and the ritual. Now that she'd recognized the influence over everyone's emotions as being false, the magic was already dissipating. She suspected this next part of the test wouldn't be so simple to overcome.

Malek took her hand and murmured, "I'll be with you every step of the way."

She smiled up at him, grateful he was willing to accompany her. He might not be able to help, but his support helped strengthen her resolve. "I'll need to suppress our bond so I don't accidentally draw upon your power. If you have any insight during the course of the ritual, you can share them with me. Dagmar is technically sworn to serve my family's line, but I don't know the details of that obligation. Until we can be sure about her, try not to arouse her suspicions about your identity."

"I'll help you however I can," Malek murmured. He lifted her hand and kissed her knuckles. "I'll follow your lead as much as possible, but there are limits. I won't allow anything to happen to you."

"I know." She moved into him and brushed a light kiss against his lips. "I'm glad you're going with me, Malek."

"I'm still tempted to take you away," he whispered, running his thumb over her hand. "I'd follow you to the underworld and back if it kept you safe."

"Let's hope it doesn't come to that," she said and led him through the doorway.

Chapter Eight

Dagmar grinned at Sabine the moment she crossed the threshold. "Oh, good. You passed the first test. Mum said I might have to wait a few hours before you figured it out. I was hoping it wouldn't take that long." She gestured at the nearby seating area. "Go ahead and make yourself comfortable. It'll take me a few minutes to get everything prepared. I hope you like the room. It's one of my favorites. The colors are so pretty compared to the other suites."

"It's lovely, Dagmar. You've cared for everything beautifully," Sabine said, sweeping her gaze around the room.

The ritual room wasn't what she'd been expecting. It appeared much like a living area found in most residences in Faerie. In fact, it reminded her of her mother's sitting room back home. The silver and deep-blue colors belonged to her mother's line, and nowhere else in Faerie could such a combination be found.

Crystal chandeliers cast their dancing silver lights upon the walls and furnishings. Elegant and plush seating had been artfully arranged throughout the room. Subtle traces of welcoming magic filled the air, inviting people to sit and relax.

Sabine tried to ignore the pang of homesickness that filled her as she ran her fingers across the midnight-blue fabric draped over a lounging bed. Her mother had told her these rooms had once been accessible directly from their home in Faerie.

Unfortunately, the knowledge of how to create new doorways to the in-between had been lost for generations, ever since the gods had abandoned the world. The few doorways that still remained could only take them to predetermined destinations, and most of them were well hidden. It was only by sheer luck she'd found a few of them over the years.

Dagmar walked to a low table on the far side of the room, which contained a collection of baubles and trinkets. She removed a dark-blue cloth and revealed a large clear crystal situated in a silver stand. A circular design, inlaid with a triangular pattern, had been etched on the floor around the table. Dagmar walked around the circle, placing several small red crystals over top of it before turning her attention back to Sabine.

She clasped her hands together and said, "Okay. Before you enter the circle, you have to remove all metals, clothing, jewelry, and anything other than what you come by naturally. Then you can step inside the circle."

Sabine swallowed and stepped away from Malek. She removed her weapons and handed them to him, and he placed them on a nearby table. Her fingers shook slightly as she unlaced the bindings on her shirt and removed the rest of her clothing. Her nerves were getting the better of her, and she needed to calm herself. He took her clothing, giving her hands a reassuring squeeze before putting her garments beside her weapons.

Dagmar gestured toward the crystal sitting on the table. "Only the true queen of the Unseelie can activate the crystal. You can try to use any of the items within the circle to connect with the magic of Faerie. Your guard can give you advice, but he can't enter the circle. If you're a pretender, the protections of this suite will strike you down where you stand." She winced. "Sorry. I don't make the rules."

Taking a steadying breath, Sabine entered the circle and approached the table. The prickle of foreign magic caressed her skin as she passed through the crystal barrier, but it wasn't unpleasant. She'd participated in similar tests during her youth, but most of them hadn't ended with death if she failed.

She studied the items on the table but was careful not to touch anything. The crystal was larger than her hand, smooth and polished like a precious gem. It was pretty but unremarkable in its current form. The lack of color was the most telling thing about it. It wasn't blue, which would indicate it was dormant. An active magic worked within it, but that was all she could determine simply by looking at it.

Sabine turned her gaze to the other items. Two silver bowls were on each side of the table. One of them was filled with clear liquid while the other held a small sample of soil, possibly from the Silver Forest. She leaned over and sniffed the bowl containing the liquid, but it was completely odorless. Water, maybe?

A small brazier and feather sat beside the bowls, while a silver box was tucked farther back in the corner of the table. The box was decorated with an unusual lattice design, a stunning piece of artwork on its own. She peered inside the open box and found a ceremonial knife lying on a velvet cloth. The hilt was affixed with glowing red gemstones, the color reminding her of blood.

Sabine paused, considering it carefully. A knife would be

necessary if she needed to create a blood sacrifice to power the spell. The rest of the items could be used as focus devices to harness each of the elements toward the crystal. It was the simplest and neatest solution.

She started to reach for the knife but froze. No. Something was wrong. She swallowed and pulled her hand away, sensing this entire thing was a trap.

"Dammit," she muttered, frustrated by the puzzle in front of her.

"Are you all right?" Malek asked from his place outside the circle.

She nodded. "Yes, I'm just trying to figure out what's expected of me. Something about this isn't quite right."

Malek was quiet for a moment. "All right. Talk it out with me. What's on the table?"

"Other than the crystal, all four elements are represented in the form of water, soil, a feather, and brazier," Sabine said, her gaze gravitating toward the box again. "There's also a silver box containing a dagger, possibly for a blood sacrifice. The dagger has glowing red stones in the hilt. I think they may be power crystals."

"Are you supposed to use all of them?"

She hesitated. "I don't know. There could be multiple ways of activating the magic within the crystal or just one."

"All right," Malek said, moving closer to the circle but remaining outside of it. "If this test is designed to determine whether you're the true queen of the Unseelie, your blood is probably the key to unlocking it."

She nodded, having already come to that conclusion. "I agree, but it doesn't feel right to me. Blood is used as a sacrifice to power magic, not to determine the rights of succession."

Malek frowned. "How is succession determined?"

Sabine considered his question. The Wild Hunt always

proclaimed the right of succession, even over the wishes of the current monarch. She'd encountered the Wild Hunt thrice, and that was twice more than most people. The Hunt might be able to track her using ties of blood, but something else had proven to the Huntsman her right to rule. It was strange she'd never wondered about it until now.

"I believe it's determined by right of birth and the type of power you possess. Those with the closest ties to the gods have the purest form of magic."

Sabine stared at her hands, remembering the last time the Wild Hunt had sought her out. She'd had to expel her magic into the ground, draining it almost entirely. Only after she'd sacrificed her magic completely had the debt been resolved.

She froze. Lifting her gaze, she studied the items on the table in a new light. "That's it. They're clues *and* a trap."

"What is?"

"All of it," she said, gesturing at the table. "None of this is real."

Sabine waved her hand, stripping aside the glamour crafted with Unseelie magic. A rush of magic trailed along her skin, causing it to prickle in awareness as the power subsided. If she had been anything other than the queen of the Unseelie, she wouldn't have been able to discard the illusion with such ease.

Each of the items sitting on the table were actually crystals, pulsing in red and black colors. Their appearance had been modified to hide their true intent. If she had touched any of them, she would have died instantly. Only the clear crystal in the center remained unaltered, and this was the true part of the ritual.

Sabine's mouth curved into a smile. "I know what needs to be done."

Malek frowned. "Are you sure?"

She nodded. "The right of succession has already been determined. I simply have to claim it as *mine*."

Pressing her hands against the cold crystal, Sabine closed her eyes. She took a steadying breath, remembering the mental exercises she'd learned in her youth. She exhaled slowly, allowing the serene quiet to fill her mind. It was a place between waking and dreaming, a place of visions and forbidden magic. The etchings on her skin warmed and a gentle wind caressed her hair, bringing with it the strong scent of night-blooming flowers.

Sabine abandoned all pretenses and opened her eyes. It was time to accept the person she'd been born to become. She was both Seelie and Unseelie, a creature of the light and dark. Her magic was as multi-faceted as the crystal in front of her. The ground trembled under her feet, and she channeled her power outward, using the crystal as a focus for her might.

Magic erupted from her, and she threw her head back, unleashing all her reserves. Burning pain shot through her fingers and up her arms, the marks on her skin pulsing in time with her heartbeat. She cried out as she fused her power with the crystal, merging her mind with the magic of Faerie.

It embraced both aspects of her power, disregarding the boundaries that had divided the Fae into light and dark for millennia. For a brief moment, a flash of understanding and awareness filled her. The line separating the Seelie and Unseelie Fae had deepened with every dispute, until their very survival was now threatened by greed and ambition.

The dwarves, demons, merfolk, and others who claimed alignment with the Unseelie weren't immune either. They had once been unified in their intention to protect the world but were now separated by cultural differences and misunderstandings.

The magic contained within the crystal in front of her

was a reminder of their shared origins. They'd chosen to divide themselves into different facets of their powers, fracturing their strength when they were stronger as a whole.

A profound sense of loss gripped her. They'd somehow forgotten.

The crystal in front of her began to glow with a silver-and-gold light. Sabine staggered but didn't release it, sensing Faerie wasn't finished with her yet. In the distance, she heard something that sounded like the ringing of bells, an announcement or proclamation of some sort.

Power rushed out of the crystal and back into her. Her back went ramrod straight, and she inhaled sharply against the onslaught. It was both foreign and familiar at the same time, tugging at the edge of her memory. Somewhere in other parts of the world, the Unseelie had heard her call. They were all reaching for nearby crystals, channeling their power toward her and infusing her with their strength.

It went beyond that. She felt the awareness of the dwarves through the crystals they created. The cool power of the merfolk flowed through her too, brushing against her absorbed power. A heated blast of demonic might rushed over her, but it was the call of the Fae that spoke to her the loudest.

Tears sprung to her eyes, and elation rushed through her. These were her people, her family, her entire reason for surviving. She was their protector, their leader, their *queen.* Until now, she hadn't fully understood. They were one. A single heartbeat, all beating with a singular purpose. *They were Unseelie.*

The mantle of responsibility settled heavily upon her shoulders, and the magical containment field around the table faded away. She released the crystal and lowered her head, her emotions raw and untethered. Her legs started to give out, but Malek was suddenly there, pulling her into his arms. She leaned heavily on him, grateful for his strength.

She stared down at herself, somewhat surprised to find she was fully clothed. Faerie had adorned her with clothing fit for a queen. Her midnight-blue dress had intricate silver stitching in a pattern reminiscent of moonlight. She touched her head, the weight of the crown a reminder of the burden she now carried.

Sabine looked up and into Malek's captivating blue eyes, the color reminding her of the sky at twilight. He was gazing at her in wonder, the love and adoration in his eyes mirroring her feelings for him. She lifted her hand and brushed her fingers against his cheek, marveling at the sense of rightness at having him with her in this moment. Faerie had even chosen to adorn him in new attire, only slightly less brilliant than her own.

"You're all right?" he asked, searching her expression.

She smiled and nodded, pulling him down to kiss him. "Yes."

She turned and found Dagmar on her knees, her head lowered in fealty. The dwarf peeked up at her with a wide grin and said, "Welcome to Razadon, Queen Sabin'theoria. I think Faerie's pleased you've finally arrived."

Chapter Nine

"We've tried to account for everything you might need while you're here, but we don't get visitors from Faerie often anymore. Maybe three times a century if we're lucky. But only the royal family is allowed to stay in this suite. It's special."

Sabine absently listened while Dagmar continued boasting about the suite of rooms where they'd be staying for the duration of their visit. Once the ritual had been completed, Rika and Blossom joined her and Malek. Faerie had also adorned them in new clothing, and their old ones had been spirited away to an unknown location. Dagmar said such things happened all the time and their belongings would eventually turn up freshly laundered and folded in their rooms.

"Everything's so pretty in here," Rika said, leaning close to a crystalline lantern designed to reflect the current phase of the moon on the far wall.

Blossom zipped around, exploring every inch of the room. She peered under and behind the furniture and even studied inside the crystal chandeliers. She lifted her head and called, "No evil dust bunnies up here."

Dagmar's eyes widened. "I would hope not. I had to drag the ladder out just the other day to clean inside them. This entire wing has been my clan's responsibility for eight generations now. We take our duty very seriously." She gestured toward two hallways on opposite sides of the room. "To your left are the servant's quarters, kitchens, and laundry areas. Since you don't have much of a staff with you, my clan will happily fill in. To the right, you'll find the main bedchamber, bathing room, and five more dignitary rooms. Faerie sometimes changes the layout or number of rooms without telling us, so it might be a little different."

Rika made a soft noise of exclamation, her wings fluttering even more frenetically. Malek gripped her shoulders and pushed her back down. "Calm yourself, little butterfly."

"Sorry. I got excited," Rika said with a sheepish grin before turning back toward Sabine. "Is it safe for Blossom and me to explore? I've never been in a magical place before."

"I'll make sure she doesn't fly away, Sabine. Pretty please?" Blossom pleaded, clasping her hands together and fluttering her wings wildly.

"Go ahead, but try to keep out of trouble," Sabine said with a smile.

With a loud whoop, Blossom took off down one of the hallways. Rika paused long enough to dart a grin at Sabine and Malek before following the pixie. Sabine stared after them for a moment, but it was difficult to share their enthusiasm. Her thoughts kept straying to Bane, locked away and temporarily out of her reach. She needed to talk to him. Unfortunately, they needed to play Razadon's political game first.

Turning back toward Dagmar, Sabine asked, "Do you know when the council will be meeting?"

"I'm not sure," Dagmar said, glancing at the entrance door. "They probably wanted to wait until you finished the ritual. I'll send a runner to find out. I'll also have my cousins arrange to have a meal prepared for you. Is there anything you don't like? Mum said the Fae eats lots of plants. Is that true? We have some really tasty lizard recipes, and we can stuff them with plants."

"Perhaps a variety of things would be best," Sabine said, considering Malek's heavier meat-eating tendencies. "I'd like to check on my demon friend at the earliest opportunity. Would you know where they're holding him?"

Dagmar bit her lip. "He's probably being held in our prison. Um, I can try to figure out how to put in a request, but, um..." She leaned closer and whispered, "I'm not supposed to go there since I'm not part of the Warrior Guild. I think you need to talk to a council member to arrange a visit. Do you want me to send someone a message?"

Sabine hesitated. "Yes. Can you send a message to Astrid? Let her know I'd like to speak with her at the earliest opportunity."

Dagmar blew out a breath, her shoulders slumping in relief. "Whew. I can definitely do that. Some of those warriors who run the prison get really grumpy. I'll run over to Astrid's steward and arrange everything so you can meet with her. If you need anything while I'm gone, just touch the crystal and say my name."

Sabine nodded at her, and Dagmar headed out of the room. Malek walked over to a large silver table. Several rolled parchments and a few packages were sitting on top of it.

He picked up one of the boxes and asked, "What are these? They just appeared out of thin air."

Sabine frowned and approached him. He was holding a square box covered with dark-blue paper. It had been etched with tiny silver stars, which sparkled in the light. She took it from him, a trace of glamour coating her hand from the shimmering effect. She smiled and rubbed her fingertips together, impressed by the sender's talent in crafting such an illusion.

"It's a coronation gift," she murmured, opening the box and finding a small crystal globe. She picked it up, staring in wonder at the living world contained within the globe. It was a piece of the Silver Forest, forever preserved by the magical containment embedded within the crystal.

The trees glowed silver in the moonlight, and the dark-blue sky contrasted sharply against it. A splash of colors from the rare flowers that dwelled there completed the captivating effect. Sabine ran her fingers along the crystal, allowing the magic that had lovingly crafted such a gift to flow over her.

Malek reached into the box and pulled out a small card. He studied the elegant script and said, "It's from Averia and her family."

Sabine smiled at her childhood friend's name, unsurprised such a treasure had come from Averia's family. "Go ahead. You can read it."

Malek opened the card and said, "Dearest Sabin'theoria, we have long awaited the day you would return to Faerie and take your rightful place. Knowing this day has finally come fills us with unrepressed joy. We wish you continued good health, prosperity, and a swift end to your enemies. We remain forevermore your faithful servants and allies."

Sabine placed the globe back in the box, trying to suppress the unease that filled her. She ran her fingers along the edge of the box and murmured, "Then it's begun."

"What?"

She lifted her head to meet Malek's gaze. "All of Faerie knows I'm in Razadon. These gifts and messages are from people who are seeking my favor. Lines will be drawn, alliances will shift, and my father will make plans to redouble his efforts to kill me. Be careful opening any more of them. Some might be traps."

Malek scowled and tossed the card back inside the box. "What can we do to mitigate the damage?"

She shook her head. "At this point, I don't know. We either have to ride the wave or be crushed beneath it. By announcing to the dwarves I'm the Unseelie queen, I've set things in motion that can't be undone. My situation is even more precarious now."

"That's why Balkin hid you away in Akros and not in Razadon," Malek guessed aloud, picking up another scroll and glancing at the sprawling script before putting it back down unopened.

She nodded and closed the box containing Averia's gift. "If I had gone to any location where the first races dwelled, word would have gotten back to my father. Balkin chose Akros because it was close enough to Faerie so he could check on me without arousing suspicion, but it's also far enough away to avoid running into anyone who might have ties to the Fae. No one would have suspected I was hiding in a mostly human city."

Malek took her hand in his and ran his thumb over it. "All right. We need to reassess our priorities. I'm assuming rescuing Bane is at the top of it."

She nodded. "Yes. Not only does he mean a great deal to me, but I need his help. Balkin trusts him, and Bane understands the inner workings of dwarven politics far better than I do. While we're here, we should be safe enough from my father, but we can't risk staying too long. My father may have spies among the Unseelie who are seeking to curry his favor. They'll likely be arriving in person within a few weeks, if some aren't here already."

Several more rolled parchments and a few packages had materialized on the table while they were talking. Out of curiosity, she picked up one of the notes. Not sensing any malicious magic, Sabine broke the seal and scanned it quickly. It was another message praising her ascension as queen. The author also insinuated they would be interested in forming an alliance.

The name at the bottom wasn't familiar. She frowned, suspecting it was likely from one of the lesser nobles who had little dealings with the court. She dropped it on the table and rubbed her temples. Balkin would know which of these families could help strengthen her position and which ones were liabilities. In the meantime, she could have Dagmar or one of her family members sort through them and prioritize each message. Her mother had used a trusted advisor to handle such matters, but Sabine hadn't expected to need one so soon.

Malek frowned. "Where are they coming from?"

"We can't navigate the in-between without doorways, but Faerie has a way of transporting items and notes. Pretty soon, we'll be inundated with hundreds of messages and requests."

Another note appeared and Sabine stilled, recognizing her family's crest. She picked it up and broke the seal, but it was blank. Sabine took a shaky breath and ran her hand over the parchment, removing the intricate glamour masking the contents of the message. Her heart dropped into her stomach as she read it.

My foolish queen and daughter of my heart,

Are you mad? Have you completely lost your mind? While I'm enjoying seeing the frenzy your pronouncement has made upon the Seelie court, you are not in a position to formally claim your throne. I can only assume the situation must be dire for you to have taken such action. You have announced to the world you are now a threat.

Renewed attempts to end your life will likely be forthcoming, even from those you are currently seeking shelter with. Do not trust anyone.

I'm sending a trusted representative and honor guard to assist with damage control and also to manage your holdings there. They will leave within the hour, but it may take weeks for them to arrive. In the meantime, I will do what I can from here.

Stay well, my darling kitten.

- Balkin

She showed the message to Malek, and his expression darkened as he read it. When he finished, she walked over to a candle and set the parchment on fire. She dropped it on a tray and watched as the smoke billowed, destroying the paper and message it contained.

Malek stared at it, his jaw hardening. "More assassination attempts than what we're already dealing with? The Wild Hunt's parked outside the damn door."

"Yes, which is why we can't wait around for this honor guard," Sabine said, turning away from the ashes. "Let's locate the bedrooms and figure out how we're going to free Bane."

She headed down the hall toward the bedroom suites and began opening doors. All the bedrooms contained similar elegant furnishings. Toward the end of the hall, she opened the last set of double doors and paused inside.

A large sunken living area with lounging chairs and low-seated tables took up the majority of the space, but it was the artwork that captured her attention. Incredible murals painted with rich tones lined the walls, the edges inlaid with gold, silver, and precious gems. In between each panel were flowering vines she'd never seen outside the Silver Forest. The deep green colors were interrupted with splashes of silver, and the energy contained within those plants filled her with a pang of homesickness.

Everywhere she looked, she caught sight of another reminder of home. From the elegant craftsmanship of the crystalline accents to the deep blues and silver tones of the décor, it was as though she was back at her mother's palace.

Laughter trickled out of a side door. Rika and Blossom stumbled into her bedroom a moment later, wide smiles on both of them.

"This place is amazing!" Rika said, her eyes bright with excitement. "There's a huge underground spring in the other room, and there are plants everywhere. Blossom said the flowers here can sustain her for years."

"Barley spoke to me, Sabine!' Blossom shrieked, throwing her hands upward in a cheer. "I can talk to all my brothers and sisters. The plants are all from Faerie!"

"That's wonderful news," Sabine said with a smile and held out her hand for Blossom to land. The lock of hair Sabine had gifted her had been woven into a necklace and matching bracelet. "If you speak with your family, I'm going to need you to keep abreast on the happenings in my father's court. Balkin sent a message warning us to expect trouble."

Rika's smile faded. "We're still in danger?"

Sabine nodded. "Yes, but we're all going to be cautious. While we're here, we all need to play certain roles. Between the four of us, we should be able to appeal to the different groups within Razadon. Our first priority is to free Bane. After that, we'll need to figure out a way to avoid the Wild Hunt. They can't pursue me while I'm in the city, but they'll be waiting for the moment I step outside."

"What do you want us to do?" Rika asked.

"To start, I'd like you to act as my lady-in-waiting," Sabine replied, wishing she'd had more time to coach Rika. "We'll need to improvise much of it, but this should allow you to intermingle with the servants. I'll explain to Dagmar your training has just started, and I need her assistance to guide you. That should put you in a position to overhear gossip while you shadow her."

Rika nodded. "I can do that. I don't think Dagmar's much older than me. We should get along fine."

Sabine smiled at her and then turned to Blossom. "I'd like you to try to locate the council members and listen in on their conversations. You have the best chance of getting close to them."

"That sounds like fun!" Blossom said immediately, but her smile faded a moment later. "Will my glamour work here? When we were in Karga, I couldn't get close to their magic crystals without them detecting me. Will they be able to find me here?"

Sabine frowned. "I'm not sure. You'll need to be careful to avoid detection. I'll give your magic a boost, which may help, but it's no guarantee. If you speak to the goddess, she may be able to tell you how to travel more easily to various places within the city. My mother told me there were doorways to the in-between in Razadon that were still active, but she didn't know their location."

Blossom nodded. "I think the cave trolls are sort of like pixies. We share similar magic. They might talk to me if I can find some. Maybe they know about the doorways or the super-secret ways to sneak around."

"That's a good idea," Sabine replied and then turned toward Malek. "I don't have any right to ask you to help me, Malek. Our bond doesn't make you beholden to me."

"You're not asking me anything," he said, taking a step toward her. "I've already established myself as a trader, sweetheart. I can work my contacts here to get information about Bane's situation. If there's a way to free him, we'll find it. In the meantime, it might be best if I remained at your side. You're a remarkable power, but even a queen usually has a bodyguard."

A wave of relief rushed through her. "How much do you know about Razadon and dwarven politics?"

Malek hesitated. "Probably not as much as you, at least not in dealing with the council. My interactions with them were a bit on the shady side."

She frowned. "What do you mean?"

"Dwarves view things like smuggling differently than other parts of the world," Malek admitted with a shrug. "Bartering, negotiating, and bragging are cornerstones of dwarven culture. They're willing to overlook a great deal of underworld dealings if it's profitable. If anything, they respect creativity when it comes to commerce."

"That's why you're one of the few traders who's allowed to enter the city," she mused, regarding Malek in a new light.

He chuckled. "Yes. My reputation has been carefully cultivated. I've met a few of the councilors, but they mostly went through intermediaries when they were buying or selling items. Hargrim Icemail was my sponsor each time I've entered the city. He'll probably be drinking at his favorite pub later tonight. I can meet up with him then. He might know something that can help, and if not, a bribe will certainly encourage him to find out."

"What's a sponsor?" Blossom asked.

"If you're not a dwarf, you must have someone currently living in Razadon sponsor you for the duration of your stay. If you do anything wrong or commit any crime, they accept responsibility."

Blossom blinked at Sabine. "Is Dagmar your sponsor?"

Sabine shook her head. "I don't believe so. My family's position changes the dynamic. I know Dagmar's beholden to my family through the treaty signed generations ago, but I don't really know much beyond that." Sabine blew out a breath and rubbed her temples. "Navigating the ins and outs of this political mess is going to be a nightmare."

Malek pressed his hand against Sabine's back. Turning toward Blossom and Rika, he asked, "Have you two finished exploring?"

"Not yet," Rika said with a grin. "We still have to check out the servants' quarters. Everything here is amazing."

"All right. Why don't you two go finish investigating?" Malek suggested. "We'll need to finish ironing out the details soon enough, but I think Sabine could use a break before the council is convened. I also need to speak with her about some private matters."

Blossom saluted him. "Aye, Captain! We're on it! If there are any spies or traps in our midst, we'll find and eliminate them!"

Both Rika and Blossom grinned at each other and raced out of the room.

Malek's mouth twitched in a smile. "I don't think Blossom was kidding about hunting down any threats. At least they're enjoying themselves."

"I think Rika's pretending more than anything. She's worried about Bane," Sabine said and studied the room again. She walked to one of the closed doors and opened it to find a large bedchamber. The bed itself was positioned in the center of the room and had been crafted from the boughs of a tree from the Silver Forest. Her breath caught, and she ran her hand up the carving, feeling a tingle of magic float over her.

Malek placed their bags beside the bed and asked, "How tired are you?"

"Exhausted, but I won't be able to sleep for a while yet."

He captured her hand and pulled her toward him, wrapping his arms around her. Malek's eyes roamed over her, his brow creased with concern. "You've been using a lot of magic today. Are you sure you're all right?"

She ran her hands up his chest, the heat from his body more than a little enticing. A few months ago, she wouldn't have been standing after expending so much magic.

"Better than I expected, but I think that's because of you and the goddess. Even with the power boost, it's going to be difficult hiding my weakness from the council. If there were any way to wait without consequences, I would. But if Balkin's right about us being in danger, we can't allow anyone to know how little magic I have left."

"That's what I thought." He pressed his forehead against hers. "I'd like to share my power with you, Sabine. I won't need it while I'm here, and I think you will."

"Malek, I'm not sure it's safe for you," she whispered, her heart fluttering at his generous offer. If anyone found out his identity while he was here, his life would be forfeit. He needed access to his magic if he had any intention of escaping Razadon with his life.

"Why don't you let me worry about that, sweetheart? You have enough to deal with."

She hesitated and then relaxed against him. No one had ever offered her such a reprieve until she'd met him. "Sometimes it feels as though you're too good to be true."

Malek winced. "Not by any means, but I would still like to give you some of my power."

Something in his voice gave her pause. "What's wrong, Malek?"

He cupped her face and trailed his thumb along her cheek. "There are things I need to share with you, but not when you're this tired. It's something I've been wanting to tell you for a while, but the timing hasn't been right."

Her brow furrowed, and she searched his expression. "Are you all right?"

His eyes softened. "Yes, but more so because you're beside me." He tucked her hair behind her ear and then slid his hand down, caressing her neck. "I love seeing you like this, without your glamour. The real you."

Sabine smiled up at him. He was one of the few who had seen her without her glamour when she'd still been in hiding. It seemed like such a long time ago, even though it had only been a few months since they met. It reminded her of another time when he'd kept things from her—like the fact he was a dragon.

"This thing you want to tell me," Sabine said, looking up at him with concern. "Should I be worried?"

"No," he promised and kissed her lightly. "I simply need to explain some things to you. Whether I share them with you now or later won't change anything. You have a right to know, but I don't want to add more to your burden than you're already carrying."

"You're not a burden," she whispered, curling her hands in his shirt. "I'd like to be here for you, just as you've been for me."

He closed his eyes and took a deep breath. When he opened them again, the love in his eyes was staggering. "Later, sweetheart. Please. We don't have time for a full discussion, not when Dagmar could be back at any moment."

She nodded. "Whenever you're ready, I'm willing to listen."

"Sabine, I—" He paused and then muttered a curse under his breath. "You have no idea what you do to me."

This was such a dangerous path to tread upon, but she couldn't resist the promise of everything he offered. In a soft voice, she whispered, "No more than what you do to me, Malek."

Malek glanced toward the door. "I'll need to remove my

warding medallion to share power with you. Can I remove it safely in here without alerting anyone?"

"It's probably safe, but give me a moment," Sabine said, reluctantly pulling away from him and his captivating heat.

She closed the bedroom door and pressed her hand against the crystal located nearby. Infusing her magic into the device, Sabine sent Faerie a silent request to enable a ward to shield their presence. A flicker of acknowledgement flittered through her mind, and her skin prickled from the magic encasing her bed chamber.

This next part would be a bit tricky. Faerie could be a fickle mistress at times. Framing her thoughts carefully, Sabine informed Faerie that even though Malek and Rika were foreigners, they also sought sanctuary. Any harm to them would also harm her, and she was oath-bound to protect them. She focused on her memories, allowing Faerie a glimpse of everything they'd been through together and how much she'd grown to care for them.

There was a pause, as though Faerie was considering her request. A glimmer of desire passed through her, and Sabine paused at the realization Faerie craved these memories. Faerie was alive, but not in the conventional sense. In some ways, it was almost childlike, wanting to understand and learn more about the world. Sabine hadn't fully realized it held such needs, but it made sense if it possessed an awareness like the treeheart back in Atlantia.

She sent out a reassuring thought, promising to share more of her experiences with Faerie. A gentle embrace of power wrapped around her before dissipating. The crystal turned green, and Sabine removed her hand.

Turning back to face Malek, Sabine said, "No one can enter or detect any magic inside this room. You can remove it."

He nodded. Malek reached up, unfastened the warding

medallion, and placed it on the table beside the bed. She took a deep breath, inhaling the strong scent of burnt leaves that always surrounded him.

Sabine walked across the room toward him, admiring the strong lines of his physique. Being with him like this felt right. It was strange to realize how much she'd come to depend upon him. Since the moment he'd walked into her life, she hadn't experienced the pangs of loneliness that had plagued her over the last ten years. Instead, each moment seemed to bring a new emergence of joy and hope for the future, no matter what obstacles they faced.

She reached for him, and he wrapped his arms around her, pulling her close. There was no use denying it. She'd fallen in love with a dragon. They'd known each other for such a short amount of time, but it didn't matter. The obstacles they'd faced had shown her who he truly was, and that was the man she'd come to adore.

"If you keep looking at me like that, I'm not sure you'll make it to your council meeting," he murmured, his voice husky.

"Are you offering an alternative?" she asked with a teasing smile, winding her arms around his neck. For just a few minutes, she wanted to forget the worries plaguing them and get lost in the moment—with him.

His gaze heated and he lowered his head, caressing her with the delicious heat of his draconic power. It swirled around her, fueling the flames of the fire that burned within her every time he was near. Every touch became a powerful caress, and he eased her back on the bed. His kiss became more demanding, and she gasped, wanting everything he offered and more.

Dragonfire surrounded her, burning her from within, but she'd gladly surrender to his heat. Malek's power poured into her, burning away her subterfuge until the naked emotions of her feelings were exposed. She returned his kiss, telling him without words how important he'd become to her. She wanted him, more than she'd ever wanted anything. His hand fisted her hair, and he consumed her mouth while his power continued to stroke the flames of her desire.

Unable to resist him or the promise in his touch, she met his power with her own. Wave after wave of magic coursed through them, and everything faded away but him. In that moment, Malek became her entire world, her sole focus, and it still wasn't enough.

His hand slid up her thigh, pushing her dress upward as he caressed her skin. Need, unspoken and irrefutable, welled within her, and she pushed him down on the bed and rose over him. Her silvery hair was like a curtain, shielding them from the world as she gazed down at the dragon she loved. His hands rested on her hips, holding her to him and the hard ridge of his desire pressed against her core.

"Sabine," he groaned, his voice heady with a need that matched her own.

She leaned over him and brushed her lips against his. "Will you surrender to me, Malek?"

"Not a chance, sweetheart," he murmured against her mouth. "But you're welcome to try your power against mine."

Her mouth curved upward, thrilled with the challenge he offered. She pushed up his shirt, needing to touch him. He sat up and pulled it off, then tossed it aside before yanking her back down toward him. He rolled with her while they battled for supremacy, neither considering themselves the loser as they lost themselves in the magic of the moment.

Her hands threaded through his hair as his mouth kissed its way down to her breast. She gasped, the erotic heat fracturing her thoughts as he nibbled and licked every inch of her. She was helpless in the face of the power he held over her, but part of her was dimly aware she was holding him in her thrall as well. She needed this—needed him. This was more than simply magic. This was the gift of sharing power, the gift of sharing the essence of oneself to strengthen and enhance their partner. It was the gift of love, and there was no greater magic in the world.

"Malek," she whispered, needing him and everything he could offer.

He lowered his head to kiss her again, but the stubborn man wasn't heeding her demand. She pushed him back down, rose over him, and lowered her body, taking him into herself. She rode him, meeting every exquisite thrust with a wave of power that consumed them both. His gaze was heated and predatory, claiming her with more than his touch. His hand fisted her hair as he rose to claim her mouth once more.

Power fused them together. Like the ritual that had bound her to the Unseelie and proclaimed her queen, her love for this dragon bound her to him. The bond between them flung wide open, and magic surged between them until they could no longer tell where each one began and the other ended.

Malek thrust one last time, and Sabine's thoughts shattered, like the crystals carried on the wind of the storm. Malek followed her a second later with a rush of heat that seared her from within. With a gasp, she collapsed on top of him. Boneless and unwilling to leave his embrace, she reveled in the afterglow of their spent passion. He held her tightly, and she lay there for a long time, wanting to stay in this moment forever.

His hand trailed up her naked back, his touch both gentle and possessive. It was dangerous to allow a dragon to hold such a claim over her, but she couldn't find it within her to protest, especially given what they'd just shared. If she were honest with herself, Malek belonged to her, and she'd become part of him in return.

When she started to stir, Malek rolled them over and propped himself up on his elbow to look down at her. He traced his fingers along the side of her face, the tenderness in his gaze making her stomach flutter. "You take my breath away, Sabine. Seeing you like this… I never imagined anyone like you could possibly exist."

She pressed her hand against his strong jaw, needing to touch the man who had broken through the strongest of her barriers. "I've often thought the same thing when I look at you."

"I keep losing control around you," Malek admitted, his hand caressing downward along her side. His touch was impossibly gentle, as though she'd been crafted from the finest crystal. "I wasn't too rough, was I?"

She smiled. "I'm not human, Malek. I don't break easily."

"You're also not a dragon," he reminded her with a grin.

"No. But if that's the result, I'm hoping you'll lose control again soon," she murmured, winding her arms around his neck. "I probably shouldn't tell you I've been wanting to do that for a while now."

He chuckled. "I probably shouldn't tell you I've been wanting you for twice as long."

She laughed and kissed him lightly. "I think I prefer that method of sharing magic over simply sharing a kiss with you."

"I'm always happy to accommodate the new Unseelie queen's request," he murmured and brushed his lips against hers again.

The reminder of her new situation slammed into her. She squeezed her eyes shut and muttered, "Don't remind me."

He paused. "You don't want to be queen, do you?"

Sabine opened her eyes and found a weighted intensity in

his gaze. She had the impression his question wasn't an idle one. Uncomfortable with the emotions he evoked, Sabine sat up and reached for her dress, taking the opportunity to gather her thoughts.

She pulled the dress into her lap, running her fingers over the soft material. "Sometimes what we want in life has no bearing on what duty demands."

"That wasn't what I asked."

Sabine looked at him. Malek was still lounging on the bed, and the sight was enough to tempt her into exploring every inch of his hard body again. She swallowed and turned away, not trusting herself when he was so close. He could easily strip away all her hidden truths, just like her glamour hid her true self from the world.

Malek sat up, the bed moving beneath her. He lifted her hair and placed it over her shoulder, exposing the nape of her neck. He pressed a soft kiss against her skin, causing it to prickle in awareness. She took a shaky breath, her resolve wavering. Part of her reveled in the freedom of traveling with him and seeing the world, but it was temporary—just like their relationship. Each moment spent with him was precious, and she was carefully storing each of these treasured memories.

As she traced her fingers along the silver threading on her dress, Sabine considered his question, wanting to give it the weight it deserved. She didn't know if she'd enjoy being queen. An alternative wasn't something she'd ever contemplated. It was her destiny, an expectation, an obligation. She couldn't afford to consider any other options. If she didn't assume the throne, she would be killed. It was that simple.

"I don't know," she admitted in a soft voice. "I'm worried about letting my people down. I'm not sure I'm up to the challenge of withstanding my father's schemes."

"Those are fears, not desires," Malek replied, wrapping his arm around her waist.

Sabine smiled at his ability to always cut to the heart of things. "You're right, but your question is impossible to answer. Becoming queen was something that was always expected of me. In some ways, the idea was abstract—a beautiful dream of sorts—but something so far in the future, it wasn't quite real."

"That's fair," he said and kissed her neck again. "Although, I would have preferred if you hadn't risked certain death to accept your crown. Being unable to reach you during the ritual was one of the most difficult things I've ever experienced."

Sabine paused, recalling the moment she'd sent her power into the crystal. The connection she'd felt when her people joined with her had been one of the most beautiful and powerful experiences of her life. It had opened her eyes in so many ways.

"I think Faerie knew it needed to be presented as a choice, even if the alternative meant death. If I had refused, it wasn't just me who would have suffered. My people would have too. By accepting the crown, our fates became intertwined."

"I'd never considered it like that," Malek said quietly, his hand trailing across her stomach in a slow caress.

She hadn't either. Sabine relaxed against him, running her fingers along his arm. "Dragons don't have kings and queens, do they?"

"No," he said with a sigh. "Our social structure is probably closest to the dwarves. We have clans like they do, divided into the types of dragons we are and the powers we possess. It's based on our family trees more than anything."

She turned to face him. "All dragons have different abilities?"

He hesitated and then nodded. "For the most part, yes.

Many of us are elemental, and our powers are tied to our alignment. Many dragons are only strongest with one or two elements, but we have some ability with most of them."

"I've never heard that before," she said, trying to recall everything she'd learned about dragons as a child. Some of the Fae had dedicated their lives to studying their most ancient of foes, but Sabine was starting to realize a great deal of that knowledge was rooted in fear and supposition.

Malek ran his hand down her arm. He captured her hand and pressed a kiss against it. "It's not common knowledge, sweetheart. While many of us can guess each other's abilities, we don't openly discuss them. Even among our own people, we don't trust easily and any weakness can be used against us."

"Like the demons," she said, surprised by the similarities. In many ways, Malek had more in common with the first races of this world than she'd expected.

"In some ways, but our abilities don't change whether we're above ground or below."

Sabine considered the crystal again. Faerie had chosen a crystal vessel for a reason, and not simply because she was in the dwarven realm. In some ways, the facets of power possessed by each race mirrored those edges of the crystal. They had been divided into different aspects for a reason. Sabine glanced down at the mark on his wrist again, an uncomfortable suspicion flittering through her mind.

A light knock on the door brought her back to awareness.

"One of these days I'm going to get you alone for longer than an hour or two," Malek muttered and picked up the warding medallion from the nearby table.

"Sabine?" Rika's tentative voice called from outside.

"Just a moment," Sabine said and leaned forward to give Malek another quick kiss. While he fastened the warding medallion around his neck, she slipped her dress back on and smoothed out her hair with a trace of magic. With a glance at Malek to ensure he appeared as nothing more than a partially dressed human, albeit a delicious one, she headed toward Rika's voice.

Sabine pressed her hand against the crystal panel and mentally instructed it to relax the wards around the room. The magic fell away, and Sabine opened the door.

Rika was standing there, her face pale and her eyes wide with worry.

"Rika? What's wrong?" Sabine asked, taking a step toward her.

Rika glanced down the hall and then back at Sabine. "Dagmar's back. She's still waiting to hear official word, but… It's bad, Sabine. Really bad."

"Talk to me, Rika," Sabine said, trying to bury her alarm. "What did she say?"

Rika's eyes welled with tears. "There isn't going to be a trial, Sabine. The council already made their decision."

"What are you talking about?"

Rika took a shaky breath. "They're going to execute Bane in three days."

Chapter Ten

Malek finished equipping his weapons, watching as Sabine's entire body tensed. He'd suspected the dwarves might try something like this, but he'd thought Sabine's status would give them pause. He needed to reach out to Hargrim, the dwarf who had sponsored him on previous visits, to find out what rumors were circulating around Razadon. The dwarves had to know neither Sabine nor the demons would take this well.

The mark on Malek's wrist burned. He clamped his hand onto his wrist to stop Sabine from pulling power from him. Something wasn't right. Sabine's skin was glowing, flickers of silver and gold light erupting from the etchings on her skin. He'd begun to realize they flared with power whenever her emotions were riled, but rarely that gold color and never in conjunction with the mark she'd gifted him.

"They will not touch him," Sabine snapped, turning on her heel and storming down the hall.

Rika squeaked and jumped out of Sabine's way, scrambling backward. Malek couldn't blame her. For all Rika's resilience, she was still human and had been taught to fear the Fae. Hell, he knew Sabine fairly well, and even he was a little taken aback.

Malek ran after Sabine and caught her before she could take out her anger on Dagmar. He grabbed her arm and urged, "Sabine, wait."

She jerked away from him and narrowed her eyes. Any sign of the soft and passionate woman he'd held in his arms mere minutes earlier had fled. If anything, her features had taken on a harshness he hadn't seen since the goddess last made an appearance.

"You overstep yourself, Malek. Regardless of what you and I have shared, Bane is mine to protect. I'll turn this mountain to rubble before I allow anyone to harm him or this land."

Malek paused, both surprised by her demeanor and the cold inflection in her tone. The gold light trailing along her skin was becoming even stronger. While Sabine's sense of righteousness seemed to emerge when those she cared about were in danger, this gold glow and tapping into his power was out of character.

"What's going on?" Malek asked in a low voice, taking a step toward her.

"You dare think to challenge me?" she demanded, the golden glow becoming even stronger. Even her facial features were becoming sharper and more angular, the shadows deepening and growing around her. It could be a trick of the light, but he didn't believe it. Something was definitely wrong, and he needed to proceed carefully. The goddess had made no qualms about her hatred for dragons.

"I won't try to stop you, but I will urge you to caution," he said, glancing behind her for any sign of Blossom. Unfortunately, the pixie was nowhere in sight and couldn't act as a mediator. He couldn't risk allowing Sabine to leave this hallway until he knew what was wrong with her. "Threatening to kill the dwarves outright isn't like you, Sabine. You've always wanted to protect the innocent. How many innocent lives will be destroyed if you take out your anger on everyone compared to the few who are responsible for this decision?"

"Caution? You expect me to restrain myself when they've befouled this land?" Sabine asked in disbelief, her skin glowing with power as her temper continued to build. "These dwarves intend to use Bane as a scapegoat. My people entrusted this mountain to them, and they *will* shoulder the responsibility for their negligence or lose all rights to it. Their actions are the reason Bane harmed their people."

"I agree with you," Malek snapped, not bothering to hide his anger. "I'm not your enemy, Sabine. The fact Bane is a demon is simply an excuse, just as they would blame my heritage if given the opportunity. I intend to do everything within my power to help rescue Bane, but if you walk out there like this, you'll destroy any hope in getting Dagmar to willingly aid us."

She arched her brow. "You believe I would harm a servant, simply for being a messenger?"

Malek swept his gaze over her again, his frown deepening as his misgivings increased. The Sabine he knew never referred to anyone as her servant. She'd always referred to people as her companions, allies, or even friends.

"Not normally, no. But a few minutes ago, you received a major power boost. Now you're glowing and not in the way you normally do. Look at your markings, Sabine, and tell me what's going on. You're not acting like yourself. You've always placed the welfare of innocents above everything."

Sabine's brow furrowed as his words penetrated. She looked down. Her eyes widened in shock and horror as she studied the markings on her arms. The gold light flickered, almost warring with her silver glow.

Her voice wavered slightly as she whispered, "I don't understand. How is this possible? Only the gods' power flares gold."

Malek took another step toward her, needing to close the distance between them. Whatever was happening wasn't her doing. "I feel a pressure within me as though you're trying to force more power from me through our bond."

Sabine paled and shook her head. "No. I wouldn't betray your trust in me like that."

The fear in her lavender eyes stripped away the last of his doubt. Malek cupped her face, her loose hair brushing against his hand. This time, she didn't pull away from him. "It's Lachlina, isn't it? She's affecting your emotions, just like Faerie did to all of us earlier. You need to fight it, sweetheart."

Blossom flew down the hallway in their direction, her dust tinged red in agitation. "Sabine, the goddess is really angry! She says the corruption is coming back."

Sabine whipped her head in Blossom's direction. "What? How?"

"I don't know," Blossom said, fluttering her wings furiously. "She says the imbalance will penetrate the foundation of the world. She's demanding you stop it, or she'll destroy the mountain."

Malek frowned, worried by how closely the goddess's edict aligned with Sabine's earlier words. It was almost as though Sabine had opened a window for the goddess once she became angry. "Can you sever her connection to you, Sabine?"

"I must," Sabine said with grim determination. She withdrew her dagger and thrust it in Malek's direction. "If I fail, you'll need to cut Lachlina's mark from my skin. There's no guarantee it'll work, but we may not have a choice."

He froze. The thought of harming her in any way was

anathema to him, but he didn't know how he could refuse her request. If Sabine couldn't gain control over the goddess, more lives would be in jeopardy.

"Promise me, Malek," Sabine pleaded, gripping his arm tightly. "She'll kill everyone within Razadon if she brings the mountain down on top of us. We can't let that happen."

He squared his shoulders and gave her a curt nod. "You have my word. I'll cut the mark from your skin if you aren't able to stop her."

Sabine took a deep breath and closed her eyes. Her markings pulsed even more rapidly, the glow becoming almost blinding. Sabine's entire body went rigid, her skin glistening from the exertion of an internal battle he was unable to protect her from.

Blossom landed on Malek's shoulder. "This isn't good, Malek. The goddess is really angry. Bad things happen when the gods get angry. I don't want her to hurt Sabine."

Malek frowned, searching for any sign Sabine's efforts were working. It was slight, but it appeared the golden hue was fading from Sabine's skin. The silver glow, which had always reminded him of moonlight, trailed along her skin even more brilliantly. Her features were softening, the harsh lines fading away and reminding him once again of the woman he loved.

Rika angled closer to him and whispered, "Is she doing it? I see all sorts of magic moving around her, but I can't tell what's happening."

"Lachlina's influence is lessening," Malek said and took Sabine's hand. He turned it over to expose her wrist and the chalice symbol where the goddess had marked her. The gold was still prominent, but even that was dissipating. He ran his thumb across the symbol, but he didn't dare touch her with his power.

After several minutes, Sabine opened her eyes. She

clutched her head and took a ragged breath. Whatever she'd done had cost her a great deal. Malek frowned in concern. She couldn't afford to expend more power if they were going to survive Razadon.

Rika took a step toward her. "Are you all right, Sabine?"

"I'll be okay in a few minutes," Sabine said, but her voice was strained. "Blossom, tell Lachlina I'll agree to investigate this corruption, but it will be on my terms or not at all. I will not be a hostage to her influence."

Blossom nodded and closed her eyes, presumably to communicate with the renegade goddess.

Malek wrapped his arm around Sabine's waist to steady her. No matter what had just happened, she still needed to meet with Razadon's leaders and advocate for Bane's release. "Do you need more power, sweetheart?"

"No, it's too risky. Your power calls to my Seelie magic," Sabine said, leaning against him. "Lachlina's grasp is tenuous at best, but she can't be allowed control of our bonds again. I didn't even realize she was doing it this time. If you hadn't stopped me and made me question myself…" She lifted her head, her eyes softening as she gazed up at him. "It would seem I owe you another debt, Malek."

The weight of her words stood between them. Malek immediately rejected her offering, not wanting to upset the precious balance they'd managed to find.

"There is no debt between us, sweetheart. You stopped me earlier when I was ready to steal you away." He ran a hand down her arm, the golden glow hardly noticeable. "I can barely see her presence now."

She looked down at herself. "Yes, but we need to find a way to prevent this from happening again. I don't know who we can trust enough to help us find a solution. My magic is changing, and it seems to be getting worse. I don't believe the goddess realized her thoughts were merging with mine. She's getting stronger."

Malek frowned. The first time he'd seen Sabine's skin flare gold had been in Atlantia when the goddess had taken control of her. Then it had happened again on his ship. He was beginning to wish Sabine had never tied herself to that damn chalice, regardless of the cost to his people.

"I think her connection to you may be linked to your emotions," Malek said, wondering if Bane might have some insight. The demon had been concerned about Sabine's magic changing and becoming more Seelie. It was possible Lachlina's influence could be affecting Sabine in more ways than they'd anticipated.

"I don't think Lachlina particularly cares about Bane," Sabine said with a frown. "She's willing to use his power for her own purposes, but she doesn't feel protective over him like I do."

"I think it's a little deeper than that," Malek said, considering the possibilities. "I believe the intensity of your feelings may be the catalyst. If you're both aligned in your emotions, no matter the reasons, you may be opening a doorway to allow your powers to merge. I've seen flashes of it before, but never this intense."

Sabine absently rubbed the chalice symbol on her wrist where the goddess had marked her. "I can't risk losing control again and allowing Lachlina to manipulate my alliances and blood bonds. The Unseelie vowed never to be their slaves again, Malek. Through me, she has access to all of them and more—the lion clan of the Beastpeople, the merfolk, Rika, the pixies, Bane, and you."

"Not necessarily," Malek said, considering the strange pressure he'd experienced. "I was able to resist her pulling more of my magic through our bond. It wasn't the same when she killed those hunters, possibly because of how we changed our connection. You made us more balanced, Sabine."

A shred of hope flared in her eyes. "You believe you're immune?"

Blossom's wings fluttered. "Maybe that's why the gods don't like your people, Malek."

Malek paused with surprise. The magic of this world had originally drawn his people here, but he didn't know all the details about what had begun the conflict. "I don't know, but I believe Sabine also has the power to resist her. The only times I've seen flashes of Lachlina's influence was when Sabine allowed it or her emotions ran high. The minute Sabine realized what was happening, the gold faded."

"You may be right." Sabine's shoulders relaxed, and she glanced down the hallway in the direction of the common room. "Malek, I need to meet with Razadon's leaders right away. Even if they're not planning on harming Bane for three days, we can't afford to leave him in prison."

Malek frowned, knowing Sabine was right. The dwarves might be trying to test Sabine's strength and ability to rule by threatening to execute her trusted advisor. Allowing Bane to remain imprisoned would be a tremendous show of weakness.

"I don't want him to stay there either," Rika said, clasping her hands together. "I was afraid of demons until I met Bane, but he's not like what the stories say. These people really want to hurt him, Sabine. We can't let that happen."

Sabine nodded and placed her hand on Rika's shoulder. "I know. He's grown to care about you a great deal, Rika."

Rika's eyes glistened with moisture, and she averted her gaze.

Blossom landed on Rika's shoulder and patted her hair before turning back toward Sabine. "I don't like it when Bane calls me a bug, but he helps with your Unseelie magic,

Sabine. If the dwarves think you're not Unseelie enough for them, they might try to kill you or even worse—surrender you to the Wild Hunt."

A cold chill gripped Malek. He turned back toward Sabine and demanded, "Is that true?"

She sighed and then nodded. "We're walking a dangerous line here. Not only do we need to keep up appearances to suggest I'm a formidable power, but they can't know how much our bond has changed my magic. Bane helps strengthen all of us, and he helps bolster my Unseelie side."

Malek blew out a breath. "Okay. Can we have them call a council meeting right away?"

"We can try, but I need allies first. Astrid's our best chance since she had a relationship with my mother. It may require a bribe or some other concession, but Astrid is a highly respected council member. We'll need her on our side." Sabine paused and then admitted in a quiet voice, "I can't risk losing control of my magic, Malek. Not here, and not if I intend to keep my throne."

He frowned, the waver in her voice causing his protective instincts to flare to the surface. He drew her in his arms, unable to resist holding her. "Can I do anything to help?"

She lifted her head to meet his eyes. "The dwarves respect strength above all else. I'll need to rely heavily on my power to keep up appearances while I'm here. Bane can temper my magic and keep it in check, but not while he's imprisoned. Until he's freed and can act as my anchor, would you be willing to accompany me and fill that role? If Lachlina influences me again, you're the only one who might be able to get through to me."

"You don't ever have to ask," he murmured, running his hand down her back. "I'll reach out to my contacts later tonight when you're safely back in the embassy. Will that work for you?"

Sabine nodded, her slim form trembling slightly in his arms. The sudden insight into her vulnerability gave him pause. Lachlina had truly scared her.

Malek caught Blossom's eye and nodded toward the bedroom in a silent request to give them a moment alone. The pixie gave him a salute and then whispered something in Rika's ear. The seer nodded, and the two of them disappeared into Sabine's bedchamber.

"Where are they going?" Sabine asked, glancing toward her bedroom.

"They'll be right back," Malek said, pulling Sabine even closer. She fit him so perfectly, her body molding to his. "Take a moment to center yourself and make sure Lachlina's really gone, sweetheart. We'll leave as soon as you're ready."

She nodded and curled her fingers into his shirt, resting her forehead against Malek's chest. The scent of night-blooming flowers surrounded him, and a sense of rightness filled him at having her this close.

A fortifying wave of magic brushed against his skin, but it wasn't directed at him. He realized Sabine was focused inward and trying to reinforce her mental barriers. Touched and awed by her trust that he would protect her, Malek ran his hand up and down her back in a gentle caress. When she eventually relaxed in his arms, something inside him eased as well.

Rika cleared her throat and held out Sabine's crown. "I hope it's okay, but Blossom and I thought you might need this when you go out in public. She said it was the same crown your mother wore."

Sabine pulled back slightly and accepted the elegant silver circlet. "Yes. The Crown of Shadows and Twilight can change its appearance to suit its whim. My mother often wore it in this form. I'm assuming it chose to appear this way to remind the dwarves I'm her heir."

Rika's eyes widened. "Is the crown alive?"

"Not exactly," Sabine said quietly, running her fingers over the intricate silver design. "It's Wild Magic, and objects of power often develop their own awareness. No one knows exactly how the magic works."

"My parents told me it sometimes has red stones in it," Blossom said, perched on Rika's shoulder. "A few times it was made from flowers, but Queen Malia didn't like that much. She said it was too Seelie."

"May I?" Malek asked, gesturing at the crown.

Sabine hesitated but then held it out for him. He took it from her, and a slight tingle of magic brushed against his skin as though the crown were testing him. It warmed in his hand, but it wasn't unpleasant.

He held it up to the light, admiring the details and workmanship. The silver was as thin as a spiderweb in some areas, sloping gracefully in artistic patterns that represented the phases of the moon. Dozens of midnight-blue gems decorated the silverwork, but the center stone was breathtaking.

Like the other gems, this one was also blue, but the color was deeper and richer somehow. It had the appearance of the night's sky when the sun had just slipped past the horizon. Within its depths, Malek caught a glimpse of silver and gold flecks. They pulsed with a strange light, as though the gem contained the essence of stardust.

Malek turned to find Sabine watching him, with a small smile playing upon her lips. It suited her, he realized. She was as exquisite as the crown, a priceless and rare treasure unlike anyone he'd ever met. The crown warmed in his hand, and he glanced down at it in surprise. He could almost detect a hint of emotions emanating from it—desire and longing. It belonged with Sabine and would never suffer another to possess it. He suspected the only reason it allowed his touch was because of his feelings for the woman in front of him.

He lifted the crown and carefully placed it upon Sabine's head, marveling at how he'd ever doubted she was anything other than Fae. It had never been more apparent Sabine had been born to wear this crown. No matter how much she might return his feelings, she was the equivalent of the stars in the night sky. Trying to steal her away would destroy her light, and he could never do that to her, no matter how much he wanted to keep her to himself. Their only option was to find a way to live in the light—together.

He slid his hand downward along her soft skin and caressed her cheek. "I've never seen a more beautiful queen, Sabin'theoria."

Her lavender eyes softened, and she pressed her body against him. "I'm glad you're here with me, Malek."

He lowered his head and kissed her. From the way she responded to his touch, it was clear her feelings for him ran just as deeply. She was his. He knew it with every fiber of his being, even if she hadn't said the words. He didn't know what this meant for their blossoming relationship, but he'd go to the ends of the world for this woman.

He broke their kiss and searched her expression. "Are you ready to do this?"

She pressed her hands against his chest and nodded. "I am now. Let's go speak with Dagmar and arrange to meet with Astrid. We need answers."

Chapter Eleven

Sabine accompanied Dagmar down the main thoroughfare of Razadon. The dwarves who had stood outside the Faerie embassy during the ritual had become part of Sabine's personal guard. They were now positioned around her, moving curious onlookers out of their path—sometimes with a little more force than necessary. Dagmar had explained that Sabine's protection fell under the terms of the treaty signed generations earlier, and these four warriors were all members of the Faerie embassy.

Malek kept pace beside her, his hand never straying far from the hilt of his sword despite Dagmar's assurances. Sabine could relate; she'd learned years ago never to blindly trust the safety of her loved ones to outsiders, which was why she also wore some of her throwing knives under her dress. Unfortunately, the heavy material and design of her garment would make it challenging if she needed to use them.

Even Rika had been armed with a small dagger, which she wore openly on her side and within easy access of Sabine's grasp. Bane had been showing Rika some basic moves since they'd left Karga, but the young seer still had a great deal to learn. If a problem arose, at least Sabine and Malek would have another weapon at their disposal. She just hoped Rika had enough control over her wings to try to avoid danger.

"Is there anything I need to do when we get there?" Rika asked, her wings twitching slightly. Malek placed his free hand on Rika's shoulders to keep her on the ground.

"Suck in your gut and pinch your butt cheeks together!" Blossom instructed Rika from her perch on Sabine's shoulder. "Tuck in those wings!"

Rika threw her a quick grin and tucked her wings tightly against her back. "Got it!"

Sabine glanced at Blossom and asked, "That actually works?"

Blossom shrugged. "Maybe a little, but it's more fun watching her walk funny."

Sabine bit back a smile at the sight of Rika waddling down the corridor. "I see your point."

"Don't worry about a thing when we arrive," Dagmar said to Rika, her footsteps bouncing lightly on the tiled walkway. "I'll tell you who everyone is, their position, and everything else you might need to know. I've been studying up on everyone's family history for years. Although, I had to do a quick refresher earlier on Badac Coinbasher's successor, but we won't need to worry about him while we're visiting Astrid. She's the leader of the Powerbroker Guild, and Badac was the leader of the Tradesmen Guild."

Sabine glanced at Dagmar. "Badac Coinbasher was the Elder who was killed, correct? Did you know him?"

Dagmar wrinkled her nose. "Yep. He was a right ogre's tit, if you don't mind me saying. His breath smelled like boiled goblin pus too. It was enough to knock you over."

"Eww," Rika said, making a gagging noise.

"I wonder what he ate," Blossom said, holding on to

Sabine's hair. "I once heard about a dwarf who knocked an entire family of pixies unconscious by breathing on them. Maybe you guys should grow some mint down here."

"No kidding," Dagmar replied with a cheerful grin, her red braids swinging with every bounce. "No one liked Badac, but he kept his guild's pockets lined with coin. His replacement is Hargrim Icemail, but he didn't have anything to do with the decision about your demon friend. If we do run into Hargrim, I can name all his ancestors back eleven generations, but I'm a little shaky after that." She patted her oversized pocket and winked. "Don't worry. I've got notes. Might have a sandwich in here too, but that's supposed to be a secret."

"Do you have any plants in there?" Blossom asked, taking flight and zipping around Dagmar to sniff her clothing.

"Sorry. No plants."

Malek arched his brow. "Were you talking about the same Hargrim Icemail who managed the surface trading?"

Dagmar nodded. "Aye. You know him?"

Malek let out a low whistle. "I do, and fairly well. Hargrim Icemail always swore that if a giant ever sat on his cousin, he'd turn every council meeting into an excuse to get piss-faced drunk to celebrate."

Sabine frowned at Malek. "He was your sponsor?"

Malek nodded. "Yes. I was planning on meeting up with him later tonight. Given the news of his recent rise in standing, I'm not sure he'll be sober enough to recognize me."

Dagmar grinned. "Sounds like him. When Hargrim heard his cousin ended up dead, he immediately went to the tavern and bought a round for the house. He was there celebrating when his wife showed up. Kavish grabbed him by his ear, hauled him out of the tavern, and threatened to shove her boot up his arse if he didn't get home. You could hear her shouting about how he was a damn fool who was going to screw up the council the entire way home."

The clang of metal weapons clashing against each other filled the air, followed by loud cheering. Sabine slowed her footsteps, catching sight of what appeared to be some sort of fighting ring. Several groups of armored dwarves were fighting against each other, while a large group of onlookers shouted their encouragement. The fighters weren't holding back either; some were bleeding heavily or had fallen to their knees in defeat.

"What's going on over there? Is that a tournament?" Sabine asked, gesturing at the commotion.

Dagmar glanced over and then hunched her shoulders. "Um… they're, ah, competing for rights to battle in the upcoming combat."

"Uh oh," Blossom muttered. "I've heard about these things."

Sabine frowned, an uneasy suspicion entering her mind. "What combat?"

"Demons always choose death by combat," Dagmar admitted with a wince.

"What?" Sabine demanded, halting in her tracks.

Blossom landed on Sabine's shoulder and patted her hair. "Want me to dust them? If they're all busy trying to scratch under their armor, they won't be able to fight." She cocked her head. "Actually, it might be kinda fun to watch it happen. I bet I could have them all rolling around on the ground in less than ten minutes. Wanna take bets?"

Sabine's mouth formed a thin line. "I'll keep it in mind."

"I'm so sorry," Dagmar said in a rush. "I forgot they were going to be competing. I guess we should have gone a different direction through the caverns. Maybe nothing will happen, and your demon friend won't be bludgeoned—er, beaten, no wait. Um…" Dagmar grimaced and then gave

Sabine a wobbly smile. "You know us dwarves. Any excuse for fighting. Or drinking. Or having a good time really. Wait. That didn't sound good either, did it?" She slapped her forehead. "By the stone, I'm making a mess of this."

Malek took a step closer to Sabine and placed his hand against her lower back. She took a steadying breath and turned away from the combat. No matter how much Sabine wanted to put a stop to their practice battle, she wasn't here to change their culture. She would, however, ensure Bane never stepped foot inside that ring.

Straightening her shoulders, Sabine gestured for Dagmar to continue to lead the way. "It's fine, Dagmar. Astrid's waiting for us."

"Right. Got it," Dagmar said, snapping to attention. "Best not to make the leader of the Powerbroker Guild wait. She can be a little scary. Good thing we're close now."

They turned down a side street, taking them away from the combat ring. The area wasn't as populated, and the street was lined with what appeared to be a number of residences.

The dwarves might be small in stature, but they more than made up for it with their grandiose architecture. The buildings were all side by side, as many as two or three stories in height. Each façade featured decorative carved stonework, with elaborate scenes depicting facets of daily dwarven life. Flickering crystalline lanterns illuminated the path, painting a variety of colors upon the stone and almost giving them the illusion of movement.

Under normal circumstances, Sabine would have loved to take the time to explore everything Razadon had to offer. She'd been fascinated by dwarven culture ever since she was a child. Unfortunately, her concern for Bane overshadowed any enjoyment she might find.

"I don't think I've been down in this area before," Malek said, looking up at the buildings.

"The homes of the various guilds are in different areas of the city," Dagmar explained. "Only powerbrokers live in this district. Your friend, Hargrim, lives closer to the main market area with the rest of the tradesmen."

Dagmar led them to one of the largest residences on the street. Fractured crystals in a rainbow of colors had been fastened into the large double doors, creating a stained-glass effect. A small crystal panel like the ones Sabine had seen inside the Faerie embassy had been embedded into the stone wall beside the door. Dagmar pressed her hand against the panel, and a bell chimed loudly from within.

The door opened a few moments later, revealing an older dwarf nearly as wide as he was tall. His silver beard reached almost to his waist and had been braided with several glowing crystals.

He grinned widely at Dagmar and slapped his thigh. "Well, crap on a crystal! Look at this here party. Get in here, girl, and bring your friends. Astrid's had the household in a tizzy for the past several hours."

"And that means you can't sneak any of her good ale until she's distracted," Dagmar said with a grin.

He winked at her. "Caught me."

Dagmar laughed and hugged the older dwarf. "Heya, Uncle Elgrin. Looking good. Think your beard's grown another hand's length."

"Aye. Still haven't forgiven yer aunt for cutting it off," he grumbled.

Dagmar grinned. She turned toward Sabine and explained, "He got his beard caught in the power crystal mixing vat when he was drunk."

Blossom leaned close to Sabine's ear and whispered, "How long do you think it was before?"

Sabine shook her head, wondering if any of the dwarves tripped over their beards. It might be a mark of their status, but their lengths and the pride they went to for the sake of their beards was a little peculiar. They were the only original race capable of growing facial hair, which might explain their fixation.

Elgrin stepped aside, allowing them to enter. The doorway was low enough that both Sabine and Malek had to duck to pass through. Once they were inside, however, they were able to stand fully upright. Even if they tried, neither of them would have been able to touch the ceiling with their fingertips.

Sabine paused inside the entryway to Astrid's home, marveling at the artistry and craftsmanship. She wasn't sure what she'd been expecting, but she found herself both charmed and captivated by the warm and inviting interior. A large stone fireplace, almost deceptively simple in its design, took up most of the far wall. A few small embellishments only served to draw attention to the crackling fire that erased the chill from the air.

Crystals hung from the ceiling like hundreds of snowflakes caught in midair. Each one captured the light from the flames and reflected them onto the painted walls. Detailed murals depicted aspects of the Powerbroker Guild, from harvesting the crystals in the caverns to infusing them with magic.

The furniture was lower to the ground to better suit the dwarves' shorter stature, but it appeared heavy and extremely well built. Most of the pieces had been fused together with a combination of stone, crystal, and even wood. Each piece had obviously been crafted by a master artisan and then lovingly cared for over the years by the residents.

"You gonna introduce me to yer friends, Dagmar girl? Not every day the new Faerie queen comes callin' with a giant pixie and a human in tow."

Dagmar's face reddened. "Oops. Sorry. Um, Queen Sabin'theoria, please allow me to introduce Elgrin Onyxborn, my great uncle on my mum's side. Uncle Elgrin, this is Queen Sabin'theoria."

"You must call me Sabine," Sabine said with a smile. "I'd rather not stand upon formality when my mother spoke so highly of the Onyxborn clan. I grew up hearing stories about your remarkable crystal caves, and my beloved Beastman protector still safeguards the pendant you sent me as a nameday gift."

"Aye. That was a fine piece of work and worthy of a Faerie princess." Elgrin grinned and puffed out his chest. He gave her an approving nod and said, "We'll get along just fine, Sabine. Just fine."

Dagmar gestured toward Malek and Rika. "Her companions are Captain Malek Rish'dan of Obsidian's Storm, and Rika, Seer of Karga. Blossom, the pixie, is on her shoulder."

"It's a pleasure," Malek said, nodding in greeting. Rika gave the dwarf a shy smile, her wings fluttering wildly.

"Well, I'll be damned. A ship captain and a seer? And check out those wings. Antennae too. Never seen such a thing in all my years. What crafty bit of magic is that?"

Rika's cheeks reddened, and Malek pressed on her shoulder again to prevent her from flying upward. Heightened emotions or embarrassment seemed to make it more difficult for Rika to control her wings.

In a hushed voice, Dagmar said, "Rika's a butterfly, not a pixie, Uncle. The pixie's playing hide-and-seek in Sabine's hair."

"Hiya!" Blossom said with a wave, peering out from beneath Sabine's hair. "Some people call me Lady Blossom, but you can call me Blossom."

Sabine sighed. Blossom was determined to adopt this new

title. Pretty soon, all the pixies in Faerie were going to flying around referring to themselves as ladies or lords.

"Hah! No lie? I wonder who can fly higher, the seer or the pixie?" Elgrin asked, stroking his beard. "I wouldn't mind placing a wager on the outcome of that game."

"No wagers," a woman's voice called from a doorway on the opposite side of the room.

Sabine turned as Astrid swept toward them. The woman gave Elgrin a disapproving look and said, "You'd gamble away the clothes off your back if I didn't send Thetar chasing after you all day. Now unless you intend to stick around and conduct business like the patriarch of this family, get out of my hair and stay out of my larders."

Elgrin grunted and leaned forward, whispering conspiratorially, "Don't let her meanness fool ya. She ain't nearly as hard as the crystals she loves so well."

Sabine bit back a smile, taking an immediate liking to the older man. Dwarves always placed familial relationships above all others, a concept Sabine had always envied. Relationships among the Fae were much more complicated and often adversarial, especially when they were vying for power.

Astrid scowled and stalked toward them. She scanned Sabine up and down and said, "Well, girl, it looks like you finally claimed yer rightful place, and none too soon. I was wondering when you'd show up on my doorstep. Those idiots on the council thought to take advantage of yer inexperience. I'd be lying if I said I wasn't looking forward to watching you put them in their place."

Without waiting for a response, Astrid turned on her heel and headed into another room.

Dagmar swallowed audibly and said, "Welp, she's definitely in a mood."

Elgrin motioned for Dagmar and Rika to follow him. "Come along, you kids. Let's leave these fine folks to handle their business in private. No need for us to get underfoot when we can raid the larder while Astrid's distracted."

Dagmar's eyes lit with hopeful excitement, but Rika hesitated and turned to Sabine instead. "Is that okay?"

"Go ahead, but I think Blossom will stay with me for now," Sabine said, giving Rika a reassuring smile. Despite Rika's inexperience, she'd already demonstrated an insightful and warm nature people naturally responded to. Mingling with some of the other household members without Blossom's presence might allow Rika to gain a bit more confidence in her abilities.

Dagmar and Rika exchanged mirrored grins and followed Elgrin into the kitchen areas, while Sabine and Malek headed toward a small sitting room.

Thetar, the dwarf who had challenged her when they'd entered the city, was sitting in a chair with his boots propped up on the table. His arms were clasped behind his head, and he grinned at them.

Astrid was pacing the length of the room, her mouth turned downward in a frown. She lifted her head at the sound of their footsteps and motioned for them to have a seat. "Make yourself comfortable. You remember Thetar, I'm sure."

Sabine scanned the dwarf up and down, giving him a wry smile. "Looks like you found someone to braid another crystal into your beard."

Thetar let out a loud laugh and stroked his beard. "Aye, girlie. But if you still want to give it a tug, I'd be happy to oblige."

Astrid halted and glared at the other dwarf. "Talk that way to Faerie's newest queen again, and I'll make sure yer face is as well shorn as a baby's butt. Now get yer damn boots off my table or I'll have you licking it clean, you buffoon."

Thetar chuckled, removing his boots and placing them firmly on the ground.

Blossom giggled. "I think I like her."

Astrid huffed and gestured at the chairs again. "Sit, sit. You're too damned tall as it is. No need to keep towering over the room. Yer shadows are bigger than my floor."

Taking the dwarven woman at her word that they should make themselves comfortable, Sabine rested her hand against two of the chairs designed for much shorter individuals. Infusing a trace of her magic into the heavy wood, she reformed them into a size that would better suit her and Malek.

Astrid snorted. "Just like yer mum. She hated our furniture too. Always said she'd rather sit on the floor than squat like a troll."

Sabine took a seat and said, "Perhaps we're alike in some ways, especially when those under our protection are threatened."

"Yep," Blossom said in agreement. "Sabine is one of the best friends I've ever had. She even threatened to kill a couple of demons if they tried to eat me."

Malek sat beside Sabine and adopted a more laid-back pose to mirror Thetar's demeanor. Thetar might be acting as Astrid's bodyguard, but his body language was mostly relaxed. Only a slight rigidity in his shoulders indicated he was keeping a close eye on both Sabine and Malek.

Astrid sighed and sank into another chair. "I warned those idiots you wouldn't tolerate the demon's execution, but they're convinced yer nothing more than a child. Given yer sudden arrival and lack of honor guard, most of the council assumed you were here simply looking for sanctuary."

"A dangerous misconception." Sabine leaned back, drumming her fingers on the arm of the chair. No matter what relationship Astrid may have had with Sabine's mother, she needed to tread carefully. She didn't have a formal alliance with Astrid, and until one was in place, she couldn't completely trust the dwarven woman's motivations.

Blossom flew off her shoulder to investigate a cluster of crystals mounted on the wall on the far side of the room. She peered into the facets, sticking out her tongue and making faces at herself.

Astrid shrugged. "It was only dangerous if you proved to be yer mum's daughter. Many argued you were merely a hapless girl running away from her father like a naughty child. The King of the Seelie named you murderess and exile. Who are we to dispute such things?"

Thetar snorted. "Then you brought the damned Wild Hunt to our doorstep. There was talk about tossing you back out the door."

Astrid reached over and slapped Thetar on the back of his head. "Shut up, fool."

Malek straightened in his chair, his entire body stiffening at the insult. Sabine placed her hand on Malek's arm directly over the mark she'd given him. She'd expected people to talk, but not for them to make such accusations to her face.

Sabine sent a small pulse of power along her markings and warned, "I would be careful of repeating such slanderous remarks. My mother may have counted you and your clan as allies, Astrid, but our relationship still must be determined. No matter how informal we may be with each other, you are still speaking to the queen of the Unseelie."

Astrid fell silent, but her eyes widened slightly when she caught a glimpse of Malek's wrist. The dwarven woman quickly averted her gaze. She was no doubt wondering what had possessed Sabine to gift such a significant mark to someone who appeared nothing more than a human ship captain. Good. Keeping the dwarves off-balance was going to be necessary, especially since Sabine's anger was simmering just below the surface. Unfortunately, it was now obvious Malek meant more to her than if he were a simple bodyguard.

Astrid turned back to meet Sabine's gaze, but there was a coldness in her eyes. "Perhaps, but how you came to inherit is another matter. Our people place great store on family ties. An alliance with an ambitious girl who murders her mum is not necessarily desirable."

Anger, white hot and volatile, surged within Sabine. Her hands curled into fists, her nails biting into her palms as she struggled to wrest control of her magic. Thetar straightened, his hand lingering a little too close to his weapon.

"Be careful," Malek warned, his voice holding a jagged edge. Sabine wasn't sure if the warning was for her or Thetar, but it likely applied to them both.

Blossom poked her head out of a vase and flew toward Astrid, her wings tinged with red. "Sabine didn't hurt her mom! Take it back! Take it back right now!"

"Blossom," Sabine said sharply, motioning for the pixie to stop.

Blossom flew to her and hid under her hair. She patted Sabine's neck and whispered, "She shouldn't say things like that about you."

Sabine took a deep breath and studied Astrid carefully, trying to determine the older woman's motivations in provoking her. Some part of Sabine knew this wasn't a test of power. She was beginning to wonder if Astrid was truly grieving the loss of Sabine's mother.

The dwarves had often accused the Fae of twisting the truth almost to the point of lying, but there was one way for Sabine to prove she was beyond reproach. It might be the only chance she had to secure an alliance with the dwarven woman.

Trusting her instincts, Sabine lifted the hem of her dress

and withdrew one of her throwing knives. Thetar's hand went to the hilt of his axe, but Astrid held up her hand in a gesture for him to hold.

Sabine pricked her index finger and allowed a drop of blood to well to the surface. Power rose sharply and swiftly within her. A sudden wind whipped through the room, carrying with it the scent of major magic and night-blooming flowers.

Infusing her voice with power, Sabine said, "By blood and magic, and by my rights to both, I swear upon the last memory of the gods: I did not kill nor plot the murder of Queen Mali'theoria."

The blood on her fingertip disappeared, absorbed by the magical oath she'd uttered in front of witnesses. Such a thing was never done lightly, and Astrid stared at her in stunned disbelief.

"You would make such an oath to me? Why?"

Sabine sheathed her throwing dagger and smoothed her dress. "My mother spoke fondly of you, Astrid. I don't know the exact nature of your relationship with her, but I know she admired and respected you a great deal. I would not have someone she once viewed as an ally believe her daughter might be responsible for her death."

Astrid's eyes shone with grief, and the older woman blinked several times. Thetar settled back in his chair and pressed his fist over his heart in a gesture of respect. Sabine tilted her head in acknowledgment of his unspoken words.

After a moment, Astrid said, "Yer mum was a hard and complicated woman, Sabine. I often hated her as much as I admired her." She paused, a faraway expression on her face. "Even with our differences, I also counted her as more than an ally. She was possibly… a friend. I'm pleased the rumors about you are unfounded."

Sabine lowered her gaze, a myriad of emotions rushing

through her. Queen Mali'theoria had often ruled with fear, and many hated her for that reason alone. Sabine's own feelings for her were tangled in a mixture of regret and sadness. She hadn't expected to hear someone speak with such affection about her mother.

Blossom patted Sabine's hair affectionately, likely sensing her conflicting emotions. Without a word, she began braiding Sabine's hair. It was a task that would keep the pixie busy for a time and also serve as a calming influence for both.

She couldn't help but wonder if her mother had cultivated her cold and callous reputation out of necessity. Sabine had hoped to be a different kind of ruler, but she wasn't sure if that would be possible. Even her brief foray into living among demons had shown her some sacrifices might be necessary. Forcing her will over Bane was distasteful, but his nature didn't allow an alternative. Perhaps there were aspects to Sabine's mother she hadn't realized, and Sabine had been overly harsh with her judgment.

Malek reached over and placed his hand over hers, a reminder she wasn't alone. Decorum demanded she pull away and even chastise him for his liberties while she conducted a meeting to secure a political alliance, but she wasn't inclined to follow protocol. Malek offered her strength and compassion she desperately needed.

Astrid waved toward the man sitting next to her. "Thetar, get off yer ass and see where the damn refreshments are hiding. A woman could starve while waiting for the kitchen staff to get their heads out of their bums. Oh, and have them grab the spiced ale in the larder. Get something for the pixie too."

"Yer assuming anything's left with Elgrin bein' home," Thetar muttered and stood. He adjusted his belt buckle and flung open the far door. For such a loud man, he spoke quietly to the person who was standing right outside. The distraction gave Sabine a few moments to compose herself, which was likely what Astrid had intended.

Sabine squeezed Malek's hand and gave him a reassuring smile before pulling away and folding her hands in her lap. She lifted her head to regard the dwarven councilwoman, who was watching her with a shrewd gaze.

"I met yer daddy once," Astrid said, leaning back in her chair.

Blossom squeaked and tugged on Sabine's hair a little too hard. Sabine stiffened but didn't respond to Astrid's words. No discussions concerning her father had ever heralded good tidings.

Astrid rubbed her chin and said, "Didn't like him. Pompous ass who enjoyed torture a little too much. I'd say he enjoyed bloodletting even more than most demons. Granted, this was before he and yer mum were paired together. I doubt he changed much afterward, but I never went back to Faerie, so I can't say either way."

"I didn't know him then, so I cannot make any comparisons," Sabine said in a cold voice. She hadn't come here to discuss her father, and even speaking his name was unsettling.

Astrid nodded. "See, torture's a curious thing. It poisons something inside when you hurt someone else. Sometimes it's necessary, sure. But on some occasions, torture is done for sheer pleasure."

Malek arched his brow. "You're suggesting he enjoyed it."

Thetar walked back to the chairs and sat down. "Hah. I'd say the bastard more than enjoys it. I've heard he stalks the human children living outside the Silver Forest. He offers them pretty trinkets to lure them into the forest and then drains their essence while donning their skin."

"He does bad things to pixies too," Blossom said in a quiet voice.

Sabine's hands curled into themselves again, her nails digging into the meat of her palms. The pain was enough to distract her from the revulsion their words had evoked. She knew some of Faerie's creatures, including the Fae, enjoyed eating the tender meat of human children and pixies. Rumors about her father's habits had been circulating for years, but Sabine's absence from Faerie had given her a brief respite from listening to the horrors.

Sabine held Astrid's gaze and said, "I wouldn't have thought the dwarves cared much about the plight of human children."

"Not normally, but I don't like the thought of what yer daddy's doin' to them," Astrid said with a shrug. She nodded toward Sabine's clenched hands. "From the looks of it, you don't either."

Sabine forced her body to relax. "Horrors exist in all Faerie courts, just as they do in Razadon. I haven't had any direct contact with my father for more than ten years. Even before we left, I wasn't privy to the inner workings of his court."

Astrid nodded. "Didn't expect you did. But now that you've taken your throne, I'd be remiss in not sharing what I know. It's not just humans who have gone missing near the Silver Forest. Trolls, orcs, goblins, and other creatures living nearby have begun disappearing. Mostly those with Unseelie ties."

Sabine stilled. "What are you suggesting?"

Astrid held her gaze, a burning hot anger flickering in the depths of her irises. "The last time so many living creatures disappeared near the Silver Forest was during the war. Instead of animals that emerged from the forest, the dragons faced an army of Beastpeople. Tell me, Queen Sabin'theoria, who is yer daddy's enemy now? What need would he have for an army?"

Blossom gasped and took flight. "He's going to kill you, Sabine! He's going to send your own people after you!"

Sabine stood abruptly, unable to sit still. She paced the floor of the sitting room, reeling from Astrid's suggestion. It couldn't be true. Her father's power wasn't absolute. He was still beholden to the Faerie council, which represented all the creatures of Faerie. Even if he wanted her dead, the idea he was stealing her people's lives to twist them for his own purposes was a depravity of the highest order.

She paused and looked at Astrid. "How sure are you about this?"

Astrid stood and walked to a desk in the corner of the room. She unlocked the top drawer and pulled out a small box inlaid with several crystals that swirled with various colors. "I haven't seen anything firsthand, but the last dwarven emissary who visited Faerie brought these to me."

The dwarven councilwoman walked to Sabine and offered her a small stone. It was unremarkable at first glance, appearing like any other ordinary rock found within the Silver Forest. The only difference was the archaic rune inscribed on the bottom of it. Sabine picked it up, her eyes widening in surprise at the powerful magic that pulsed in her hand.

Blossom fluttered over and sniffed at it. "Hey, I've seen these in the forests before. They smell different than regular rocks, like dusty magic and blood."

Sabine ran her thumb across the stone and lifted her gaze. "It's a memory stone, isn't it?"

Malek rose from his chair and walked over to look at the stone. "Is that like Faerie wine? It contains the memories of the dwarven people?"

Astrid inclined her head. "Aye. We have several such

stones placed within their forests, just as the Fae have left their spies here for centuries. Our treaty may be with the Unseelie, but it doesn't include the Seelie. We've found it handy to keep an eye on them."

"Blossom, go to Malek," Sabine ordered, not wanting the pixie to accompany her to a place of memory. It would be hard enough to navigate unfamiliar magic alone, but taking Blossom along would be even more challenging. Sabine needed to conserve her power.

Blossom nodded and landed on Malek's shoulder, her wings twitching slightly in agitation.

Sabine steeled herself and closed her eyes to better concentrate on unlocking the magic contained within the stone. While the Fae could infuse their memories into the plants, trees, and other aspects of the land, their ties to the stone were tenuous. The dwarves had a different brand of magic, but it all originated from the same source—the gods.

Sabine allowed the magic to flow over her. It was inflexible like the stone but smooth and polished as though crafted by a master. She opened her eyes and found herself back in the Silver Forest. Tall trees towered overhead, while the sunlight dappled through their dark-green-and-silver canopy. Sabine heard the faint sound of a river somewhere nearby, but it was the cave in front of her that caught her attention.

She approached the rocky outcropping, stopping short at the sight of a large creature ambling out of the cave. It was one of the forest trolls, the elusive creatures that rarely emerged from their homes during the day. They were quiet and shy, preferring solitude for the most part. Its skin was covered with layers of green-and-brown moss, which allowed the troll to better blend into its surroundings. Sabine had known a few of them as a child and had even received gifts in the form of pretty rocks or flowers.

The one in front of her lifted its head to stare directly at her, its silver eyes glowing with a strange light. Sabine frowned. Troll eyes were typically green or a soft brown, but she'd never witnessed one in the throes of power before.

"*See me,*" it growled in a low voice as though the words had been ripped from him.

She stared in shock. Some sort of magic had traversed the boundaries between memory and reality. Only the most powerful Memorywalkers had such a talent.

"I see you," Sabine said and moved closer to the troll, lifting her hand to touch its moss-covered skin. A frisson of awareness passed through her, and she recognized the heavy layer of Calling magic surrounding the creature. Someone had summoned this troll from its daytime slumber and was holding it in their thrall.

Footsteps emerged from the far side of the clearing, and Sabine turned and saw several hooded figures approaching. She tensed, her heart pounding in her chest as she tried to resist the urge to flee from the memory. The images of the seven individuals flickered in the sunlight, as though heavy layers of glamour had been used to mask their identities. The similarities between this group and the ones who had murdered her mother were too familiar.

Sabine watched with helpless frustration and revulsion as the individual leading the group stood in front of the troll. His cloak hid his features, but the cut of his clothing and paleness of his skin marked him as Fae. He withdrew a knife from the folds of his robe, the sunlight catching the metal of the blade. The other cloaked individuals approached, chanting words of power as they formed a circle around their intended sacrifice.

"No," she whispered in shocked horror as the leader waved his hand, sending the troll to his knees. She had to force herself to remember this was a memory. Nothing she did here would change the outcome, except draw the attention of those who still lived.

In a rising tidal wave of Seelie magic, the man raised his knife and sliced through the troll's chest and shouted, "Sacrifice!"

The creature let out a bellow of pain, loud enough that even the trees shuddered. Green blood spattered the floor of the forest, coating the fallen leaves. The troll thrashed wildly, trying to escape the magic containment, but it was no use. The group surrounding him took a step forward, using their own enchanted weapons on the troll.

With each slice of the troll's skin, the figures dipped their fingers into its blood and then began to peel away his skin. The troll was aware of everything they were doing to him, but he couldn't break free of the enchantment. The only thing he could experience was agony as his sacrifice fueled their magical working.

Unable to watch any longer, Sabine blinked back her tears and stumbled away as the troll's death scream filled the air. She pressed her hand against the trunk of a tree, breathing heavily and trying to fight back the nausea.

They couldn't steal the troll's magic outright, but they could use its ties to the forest to amplify their own power. Such was the nature of the Fae; they were the ultimate authority of the forests, and no one was safe once they entered the Fae's dominion.

Chapter Twelve

With a shaky breath, Sabine opened her eyes and found herself once again in Astrid's sitting room. She felt sick, but more than anything, a burning anger was taking root deep inside her. That troll had been one of her subjects, and even though she'd never met him, she was ultimately responsible for his protection—a task she'd failed. His murder was a brazen declaration of war by the Seelie, who had made no secret in slaughtering someone under her protection.

"They knew your people were watching," Sabine said, her hand tightening around the memory stone as she recalled the way the troll's eyes had met hers. "This was a show, a performance put on in the hopes you would pass the message along to me."

"Aye," Astrid agreed, her mouth tightening. "The placement of those stones is not common knowledge. We believe the Seelie have managed to install spies even in Razadon."

Sabine's jaw clenched. "How many are dead?"

"Dozens," Astrid said in disgust, gesturing toward several stones still in the box on her desk. "We have memories of several, but there is evidence this group killed many more than we have recorded in the stones."

Thetar walked to his chair and sat, then propped his boots back up on the table. "They weren't all killed. Some of them were changed. They walked outta those circles wearing different skin than when they entered."

A cold chill went through Sabine. Such magic was never used without the council's approval. Even with her absence, there were several Unseelie who held leadership positions. She couldn't imagine any of them allowing Seelie magic to change creatures of the dark.

"I will need to see all of the stones," Sabine said and offered the stone back to Astrid. She had no desire to witness any more of these memories, but each one would have to be carefully studied for clues to help identify the culprits.

Astrid nodded. She took the memory stone from Sabine and placed it in the box with the others. After closing it, she handed it to Sabine.

"Bad magic, very bad magic," Blossom exclaimed and flew to Sabine, her eyes glistening with tears. The pixie landed on her shoulder and hugged her neck tightly. "It hurt you, and I couldn't protect you."

Malek took a step toward Sabine and asked, "Are you all right?"

She managed to nod, unable to explain how deeply the vision had affected her. She handed him the box for safekeeping, and he pressed his hands against hers and squeezed them gently. The contact helped fortify her, but it was the concerned look in his eyes that threatened her resolve. She couldn't risk losing her composure here, not until they were back in the relative safety of the embassy.

Turning back toward Astrid, Sabine asked, "What makes you believe my father is responsible for this?"

Astrid walked back to her chair and sat. "Rumors mostly.

The stones never recorded him, but the Master of Illusions wears many faces."

Sabine took her seat, the memory of the troll's screams forever etched into her mind. "He does, but many Fae are proficient with glamour. I can confirm Seelie magic was used in their ritual, but I would have to revisit the memory again to discern more."

Astrid sighed. "I figured as much. If yer mum had lived, I would have handed those stones to her to deal with that ugliness. Some of the families living close to the Silver Forests have requested sanctuary within Razadon, but this isn't a matter for the dwarves."

Sabine frowned. "Is that why you've chosen to close Razadon to all outsiders? Or is it because of the suspected Seelie spies?"

"Dammit," Astrid muttered and reached over to grab Thetar's ear. "Get up and find out where our damn drinks are. If I find out my louse of a father has emptied every cask in my cellar, I'll see both of you polishing my floor with yer beards."

Thetar grunted and scrambled to his feet. He shot an annoyed glare at Astrid but headed toward the door. He flung it open and shouted, "We're parched in here. Get yer asses in gear and get us some brew, or I'll string you up by yer toes over the sewer pits."

He kicked the door shut and stomped back to his chair.

Blossom leaned close and whispered, "I want to see dwarves hanging over the sewer pits. Can I go sabotage their casks?"

Sabine blew out a breath. All she needed was for Blossom to start causing mayhem in Astrid's home. The dwarven woman would throw them out and then they'd be out of luck trying to find a way to rescue Bane.

Sabine lifted her hand and made a show of patting her

hair. In a quiet voice, she asked, "Hmm. Is that a knot in my hair?"

"Oooh, I'll find out," Blossom exclaimed and started braiding her hair again. Malek coughed discreetly to hide his laugh.

Astrid settled back and interlaced her fingers over her stomach. "Now then, let's get back to the business of why you wanted to see me. You can do whatever you wish with those stones. That's an Unseelie matter to handle, a suitable task for the new queen."

Sabine paused, considering Astrid carefully. The dwarven councilwoman had obviously decided not to answer her question about the reason why Razadon had been closed. She could force the issue, but it wouldn't endear herself to the older woman.

Queen Mali'theoria had often said the dwarves needed to be reminded of their oaths to the Unseelie more frequently than any others. Her mother had made it a point to travel to Razadon every ten or fifteen years. These visits were always brief, but the former leader of the Unseelie had a reputation for making her point clearly and decisively.

The dwarves were simply tenants within this mountain range and charged with safeguarding it, provided they met the terms of their obligations to the Fae. It would be up to Sabine to remind them, or risk losing Razadon as a way to bolster her throne.

"*You* are just as Unseelie as I am," Sabine reminded Astrid sharply. "The treaty signed centuries ago bound us together by blood and magic, just as it bound together *all* the races who chose to embrace the darkness. We are all Unseelie, acknowledged as such because we rejected our captors and shattered our chains. My people fought alongside yours for centuries, breaking down the barriers that divided us as Fae, dwarves, demons, and more. We may be creatures of the dark, but we are bound together by a light more brilliant than what shines within the most powerful Seelie."

Thetar snorted. "Pretty words, but that's all they are. Since when do the Fae care about anyone who isn't one of their own kind?"

Sabine stood and lifted her hand, curling it into a fist as she wrapped a strong band of magic around Thetar. She yanked him from his chair and threw him down in a prone position on the ground.

Narrowing her eyes on him, Sabine said, "How dare you suggest that troll and others who sacrificed their lives are any less important than those of us in this room? You are Unseelie, and those trolls are our kin. You *will* respect their memory or join them as the treaty demands."

Malek stared at her in surprise, but he remained silent. Blossom snickered and continued braiding.

Thetar rolled over and grinned. "Damn. She's just like her mum, ain't she?"

Astrid studied Sabine for a long time and then inclined her head. "It would appear so. Better get off the ground and mind yer manners, Thetar. Queen Mali'theoria taught her daughter well."

Sabine took her seat and said, "Indeed, and I'm sure you know the reason I came to see you. My mother never would have tolerated such disrespect by allowing one of her trusted advisors to be sentenced without a trial, and I happen to share her opinion in this matter. The insult of Bane's imprisonment will have to be answered, Astrid."

Astrid sighed. "Aye. I suspected as much. Those blasted fools on the council have made a right mess out of the situation. While I don't approve of their actions, I'd rather not have my people cleaning blood from the floors after you knock their heads together."

Someone lightly tapped on the door, interrupting the

conversation. Astrid called for them to enter, and a young man slipped into the room carrying a tray filled with several dishes. Astrid impatiently waved him over, and he placed four mugs on the nearby table. Beside them, he put several large bowls and then quickly left the room. Blossom abandoned Sabine's hair and flew to the table to investigate.

Sabine studied the crystal bowls, impressed by the design and talent of the artist. Each bowl appeared to have been formed from one solid crystal, with no other marks or etchings to detract from its remarkable craftsmanship. The most unusual aspect were the wisps of red swirling within the crystal, a sign that demonic magic had been used to keep the contents heated. It was a clever bit of magic, merging the use of power crystals into something both functional and beautiful.

"Wings!" Blossom shrieked, throwing her hands in the air and zipping around the room. "They have wings! They cut up pixies and served them to us!"

Sabine frowned, catching sight of something wiggling inside one of the bowls. She leaned forward to take a better look, her stomach recoiling at the sight of live insects. It might be normal for the dwarves, but Sabine preferred her food not to be moving when she ate it.

She sighed, sent an apologetic look toward Astrid, and said, "Blossom, enough. They're not pixies. Take another look."

The pixie stopped suddenly and dropped onto the table. She crept toward the bowl and peered over the rim. "Ew. They're bugs?"

"Good bugs," Thetar said, grabbing one and slurping it down.

Blossom poked at them and cocked her head. "Some bugs help the garden. We don't eat them. That's gross."

Astrid arched her brow. "Are all pixies so excitable?"

Sabine smiled. "Most of them, yes."

"Huh," Astrid said, reaching for her mug and taking a long drink. "Help yourself. We've got mushrooms if yer not inclined to eat bugs, little pixie."

The dwarven councilwoman gestured toward another bowl filled with a variety of colorful cave mushrooms. These had been cooked to a crisp with sprigs of blue plants mixed into it. That was probably a safer bet, but Sabine wasn't particularly hungry, given the previous direction of the current conversation.

Unfortunately, such an invitation couldn't be refused without insulting their host. Sabine picked up her mug and took a sip of the strongly spiced ale. She didn't drink dwarven ale often, finding it far too harsh, but this one was surprisingly pleasant. The realization gave her pause. Astrid either wanted to impress her, or she was seeking to curry favor with Faerie's newest queen. Even the mug itself was a work of art, a heavy silver vessel with detailed leaves carved into the side. Several emeralds had been embedded into the silverwork, the stones catching the nearby light and making the silver leaves appear almost green.

Malek must have been familiar enough with their ways as well because he followed Astrid's direction and picked up his own mug. He settled back in his chair and took a long drink. They'd even brought out a silver thimble for Blossom with a drop of honeyed ale inside. The pixie took a drink and giggled in appreciation of the rare treat.

Taking the opportunity to gather her thoughts, Sabine picked up one of the mushrooms and nibbled on it. The flavor was earthy and a little nutty, and the spiced wine brought those flavors to the forefront, making the combination even more enjoyable.

"It's excellent," Malek said, lifting his mug in salute.

Thetar belched and nodded. "Aye. Better than what you'll find in the main room of any of the local pubs."

Astrid ignored them and focused on Sabine. "Now, then. How do you intend to handle this mess with the demon?"

Sabine took another sip of her drink, taking the opportunity to decide on a suitable response. "While I might respect your council's initiative, the fact remains that my sworn subject and blood-bonded protector has been imprisoned and sentenced without a trial."

Astrid nodded. "Aye. Idiots thought if they moved quick enough, they'd be able to execute the demon before you completed the ritual proclaiming you queen. The fact you did it so quickly will only be to your benefit, but you'll need to act soon or lose any advantage it might have afforded."

Sabine studied Astrid carefully, recalling Balkin's warnings about not trusting anyone. "I can't help but wonder what you hope to gain by aiding me."

Astrid paused, her gaze turning calculating. "I haven't offered to aid you yet, have I?"

Sabine smiled. "Then perhaps I should ask what aid you can offer and what favor you expect in return."

"Clever girl," Astrid said with a laugh. "In truth, I'd hoped you came here to barter. I have a number of talents and resources at my disposal. Tell me what you have in mind, and perhaps we can come to an arrangement. I wouldn't be opposed to acquiring a few new power crystals, the first of many to be infused with the magic of the new queen."

Sabine took another sip, watching Astrid grab another handful of the squirming insects. She popped them into her mouth and chewed, crunching loudly. Malek put down his mug and reached for the bowl.

Blossom squeaked, flew to Malek, and smacked his hand. "No! No bugs! You can't kiss Sabine if you eat anything with wings. It's a new rule!"

Malek arched his brow. "But it's acceptable to kiss her if I don't?"

Blossom nodded. "You've got it. Just say no to bug breath."

Malek chuckled and held up his hands in defeat. "While I'm sure they're delicious, I'm afraid I'll need to forego eating anything with wings or else risk the pixie's wrath."

"Try the mushrooms," Sabine suggested and then turned toward Astrid. "Your cooks are a credit to your household, Astrid. I haven't had spiced ale this marvelous since one of your ambassadors visited us in Faerie."

The councilwoman inclined her head at the compliment and took another drink. "That particular ale was also one of your mother's favorites."

Sabine paused, considering Astrid's hospitality in a new light. The fact Astrid had chosen to serve Sabine's mother's preferred drink was a kindness she hadn't expected. She had to remind herself not to allow the gesture to affect her mission.

Malek reached over and grabbed a mushroom from the bowl. After breaking off a small piece, he offered it to Blossom. Her eyes widened, and she snatched it from his hand. She shoved the entire piece into her mouth. With her cheeks bulging with glee, she held out her hands in a silent entreaty for more. Mushrooms were considered a delicacy among the pixies, and they often planted large circles of them in the forest where they would dance and sing to make them grow.

Bringing her thoughts back to the previous conversation, Sabine said, "Like my mother, I'm a woman who enjoys frankness, so I won't dance around the subject. I want the council to release Bane. Immediately."

Astrid swallowed her bugs and leaned forward to rest her elbows on the arms of her chair. "If it weren't for yer age, I'd swear I was speaking with yer mum. And as I would tell her, I'm one voice in the Council of Ten. You either need to enforce yer will over the combined strength of Razadon's dwarves or convince the other nine guild leaders to release the demon."

Sabine frowned. The second option had a greater chance of success, but it would likely require a great deal of negotiations and favors. Until Sabine knew what they were up against, she couldn't agree to anything. Like the Fae, the dwarves were beholden to their laws. If there was a loophole somewhere, she might be able to exploit it.

Sabine took a sip of her ale, deciding how to proceed. Once she began bartering with Astrid, it would be unlikely she could elicit more information out of the guild leader. Astrid wouldn't want to allow Sabine the upper hand.

Determined to gather as much knowledge as possible, Sabine asked, "What exactly are the charges against Bane?"

Astrid cocked her head, a gleam in her eyes. "Interesting. I figured you'd immediately jump into negotiations. That you'd even ask such a question shows you know much about our ways."

Sabine folded her hands in her lap and didn't respond. She knew very little about their ways, but she wasn't about to give Astrid the advantage.

Astrid took a drink of her ale before answering. "No one actually saw yer demon kill Badac Coinbasher. He'd need to be brought up on separate charges for that offense, which would require a trial. However, he killed at least three others in front of witnesses. The Council of Ten believes we're within our rights to execute the demon since these deaths were a violation of the treaty forged with the denizens of the underworld."

Thetar snorted. "Badac the Bastard needed killing. His death was no great loss. Hell, I'm inclined to send someone down to the prison to give the demon a flask of ale."

Astrid reached over and smacked the back of Thetar's

head hard enough that he spit out the worms he'd been slurping. "Mind your manners, Thetar. The man was still an Elder, no matter what headaches he caused."

Sabine only knew a little about the treaty between the dwarves and their neighboring demons. To the best of her recollection, fighting between the dwarves and demons was only permitted during certain times of the year. It was usually prearranged and a method to resolve disputes between the two groups that otherwise couldn't be resolved. Any issues that occurred outside that window had to be handled during the next Twilight Trial or through a sanctioned duel.

Sabine shook her head. "While Bane may have ended some of your people's lives, he cannot be held responsible for those deaths. The magical corruption that drew us to that location sent him into a bloodlust. Your own men were influenced by that foul magic and would have likely turned on each other if I hadn't stopped the corruption."

Astrid's hands tightened on her mug. "I've heard rumors indicating such, but without proof, no one will give yer claims any weight. It's difficult to dispute eyewitnesses, especially when the bodies of our men are still warm."

Sabine pressed her lips together and frowned. Somewhere in Razadon, families were mourning the loss of their loved ones. She didn't want to diminish their grief, but they were blaming the wrong person.

Blossom leaned over the bowl of mushrooms and dug around in it. She plucked one of the blue sprigs out, sat down, and licked at its leaves. She tossed it aside and grabbed a different one, tasting it in the same manner.

Malek leaned forward and asked, "I'm not as familiar with many of your ways, but what sort of proof would they consider? I'm sure we'd all like to resolve this situation as peaceably as possible."

Astrid cocked her head to study Malek. "Fancy yerself a bit of a peacemaker, eh?"

Malek smiled. "Better than allowing the councilor's blood to stain your floors."

Astrid laughed. "Very well. In that case, I'd suggest finding the actual source of the corruption if the demon's not to blame."

Blossom darted her gaze back and forth between Astrid and Sabine. She climbed into the mushroom bowl and began pulling the leaves off the remaining plants. She held up each one, sniffed it, and either stuffed it into her pocket or tossed it back in the bowl.

Sabine placed her mug on the table and asked, "Do you know what's causing the corruption affecting this land?"

"No."

Sabine leaned back, considering the older woman carefully. For the most part, Astrid had been forthcoming, but the rigidity in her shoulders and her curt response made Sabine suspicious. She could keep prodding, but Sabine doubted Astrid would share anything she wasn't willing to divulge.

Deciding to take a gamble, Sabine asked, "Are we back to playing word games, Astrid? If you seek to negotiate a gift of power to infuse into your crystals, you shouldn't try my patience when my beloved companion is being threatened with death. You have a duty to protect this land. If you know something, you are oathbound to share it with me."

Astrid sighed and rubbed her temples, appearing far older than she had just moments before. "May my ancestors forgive me, but yer right. The rest of the councilors likely won't see it that way. All I can tell you without violating any oaths is that I've heard rumors about magical experiments being conducted outside our city walls."

Sabine straightened. "What can you tell me?"

Astrid shook her head. "Not much. For almost a year, we've been having issues with trolls and orcs asking for sanctuary. We've refused them entry while we try to ferret out the Seelie spies in our midst. If that wasn't bad enough, about two months ago, visitors arriving by ship began getting sick or even dying. We didn't know what was causing it, so the council agreed to close our doors and halt all trading before the situation got out of hand. We send out regular patrols to search for any hint of who's causing mischief, but so far we haven't had any luck."

Blossom clutched a leaf tightly against her chest, her eyes wide with worry. "Oh no! Esme's still on the ship. We have to hurry and warn her! She might be in danger!"

Malek cursed under his breath, his entire body rigid. The anger emanating from him filled the room. "I need to get a message to my crew immediately. If something is still killing people outside the city and they aren't allowed entry, they'll need to depart at once."

"We'll send a runner to yer ship immediately," Astrid said and motioned for Thetar to handle it. "The fault is mine, so no debt is due for my assistance in this matter. I should have told you the moment you arrived in the city. It seemed prudent to disperse the mob of idiots first."

Thetar stood and asked, "Yer ship's at the main dock?"

Malek nodded. "My first mate's name is Levin. You can give him the message and let him know he needs to set sail without us. I made arrangements with him already if we didn't return in a week's time."

Thetar headed for the door, flung it open, and yelled for someone named Eikil. The man who had served them earlier appeared a moment later, listening intently while Thetar ordered him to put together an armed escort to dispatch a messenger to Malek's ship.

Astrid frowned and said, "No mistakes, Thetar. See to the

patrol assignment personally. I want all of my men returned unharmed."

Thetar nodded. "I'll make the arrangements the moment we're done here. I'll have them use one of the other exits to avoid the Wild Hunt."

Blossom flew over and landed lightly on Sabine's shoulder. "It'll be okay, Malek. Esme's one of the best witches I've ever met. She won't let anything happen to the crew. She can make one of those powerful wards again to protect them."

Malek nodded, but Sabine knew he would continue to worry until his crew was away safely.

Determined to wrap up the conversation as quickly as possible, Sabine asked, "What else can you tell me about the rumors concerning the corruption?"

Astrid shrugged and picked up her mug again. "Most of them suggest the demons are responsible, which is partly why the council was so quick to sentence yer friend."

Malek frowned. "Are there any other demons within the city?"

Astrid shook her head. "No. On occasion, we have gatherings between ourselves and the demons, but they're not allowed within Razadon outside of the Twilight Trials. In fact, since we closed our doors, we have very few non-dwarven folk staying in the city."

Sabine thought back to the magical storm and how the powers of different races had been fused together. As far as she knew, no one other than the gods or the dwarves had the ability to blend and merge magic in such a manner. She still wasn't sure of the intention of the magical working, but Badac's death was the strongest lead they had in finding who was responsible.

"The corruption that brought us here originated from the ritual that killed Badac. Do you know what he was doing outside the city or who he was meeting with?"

Astrid paused, considering the question for a long time. She placed her mug on the table and said, "That question was raised in the council. When trade was open, Badac would often visit the trading plaza outside the city's entrance. He shouldn't have had any reason to be there with trade shut down. Someone in his guild would probably know better."

Sabine exchanged a look with Malek. His connection to Hargrim might yield additional information. He gave her a barely discernible nod, indicating he agreed with her assessment. Turning back toward Astrid, Sabine asked, "How many council members will follow your lead if a vote is called?"

Astrid arched her brow. "Are you ready to barter?"

Sabine inclined her head. "I may be interested, depending on how many votes you can sway in my favor."

Astrid gave her a wide grin and leaned forward. "Out of the ten seated on the council, two others owe me votes of my choosing. However, to free yer demon, you'll need a majority."

Sabine frowned. If Malek could convince his former sponsor to vote in their favor, that would be four of the six they needed. She glanced over at Malek, who gave her an encouraging nod.

Trusting Malek's instincts, Sabine asked, "Can you arrange for enough favors to sway two more votes to your side?"

Astrid paused, considering the request, and then shook her head. "I can't make any promises. The dwarves he killed were well liked. With the closure of our city, our people have been demanding entertainment in some form or another. A tournament to kill the demon would help satisfy their need for vengeance and provide a distraction."

Heat rushed through Sabine's body. "Your council leaders would be willing to execute Bane simply to provide Razadon's citizens an afternoon of *entertainment*?"

Blossom squeaked and flew to Malek's shoulder. "Uh oh. If things go bad, grab the mushrooms."

Sabine gave Blossom a sharp look, but the pixie merely held out her hands in a helpless gesture.

"What? They're mushrooms, Sabine. Mushrooms!"

Astrid ignored Blossom. She peered down her nose at Sabine, the light catching the glint of crystal beads braided into her hair. "The demon assassin is hardly an innocent."

Sabine's hands tightened on the armrests of her chair. "Innocent, no. But Bane isn't responsible for what occurred outside your city's walls. The fact that Razadon's rulers would turn a blind eye to the corruption in lieu of a convenient scapegoat is unacceptable."

"Unlike the Fae, our right to lead our guilds is not inherited," Astrid said, her mouth twisting into a scowl. "It's fought and won every day through our life's blood, our sweat upon the stone, and the tears of those we've conquered. If we fail to honor the demands of our citizens, every representative on that council will be crushed into dust by the weight of thousands of dwarves."

Sabine clenched her jaw. If the council leaders were so influenced by the wishes of their people, they would likely defer to the more popular decision. Bane didn't have any friends here, and finding allies would be more challenging than she'd expected.

Malek frowned and put his empty mug on the table. "You don't know me, Astrid, but I've traveled from one end of this world to the other and experienced more cultures than I imagined were possible. The one thing that's stood out is how much we all have in common, despite our differences. Even when the right to rule is inherited, a weak or foolish leader doesn't hold their position for long."

"I suppose you have a point," Astrid admitted with a sigh

before turning back toward Sabine. "Make me an offer, and I'll consider it."

Sabine nodded. "In exchange for providing me three votes on the council to be used at my discretion alone, I shall provide you with enough magic to fully charge one palm-sized power crystal."

Thetar choked on his ale, placing his empty mug on the table.

Astrid scoffed. "You can't be serious. I doubt even one crystal per vote would be enough to reimburse me for the cost of such favors. I require no less than ten power crystals for my efforts in securing the necessary votes, and even that's no guarantee."

Sabine didn't respond. Instead, she folded her hands in her lap and waited. She had no intention of increasing her offer. Bartering was something of an artform. If Sabine was going to force the dwarves to treat her as queen, she couldn't afford to cheapen herself or her abilities.

Blossom's wings perked up. "Ohhh. You should take the deal. If you knew about Sabine's magic—"

Sabine held up her hand to stop Blossom from saying anything prematurely. The pixie clamped her mouth shut, a wide grin on her face. Sabine forced herself not to respond to Blossom's enthusiasm. The little pixie loved secrets and magical displays in any form, and she was probably hoping Sabine would treat them to such.

If Sabine could convince Astrid of the rarity and potency of her magic, her reputation would grow and the need for other grandiose displays of strength would lessen. Sabine had learned at an early age that someone's threat could be even more powerful than the truth. She just hoped the goddess would cooperate with her and this wouldn't end in a battle of wills.

From the corner of her eye, she saw Blossom whisper

something into Malek's ear. He met Sabine's gaze, his eyes full of concern. He gave her a brief nod, indicating he understood what she was considering. At least he wouldn't be alarmed if she had to call upon Lachlina's power.

Astrid sighed heavily. "Ah, you disappoint me. Well, if we can't come to an agreement, I shall be unable to secure the votes you desire."

Malek cleared his throat. "I don't think you realize the generosity of Queen Sabin'theoria's offer. I can guarantee no one within Razadon has a power crystal that would compare to one the new Unseelie ruler could offer you."

"Perhaps, but it's unlikely," Astrid said with a shrug. "Yer mum provided me dozens of power crystals over the years. Yer magic is still relatively new, whereas yer mum had centuries to hone her abilities."

A light tapping on the door interrupted them again, and this time, a young blonde woman entered the sitting room. She carried another tray filled with mugs and a new selection of various foods. She began switching out the empty mugs and collecting the empty dishes, the metallic bands around her arms jingling as she walked.

A strange pressure built within Sabine and beat against her temples in warning. The goddess was growing impatient. Sabine clamped down tightly on the connections she shared with her friends and loved ones.

She sent a silent thought to the goddess, asking for her cooperation and patience. Silence was her only response, but Lachlina's power continued to pulse against Sabine's thoughts. It was time to end this while she was still in control and before Lachlina tried to force her hand.

"I will give you another choice, and you have until the next council meeting to decide which option you choose," Sabine said, infusing her voice with a trace of her building magic. "In exchange for one power crystal, you will either secure the votes we discussed or provide me with the names of those who are responsible for the corruption."

The young serving girl froze, darting a fearful glance at Sabine. Blossom leaned forward on Malek's shoulder, her wings quivering in anticipation.

Astrid snorted. "If I knew who was responsible for the corruption, I'd kill them myself for meddling in my trading business. The merfolk have taken off for the northern seas, which limits the number of power crystals I'll have in stock for the remainder of the year. Until this mess is cleaned up, they likely won't be back."

Malek frowned. "I've never seen power crystals for sale in any of the trading kiosks."

"Are ye daft, man?" Thetar asked, shaking his head. "The damn humans would end up blowing up our mountain the first time they fumbled with a power they didn't understand. We only offer them to other magical races."

"That's not true," Blossom protested. "The humans in Karga had one. It was a big purple one. We had to melt it so they wouldn't kill everyone during their burning festival."

Astrid's gaze whipped toward the pixie. "That's not possible."

"Blossom speaks the truth," Sabine told her. "I saw the remnants myself. We destroyed it before the humans could use it."

Thetar darted a worried glance at Astrid before turning back toward Sabine. "You didn't happen to see a maker's mark on it before you destroyed it, did ya?"

Malek shook his head. "No, but we weren't looking for one."

Astrid didn't reply, her mouth forming a thin line. The serving girl refilled the dwindling bowl of insects, and the crystalline light in the room illuminated the small crystals braided into her blonde hair. It was a costly accessory for someone who might not be a blood relative, and a sign of the substantial wealth of Astrid's family.

Sabine frowned. A great number of problems in the southern lands could all be laid at the dwarves' feet and specifically the power crystals. She wouldn't accuse Astrid of having a hand in it, but Sabine suspected the councilwoman knew more than she claimed. There might be a way to provoke Astrid to reveal something.

She leaned forward, watching Astrid's and Thetar's body language carefully as she spoke her next words. "I would expect the council to be more concerned. Human sailors are being murdered or forced to turn away from your beaches. Someone also sold humans a power crystal to help select sacrifices during Karga's burning festival. I'm seeing two things in common: Razadon and dead humans. Tell me, Astrid, who among your people has issues with those not native to our world?"

Astrid's jaw clenched, and she shook her head. "I have no issue with humans, and I wouldn't tolerate my household engaging in such activities. I may not know what happens in all aspects of my city or guild, but my family is innocent of any wrongdoing."

Malek shook his head in disbelief. "I don't think Sabine is suggesting such a thing, but we're both wondering why you haven't tried to get to the bottom of it. The longer the corruption goes on, the more difficult it will be for Razadon's trade to recover. Like them or not, humans are critical to our world's trading system, and Razadon's a major player in that game. I would think the entire council would be more determined to discover what's making the sailors sick."

"You'd think so," Astrid muttered and accepted a mug of ale from the serving girl. "Most of the bulbous oafs on the council need more of an incentive to investigate rumors.

The guilds who rely on sea trade have voiced some concern, but it's only a low rumble right now. The longer the city remains closed to trade, the louder their voices will get. They'll probably get off their asses and do something in a few months or even a year, unless I can kick them into gear."

Sabine straightened, her anger and that of the goddess rising sharply to the surface. She allowed her markings to flare silver and gold, for once in full agreement with Lachlina's wishes. The indifference these dwarves were displaying for the corruption was unacceptable. They might be well known for playing political games among themselves, but the land was suffering while they dallied. The balance *would* be restored, no matter the cost. If they needed an incentive to act, she would provide it.

Sabine infused more power into her words, her voice sharp and biting as she said, "You will do two things, Astrid Onyxborn. The first is to call a council meeting tomorrow and ensure a representative from each guild is present. As spokesperson for the Powerbroker Guild, you are oathbound to summon a council if cause has been presented." She leaned forward. "*I* am that cause."

Astrid's eyes widened. Her mug fell to the floor with a clatter, spilling the contents across the tile. The young serving girl gasped, stumbling backward and dropping her tray. Dishes crashed to the ground, and the dwarven woman pressed herself against the wall. Even Thetar was slack-jawed, gaping at Sabine in shock.

In a shaky voice, Astrid whispered, "How is this possible? You carry the power of the gods."

Sabine inclined her head, allowing Lachlina's power to take hold. The power surged within her like a tidal wave trapped barely under the surface. If she didn't bank it soon, she ran the risk of drowning under its weight. "I do, and all of Razadon will be informed of such if this corruption is not stopped."

Malek shot Sabine a warning look, but she held up her hand to indicate it was under control. If the dwarves respected strength above all else, she'd show it to them.

Astrid swallowed, a sliver of fear in her gaze. "And yer second request?"

Sabine stood, her crown a heavy weight upon her head. She managed to take a full breath, struggling to push down Lachlina's power and still maintain her illusion of control. "Make no mistake, Astrid Onyxborn. These are demands, not requests. While I have no desire to make enemies of you or your family, I *will* see an end to this corruption."

Astrid considered her for a moment and then nodded. "Very well, Queen Sabin'theoria. I and mine have no intention of violating the treaty. I will aid you in stopping the corruption. What is yer second demand?"

She swallowed. "I wish to speak with the demon Bane'umbra Versed."

Astrid rose from her chair. "It's within my power to honor both requests. If you'll come with me, I can take you to the demon."

Malek stood and moved to stand next to the door, but Sabine hesitated. No matter how impatient she was to see Bane, she didn't want to run roughshod over someone like Astrid. The older woman had done her several kindnesses already, not only with sharing information but also by welcoming them into her home beyond what protocol demanded.

"A moment, Astrid," Sabine said, stopping the woman before she could leave the room.

Astrid turned to regard her, her bearing regal and uncowed even though Lachlina's influence had obviously shaken her. The dwarves had a complicated relationship with the gods, but Lachlina was the one who had nurtured them in their mountain home. She'd taught them how to use their crystals to harness magic they could never hope to possess.

Sabine held out her hands in a peaceable gesture and said, "Cleansing this land is my first priority, but the demon you're holding has been my ally and friend for ten years. There are no lengths I won't go to protect those who are mine."

Astrid cocked her head. "Is this yer way of apologizing before you drop the mountain on our heads?"

Sabine shook her head sadly. "No, and it's my sincere hope it doesn't come to that. The dwarves, and especially your family, have proven to be honorable allies to the Unseelie. When you consider my earlier offer and make your decision, I would like you to remember that friendship was what brought me to your home. I swear by the blood of my ancestors, if you align yourself with me and mine, you'll be gifted with much more than a crystal containing the magic of the absent gods." She paused and gave Astrid a genuine smile. "I would very much like to one day call you a friend, Astrid."

A hint of a smile touched Astrid's mouth. Her eyes brightened, a gleam of approval and admiration filling them. The dwarven woman inclined her head and said, "Aye. Just like yer mum in more ways than I expected. I daresay she'd be proud." Astrid paused, her expression becoming thoughtful. "I'm beginning to think she could have learned a thing or two from you. Perhaps she would have lived longer if she had."

Emotion choked Sabine, and she turned toward the door where Malek was standing. No matter what memories Astrid shared, Sabine's mother, just like her father, had plotted Sabine's death. Sabine might not ever learn her mother's motivations, but it didn't make them any less real.

Astrid cleared her throat. "Come along. I'll take you to see yer friend, and I'll consider the rest of yer words carefully. I have to warn you though; our prison is anything but pleasant."

Malek took Sabine's arm, the heat from his body doing little to ward against the chill taking root in her soul. She leaned against him for a moment, desperately needing the strength he offered. If the dwarves ever learned how dependent she'd become on a dragon, her newfound reign as ruler of the Unseelie would become the shortest in history. It wouldn't matter if the renegade goddess had gifted her with additional power. She would still be dead.

Chapter Thirteen

"I got to see one of the infusing stations for the power crystals," Rika said, her butterfly wings fluttering in excitement. Malek placed his hand on Rika's shoulder to remind her about keeping her feet on the ground.

"Wait until you see the crystal caverns," Dagmar replied with a wide smile. "Some of the crystals are nearly as tall as buildings. Astrid always cultivates the best ones, and I'm not just saying that because she's my cousin. She even knows how to mix and match magic to make different colored crystals. The caverns are normally closed to outsiders, but the Faerie queen is allowed to visit."

"Maybe we'll have time to check it out before we leave," Malek said, continuing to walk beside Thetar along the busy streets of Razadon.

Astrid and Sabine were a few steps in front of them, talking in quiet voices to each other as they headed toward the prison. Blossom was perched on Sabine's shoulder, but the pixie kept flying back and forth between them to give Malek updates on the conversation. So far, they'd spoken of rather mundane topics, like commerce and travel between Razadon and Faerie.

The four armed guards who had escorted them to Astrid's home had fallen into a protective circle around the group, using their elbows and threat of weapons to keep curious onlookers away from them on the crowded street. More than a few had tried to approach, their fascination with the new Faerie queen and her companions overpowering common sense.

Blossom landed on his shoulder again and said, "Booor-ing. They're talking about crystals and magic again. Sabine doesn't want me to go off and explore yet. I hope the prison's more exciting."

Malek made a noncommittal noise. He'd be happier once they were completely out of Razadon and he could see about erasing some of the shadows from Sabine's eyes. She'd handled the meeting with Astrid better than he'd expected, but it was obvious the discussion concerning her mother had affected her deeply.

Sabine wasn't ready to assume her throne, and Malek was at a loss on how to help her. Sabine's newfound leadership might make it easier to secure the portal and protect his people, but it had likely made her loyalties to the Fae even stronger. He wasn't sure what this would mean when he shared his intentions in controlling the portal, but that would have to come later. He only hoped she would remember he'd stayed by her side and supported her when her own people had abandoned and betrayed her. He wasn't about to walk away from her.

No matter what issues he had with Bane, the demon was better suited to navigating the political minefield of her new title. For that reason alone, Malek was determined to do whatever was necessary to ensure Bane survived.

"Noticed ya weren't too eager to get back to yer ship,

even though it's setting sail without you," Thetar said, darting a quick glance at him. "Curious about what a human ship captain's doing abandoning their crew and chasing after a Fae."

"It wouldn't be the first time such a thing has happened," Malek said with a shrug. "Humans have been intrigued by the Fae for centuries."

"Ah. The new tree-loving queen's got a taste for human twig and berries, eh?" Thetar asked, elbowing Malek in the side and waggling his eyebrows in Sabine's direction.

"Sabine found a human who has berries?" Blossom asked, her eyes wide. "She didn't tell me. What kind of berries? What color? Red? Blue?"

Thetar snickered. "Don't think the ship captain would be chasing her around if his berries were blue. Nah, I think if he's willing to give up his ship, she knows what she's doing with a human twig."

Malek narrowed his eyes on the obnoxious dwarf and snapped, "Better than a dwarf-sized one."

Blossom crossed her arms over her chest. "I don't think you're talking about real berries, are you?" She smacked her forehead. "Wait. Are you talking about a thorn and seeds? Gah. Big people are so weird."

Thetar guffawed. "Thought I'd damn well piss myself when that queen of yours started glowing. Bet she's hot in bed if she's got enough power to light up like that. Wouldn't mind a little taste myself."

The warding medallion around Malek's neck heated in warning. He scowled and glared at the man. "Watch it, Thetar."

"Better listen to him, Thetar," Blossom warned, fluttering her wings. "You really don't want to make him mad."

Thetar rubbed his crotch. "Maybe I'll find out for myself

how hot she is. Perhaps I'll see about sneaking into her room tonight and slide her dress—"

Malek's fist struck out and slammed against the dwarf's jaw. Thetar went flying and hit the ground with a loud thud. Thetar grunted, spitting out a mouthful of blood along with at least one broken tooth.

"Hit him again, Malek!" Blossom cheered and launched herself into the air. Rika and Dagmar gasped and backed up quickly.

Malek ignored them and leaned over the fallen dwarf, tempted to do much more than hit him. In a low voice, he warned, "Go near her or talk about her like that again, and you won't be getting back up."

Thetar rubbed his jaw and grinned through blood-stained teeth. "Aye. Figured you were hiding something, and it looks like I was right. Fae don't mark their human pets, and you definitely aren't human."

"Tricky dwarf," Blossom muttered, hovering over Thetar. "Maybe you should hit him with your other hand, Malek. My brother always told me to make sure they don't get back up."

Malek barely resisted the urge to curse at his lapse in control. Sabine and Astrid had both stopped at the sound of the commotion and turned around to see what had happened. Blossom flew to Sabine and whispered something in her ear.

Sabine walked toward him and arched her brow. "Problem?"

Malek shrugged. He gestured at Thetar, who was slowly climbing to his feet. "These surfaces can be slippery when they get wet."

Thetar let out a loud laugh. "Hah. Ship captain cold-cocked me. Can't say it wasn't deserved. I'll have to buy him a drink later to make up for it."

Astrid huffed and walked over to Thetar. She reached

down, grabbed him by his ear, and asked, "Haven't you caused enough trouble for one day? See if you can keep yer damn mouth shut for the next hour. I swear, how I ever let yer mum talk you into acting as my second..."

Astrid continued berating Thetar, her voice carrying well over the din of the passersby. Malek stared after them, suspecting the crafty councilwoman had instructed Thetar to provoke him.

Blossom giggled and flew to Rika and Dagmar, telling them what had happened.

Sabine's mouth quirked in a small smile, her eyes dancing with amusement. She took Malek's arm, her touch sending a teasing tendril of power along his skin. He inhaled deeply, catching the scent of night-blooming flowers that always surrounded her. It immediately both calmed his draconic instincts and incited his desire to keep her safe from anyone who would harm her either in words or actions. Damn. He needed to get himself under control.

Sabine smiled up at him and asked, "I'm assuming you felt the need to defend my honor?"

Unable to resist touching her, Malek tucked a strand of her silvery hair behind her pointed ear and said, "Even if you didn't have a pixie whispering in your ear, I'm guessing you wouldn't have bought the slip and fall comment."

"No." Sabine leaned in and kissed his cheek, taking the opportunity to press her hand against his warding medallion in a silent warning. In a soft voice, she whispered, "They're testing you, Malek. Be careful."

Malek's smile faded, knowing his earlier assessment was correct. Thetar and some of the other dwarves would continue to provoke a reaction to uncover his secrets in an effort to identify Sabine's weaknesses.

His contacts in Razadon knew he wasn't fully human, but Malek had never volunteered details about his history or background. Part of the reason he'd decided to adopt the ship captain persona was to take advantage of their wandering-nature stereotype. Since donning the disguise, no one thought twice when he evaded questions about his origins or neglected to offer any personal information. Visits to various ports rarely lasted longer than a week or two, and they were usually moving on by the time people became suspicious. Traveling with Sabine had pierced that shroud of anonymity. No one would assume he was strictly human once they realized how close he was to Faerie's newest queen.

Malek gave Sabine a barely discernible nod, indicating he understood her warning. He could handle himself in most situations, but his deepening feelings for her had changed everything. For the first time in his life, he found himself fixated on someone else's welfare, even above his own. Part of him knew Sabine was capable of taking care of herself, but it didn't negate his desire to protect her. If anyone learned the truth about him, it would be just as dangerous for her as it was for him. He needed to learn how to balance his draconic instincts with the more rational side of himself before he jeopardized everything.

Astrid motioned for the guards to follow her, and everyone headed in the direction of the prison again. This time, Astrid was keeping Thetar close by her side.

"Are we going to be able to bring Bane back with us?" Rika asked, her eyes shining with hopefulness as she gazed up at Sabine.

Sabine shook her head. "I'm afraid not yet. This is just a short visit to make sure he's all right."

Rika's wings drooped. "Oh. I thought that's why we went to see Astrid."

Blossom landed on Rika's shoulder and patted her hair. "Don't worry. If anyone can save him, Sabine will. I don't think Bane would have agreed to go to prison if he didn't think Sabine could get him out."

Dagmar glanced back and forth between them. "You know, there are some crystals that grow near the prison. I bet Astrid would be willing to let us collect one or maybe even two. They don't have magic inside yet, but they're still shiny and pretty. We could even see about having them made into jewelry. Wait until you see the market tomorrow. I'll get one of my aunts to take us when she goes shopping."

"What about mushrooms?" Blossom asked. "Maybe we can find a mushroom ring and convince Sabine to show us the healing properties. We can teach Esme something when we see her next."

"I guess," Rika said, but it was obvious her thoughts weren't on planning more activities. Sabine's gaze roamed over the young seer, but she didn't comment.

Malek reached down and squeezed Sabine's hand. In a low voice, he whispered, "She'll be fine, especially once Blossom and Dagmar finish distracting her. I don't know about Dagmar, but that pixie won't give up until Rika's smiling and laughing again."

Sabine nodded. "You're right. I don't think her worry is strictly for Bane though. She's been forced to handle many changes in a short amount of time, and I'm not sure how well she's adjusting. Will you keep an eye on her while I'm with Bane? Astrid mentioned only one person would be permitted into his cell."

Malek hesitated, not liking the idea of being separated from Sabine while deep inside a dwarven prison. He'd heard rumors about them for years and how they had the ability to change magic users. It was bad enough Sabine wanted to visit the prison, but Malek wasn't sure he'd be able to let her leave his sight.

Sabine looked up at him, searching his expression.

"Malek?"

Damn. He didn't want to agree, but Sabine would likely object to his reasons. He glanced at Rika, who was still talking to Dagmar about crystals. Malek blew out a breath and muttered, "I'd rather not leave you without someone to watch your back."

Sabine didn't answer right away. They stopped at what appeared to be a large crystal lift, similar to the one they'd used while they were in Atlantia. Crystals had also been a major focus in that city, and he couldn't help but wonder if the dwarven crystals were used in all parts of Faerie.

Astrid shooed the guards and said, "You can wait here and catch the next lift. We're not riding down with sweaty men who haven't washed their armor in the last month. Last thing the new Faerie queen needs is to get sandwiched between the stench of beard sweat and stale beer."

The dwarves chuckled and moved aside, allowing Astrid to enter the lift along with Thetar. Sabine and Malek both joined them, while Rika and Dagmar took up the rear. Rika's enthusiasm was already beginning to shine through, and she kept peering over the edge into the darkness below.

The lift was larger than the one they'd traveled in before, capable of carrying at least two dozen individuals. He'd ridden on some others while in Razadon, but this one was infused with darkened swirls of power that moved through the crystal, like snakes trying to break free. Astrid pressed her hand against the panel and it began to move downward, taking them down to the bowels of the city.

Blossom landed on the crystal railing and flattened herself against it. She beat her wings, scattering glittering pixie dust onto the surface. Tendrils of green-and-blue magic separated from inside the railing and pressed against the crystal, reacting to whatever Blossom was doing with it.

Sabine frowned and motioned for Blossom to stop. The

pixie stuck out her bottom lip but flew upward and landed on Sabine's shoulder.

She scooted under Sabine's silvery braids and whispered loud enough for Malek to hear, "I smelled Fae magic and maybe some merfolk too. I think they also used some troll blood or something else I don't recognize."

Sabine remained silent, but she turned her attention to the railing. Malek didn't know much about the magic of trolls. They weren't one of the original races as far as he knew.

Malek studied the railing again, paying closer attention to the flow of the magic contained within the crystal. It seemed to be floating in and out of the large control panel Astrid had used to engage the lift.

He turned toward Astrid and asked, "I've noticed those crystal panels in quite a bit of construction. Are they all dwarven made?"

Astrid's gaze sharpened on him. "Aye. I'm assuming yer referring to panels we've installed in Faerie?"

Malek nodded, not bothering to explain about the independent pocket of Faerie they'd visited while trying to save a missing merfolk woman. "Yes. There are small differences, but it's similar."

"The dwarves make almost all the building materials," Dagmar said, earning a frown from Astrid. "We've even installed some of them in the underworld. They don't seem to work very well down there. At least, they're always breaking and someone has to draw the short crystal to fix them. They don't break them a little bit either. Those demons somehow manage to crack the crystal faces of the control panels all the time. Mum thinks they probably hit them or throw people into them. Why, just last month, I saw one that had—"

"Take a breath, girl," Astrid said and rolled her eyes

upward. "I swear, cousin mine, you'll learn how to keep yer mouth shut even if I have to seal it for you."

Dagmar's eyes widened and she sputtered, "But I thought it was okay to tell them. She's the queen of the Unseelie. Shouldn't she know all this? I mean, I thought everyone knew where things were made. We get lots of stuff from Faerie too. And our bug crunchies come from the underworld. Oh, and the hot water for the bathing pools."

Sabine lowered her head, but not before Malek caught a glimpse of her smile. He chuckled and said, "That's all right. I think I get the point."

Sabine's eyes fell on the crystal panel, her expression turning thoughtful. Malek arched his brow at her, but she shook her head and murmured, "Later."

Malek nodded and leaned over the side of the lift. Razadon descended deep below the ground, with crystalline lanterns twinkling like thousands of stars in the night sky. The city was enormous, with winding paths and magical lifts stopping at every level. Stores, homes, and various districts lined the winding paths to form a sprawling subterranean empire unlike anything Malek had seen anywhere else in the world.

It was colder here, the temperature dropping the farther they descended. If he'd been anything other than a dragon, it might be uncomfortable. He glanced at Sabine and Rika, but neither appeared troubled by the temperature. The clothing Faerie had provided them must have some component woven into the fabric that offered additional protection in the subterranean climate.

The lift stopped suddenly, and the door swung open to allow them to exit. Astrid led the way, and Malek offered Sabine his hand, helping her to descend from the lift with her heavy skirt. Rika and Dagmar fell into step behind them, while Thetar took up the rear.

This level was more somber, with fewer lanterns and deeper shadows. The dwarves who walked the streets did so with hunched shoulders and heavy footsteps.

Large archways with names carved into the stones lined the path, towering overhead. Malek's hand immediately went to the hilt of his sword, and he systematically swept his gaze over the area searching for would-be assailants. There were hundreds of places for an enemy to hide, and an assassination attempt could come from anywhere.

"What do those names represent?" Sabine asked, gesturing toward the stone markers. Blossom took flight, flying upward to investigate them.

"They're names of prisoners, their crimes, and their sentences," Astrid explained. She pointed at a dozen other stone tablets, angled precariously on a ledge over the entrance of the prison and throughout the courtyard ahead. "We've also kept records of all the judges who issued verdicts upon each prisoner who passed through these walls."

"Hey, there's lots of room up here on these stones," Blossom called. "You need more prisoners!"

Rika frowned. "Is Bane's name up there?"

"Not yet," Dagmar told her. "It's usually recorded after they're sentenced. He won't be executed for a couple days, so they'll do it then. We have a big feast at the end of the tournament. There's usually a party, the pubs open all their doors, and we celebrate into the night."

Rika paled, her eyes wide with horror. "They're going to celebrate killing Bane?"

Sabine frowned at Dagmar and placed her hand on Rika's shoulder. "I'll make every effort to ensure such an event doesn't come to pass, Rika. Bane has lived more years than you and I combined. I fully expect he'll continue to live many years beyond a normal human lifespan."

Rika swallowed and nodded, but she didn't appear

convinced. In all honesty, Malek wasn't sure Sabine would be able to save him. From everything he knew about the dwarves, they were a stubborn and proud people. Sabine might be able to threaten them up to a point, but eventually, she'd need to show her teeth. If it came to that, he wasn't sure Sabine had enough power to take on thousands of dwarves in their own home.

Astrid pinned Dagmar with her glare. "Shut yer fool mouth, girl. Demon or not, they consider him a friend."

Dagmar winced. "Uh, er, I didn't mean… Sorry. I'll be quiet."

They approached a large double door, the heavy wood inlaid with various crystals that pulsed with power. Most of them contained variations of purple, red, and black swirls of color. Sabine moved closer to Malek, and he glanced at her, his heart soaring at the realization she'd done it to keep anyone from detecting his draconic power. If someone had suggested a few months ago that one of the most remarkable Fae women he'd ever met would try protecting him, he never would have believed them.

Unable to resist her, he brushed the backs of his fingers against Sabine's hand. Her lips curved upward slightly, and her lavender eyes gazed up at him with unspoken affection. There was no use denying it; he'd fallen completely in love with her. Even the dragon side of him understood everything this woman represented and had chosen her as his intended mate.

Blossom returned to Sabine's shoulder just as Astrid pressed her hand against the crystal panel adjacent to the prison door. With a loud creak, the heavy door swung open. Two armed dwarves stood in the entrance and snapped to attention at the sight of them.

A young man with a short reddish beard saluted Astrid. "Welcome to Hivenforge, Councilwoman Onyxborne. The name's Osten, and ah..." His eyes widened at the sight of Dagmar, his face flushing red. "Dagmar! What are you doing here? Did you, uh, come here to see me?"

Dagmar gave him a finger wave. "Heya, Osten. Nope. Just here escorting the Faerie queen and Councilwoman Onyxborne to the prison. You know, the usual day's work."

"Yeah? You're pretty important, aren't you?" Osten said, staring at Dagmar with unmistakable longing.

Astrid scowled and snapped her fingers at the moon-struck dwarf. "Do you think I'm interested in hearing your bumbling over my cousin? Move aside and let us pass."

Osten hesitated, looking at his companion for confirmation. "Do we let them enter?"

"Nope," the older guard said, causing something thick and yellow to dribble out of his mouth and down his beard. His beard was the color of burnt umber and straggly, and his belly was nearly as wide as he was tall. A short spear was tucked into a loop at his side, but he made no move toward it.

Blossom gagged and flopped down on Sabine's shoulder. "Eww! His breath smells like he's been licking a dead toad!" She gasped and pinched her nose. "I feel it in my eyes, Sabine. It's lethal! Worse than bug breath!"

The stinky dwarf scratched his overly large belly and asked in a bored tone, "You got official business here, Astrid?"

"Not with you, Gorgin," Astrid said and motioned for them to move aside. "I need to speak with the warden. Queen Sabin'theoria needs to see one of the prisoners."

The young dwarf's eyes widened, and he immediately moved to the side. Gorgin, on the other hand, merely continued to scratch his stomach. He eyed Astrid up and down and then turned toward Sabine. "So that's the Faerie princess all grown up, eh?"

Astrid crossed her arms over her chest and tapped her foot impatiently on the ground. Tiny power crystals had been affixed to her boots, so the motion caused them to clink together. "If the Faerie queen doesn't knock some sense into you, I will. Now move aside, so we can speak with the warden. I have no interest in dealing with more fools today."

Thetar chuckled and patted the handle of his axe affectionately. "Yer not important enough to bribe, Gorgin. If you make us move you aside, they won't find all the pieces of yer body when I get done with you."

Gorgin grinned, showing yellowed teeth that were beginning to turn brown. He spat a glob of something thick and yellow onto the ground, narrowly missing Rika's boots.

Rika squeaked and jumped backward, her wings fluttering in agitation. Malek grabbed her shoulders and pressed down, forcing her back to the ground. "Easy, little butterfly. We don't want you to fly away on us."

Rika gave him a grateful smile. Leaning in close, she whispered, "Blossom's right. His breath does smell really bad. Like moldy cheese or worse."

Malek bit back a smile and winked at her. Sabine lifted her hand and sent a burst of magic outward, knocking the stinky dwarf aside. He wobbled and fell to the ground, staring up at Sabine in surprise.

Without sparing him a glance, Sabine lifted the hem of her dress and stepped over the bemused dwarf. Astrid chuckled and followed her into the large, enclosed courtyard.

The prison itself was vastly different from the rest of Razadon. The walls were nearly black and crafted from some material Malek had never seen before. At first glance, he thought it might have been volcanic rock, except for its strange glittering effect. He leaned in closer and caught sight of flecks of crystals, which had been somehow crushed into the stones. As he passed by them, he sensed their pulse of power even through the warding medallion around his neck.

More armed dwarves stood watch in the courtyard, eyeing the group's approach suspiciously. Astrid held up her hand, which was likely the only reason they were able to enter unhindered. Faint screams and cries for mercy reached his ears from somewhere deeper in the prison. Malek glanced at Rika and found her eyes wide and shoulders shaking slightly. Even Sabine appeared slightly pale, but she held her head high. No one who didn't know her well would ever know she'd been affected.

Malek frowned, his hand still resting on his sword. If there had been any chance in talking Sabine out of doing this, he would have taken her away in a heartbeat. The courtyard branched off in several directions, but the doorways were sealed and affixed with runes that shone with various colors.

Sabine halted in the middle of the stone courtyard and asked, "Where is Bane's cell?"

Astrid walked to one of the doors. The glowing symbol etched into it pulsed with grey and purple colors. Astrid pounded her fist on the door and shouted, "Get out here, Tinthorp! You've got visitors."

A moment later, the door flung open and a red-faced dwarf emerged. A nest of blond curls sprung out from the top of his head while his beard had been braided into intricate designs. His clothing had been crafted from a much finer material than that of the other prison guards, and each of his shirt buttons appeared to be made from a precious metal and affixed with tiny diamonds. His entire demeanor reeked of self-importance.

He lifted his head, peering down his nose at Astrid. "What the hell do you think yer doin' here, Astrid? You may be the councilwoman for the Powerbroker Guild, but you have no standing in my prison."

"Oh, go stuff yerself, Tinthorp," Astrid muttered, crossing her arms over her chest. "Queen Sabin'theoria's here to see her demon to make sure he's unharmed. We need you to open his cell."

Tinthorp swung his gaze toward Sabine, not appearing overly impressed. "I'm under orders. No visitors without an official order."

"Yer daft," Astrid snapped, glaring at him. "Where do you think those orders come from? Open up the damn cell, or I'll see you demoted and shoveling cave troll shit by this time tomorrow. I'll take her to see him."

Tinthorp shook his head and gestured at their group. "Even if I agreed, only one approved visitor can go into a cell. You know the rules, Astrid."

Astrid frowned, turning toward Sabine. "The magical protections in this place are sensitive. I'm afraid he's right. I can go with you part of the way but not inside the cell if you want to see yer demon."

Malek took a step closer toward Sabine and said, "Absolutely not. She's not going alone."

Thetar snorted. "Human, my ass. Whatever he is, he's got some balls on 'im."

Before Sabine could object, Malek took her arm. In a low voice, he said, "I'm not allowing you to step foot inside a prison cell without me there to make sure you walk back out. This isn't negotiable, Sabine. Bane wouldn't want you to do this without me either, and you know it."

Sabine held his gaze for a long time. Finally, she turned toward Astrid and said, "I'm entitled to an armed escort anywhere I choose within the confines of your city. Otherwise, you and all of Razadon will be required to guarantee my safety. Are you prepared to offer me such assurances?"

The councilwoman studied Malek thoughtfully and then gave Sabine a curt nod of agreement. She turned to face the warden and said, "Are you willing to put the lives of yer family on the line to ensure the Faerie queen doesn't stub her toe while she's here? I'm sure a blood oath would suffice."

Tinthorp sputtered. "This is outrageous. You can't be suggesting such a thing."

Astrid shrugged, but her eyes gleamed with humor. "Queen Sabin'theoria's right, and there's not a damn thing anyone can do to stop her. It's one of our oldest laws. I'm not prepared to jeopardize my house and clan on the random chance the Faerie queen gets a splinter. Unless yer willing to do the same, Tinthorp, let her and her man head down to the cell."

"Fine, but yer claiming responsibility if things go bad," Tinthorp muttered. He hitched up his pants and started heading down the hall. He pointed at two guards standing nearby. "You two, follow me. The demon has a visitor."

Blossom flew to Rika's shoulder and said, "I'll stay here with Rika. Maybe we can find some mushrooms."

Astrid caught Sabine's eye and nodded toward Rika. "I'll keep an eye on them while you handle business. I'm assuming you won't need a blood oath for that?"

Sabine smiled and shook her head. "I leave the human seer, Rika of Karga, in your care, Astrid Onyxborne. Blossom, the pixie, will remain behind in her own care."

Blossom giggled and whispered something in Rika's ear.

Astrid snorted. "Full naming to confirm my loyalty? Yer definitely a tricky one. Yer mum's daughter indeed."

Sabine's smile deepened, and she tilted her head in acknowledgment of Astrid's words. Turning on her heel, she headed down the hall and deeper into the prison. Malek frowned and followed the woman he loved into the shadows.

Chapter Fourteen

The warden called out instructions to the two dwarven guards standing on opposite sides of the large stone door. They each gripped large metal wheels and began to turn the cranks. The sound of the heavy metal links grating across the stone interrupted the oppressive silence.

Sabine remained motionless, watching with a heavy heart as the door to Bane's cell opened. One of the guards motioned for her to enter and said, "Begging yer pardon, Your Highness, but we'll need to reseal the doors behind you."

Sabine inclined her head at his words. "I won't need longer than an hour. You may open the door again at that time."

Sabine lifted the hem of her dress and removed her knives. As part of the condition of her visit, Sabine had agreed to relinquish her weapons. Supposedly, whatever they'd used to contain prisoners within these walls had a negative reaction to foreign objects and certain metals. She could use magic while inside the cell, but nothing could escape the outside enchantments.

She lowered her dress and handed her weapons to Malek, who accepted them with a grim expression. Pressing her hand against the mark on his wrist, she infused a trace of protective power against his skin. He likely wouldn't need it, but Thetar's earlier provocation was worrisome.

Malek leaned in close and whispered, "Be careful, Sabine. I know you trust Bane, but I've heard stories about how this place can affect people when they're cut off from outside magic."

She frowned but didn't argue. His words only reaffirmed her need to ensure Bane was safe. She had no idea what sort of damage this prison had done to him, especially if it cut him off from his ability to draw upon her magic. Bane needed access to her power if he wanted to remain aboveground. Otherwise, he risked descending into madness if he couldn't return to the underworld. She only hoped she wasn't too late. Whatever magic they'd used to contain Bane in this prison had made it more difficult to sense him through their shared connection.

Squaring her shoulders, Sabine stepped through the doorway and into darkness. The sound of metal chains clanked behind her, and the outside light quickly disappeared. The door behind her slammed shut, leaving her blind and disoriented.

The air was thick and musty, with a metallic taste that coated her tongue. She pressed her hands on her thighs, choking and unable to take a full breath. Panic welled within her as each of her senses were deprived, leaving her unable to orient herself to her surroundings. She held her hands out in front of her, but she was blind. Nothing but inky darkness surrounded her.

After several minutes, the heaviness in her chest began to ease. She was still disoriented, but at least she was able to take a breath. The scraping sound of metal against stone reached her ears. She tilted her head, straining to hear anything else. "Bane? Is that you?"

There was no response, except the same metallic scraping noise. Sabine formed a small ball of light in her hand, which only provided enough illumination to see the stone steps in front of her. If Bane had been in darkness for the past several hours, anything brighter might hurt him.

Moving down the steps and in the direction of the noise, she called, "It's Sabine. Where are you?"

"You should not be here," a deep and gravelly voice said from the shadows. It sounded a little like Bane, but something wasn't right. Her heart thudded in her chest, and she moved deeper into the cell.

The air was unnaturally dense. Walking through it reminded her of tree sap, the sticky heaviness clinging to her. She sent a small pulse of power along her markings, burning the effects away from her skin. The cell appeared large enough to contain multiple people, but they'd decided to keep Bane separate from anyone else.

At the base of the stairs, Sabine caught a glimpse of a small crystalline lantern hanging from the ceiling. She reached up and infused her light source within the lantern, adjusting it until the crystals cut through the darkest of the shadows.

There were no windows to the outside world or even a way to determine whether it was day or night. The floor and walls were bare stone, with strange runes etched into the stonework. Every few steps, she caught sight of claw marks on the stone floor, as though someone had desperately sought to escape.

Bane was sitting on a small stone bench, watching as she approached with a predatory gleam in his eyes. His clawed hands gripped the edge of the bench tightly, his chest heaving as though he'd run a great distance. She stopped a handful of steps from him, anger flooding through her at the sight of the proud demon shackled in a windowless cell. They'd left him bound in darkness when they were the ones who should be punished for failing to keep their mountain free from corruption.

"This will not be," she said, using her magic to slice through the magical barrier holding Bane captive.

He roared and leaped to his feet. She had a moment of panic, realizing she'd been hasty in her decision to free him without assessing his condition first.

Bane's eyes and horns flashed to silver, and he launched himself in her direction. She barely had time to brace herself before he reached her. His claws ripped through her skin from the tightness of his grip. He roared again, throwing her away from him. She slammed into the wall with enough force to knock her remaining breath from her lungs.

Bane was on her less than a second later, his clawed hands wrapped around her throat. She slapped her hands against Bane's chest and blasted him with power. He flew backward and slammed into the opposite wall.

She gasped for air, but he was already back up and rushing in her direction. She lifted her hand, sideswiping him and crashing him into the opposite wall. He roared again and barreled in her direction.

"Enough!" she shouted, infusing her voice with another searing blast of magic. The air around them filled with prickling energy, the protections of the cell warring against her magic. Sharp pain pierced through her temples.

Bane's movements slowed, but he didn't stop his advance. From the intensity in his expression and his silvered eyes, he was in the throes of bloodlust.

She narrowed her eyes on him and shoved him backward with another blast. He shook his horned head, his expression somewhat dazed. He moved even slower toward her this time, but there was no use denying it. He was starving. Whatever this place had done to him had stolen all semblance of control.

He grabbed her arms and yanked her against him, lowering his head. His mouth was hard, hot, and almost brutal against hers. She automatically stiffened but then forced her body to relax. This was Bane. He never kissed her without reason, and if he needed such a strong show of physical intimacy to absorb her power, she was oath-bound to provide him the magic he required.

Sabine slid her hands under his torn shirt and infused her touch with more magic. The skin-to-skin contact was critical if his strength was that depleted. She sent an even stronger surge of power over him, opening the bond between them to deepen their connection. He shoved her against the wall and pinned her with his weight. He was in pure survival mode, operating on base instincts rather than logic and reason.

Recognizing he needed an even more potent form of magic, Sabine reached up to grasp one of his horns. She might not have access to weapons, but Bane had his own. Slicing her hand downward against the sharp tip, she felt her blood well to the surface and drip downward. Bane broke their kiss suddenly and turned his hungry gaze on her injured hand.

He grasped her wrist, yanked her close, and descended upon her offering. She sent her mental awareness outward, trying to gauge his condition through their metaphysical connection. Her heart fell into her stomach. He was even weaker than she'd imagined.

She wrapped her hand around the back of his neck, pulling him even closer. Her eyes closed while he fed upon her power, accepting an offering that threatened to upset the balance between them. Up until now, she'd been extremely careful with never allowing Bane or Dax to overindulge in her power. But she'd never seen them stripped completely of their magic, or the hopeless despair that dwelled within the depths of Bane's soul.

After several minutes, his grip on her finally eased, and he pressed his forehead against hers, breathing heavily. He reached down and infused his power into her hand, sealing her wound and healing her. His large, clawed hands encircled her neck again, but this time his touch wasn't harsh as he mended the injuries he'd caused.

She lifted her head and cupped his face, searching his expression. Bane's eyes had reverted to amber, and he appeared calm once again. The gods had made the demons fearsome in many regards, but their biggest weakness was being away from their volcanic home and the magic contained within the underworld.

"You've ascended to claim your throne," Bane murmured, lowering his head again and nuzzling her neck. "You've always tasted like high magic and sex, but it's much more potent now. So much power, and it's all within my grasp." His hands tightened again on her hips briefly before relaxing once again. "You should not have come here, Sabine. The dwarves will take advantage of this show of weakness. Your efforts in freeing me will endanger any hope of an alliance with them."

"You think I would leave you? Do you think so little of me?" she demanded, shocked he could consider such a thing after everything they'd been through together. "When I leave Razadon and take my rightful place, you will be by my side. That was our agreement when we forged our bond all those years ago. I have not come this far only to lose you now."

He gave her a humorless smile and ran the back of his claws down her cheek. "Do you intend to destroy all of Razadon to free one demon?"

"I've been considering it."

Bane laughed, a harsh and bitter sound. "Ah, I have missed you, little one. The hours begin to feel like days in here, especially with the shackle stripping me of my power. Even the underworld possesses more color than this place."

She frowned. "Do you need more of my magic?"

"You need to hold onto your strength, especially now that you've claimed your title. I suspect we don't have long to talk. Tell me what news you've brought. Has the council made a decision?"

"They've set your execution date three days from now," she said, her magic rising again as anger ripped through her. "Since you killed their people in front of witnesses, they believe they're within their rights to execute you."

Bane studied her for a moment and then nodded. "I assumed as much."

"I've asked for the council to gather tomorrow. I intend to make my case in your defense."

"It won't do any good, little one. The politics in Razadon are as corrupt as in Faerie." He ran a hand over her hair, absently siphoning off another trace of her magic. "When they come to formally deliver the news, I intend to demand a trial by combat."

She stiffened and lifted her head. "There won't be a trial. It's an execution, Bane, and I won't allow it. I saw them practicing in the arena. I don't know much about their ways, but it looked like they were planning on having you fight several dwarves at once."

He nodded. "Yes, as many as six at a time. Once I have killed them, more will take their places."

"How is that logical?" she demanded, finding the entire concept absurd. "They're going to allow you to kill more dwarves when they want to punish you for that same crime in the first place."

Bane chuckled. “It’s not so different compared to the fights between the Beastpeople. The Fae held those matches for centuries before they were abolished. Besides, it’ll give me a chance to take out as many of my accusers as possible. A bit of bloodletting is always good sport.”

“That’s idiotic,” she snapped and jerked away from him. She paced the darkened cell, her temper overpowering her frustration. “This entire thing is a farce. They judged you guilty before you stepped foot into Razadon simply because you’re a demon. I’ll bring this mountain down on their heads before I allow them to take you from me.”

Bane leaned against the wall and crossed his arms over his chest. “Even you cannot take on the full might of the dwarves, little one.”

“There has to be something I can do besides playing their political games,” she said, her hands curling into fists as she stared at their bleak surroundings. “I just came from Astrid's home. She may be able to secure a few votes on the council, but I don't have enough yet for a majority. There must be a way to prove you’re not responsible for what happened or how the corruption began. I thought you might have some ideas, which is why I insisted on them allowing me to see you.”

Bane fell silent. After a long moment, he said, “We need to speak frankly about the future, Sabine.”

She turned toward him. “What?”

“You need to find Dax in the underworld.” He pushed away from the wall and prowled toward her. “You will need to secure the demons as your allies if you intend to safeguard your throne. You must put aside your reservations and bind Dax to you. With his help, you can bend the rest of the demons to your will.”

Sabine stared at him in disbelief. “Are you that eager to die? You’re talking as though you’ve already given up.”

"Never," Bane snarled. "I will go down fighting—a true warrior's death. Life and death are simply alternative sides of a coin."

She narrowed her eyes. "And I've been transmuting coins since I was old enough to walk. I'm *not* giving up. With or without your help, I'm going to find a way to get you out of here—even if I have to cheat to ensure it happens."

Bane considered her and then chuckled. "Razadon will likely be turned upside down by the time you get through with them." He paused, his expression becoming more serious. "If this does not turn out the way you hope, you must travel to the underworld using the passages below the mountain. Our bond will allow you to find and access the doorway to the underworld, but you must locate it before my execution. Dax will know the moment you cross over into our realm, and he will seek you out."

Sabine took a steadying breath, refusing to give into her fears. "I'm not giving up on you, Bane. I came here because I wanted your help. You have insight into dwarven culture and their laws. I need your guidance. You're the only one of us who knows these people."

When he didn't respond, she took a step toward him, trying to blink back the tears that threatened. "If the end comes to pass like you expect, you have my word I'll seek out Dax." She lifted her hand and pressed it against his cheek. "I still need you, my protector. Help me find a way to save your life. Call it a weakness if you must, but I don't want to lose you."

"It's only a weakness if you ignore what must be done." Bane lifted his clawed hand and caught one of her tears that had escaped. He studied it with a strange sort of fascination. Lifting it to his mouth, he accepted her offering. His eyes flashed to silver before he closed them as though savoring her pain.

When emotions became their own form of magic, they often spilled in the form of tears. She waited, knowing he needed a moment to gather himself. Demons always felt things more deeply than they admitted. Even so, her tears on his behalf had reinforced the shift of power in their arrangement. His death would hurt her deeply, but he likely hadn't realized how much until now.

"You have become far too Seelie," he murmured. "I can taste honeyed sunlight in your tears."

"You're wrong," she whispered, cupping his face. "Look at me, Bane. *See me.*"

He opened his amber eyes and stared down at her. She sent a pulse of magic along her markings, and her skin glowed.

"I am both, light and dark, Seelie and Unseelie," she told him, infusing her voice with power. "I am both sides of the coin, life and death. I bound you to me because you understand how easily the coin can be turned—far better than Dax. I need *you* right now, not your brother."

She sent a sharp stab of power through her hands and into him. His back went ramrod straight, his eyes shifting to silver again. He growled, causing her skin to prickle in awareness.

She narrowed her eyes on him, refusing to give in to fear. He was hers, bound to obey and protect. But more, he was her friend. "You *will* help me fight this battle, Bane. I will force you to obey me if necessary, but I will get the answers I seek."

Bane's mouth curved upward in a cruel smile, putting her in mind of his brother. "The idea of you subjecting your will over mine again is rather intriguing, little one."

"Stop playing games," she snapped, lowering her hands. "Killing dwarves aside, I know you don't wish to leave my side. Talk, and tell me what you know. How can we prove you weren't responsible for the corruption?"

Bane sighed and wrapped his arms around her to draw her against him once again. He siphoned off more of her power, and Sabine sent a stronger wave toward him. If she had to leave him here alone, she would ensure he was as comfortable as possible. Removing the shackle would slow the progress of his mental decline, but it was a temporary measure. She was tempted to blast his way free of this place, but only death would greet them once they stepped foot outside of Razadon. The Wild Hunt was still waiting.

Bane pressed his face against her neck and breathed in deeply. "The archivists in Razadon have catalogued the knowledge of the dwarves for millennia. Beneath this mountain, they have stones detailing their history and beyond. It would take you several lifetimes to sort through all of it, but that will be your best chance in discovering the origins of the corruption."

"Then there's a chance," she murmured, wondering if there was a spell or some other way to speed up the search. It was an obscure lead but better than anything else they had at the moment.

"Slim, but yes," he replied, running his hand over her hair again. "The archivists will likely try to discourage you from a search for fear of their council's wrath. However, the treaty between the dwarves and Unseelie will allow you access to their records. You may need to insist upon it."

She nodded, hearing the chains moving the door open. Her time with Bane had been far too brief. She sent another fortifying wave of magic over him and said, "I'll get started immediately."

Bane gripped her tighter, refusing to release her. "Two more things before you go."

"What is it?"

"Be careful with the dragon, Sabine," Bane warned, his eyes flashing silver briefly. "I know you care deeply for him, but I believe he's hiding something. Until you know what secrets he has hidden away, you cannot trust him. While you search through the archivist's records, look for a way to lessen his influence over your Seelie magic. If you take too much of his power while you're here, the dwarves will turn against you. Acknowledging your throne has given your Unseelie magic a boost, but the more you rely upon the dragon's power, the more you align yourself with the light."

She frowned, knowing Bane spoke the truth. Despite her feelings for Malek, she still knew very little about him. He might not intend her any harm, but his reaction earlier in wanting to steal her away had been worrying.

"And the second?"

He tapped her wrist where the mark of the goddess had been etched on her skin. "Be vigilant and consider the favors you ask carefully. It's not wise to fall more into debt than you already have. The Fae may have learned trickery and deceit from the gods, but they never came close to the mastery of their creators."

Sabine nodded. There was no point in worrying him about everything that had transpired in the embassy when he was powerless to aid her. It would only encourage him to turn against his jailers. If she had any hope in freeing him without violence, she needed to consider her next move carefully.

"I will keep your counsel in mind," she said and hugged him tightly. "I'll figure out a way to free you or destroy every last one of these dwarves in the process."

He chuckled and released her, taking the opportunity to run his hand over her hair one last time. "Your magic has renewed me for a time. My decline will be slower now that you've removed my bindings."

She paused, catching sight of the shackle she'd broken still lying on the floor. Placing her hand against Bane's arm, she nodded toward it. She wasn't willing to take any chances they'd try to chain him again. "Can you remove the shackle from the wall?"

His mouth curved in a wicked smile. Bane headed to where it was affixed to the wall and reached down, his midnight skin shining with a strange silvery-blue light. With a loud roar that made her skin prickle and her fear instincts kick in, he ripped the shackle out of the stone.

Bane stalked back toward her and offered it to her. She smiled and accepted the heavy restraint, the cold crystal giving her a dull headache simply from the contact. "At least they won't be using that on you again."

He chuckled. She pressed her hand against his cheek and sent another surge of power over him to replenish the magic he'd spent.

Sabine turned away and headed toward the exit, not daring to look back at him again for fear of breaking her resolve. Leaving him behind in this hell was one of the most difficult things she'd ever done. Her heart broke a little more with every step she took away from him.

Sabine walked toward the light, shielding her eyes and blinking rapidly. Still dragging the crystal chain, she climbed the handful of stairs and passed through the door, feeling the prickle of power coat her skin from the magical protections. The guards immediately turned the wheel again, sealing the door of the cell behind her.

Malek was at her side a second later, scanning her up and down. "You're all right?"

Sabine couldn't bring herself to answer him, knowing Bane was trapped in darkness and there was little she could do to help him. She took a deep breath, determined to focus on the things she could control.

She turned toward the warden and tossed the chain at his feet. "Bane's restraints have been removed. He has agreed to suffer your hospitality at my request. You will treat him as an honored guest, or your guild will suffer the consequences."

The dwarf sputtered in response, causing spittle to fly out of his mouth. "All captives must be restrained. I won't allow a demon to run wild in my prison. The idea is outrageous!"

Malek stepped in front of her and slapped his hand against the hilt of his sword. "Careful, Tinthorp. You're speaking to the queen of the Unseelie."

"That demon's a criminal! A murderer! I won't allow him unbound within these walls! Why, he's likely to possess someone or even worse!"

She narrowed her eyes on the warden and sent a sharp pulse of power along her markings. "Then allow me to be very clear. If you wish to live, you will not take it upon yourself to restrain my subject again. If your guild leader or the council objects, they can take it up with me directly."

The warden's face turned bright red. He opened his mouth to object, but Astrid let out a booming laugh from behind him.

"Well, don't that beat all. Pulled it straight out of the damned wall," Astrid said, heading toward them with a grin. She toed the crystalline shackle with her boot. "If I were you, I'd let it go, Tinthorp. If she can break our chains so easily, what do you think she'll do to you? Probably not a good idea to annoy Faerie's newest queen. Besides, the demon's on a short leash with his mistress around."

The warden's jaw clamped shut. He reached down, snatched up the shackle, and glared at all of them before stomping away.

Astrid slapped her thigh. "Not bad, girlie. Man's a bit of a twit and needs to be put in a place every now and then. Thetar and Dagmar are in the courtyard, keeping an eye on yer girl and pixie. I had a feeling Tinthorp might cause you problems, especially since he sent a runner for Brigette Barrelblade."

"Who's Brigette Barrelblade?" Sabine asked, unfamiliar with the name.

"Councilwoman for the Warrior Guild," Astrid said, her expression turning grim. "They oversee the management of the prison."

"I take it her presence doesn't herald glad tidings?"

Astrid shook her head and motioned for them to follow her back in the direction of the courtyard. "Not even close. She wanted yer demon executed immediately to avoid any complications. Yer presence is one of those complications."

"I intend to make things much more complicated," Sabine said in a dry tone.

They stepped out into the courtyard, where Thetar was having a standoff with a striking woman wearing full armor. Her blonde hair was pulled away from her face in a severe bun that emphasized the angles of her face. Another man was standing beside her, wearing similar armor, and neither appeared particularly happy with whatever Thetar was saying to them. The warden gave Sabine a smug look before trotting away and disappearing back into his office.

Astrid frowned. "Give me a moment." She moved forward to engage Brigette and her companion. They talked animatedly between themselves, using expansive hand gestures.

Blossom flew to Sabine and landed on her shoulder. In a quiet voice loud enough for only her and Malek to hear, Blossom whispered, "That's Brigette and Durgan from the Warrior Guild. She's mad because the warden interrupted an important meeting for her to come deal with an uppity Fae. I'm guessing that's you. I thought about dusting her, but I didn't think you'd like that."

Sabine frowned. "We'll keep the dusting as a last resort. What else?"

"Thetar told them you've been touched by the gods. I don't think they believe him, but she's at least listening."

"I've heard of Brigette," Malek said quietly. "Her men say she's tough and ruthless but also fair. Other than Astrid and maybe one other, I'm not sure there's another more powerful woman in all of Razadon. Be careful in dealing with her. She might try to challenge you before she'll listen to a word you say."

"I'm finding that to be a common theme among the dwarves," Sabine muttered and headed directly for them. Malek remained by her side, his hand resting on the hilt of his weapon.

Astrid gestured toward Sabine, the crystals embedded into her bracelets catching the light. "Queen Sabin'theoria of the Unseelie, meet Brigette Barrelblade of the Warrior Guild."

"Well met," Sabine said, tilting her head in greeting. "Call me Sabine. My companion is Captain Malek Rish'dan of the ship Obsidian's Storm."

"Greetings," Malek said, giving her a curt nod.

Brigette gave him a brief onceover before turning her attention to Sabine. Scanning her up and down with suspicion in her green eyes, Brigette asked, "Supposedly, you've been touched by the gods. I find that curious for someone exiled from Faerie who's taken up with a human lover. I suppose it's safe to assume Thetar's been talking out of his ass again."

Thetar chuckled. "Don't say I didn't warn you."

Astrid crossed her arms over her chest and remained silent.

Sabine kept her expression neutral, wanting to avoid another display of power if possible. Bane had taken a great deal of her magic, and fatigue was creeping into the edge of her mind. "We've all been touched by the gods in some manner. But yes, the blood of the goddess Lachlina and the god Vestior runs through my veins."

Brigette snorted. "You mean the same gods who abandoned us? Don't think yer connection to them gives you any rights to free prisoners in our city. From what the warden here tells me, you've taken it upon yerself to meddle in our affairs."

"Can I dust her yet?" Blossom whispered next to her ear.

Sabine narrowed her eyes on Brigette. "I have every right to claim justice when your city has fallen short of their responsibilities in cleansing this land. It's within *my* purview to do whatever's necessary to ensure the corruption is eradicated. If I decide Bane is necessary to complete that endeavor, you *will* release him into my custody. In the meantime, he shall not be shackled nor his magic negated in any way. If I need him to accomplish my task and you have rendered him powerless, there will be consequences."

Brigette straightened and took a threatening step toward her. "He's a demon assassin. He deserves nothing more than death for the harm he's caused my brethren. And yer nothing more than a child who thinks she can wade in here simply because she's Fae and her mommy's dead."

Sabine reared back as though slapped. Anger, red hot and molten, ripped through her. Without pausing to consider her actions, she flung her hand outward and slammed Brigette against the far wall. Clenching her fist, she tightened her mental hold around Brigette's neck and walked toward her.

Astrid inhaled sharply and stepped back, while Thetar took a protective stance in front of Astrid. Malek muttered a curse from behind her, and she heard the slide of metal as he pulled his sword from its sheath. Trusting Malek to keep her safe from Brigette's companion, Sabine ignored them and instead focused on the woman who had disparaged her.

She narrowed her eyes on Brigette, allowing her markings to flare silver and gold with power. "With one word, this so-called child has the power to coerce you into rending your own limbs from your body. Speak to me in such a manner again, and I'll see you tear out your own tongue and mount it on my wall as a trophy."

Brigette's eyes widened in shock, fear filling her gaze. Recognizing she was in danger of going too far, Sabine pulled back on her magic and dropped Brigette to the ground.

Durgan, Brigette's companion, dove toward the councilwoman. Malek pushed him back with a swift hit to the solar plexus. Durgan darted forward again, but Malek's sword slashed outward. The sharp clash of Malek's weapon against the dwarf's armor resounded through the courtyard. He quickly disarmed Durgan, forcing the weapon out of the dwarf's hand. It clattered to the ground, just out of reach.

"Step back," Malek ordered, angling his body protectively in front of Sabine.

Durgan's expression hardened as he reached for the axe affixed to his belt. "Move aside, human. I let you take a strike to play a bit, but I won't allow it again. Yer betters are talking."

"Tried to warn you. He ain't human," Thetar said with a grin, rocking back on his heels. "Not sure what he is, but he's a power of some sort. Knocked me flat on my ass on the way here."

"Stand down, Durgan," Brigette ordered, rising to her feet and rubbing her neck. She scanned Sabine up and down again, this time far more critically. "Guess I was wrong about you, Your Highness. But I'm not happy about the demon runnin' loose in his cell. Can you keep yer demon under control?"

Sabine hesitated. "I can't guarantee anything unless you release him into my custody. That said, I do not believe he will harm anyone unless he is shackled again and I continue to visit him whenever necessary."

Brigette frowned and rubbed her chin. "A straightforward and honest answer from a Fae?"

Sabine managed a weak smile. "I didn't come here to subject you to my will, Brigette. Bane traveled to your city at my direction, and he volunteered to surrender to your men of his own free will."

Brigette considered her for a moment. "Aye. That he did, but we still hold responsibility for him and his destruction. I'm already cleaning up after his mess with the bodies at our doorstep."

Sabine frowned, the edge of her vision going dark. If she didn't get some rest soon, she'd betray her weakness and end up completely at the mercy of the dwarves. But she couldn't risk alienating a potential ally while Bane's life was at stake.

Reaching for the strength of the Unseelie who had embraced her through the ritual crystal, she spun together a magical working designed to increase her awareness and understanding. It might be the only thing to get her through the next few minutes. She couldn't risk asking Malek for help.

Breathing through the power, she focused on the aura surrounding Brigette. Its edges were tinged with red and grey, signs of anger and guilt, both warring for supremacy. Sabine paused, realizing Brigette had spouted her careless and angry words from a place of grief. If she was the leader of the Warrior Guild, she'd been the one to send her patrols outside of Razadon. It was her men who had been killed, murdered by Bane while he'd been overtaken by the magical corruption.

Sabine swallowed, allowing the magical working to dissipate. She placed her closed hand over her heart in a gesture of respect and lowered her head.

"You have my deepest condolences for the loss of your men," Sabine said softly, speaking directly to Brigette's grief. "They fought with remarkable skill. Each one was a credit to you and your guild."

A flash of pain crossed Brigette's face. The warrior woman drew in a sharp breath and pressed her fist over her heart to mirror Sabine's gesture. "Aye. They were good men who retreated to the stone's embrace far too soon." She sighed and rubbed her temples. "You've caught me on a bad day. I was delivering the news to Codin Battlearm's widow when the runner said I was needed here."

Malek frowned and lowered his sword. "I imagine delivering such news would be difficult."

Brigette nodded. "Aye, but worse for Evelyn. Without a living husband or child with ties to my guild, Evelyn's wailing about being booted from her home. Codin's only been indentured to the Warrior Guild for three years. The routine patrol was his first and wasn't expected to be dangerous."

Sabine's brow furrowed. "I don't understand. Why would she be forced from her home?"

Astrid turned toward her and explained, "We provide homes to probationary members of our guilds before they become full-fledged guildmembers. Since Codin wasn't able to complete his apprenticeship, his home will be reassigned to a new prospective member."

Sabine swallowed, her heart plummeting in her chest. She'd known each of the dead men had family and other loved ones, but she hadn't considered the ramifications beyond the initial tragedy.

Malek frowned. "What will happen to her? Can she join another guild?"

Brigette shook her head. "She would normally return to her parents' home and their guild, but they've been gone from this world for several years now. She'll have to reach out to other relatives and hope they have room to take her in."

Blossom tugged on Sabine's braids and whispered, "Can we help her, Sabine? Pretty please?"

Sabine hesitated, her gaze falling on Rika and Dagmar standing a short distance away. She couldn't keep accepting responsibility for people, especially when traveling with her would likely lead them more into danger. Even so, Sabine wasn't willing to abandon Evelyn when Bane had been the one responsible for her current plight.

Malek brushed the backs of his fingers against hers. "You have all those messages to sort through, Sabine. She could stay in the servants' wing of the embassy and help you. If it works out, you could always keep her on as an assistant or find some other task."

Sabine looked up at him in surprise. It was typical to select someone from a prominent Unseelie Fae family to handle such things, but there wasn't anything that said she couldn't do what Malek was suggesting.

She gave Malek a trace of a smile before turning back toward Brigette and Astrid. "It would seem I could use some assistance in managing some household matters in Razadon. Within the next few weeks, some emissaries from Faerie will be arriving and I'll need everything put into order. If things work out, I might be inclined to extend my offer on a more permanent basis."

Brigette's eyes widened. "Yer suggesting taking her into

yer household? The girl's smart, but she doesn't have any experience. Besides, Dagmar's family's held the position as steward for Faerie's embassy for centuries. I'm sure they've got cousins aplenty who can help you."

Sabine glanced at Dagmar and Rika, who were keeping their distance but still straining to hear every word being spoken. "Dagmar and her family are doing a remarkable job with handling everything, but there are some matters which don't fall within the scope of their normal duties. I'm planning on making some other changes which will benefit Dagmar and her family. I don't believe they'll be opposed to having additional help."

Astrid gave her an approving nod. "As far as solutions go, it's a tidy one. I think you should allow it, Brigette. The girl will never be a warrior, and her extended family has already petitioned for larger quarters. Release her from service, and you've removed a potential headache."

"Aye," Brigette murmured, rubbing her chin. "Very well. I'll allow it if the widow agrees to yer terms."

"Dagmar," Sabine called, waving the redheaded dwarf toward her.

Dagmar ran over immediately, her green eyes darting between Sabine and the councilwomen. "Y-yes? Um, you need me?"

Sabine nodded. "Would you send a message to Evelyn Battlearm letting her know I'd like to speak with her? I understand she's in mourning, so I'll leave the time specifics up to her. She's welcome to join me in my quarters at the Faerie embassy at her earliest convenience."

Dagmar's eyes bugged out of her head. Ordinary citizens were rarely invited to the embassy and never to the queen's personal quarters. "Ah, er, yes. I can go let her know right now."

Rika approached them and asked, "Can I go with her? I'd like to help."

Before Sabine could respond, Blossom landed lightly on Sabine's shoulder and said, "Me too! I can go with them, Sabine. I wanted to look for plants and stuff. Remember?"

Sabine paused, realizing Blossom was asking if she should snoop around. "All right. I'll see you both back at the embassy once you're—"

Rika's head jerked up. "Hey! What's—"

Sabine followed her gaze, catching a flash of movement on the ledge. One of the giant stone obelisks wobbled, teetering back and forth. Almost as though some invisible force pushed it, the obelisk came crashing downward right over their heads.

Rika screamed. Malek grabbed Sabine around the waist and hauled her backward, just as Astrid yanked one of her power crystals from her headdress. Sabine lifted her hand and sent a powerful magic blast upward.

Her gust of wind caught the stone obelisk, shifting its trajectory away from those standing below it. The stone marker crashed against the far wall of the prison's entrance with enough force to shake the ground below their feet. The stone cracked in half, sending chunks of rubble to the ground.

Brigette shouted for reinforcements, but Malek was already in motion. With far more agility than any human, he scaled the wall and pulled himself up to the narrow ledge. He withdrew his weapon and searched the area around the remaining stones. Blossom had accompanied him, and Sabine saw her glittering figure dart in between the obelisks.

"I'll kill whoever is responsible for this," Astrid promised, shoving her unused power crystal into her pouch. She scowled and stomped to the fallen obelisk. The noise from the breaking stone and subsequent shouting had drawn a great deal of attention. Dwarves were spilling out from the prison and from the nearby streets to investigate. Brigette called instructions to the prison guards, ordering them to search the premises and find a repair crew.

Sabine's hands shook from exertion, and she curled them into fists to hide their trembling. A fierce headache had taken hold right behind her eyes, with spots streaking across her vision. She was dangerously low on magic and would likely fall into a restorative slumber soon.

Taking a shaky breath, she pulled a trace amount of power through the bond she shared with Malek, using his magic to stabilize her. Malek paused in his search and looked down at her, his gaze filled with worry. She shook her head to indicate she would be fine before turning toward Rika.

The human seer was still staring up at the ledge where Malek and Blossom were searching. Her wings twitched in agitation, and she started to lift into the air. Sabine gripped her shoulders to keep her firmly on the ground.

In a voice quiet enough to ensure no one could hear them, Sabine asked, "Did you see someone up there?"

Rika hesitated and then nodded. "I think so, but I'm not sure. It looked like a little blue creature. It was fuzzy and round, except for its long skinny arms and legs. I think it might have been one of the cave trolls Dagmar told us about."

Dagmar's eyes widened. "That sounds like them, but they don't usually show themselves to outsiders. I've never heard of a cave troll hurting anyone before. If that obelisk had hit us, we would have all been killed."

Sabine frowned and lifted her head to look up where Malek was searching. She hadn't seen anything specific, but she also didn't know much about cave trolls. The stone hadn't fallen of its own volition.

It was possible Rika's seer abilities had broken through some sort of glamour. Rika's talents were still unpredictable, but Sabine couldn't risk asking too many questions where they might be overheard. Blossom was their best chance at sniffing out other creatures who possessed the ability to hide themselves from view.

Malek caught her eye and shook his head to indicate he hadn't found the culprit. Sabine blew out a breath, watching as he climbed back down. She turned back toward Rika and Dagmar and said, "Dagmar, I know these are your people and you have a responsibility to them, but I'm going to ask you not to share this information with them just yet. I don't want to accuse anyone of any wrongdoing until we figure out what's happening."

Dagmar bit her lip and nodded. "I guess I can understand that. I mean, they're cave trolls. If they don't want to be seen, no one would see them. And they'd never hurt us. That's like Blossom hurting one of the Fae. The pixies wouldn't ever hurt one of you, right? I mean, the cave trolls are only a little bigger than her. There's no way they could move one of those obelisks. That's crazy, yeah?"

Sabine made a noncommittal noise, watching as Malek lowered himself to the ground. Blossom could absolutely hurt one of the Fae, but only under certain circumstances. If the cave trolls were similar in nature to pixies, the person who had ordered the assassination attempt would have been someone with enough power to enhance the creature's abilities. They also would need some sort of sway over the cave trolls or a blood bond, similar to what she shared with Blossom.

Malek approached them, his lips turned downward in a frown. "I didn't see anyone, but I believe that was by design. No footsteps, no sign anyone had been there. Blossom said she smelled something funny. She went to investigate and said she'd return later."

Sabine frowned. "Blossom can smell magic. She might have discovered a clue."

Malek nodded and lifted his gaze in the direction of the ledge. "The rest of the stones look like they're fixed into place, same as that one. I find it hard to believe it suddenly decided to fall while all of us were standing underneath it."

"Is someone trying to kill one of us or the new queen?" Astrid asked, walking back toward them.

Sabine turned to regard the powerbroker. "I was hoping you had the answer to that question."

Astrid clucked her tongue. "Well, regardless of their intended target, it looks like you and I have a mutual enemy. There's no way that stone fell without a good, hard push."

Sabine frowned and lifted her gaze again. "I believe you're right."

Astrid gestured to her headdress where the power crystal had been ripped off. "Not only do I owe you a debt for saving my life but also for saving my power crystal."

"It would seem I owe her as well," Brigette said, walking toward them and sheathing her weapon. "I never would have seen that damn stone before it landed on my head. If I didn't know any better, I'd say you orchestrated the whole thing yerself. It's not every day someone saves the life of two councilwomen."

Sabine stilled, realizing the culprit and Rika had done her a tremendous favor. "Indeed. It would seem a debt is due."

Astrid grinned, her eyes lighting with eagerness. She rubbed her hands together and asked, "Aye. Should we barter?"

Brigette scowled and regarded Astrid with annoyance. "Don't know why yer looking so pleased. A life debt can be a tricky thing to repay. I, for one, have no desire to scrub chamber pots for the rest of my life. Better that the stone crushed me than sniff Fae shit for the next several centuries."

Astrid snorted. "I think our new Unseelie queen has a different sort of repayment in mind."

Sabine glanced back toward the prison where Bane was being held. "Indeed. As it happens, there's a life already in need of saving."

Astrid laughed. "Aye, a life for a life. In accordance with our earlier talk, I'll secure the two other votes on your behalf. You already have mine, but the rest will be up to you."

Sabine nodded. "Who are the two?"

"Ivar Quartzman of the Jewelcrafter Guild and Ebnus Axebreaker of the Armorer Guild."

Sabine committed the names to memory and then inclined her head. "I accept. Repayment of the debt shall be made in the form of three council votes of my choosing in an effort to save Bane'umbra Versed's life."

"Acknowledged and witnessed," Astrid said, holding out her arm for Sabine.

She placed her fingers on Astrid's wrist and traced a pattern on the dwarven woman's skin. Infusing her touch with magic, she traced a triangular symbol three times. Pain lanced through Sabine's wrist as she accepted the pain of the debt marker on Astrid's behalf. The dwarven woman's new mark flared silver and then gold before reverting to silver again.

Brigette stared in shocked horror at Astrid. "You've bartered for the demon to live. Are ye daft?"

"Not at all," Astrid retorted, studying the new mark on her wrist. "I wear the mark of the gods and sign of favor from the Unseelie queen. She's kept the demon in check and already saved our lives and that of yer guild's newest widow. Suck up yer pride, woman, and make an oath to save her demon's life at the next council meeting."

Sabine turned toward Brigette and said, "The life you choose to relinquish is up to you. Either vote to release the demon into my care and walk away with my good wishes, or you may enter my servitude and clean chamber pots for the rest of your days. By all rights, your submission will lead your entire guild into servitude as well."

Brigette's jaw worked, and she glared at Astrid's wrist. "I'll find an axe in my skull one of these nights if I vote to allow him to walk free."

Astrid sighed. "She has a point. The men who died were her kin, her guildmates."

Malek frowned and took a step toward them. "No one wants your entire guild to end up in servitude either. The Warrior Guild is renowned throughout the world for their fierceness in battle and strong sense of loyalty. They follow you because they believe in you, not simply because of your skill with your weapon. Bane follows Sabine for that reason, just like the rest of us."

Sabine looked at Malek, touched by his belief in her. He gave her an encouraging nod, and she turned back toward Brigette. "Formality aside, I don't want you as my enemy, Brigette. I have enough of those already. I came to Razadon to seek out allies and to stop the corruption, not impose my will over any of you. If you vote to release Bane, it will be into my care and I will accept responsibility for him. I don't make such claims over any other demon, but Bane is my bound subject."

Brigette frowned, her gaze drifting to the fallen obelisk. Several dwarves were taking etchings of the names so they could be preserved and carved into the new stone once it was erected. Others had fanned out and were systematically searching the courtyard and ledges for any sign of wrongdoing.

"Aye," Brigette said and squared her shoulders. She unfastened the straps of the metal plates covering her arm and thrust her wrist in Sabine's direction. "I will give you one vote at the next council meeting to save yer demon's life. May the gods protect me when the rest of Razadon finds out what I've done."

Sabine inclined her head, reaching over to infuse a marker on Brigette's wrist. "I accept your debt. In accordance with our agreement, repayment shall be made in the form of one vote of my choosing during Razadon's council in an effort to save Bane'umbra Versed's life."

"Acknowledged and witnessed," Brigette muttered, pulling her wrist away. She studied the design, but the gold color was already fading to silver. "Well, I'll be damned. The touch of the gods."

Another wave of dizziness swept across Sabine's vision, and she started to sway.

Malek moved closer to her, wrapped his arm around her waist, and said, "I think we should probably head back to the embassy. I know you were expecting messages from Faerie."

Sabine threw him a look of gratitude and nodded. It was weak as far as excuses went, but it wasn't exactly a lie. "Yes. We should be heading back."

Brigette gave them both a curt nod. "I'll see you on the 'morrow. Gotta get this mess cleared out of here and the prison secured."

Without another word, she crossed the courtyard and spoke with some of the prison guards standing nearby.

Rika absently brushed her antennae from her face and looked around the courtyard. "Should we wait for Blossom?"

Sabine shook her head. "No. She'll find us later, assuming she doesn't stumble upon a mushroom ring."

Dagmar bit her lip. "Should we still go see Evelyn without her?"

Sabine hesitated, especially given the suspicious circumstances of the falling obelisk. She didn't think Rika would be in danger, but Sabine wasn't about to leave anything to chance.

Gesturing toward the four guards who had escorted them from the embassy, Sabine said, "Go ahead, but take two of the guards with you. Malek and I will meet you back in our quarters."

Dagmar and Rika both nodded and ran off to carry out their errand. Astrid swept her gaze over Sabine, studying her thoughtfully.

"I expect you know something about what happened here, especially with the pixie's disappearance," the councilwoman murmured. "For now, I'll assume you have yer reasons fer not sharing. It stands to be seen whether we'll have the sort of relationship yer mum and me did."

Sabine held Astrid's gaze and nodded. "Indeed. I hope we do, but trust takes time."

"Aye. That it does. That it definitely does."

Chapter Fifteen

Malek kept one arm around Sabine and the other on his sword as they headed back toward the embassy. Her steps became more sluggish the farther they walked, but she was doing her best to stay conscious. The two remaining guards walked on opposite sides, but Malek wasn't willing to trust Sabine's safety to unknown individuals.

"We're almost there," he murmured, recognizing slight changes on the walls as they approached the Faerie embassy. Living vines and wooden accents lined the walls and archways, in addition to the usual stone, crystal, and metal found everywhere else in Razadon.

Sabine nodded and leaned against him, her slight form trembling from the exertion. Malek was tempted to scoop her up and carry her the rest of the way, but he understood her need to maintain the illusion.

Malek led her into her private quarters, leaving the guards standing watch outside. The moment she was inside, Sabine collapsed onto the bench in the entry area. To hell with intentions. Malek lifted Sabine into his arms and headed into the main living area. She didn't protest, which only served as one more indication of her exhaustion.

"You need to take more of my power," he said, carrying her into her bedroom and kicking the door shut behind them.

"No," she murmured, leaning her head against his chest. "It's too dangerous. I just need to rest."

Malek's jaw clenched as he placed her on the bed. "Dammit, Sabine. There's a small chance Dagmar and Rika will be bringing Evelyn back here. You need your strength if you're going to keep up this charade."

Sabine blinked at him, but it was obvious she was struggling to stay awake. "I'll rest for a few minutes, but you should go talk to your friend. We still need two more votes on the council for a majority."

Malek sat on the edge of the bed and brushed her silvery hair away from her face. He lifted her hand to press a light kiss against it. "I won't leave while you're in this state, sweetheart. Either take some of my power or I'll remain here until you're feeling stronger."

"Power. We have to save Bane," she murmured, closing her eyes again. A moment later, she was sound asleep.

Malek frowned, worried about the paleness of her skin and the shadows under her eyes. At least she wasn't expending more energy trying to maintain her glamour. He unfastened his warding medallion and leaned down, then pressed his lips against hers. He breathed dragonfire into her body, his heated breath flaring the embers of her magic to life. Sabine wrapped her arms around his neck, returning his kiss with a different sort of power.

She'd once told him magic and intimacy went hand in hand for the Fae. He'd seen it for himself earlier that day. It was tempting to spend another several hours restoring her completely, but he needed to secure Hargrim's vote.

He pulled back, tracing the edge of her face with his fingertips. "I once heard a story about a kiss waking a Faerie princess. Never thought I'd experience it for myself."

She laughed, the shadows under her eyes already fading. "There are many such stories. Some of them end terribly."

"We'll have to make sure this one ends better," he murmured, trailing his thumb across her cheek.

Sabine's lavender eyes softened. The tenderness in her gaze told him everything he needed to know about her feelings, even if she wouldn't say the words back to him.

She pressed her hand against his chest and said, "I think I have time to get cleaned up before Dagmar and Rika get back. I should be fine while you're gone. No one can enter these quarters without my leave, and I don't believe one grieving widow will be much of a threat."

He hesitated. "Are you sure?"

She nodded. "Acquiring these votes is the only chance we have to save Bane without bloodshed. I can't risk drawing on the Unseelie collective unless absolutely necessary. If they don't believe I'm strong enough to hold my throne, we'll face even more threats than our current ones."

"All right," he replied and reluctantly pulled away from her. "I'll be back in a few hours. If you have a problem, send Dagmar to come find me. I'm going to see if I can find Hargrim in one of the pubs first."

Sabine nodded and stood. "Be careful, Malek. You may be targeted simply for associating with me."

"They can try," he said with a grin and winked at her before heading to the exit.

~

Malek walked toward the door of the pub, stepping aside as a drunken patron tumbled down the steps and landed on the ground with a thud. The dwarf grinned widely and saluted Malek before climbing to his feet and stumbling away. Malek shook his head and walked up the stairs.

Tapmasters was one of the largest pubs in the city, taking up nearly an entire city block. All the windows were brightly lit, with music and laughter spilling into the streets. The drinks were a bit more expensive, but the proprietor didn't have any problems commanding such prices given the quality of his brews.

Malek pushed open the heavy door and stepped inside the noisy tavern. Dozens of tables were spread out in the main room of the pub, while a large bar with a fractured crystal countertop spanned multiple rooms. The hour was approaching midnight, but the revelry was just getting started. Servers pushed aside noisy patrons while juggling trays filled with mugs of ale or mead.

Malek angled up to the bar, trying to catch the attention of one of the bartenders. A troll with leathery skin and jutting tusks approached him, leaning heavily on the counter. He peered at Malek over his hooked nose and asked, "Whady'll ya have?"

"House ale," Malek said, sliding a couple of coins toward him. "I'm looking for Hargrim Icemail. Is he here celebrating?"

"Aye," the troll said through his tusks and slid the coins off the bar. He filled a mug and passed it to Malek, nodding toward one of the side rooms. "Jasper Room. Follow the smell of piss and vomit."

Malek picked up his mug and carried it in the direction the troll had indicated. The Jasper Room was exactly as its name implied, a room where the walls had been inlaid with large pieces of the reddish-orange stone. More than two dozen people, most of them dwarves, were celebrating along with Hargrim.

The newly appointed leader of the Tradesmen Guild was a rotund dwarf with a blond beard reaching nearly to his waist. Judging by his bloodshot eyes, rumpled clothing, and the ale dribbling down his front, he appeared well and truly drunk.

"Malek!" Hargrim roared, waving his mug in Malek's direction. "Get the hell over here, boy! Thought you'd be up north. How'd you manage to sneak in our front door?"

Malek grinned and wound his way through the tables to where Hargrim was sitting. Hargrim grabbed the back of a sleeping dwarf's shirt and hauled him off his chair, then deposited him on the floor. The man grunted, scratched his belly, and resumed snoring.

"I have my ways," Malek said and slid into the newly vacant chair. "Do you think I'd let you celebrate being named guild leader without me? You promised to buy the entire pub drinks for the night. I'm here to collect."

Hargrim guffawed loudly and elbowed the man sitting next to him. "Gilgon, this here's Captain Malek. You remember me telling you that story about the exploding cask? This was the culprit."

Gilgon raised his mug and grinned. "Hah! I would have paid good coin to see ole Paggon's wife see him standing in that mess. Man hasn't cheated at cards since."

Malek laughed and took a drink of his ale. "I haven't had anyone try to cheat me since then either."

Hargrim clapped Malek on the back. "Good to see you, son. So, ya heard about my cousin losing his head, eh?"

"From what I've heard, no one's much surprised," Malek said with a shrug.

"Nah. The man was a right bastard," Hargrim said and belched loudly. He gestured at a waitress, who was serving another table their drinks, and shouted, "Another round for my friends!"

"Keep yer shirt on, Hargrim," the woman snapped, turning away with a swish of her hips.

Hargrim leaned down and said, "That there is Ingrid. She's a feisty one. Can't seem to get enough of me, if ya know what I mean."

"Uh-huh," Malek said and leaned back. Hargrim was all bluster and fiercely loyal to only one woman. "How's your wife doing these days?"

Gilgon laughed. "She'll have him herded out of here in the next hour, mark my words. And fool that he is, he'll go willingly."

Hargrim snorted and took another swig.

"Hey, I know you," a man on the other end of the table slurred, pointing at Malek.

"Oh?" Malek asked, unable to place the dwarf.

"Yer that human ship captain that's been following the new queen around. Saw you with her and that demon fellow."

"No shit," Hargrim said, arching his brow at Malek. "Smuggling ain't enough? Now yer carting around the Fae?"

Malek took another drink and said, "Just Sabine. Haven't met many other Fae willing to pay my fare."

Gilgon leaned forward. "Heard she looks just like her mum. That true?"

"Never met her mother, so I can't say."

"She does," the dwarf on the end stated. "Same bitch-ass way about her too. Came in here all uppity, trying to put us in our places. Maybe we should introduce her to whoever took care of Badac."

Malek's hand tightened on his mug, snapping off the handle. The warding medallion around his neck heated in warning. He scowled and tossed the handle aside, trying to regain control of his temper.

Hargrim reached over and smacked the dwarf on the back of his head. "Watch it, Tilgor. The lad's got a fondness for the new queen. Best keep yer tongue in check or it might end up on the table."

Tilgor sneered and stood. "I don't have much interest drinking with Faerie whores anyway."

He turned and stomped off in the direction of another table. Hargrim narrowed his gaze on Malek and jerked his head toward the main room. "Why don't we go for a walk, boy? I could use some air."

"What about the next round?" Gilgon asked, waving his empty mug in their direction.

"Do you see an apron around my waist, you fool?" Hargrim demanded. "Wave down the lass, and have her put it on my tab."

Malek left his mug on the table and followed Hargrim into the main room of the pub. He'd expected Hargrim to take him outside, but instead, the new guild leader led him toward the back room. The bartenders barely spared him a glance, which made Malek suspect this wasn't unusual.

Hargrim pushed open the door and entered the cool cellar. Casks lined the walls, all the way up to the ceiling. A few dwarves were in the back, mixing things in vats and checking temperatures. Hargrim paid them no mind, wandering even farther into the back rooms of the pub.

They passed several doors before Hargrim finally stopped in front of a nondescript door. He pressed his hand against a small crystal panel, and the door slid open. Malek followed him into a small wine cellar.

A heaviness in the air made Malek think this room wasn't used often. He glanced at some of the wines, not recognizing any of their labels. Many of them appeared to be Faerie wines, and all of them appeared incredibly old. The wines he'd purchased for trading stock bore no resemblance to these bottles.

Hargrim hummed a tune as he wandered through the wooden stacks until he got to a particular wine rack. He dragged over a ladder and climbed up the rungs, searching through the bottles. "Don't think I ever told you I knew Queen Mali'theoria."

Malek frowned and crossed his arms over his chest. "No. I wasn't aware you were acquainted."

"Aye. Met her probably three centuries ago. Got to know her fairly well." Hargrim plucked out a bottle and held it up to the light. He nodded and handed it to Malek. The bottle itself was made from crystal, not glass. Colors swirled within the bottle, making Malek wonder if it had been infused with magic.

Malek frowned and lifted his head. "What is this?"

Climbing back down the ladder, Hargrim said, "A gift. Give it to yer lady with my regards. She'll understand, I'm sure. Looking forward to meeting her, but I'll likely be too drunk for a formal introduction during the next council meeting."

"Is the wine magic?"

"Aye," Hargrim said, putting the ladder back where he'd found it. "Malia was a hard and cold woman in the end, but when I first met her, she was a different sort. If yer reaction to Tilgor's comment was any indication, her daughter's likely got that same blush about her." His mouth curved in a smile. "Similar to a new wine where you can taste the promise of power."

Malek's brow furrowed. "What do you mean?"

"Malia was a good woman. Passionate. Full of fire. She had a laugh that made every man and woman turn their heads. She tried to be fair, balancing the needs of her people with her desire to bring the Fae back to power. Not sure what happened, but she changed over time."

"How so?"

Hargrim stroked his beard. "Over the last century, she became bitter, calculating, angry, and, in the end, suspicious of everyone. Was a shame, but likely necessary to keep her throne. In the end, it wasn't enough."

Malek frowned and ran his thumb across the bottle's cork. "You believe Sabine will change?"

"Can't say," Hargrim said and shrugged. "Don't know the girl, but she's young yet. She'll need to make some hard choices if she wants to survive her da's plotting. Power changes a person and not usually for the better."

"Is that why you're planning on spending your reign drunk?" Malek asked in a dry voice.

Hargrim laughed. "Aye. If I'm drunk, no one will expect much of me. I just need to show up to the meetings."

Malek frowned and looked at the bottle again. "Sabine isn't what I expected of the Fae. There's a light inside her. When we're alone, she's quick to smile and laugh. She's loyal, almost to a fault. But she's also stubborn and consistently puts the welfare of others above her own."

"And she's got a ship captain in love with her," Hargrim said with a wry grin.

"I suppose I'm a little transparent," Malek muttered, unsurprised Hargrim had called him on it.

Hargrim nodded. "Normally there's nothing wrong with a pretty woman who catches yer eye, but I don't see good things for either of you. Might want to consider letting her go now before one of you destroys the other."

Malek froze. "You know, don't you?"

Hargrim chuckled. "I know you aren't human, and I have my suspicions about yer origins, but if I don't know the truth, I can't tell a soul. What I do know is yer a good man and a competent ship captain. You've never caused me or mine any trouble. If that changes, well, that's a conversation we'll be having at the ends of our weapons."

Malek's mouth twitched in a smile. "I've long considered you a friend, Hargrim, and I don't expect that to change."

Hargrim gave him a curt nod. "Now as to the real reason you wanted to talk. I'm guessing you sought me out fer more than a celebratory drink?"

Malek nodded. "Sabine's trying to secure as many votes as possible before the next council meeting. The demon who accompanied us here is her sworn protector. He may have killed the patrol outside these gates, but I don't believe he was ultimately responsible."

"Demons aren't usually blameless."

"No," Malek said in agreement. "But I lost several of my crew during a magical storm. I would have lost my entire ship if it weren't for Sabine's efforts in battling against the corruption that overtook us. Bane was also affected by the storm, which ultimately led to your people's deaths. Sabine was the one who stopped it from taking over the entire mountain range."

Hargrim considered him for a long time, no trace of his earlier drunkenness anywhere in his demeanor. "Yer asking me to vote to free the demon in the council meeting?"

Malek held Hargrim's gaze and said, "Sabine asked me to speak with you, but I'm asking you for the vote."

Hargrim rubbed his chin and turned to study the wall. "The dwarves are masters of stone, metal, and any mineral that can be found within the ground. We've nearly perfected the art of developing weapons and armor, but there are still flaws in our designs."

Malek arched his brow. "Your craftsmen are the finest in the world. The fact is undisputed."

"Aye, but there's the matter of raw materials," Hargrim

said with a sly grin. "I want something more beautiful than our most powerful crystal and stronger than our most resilient stone. I want to create an item that has the power to send my foes running, something that doesn't exist anywhere else in the world."

Malek frowned, a sense of foreboding filling him. "What are you suggesting, Hargrim?"

"A trade, Captain Malek," Hargrim said, crossing his arms over his chest. "My vote for the life of the demon in exchange for a dragon scale."

Malek's hand tightened on the bottle. "You can't be serious."

Hargrim snorted. "I know the power of those scales, boy. They can't be harvested without consent. At least, not in any usable form."

"Would you cut off your beard and offer it up for a demon?" Malek snapped, incensed by Hargrim's suggestion.

"Hell no. But I'm not here chasing around a Fae's skirts and beggin' favors fer a demon."

Malek narrowed his eyes. "You fully understand what you're asking, don't you? This has nothing to do with crafting an item. You want to claim a dragon's debt."

"Aye," Hargrim agreed with a grin. "One favor. To be used without question at a time of my choosing."

Malek's jaw worked, and he didn't answer. He couldn't agree to this, not without dire consequences. If he offered up one of his scales, Hargrim could summon him from anywhere in the world at any time. He could be used to destroy entire cities, shatter mountains, or even worse.

"Bet Ingrid delivered those drinks by now," Hargrim said and headed for the door. "Why don't you head on back to yer queen and give her that gift from me? Think long and hard about my offer, and let me know. A nod or wink at the council meeting will be sufficient to tell me which way to vote."

Malek stared at the bottle in frustration, wanting to throw it against the wall. The crafty older dwarf had seized upon the transparency of Malek's emotions to gain the advantage.

Muttering a curse under his breath, Malek left the wine cellar and headed back toward the main room of the pub. He heard the revelry still happening within the Jasper Room, but he didn't spare Hargrim or his companions a glance on his way out the front door. He had no idea what he was going to tell Sabine. Her loyalty to Bane was clear, but he wasn't sure she fully understood the magic and laws surrounding the dragons.

He passed by a familiar shop and stopped short, remembering Sabine's reaction when he'd given her a hairbrush and container of tea back in Karga. She'd been genuinely touched, and Malek suspected it was rare for her to receive such kindnesses without expecting something in return. If things were becoming more dangerous for Sabine now that she'd claimed her title, she'd need more weapons at her disposal than what her magic provided.

Malek pushed open the door. The crystal bell fastened to the door chimed in greeting. The shopkeeper, an older woman with her hair braided into a bun, stopped cleaning one of the displays and motioned for him to enter.

"Welcome to Brodie's Blades. I'm Verna, Brodie's wife," she said, tucking her cleaning cloth below the counter. "I was about to close up, but I'm happy to show ya my wares. Are ya looking for something in particular?"

"Actually, yes," Malek said, sweeping his gaze over a wide variety of decorative weapons. Many of these were show pieces, designed more for aesthetics than functionality. He was looking for something that was a bit of both.

He paused at a set of throwing knives, inlaid with several precious gems. Sabine already had a set, and hers were of equal or greater quality.

"You like those?" Verna asked, walking from around the counter toward him.

"I'm looking for a gift for someone. I believe she already has something similar," Malek said, moving to the next display.

Verna arched her brow. "Can never have too many knives. Why don't you tell me about yer lady friend or other things she likes? I might have some ideas."

Malek nodded, remembering when he'd first met Sabine. "A while back, I met someone with hairpins carved from a variety of different materials. They were unusual in that they allowed the wearer to fill them with poison. You wouldn't happen to have anything like that, would you?"

The woman scanned him up and down, pursing her lips. "Aye. I had a custom order made up not too long ago. With trade being shut down, the customer hasn't been able to collect them. I might be willing to sell them to you if the price is right."

"Show me what you have," Malek said, walking to the counter.

Verna headed back behind the counter and reached down to unlock a cabinet sealed with a crystal panel. She pulled out a decorative box and placed them in front of him. Malek opened it and found five distinct hairpins, each with different carvings at the end. They were even more extraordinary than the set Sabine had worn. These were inlaid with tiny power crystals, which sparkled with different colors to represent the magic they contained.

Verna pointed at each one and said, "They're each made from different materials and all hand-carved." She picked up the one with a leaf design and showed him how to unfasten the top decorative piece with the crystal. "The poison can be inserted here. Depressing the button on the side releases the poison."

Malek put down the bottle of wine and took the hairpin from her. He held it up, admiring the details. "If you don't mind me asking, who ordered these made?"

"Client confidentiality," Verna said, leaning against the counter.

Malek nodded, unsurprised by her answer. "How much for the set?"

Verna considered him for a moment. "My other buyer was going to pay two hundred gold coins for the lot."

"And your other buyer never completed the transaction," Malek said to remind her. "You could be looking at months before you collect. How about a hundred?"

Verna scoffed. "Maybe I'll have to wait a bit, but they'll eventually sell. I'll need a bit of an incentive to let them walk out my door."

"One hundred fifty," he said, his tone firm. It was a great deal of coin, but if it helped keep Sabine alive, it was money well spent.

"Deal," Verna said with a curt nod. "You want me to wrap it up for you?"

Malek nodded. "Hargrim Icemail has a line of credit established for me in the name Captain Malek Rish'dan."

Verna slid a crystal toward him. Malek pressed his palm against the panel and repeated the amount and his name. Once it flared bright white, Verna collected the crystal and placed it on the rear counter. She grabbed a piece of fabric and wrapped the box tightly, securing it with a string.

"Pleasure doing business with ya."

Malek angled his head and said, "Same to you."

He tucked the box under his arm and collected the bottle of wine before heading back outside. The streetlights were dimming due to the late hour, but Razadon never shut down completely. Over the next couple of hours, the streetsweepers and other workers would be coming out to clean and maintain the city streets.

Malek started to pass a nearby alley, but voices caught his attention. He slowed his footsteps, trying to listen.

"I heard someone tried to drop one of those stone markers on her head," a man was saying to someone.

"That'll teach that Fae bitch to come here and try to free a demon," a woman replied. "What's she thinking bringing him here anyway? Haven't we got enough problems with those damn demons?"

"I wanna know why one of us isn't good enough," someone else argued. "Sure, they'll trade with us, but we wouldn't be allowed to stand at the queen's side. I think some of the council has the right idea. We stop trading with them all together—the demons, the Fae, and the humans. Then they'll start respecting us a bit more."

Malek frowned and continued walking, careful to avoid being seen by the speakers. A sliver of suspicion worked its way through his mind. Unleashing corrupted power crystals was definitely a good way to shut down trading. The negative effects had already begun to be felt in parts of the north. They'd seen it back in Karga and in their dealings with the merfolk.

He just wasn't sure who could be responsible for such an action. Astrid had appeared genuinely frustrated. Malek had a difficult time imagining her anger was disingenuous. She'd indicated many of the other councilors had been displeased by it too. Perhaps there might be a way to discover who wasn't troubled by the corruption's effect on trade. That might lead to some answers.

A loud commotion and shouting from up ahead caught his attention, and he hastened his footsteps to see what was happening. Several dwarves were scrambling to get out of the way, so he pushed forward and caught sight of dozens of strange, furry blue creatures, no taller than his calf. They were racing through the streets, making strange chittering noises that echoed through the area.

At the head of the throng was a familiar pixie, riding atop the head of the largest of the creatures. A wide grin streaked across her face as her hands clenched the creature's midnight-blue fur. It ran with both hands and feet, its spindly arms and legs working overtime as Blossom pointed straight ahead and whooped wildly.

"Onward, Blueboy!" Blossom cheered, her wings fluttering wildly and propelling them even faster. It chittered loudly, and the other blue balls of fluff joined the chorus.

Malek stared after Blossom, who was already disappearing around a corner. He heard more shouts from other unsuspecting dwarves, but Malek simply shook his head in disbelief. The pixie appeared to be having the time of her life. She'd already won over whatever those strange creatures were. He hoped she'd have some insight to share with them soon.

Malek turned toward a woman who was still standing nearby. "Were those cave trolls?"

"Aye," she muttered and shook her head. "The world's gone mad. Never seen so many of them at one time and without their glamour no less. Raniel is going to have a fit."

Malek's brow furrowed. "Who's Raniel?"

The woman looked up at him as though he were daft. "Raniel Lorekeeper, head archivist and councilwoman."

Malek frowned at the familiar name and looked down the street again. Raniel Lorekeeper was the name he'd been given to contact for information about the dwarven artifact used to control the portal. Balkin, Sabine's Beastman, had indicated it had been in her family's possession since the portal was sealed. It appeared he now had more than one reason to seek out this Raniel.

He nodded at the woman and said his good-byes, then headed back toward the Faerie embassy where Sabine was waiting.

Chapter Sixteen

Sabine sat on her bed with Rika, tracing the edge of her new wings. Evelyn was going to stop by in the next day or two, but Sabine doubted the widow would have much of a mindset to discuss the future. At least Dagmar had explained she had options and wouldn't be out on the streets.

"Tell me if this hurts you," Sabine said, pressing against Rika's skin where her wings emerged.

Rika giggled, her wings twitching slightly. "It tickles."

Sabine smiled and relaxed her eyesight, using a trace of her power to detect magical enchantments. From everything she'd seen so far, the wings were definitely a physical part of Rika. She wasn't sure the extent of the transformation though.

Sabine lightly ran her hand along the main vein of Rika's wings. Some of the iridescent scales brushed off, coating Sabine's palm with a glittering effect. "Can you feel that?"

"Yes, but it doesn't hurt."

Sabine frowned in concern. She didn't want to cause Rika pain, but she needed to understand the extent of the seer's connection to these wings. "I'd like to make a small cut on one of the veins. I won't do it on a main vein, but one of the smaller ones. You may feel a bit of pain."

Rika looked over her shoulder at Sabine. Her brows furrowed as she asked, "How much pain?"

"I don't know," Sabine admitted, wanting to be completely honest. "If you'd rather I wait until Blossom gets back, she has more experience with wings. I've doctored a few pixies, and the smaller injuries don't seem to give them much trouble. We need to know whether the transformation is complete or if there's any part that's illusion magic. For that, I'll need to make a small cut."

Rika bit her lip and turned back around to face the wall. "I trust you."

Sabine pulled her knife from the sheath on her thigh. With as much care as possible, Sabine bent down and made a small nick on a vein at the bottom of Rika's wing. Blood welled to the surface, and Rika inhaled sharply.

Sabine stared at the blood in surprise. She quickly pricked her finger and pressed it against Rika's injury. She breathed over it, using a trace of magic to seal the wound. A pinprick of pain pierced Sabine's back, and she exhaled slowly, accepting the pain on Rika's behalf. It wasn't healing in the traditional sense, but she'd at least stopped the bleeding.

Sabine sat back, completely at a loss on how to remove Rika's wings. They couldn't even be cut off without causing her intense pain or killing her.

Rika turned around. "Is it bad?"

Sabine hesitated. "It's just not what I was expecting. When pixies break their wings, they don't bleed. Their veins are hollow. When they're extremely young or their wings are first forming, they're filled with blood. Yours are fully formed, but it bled when I nicked the vein."

Rika frowned. "What does that mean?"

Sabine blew out a breath. "It means they're part of you, just like an arm or a leg. They've made you more fragile than you normally are, and for a human, that's not a good thing. We're going to need to make this a priority and possibly restrict your movements while we're here. I'd rather you not go out on your own until I can figure this out."

"But you can fix it?" Rika asked, hope shining in her eyes.

Sabine reached over and placed her hand on top of Rika's. "I'm going to do everything within my power to correct it. I'll start with Blossom and the flowers she used for the transformation. We're also going to visit the archives tomorrow. Bane suggested we look there for information about his situation, but they may have records that will help you too. If that doesn't work, I'll reach out to Balkin and ask him to check there. His people have knowledge that isn't known outside of Faerie, especially because they were created with transformation magic."

Before Rika could comment, a knock at the door interrupted them. Sabine gestured for Rika to cover herself in case it was anyone other than Dagmar.

Once Rika had pulled her shirt back on, Sabine called, "Come in."

Dagmar poked her head in the door and said, "It's just me. Um, there's another delivery for you. My cousins and I moved all the other packages into one of the empty bedrooms like you asked, but I wasn't sure what to do with this one. It didn't arrive in the same way."

Sabine sheathed her knife and stood. "It wasn't brought here using Faerie's magic?"

Dagmar shook her head. "No, it's from Razadon. Er, well, the delivery person is from Razadon. I recognized the guild seal on the box. I think you might want to take a look. It looks pretty official. He has an armed escort and everything. The guards are keeping an eye on them outside."

"Go ahead and have the messenger wait in the main room. The armed escort will need to wait outside. I'll be out in a moment."

Dagmar nodded and ran back out of the room. Sabine helped Rika fasten the bindings on her shirt around her wings. Faerie had cleverly crafted several clothing items for Rika, which had been left in one of the spare bedrooms. The memories Sabine had shared had made an impression on Faerie. It seemed to have developed a fondness for the young seer.

"Should we wait for Malek before going out there?" Rika asked, fluttering her wings to make sure the shirt wasn't too tight.

"I'm not sure how long he'll be," Sabine said and tied the last binding. "If it's an official messenger, I'll need to address it sooner rather than later."

Sabine motioned for Rika to follow her, and they headed toward the main room.

A middle-aged dwarf was standing in the center of the room, staring slack-jawed at his surroundings. In his arms was a large box wrapped with dark paper and a red ribbon fastened to the top.

Malek had apparently arrived at the same time and was standing in front of the newcomer with his arms crossed over his chest. A bottle of wine and a small box was sitting on a nearby table, but Sabine didn't think the dwarf had brought those items.

Malek glanced at her, his eyes warming at the sight. She gave him a small smile in greeting before focusing on the dwarf.

His eyes rounded at the sight of Sabine, and he bowed low. "Ah, er, it's a pleasure to make yer acquaintance, Your Highness. The name's Opus Silverthread, Official Vault-keeper and representative fer the Tradesman Guild."

Sabine tilted her head in greeting. "Well met, Opus Silverthread. How may I be of assistance?"

Opus's mouth dropped open and clamped shut again, his face turning bright red.

Dagmar snickered and then whispered to him, "I had the same reaction, but she's nice. She won't hang you by your toes or turn you into a wooden statue."

Sabine blinked at Dagmar. Gods. Was that truly what they thought she might do? Malek's mouth twitched in a smile, and he covered it with a not-so-discreet cough.

Dagmar grinned at Sabine and said, "The Tradesmen Guild handles the most important deliveries."

"Ah, er, right," Opus stammered, his face turning an even brighter shade. He pulled out a note, unrolled it, and slowly read. "I bring greetings and salu-saluta-salutations from the Lord of the Underworld. He's asked our guild to make haste to deliver this gift. He further extends an invitation to visit him at yer earliest opportunity to celebrate yer cor-coron-coronation."

Malek's mirth faded almost immediately. Sabine swallowed and inclined her head. She hadn't anticipated receiving such a formal invitation to visit the underworld. Before she could gesture for Dagmar to take the gift, Malek accepted the box and placed it on a nearby table.

"I'll be sure to reach out to him directly with my reply," Sabine said, refusing to indicate either way whether she'd accept the demon's invitation. Opus hesitated, clearly not expecting such an answer. When Sabine said nothing more and Malek gestured toward the door, the dwarf swallowed and bobbed his head.

"Right. I'll, ah, let my guild master know the trade's been completed." Opus bowed again and hastily retreated from the room.

Malek shut the door and turned around, eyeing the box with suspicion. "Are you going to open it?"

"Yes," Sabine said, unsure what sort of gift Bane and Dax's father would give her. She walked to the table, studying the box. "I won't be able to respond until I speak with Bane, but my mother would occasionally receive living creatures from the underworld. I'd rather not allow something to die because I didn't open it right away."

She slid the ribbon off the box and opened the lid, staring at the contents in shock. One of the most striking silver chokers she'd ever seen lay nestled inside. Dozens of priceless red and black gems, mined from deep within the underworld, had been affixed to the silver netting. She reached inside the box and lifted it out, marveling at the design. It was a little ostentatious but undeniably beautiful.

It was similar to a gorget, offering a layer of protection over the wearer's neck. However, it was impossibly delicate in appearance, with hundreds of individual links connected together. It draped downward, giving it the illusion of movement similar to a waterfall. A tingle of magic coated her fingers, and Sabine realized the metal had been infused with some protective magical component.

Dagmar's eyes widened. "Ohhh. I recognize that design. It was a collaboration between the Jewelcrafter and Armorer Guilds. They wanted something that was as strong as armor, but it could still be worn as jewelry. They even had Dolan Ironside from the Weaponsmith Guild test it out. Everyone wondered why the demon king wanted it made. They thought he might take a new queen."

Rika peered inside the box. "There's more in here."

Malek reached inside and withdrew matching wristbands and even a silver dagger with a jeweled hilt. He placed the items on the table and narrowed his eyes. "Is this a typical gift for a new Faerie queen?"

Sabine frowned. It was one thing to receive a gift to celebrate her coronation or to make inroads for a potential alliance, but this seemed a little excessive given the circumstances. "I don't know. Gifts are usually presented when the new Unseelie ruler visits a particular kingdom for the first time, not when they're at another location. I'll have to complete another ritual in the underworld, and some sort of token is usually presented afterward."

Rika picked up one of the bracelets and placed it over her wrist. "I bet Bane would know."

"I don't know much about his father," Sabine admitted with a frown. "He's been ruling the underworld for centuries, but I've never met him. My mother didn't speak much about him, and she only went there maybe once every hundred years."

Malek arched his brow. "Neither Bane nor Dax told you about him?"

Sabine shook her head and placed the jeweled gorget back in the box. There was a rolled parchment in the bottom, and she picked it up. "No. They rarely spoke of their time in the underworld."

Dagmar bit her lip, her gaze darting back and forth between them. "Do you think you'll go to the underworld?"

Sabine smiled at the dwarf. "Eventually, yes. Normally, I'm not recognized as queen in each dominion until I've visited there. The only exception is the merfolk's home because it's mostly inaccessible." Her smile faded. "That's why this gift is so strange. He shouldn't be recognizing me as queen yet."

"Maybe he gave it to you because of Bane," Rika suggested, admiring the wristbands. "I mean, you named his son your protector and allow him to stay on the surface."

"Perhaps," Sabine murmured, but she wasn't sure about

that. Demons didn't put the same emphasis on familial ties compared to the dwarves.

Sabine unwound the red ribbon tied to the parchment and broke the seal. A waft of sulfur tickled her nose as she unrolled the note, the familiarity of it making her heart clench. It was Dax. A trace of his power had been used to seal the message and ensure she was the one who read it.

My dearest Sabin'theoria,

Rumors of your beauty and charm have reached me even in the darkest recesses of the underworld. Dax'than has spoken of you and looks forward to your arrival. I also eagerly await your journey to my domain so I might bestow even greater treasures upon you. Until then, may these gifts keep you in good health and serve as a reminder of my deepest affection.

Yours,

Kal'thorz Versed

Sabine read the name at the bottom of the note, and a sharp wave of power suddenly rose. It wrapped around her, the heated demonic power sliding under her clothing and caressing her skin with far too much intimacy.

"*Cesare!*" she shouted, sending out a burst of power through her markings. Her skin flared brightly, destroying the last trace of demonic magic touching her. The deep sound of laughter filled the room, sending a cold chill through Sabine.

"Salt. Now!" Malek ordered Dagmar.

The dwarf's eyes widened, and she ran toward the servants' quarters.

Malek snatched the note away from Sabine. He ripped off his warding medallion, and flames erupted from his hand. He tossed the burning note onto the floor and grabbed Sabine's arms, scanning her over. "Are you all right? What did he do to you?"

Sabine pushed down the wave of nausea and stared at the ash. "Games. He's playing games. He used Dax's blood to seal the message and hide the spell. I didn't detect the intent until I read his name."

She swallowed, shaking from the expenditure of power and another more disturbing realization. "I know Dax is back in the underworld, but I think he may be in trouble. For all his flaws, he wouldn't have allowed anyone to use that sort of spell on me. He's far too possessive."

Malek frowned, glanced toward the servants' area, and quickly refastened the warding medallion around his neck. Dagmar came running back a moment later, carrying a small bowl with salt. She skidded to a stop, looking around for the note.

Malek took the bowl and scattered the salt over the ashes, removing any trace of the magic that might remain. Sabine leaned against the table, trying to calm her racing heart.

Dagmar wrinkled her nose. "Demons are always bad news."

Sabine shook her head. "Not always. They're simply different. They only respect power, in any form. The spell was designed to test my mettle."

"Did you pass?" Rika asked, her wings twitching slightly.

"Yes," Sabine said with a sigh. "Unfortunately, that means he'll try again. I'm afraid you can expect more gifts in the coming days, Dagmar."

Dagmar wrinkled her nose again. "I'll keep an eye out and put them aside for you in a separate spot. In the meantime, I'll clean this up and get you guys a meal. My cousins have been cooking up a storm for you. I left some refreshments on the side table if you want anything in the meantime."

She headed out of the room with her red braids swinging. Malek began putting all the gifts back into the box. Rika handed him the bracelet she'd been holding and asked, "What are you going to do with these?"

"I'll keep them and use them whenever it's appropriate," Sabine said with a shrug. "They aren't enchanted with any malicious magic. Whatever his intentions, I don't believe he wants to harm me. He simply wants to test his will against mine. It's the way of the demons."

Malek closed the box and said, "I think you give them too much credit. If you fail one of these so-called tests, what do you think would happen?"

Sabine frowned and looked away. He was right, but the relationship between the Unseelie Fae and demons went back for thousands of years. If it weren't for the demon's threat, the Seelie would have claimed victory over the Unseelie a long time ago. She needed them.

Sabine walked over to the sideboard. She poured herself a glass of wine, her hands shaking slightly. Sabine inhaled and took a sip of the wine, but it did little to steady her nerves. Rika joined her and fixed herself a small snack from the basket of fruit sitting nearby.

Malek approached Sabine, lifted her hair, and placed it over her shoulder to expose her neck. His hands encircled her waist as he drew her against him. He pressed a soft kiss against her neck and murmured, "I won't allow anything to happen to you."

Rika darted a glance at them before turning back to her food, but Sabine hadn't missed the small smile on her face.

Sabine put down her glass and leaned against Malek, needing the support he offered. He helped steady her more than any wine. "I didn't get the chance to ask you how things went tonight with Hargrim."

Malek's hands tightened on her waist. "Better than I hoped, worse than I expected."

Sabine turned around to face him, searching his expression. "What happened?"

Malek's jaw worked, and he darted another glance toward the servants' quarters. "We need to talk privately."

Rika paused. "Should I leave?"

Malek shook his head. "No, you can stay. I was referring more to our dwarven friends."

Sabine frowned, immediately concerned. She walked to a nearby crystal panel and placed her hand against it, mentally asking Faerie to temporarily seal off the main room. A shimmer of light filled the doorway leading to the servants' quarters. Faerie had created a magical door, preventing anyone from entering without her leave.

Malek's eyebrows rose. "Impressive."

She picked up her wine and sat on the nearby couch. "It has its uses. What did Hargrim say?"

Malek sat beside her and said, "Before we get into that, I was intercepted by a runner outside your embassy. Astrid used one of the lesser known exits to dispatch a messenger and avoid the Wild Hunt. They managed to get our warning to Levin, and the ship's already set sail. Once it's safe for us to leave, we can meet up with them in one of the northern port cities or in the Sky Cities."

Sabine swallowed. It was harder than she'd expected to abandon Esmelle. The part-dryad witch had been like a sister to her for over ten years. "You're sure we can find them?"

Malek reached over and took Sabine's hand. "Levin and I put together a system for communication years ago. There are certain people he'll leave messages with so we can locate them. Levin cares about Esme a great deal. He won't let anything happen to her."

Sabine nodded. "All right. Tell me about Hargrim."

Malek's expression turned grim. "He's agreed to vote in Bane's favor in exchange for a dragon scale."

Sabine blanched. "He knows what you are?"

"Suspects, yes," Malek replied, his jaw hardening. "I can't agree to his terms, Sabine."

"Bane's going to die if we don't help him," Rika said with a frown. "Does it hurt a lot to take off one of your scales?"

Malek shook his head. "That's not the issue. A dragon scale acts like a debt marker. He can call it in at any time, and I will be forced to answer his call. There won't be any negotiation on the terms. He will ask, and I will have to do as he instructs, no matter how terrible the cost. If he ordered you killed, Rika, I would have to obey him."

Rika's eyes widened. "That's terrible."

Sabine stood quickly and walked back to the sideboard. She put her goblet down and pressed her hands against the table. Squeezing her eyes shut, she tried to tamp down on the fear that had been threatening to drown her since they arrived. Without the necessary votes, she couldn't hope to save Bane.

She knew Malek didn't understand her relationship with Bane. But Bane, Esmelle, and even Dax had been her family for over ten years. They'd taught her how to survive in a human city, how to protect herself without relying on magic, how to temper her power, and how to find a sliver of happiness when her family wanted her dead. She owed them everything.

Malek was right to refuse, even if it broke her heart in the process. She stared down at the table, wondering if Hargrim had made such an outlandish request for another reason. If he suspected Malek of being a dragon, he should have reported such a thing to the rest of the council. Instead, he'd allowed Malek to return to her.

"The debt isn't yours to fulfill, Malek," Sabine said,

turning around to face Malek again. "Bane is my responsibility, and I need to negotiate the terms with Hargrim myself. I didn't consider all the ramifications or how he might perceive such a request. I believe you may have presented it as a favor on your behalf, not mine."

"You're right. I mentioned I was the one asking, not you," Malek murmured, drumming his fingers on the arm of the couch. "He was testing boundaries and our relationship to determine who was in a position of power."

Sabine nodded. "It makes sense."

"I don't understand," Rika said, darting her gaze back and forth between them. "He made the offer knowing you wouldn't accept it?"

"I would accept it if I was subservient to Sabine and she ordered me to do so," Malek said, walking over to retrieve the bottle of wine Sabine had noticed earlier. He brought it to her, leaving the other box on the table. "He asked me to give this to you, along with his well wishes."

Sabine took the bottle, her eyes widening at the label. "It's my family's wine."

Malek's brow furrowed. "What?"

Sabine traced the edge of the label, reading the familiar name. The bottle had been sealed with magic, and only someone from her family line could open it. "Theoria. She was Lachlina and Vestior's daughter. When the Unseelie split from the rest of the Fae and sought refuge among the demons and dwarves, Theoria left this bottle for her descendants so we might always remember our origins."

"Why would Hargrim have it?" Malek asked with a frown. "He said he knew your mother, but if it's this important to your family, why wasn't it left here in the embassy?"

Sabine shook her head. "I don't know. I'd always thought it would have been kept in our home in Faerie. My mother must have trusted him a great deal if she left this in his care."

"Is it safe?" Rika asked, taking a step toward them.

Sabine nodded. "To me, yes. Not to anyone else. It's not meant to be drank like ordinary wine. A sip is all that's required to access the power and reconnect with my bloodline. I never would have thought to have looked for it here."

Malek placed his hand over hers. "We don't know how this will affect you. Maybe you should wait until you're stronger."

Sabine hesitated, understanding his warning came from a place of concern. This bottle had the power to change everything. She had to take advantage of it while she still had the chance.

"Normally, I would agree with you," Sabine said, placing the bottle on the table. "But this is something I need to do. It can't wait even a few hours."

"Will you explain it to me?"

She nodded. "If you hadn't helped me earlier, I would have passed out after moving that obelisk. I also wouldn't have been in any condition to fight off the trivial spell infused in Kal'thorz's note. He was playing with me, and I nearly succumbed to it. I can't afford to take any more of your magic, nor do I have the luxury of time in allowing my magic to recharge itself naturally. We don't know when the next threat is going to make itself known, and we all need to be prepared for it."

Malek considered her for a long time and then nodded. "All right. Is there anything you need us to do?"

Sabine frowned, trying to remember everything her mother and tutors had told her about the family wine. There were other such gifts, but many of them were back in Faerie or secreted away in other locations. Each had a way of connecting her with her family's power. "With just us here, I should be safe enough. I'm going to remove the barrier preventing Dagmar from coming back. This shouldn't take long, but I may slip into memories in the same way Faerie wine affects me."

Rika bent down to peer into the bottle. "It looks like regular wine."

"It's designed to appear that way," Sabine said with a smile and removed the magical doorway. "We often hide powerful magic in seemingly mundane objects. It helps to safeguard their secrets from those who would try to steal them."

Infusing her touch with a trace of magic, she removed the cork. A sharp wind filled the room, carrying along with it the smell of the forest. Sabine pricked her finger and allowed a drop of her blood to mingle with the wine. The bottle glowed briefly before dimming again.

Taking a deep breath, she lifted the bottle to her lips and then took a sip of the wine. It was rich and earthy, speaking to the most ancient part of her memories carried through her bloodline and locked within her magic. This was her heritage and the source of her power.

Light and color exploded around her. Music filled her ears, distorting her senses and touching her soul. Warmth filled her and her skin glowed as the wind became even stronger around her. It whipped through her hair like fingers, their touch achingly familiar and even loving. She felt her mother's embrace, her grandmother's, and even her grandmother's mother's. Generations of women and their power poured over her, and Sabine's eyes filled with tears as their minds touched hers.

Finally, Theoria embraced her as well. The demigoddess moved her power through Sabine and along her skin. Her touch was no less familiar, but there was a moment of hesitation when her magic touched the chalice mark on Sabine's wrist. A sharp slash of pain ratcheted through Sabine as though Theoria was trying to remove the mark. Sabine cried out, nearly dropping the bottle.

Malek took a step toward her and asked, "Are you hurt?"

Sabine shook her head and put the bottle back on the table with shaking hands. "No. It… It was a true gift, Malek. I'm not sure I can explain, but I believe that was the only gift my mother ever gave me without any conditions attached. I felt… Theoria was there. She was the first of my family's line and Lachlina's daughter."

"Did she hurt you?" Malek asked, his eyes filled with concern. "You cried out in pain."

Sabine looked down at the mark and frowned. It didn't appear any different, but something had happened. "I don't think it was intentional. She reacted to the mark somehow. I believe she was angry about it."

"But she's not alive," Rika stated, shaking her head. "How can you feel her?"

Sabine hesitated, unsure how to explain to a human. "No, she's not alive. As Fae, we're not just protectors of the land. We're also keepers of our family's knowledge and magic. That's why bloodlines are so important to us. Each Fae has the ability to tap into aspects of their origins, and that's the source of our power."

Malek took Sabine's hand and ran his thumb across the chalice mark. "You don't know why she was angry?"

Sabine shook her head. "No. I felt her essence and her power, but it's not possible to communicate with someone once they've faded from this realm."

Malek cupped her face, searching her expression. "The shadows under your eyes are gone. How do you feel?"

"Much stronger," Sabine said with a smile. The magic had renewed her more than she'd expected. She couldn't remember the last time she'd felt this refreshed.

Rika cocked her head and asked, "What happens when the bottle's empty?"

Sabine turned and corked the bottle, using a tiny amount

of magic to seal it. "Once I return to Faerie, I'll craft my own wine and infuse part of it with this one for the next generation. Each person who drinks from the bottle must contribute their memories to continue the family line."

"What should we do with it?" Malek asked, gesturing at the bottle. "I'm assuming you don't want to return it to Hargrim."

She hesitated. "I'm not sure where it would be safe. It speaks well of Hargrim that he kept it safe this long. Perhaps my mother had her reason for entrusting it to him. I suppose we can keep it in my bedroom for now and decide later. It may not be safe to travel with it."

Malek walked to the smaller box Sabine had noticed earlier. He offered it to her and said, "I saw these in a shop earlier and thought you might like them."

Touched by his thoughtfulness, Sabine smiled at him and accepted the wrapped package. She untied it and opened the wooden box, her breath hitching at the sight of remarkable hairpins. She'd lost her previous ones when they'd been forced to flee Akros, but these were even more beautiful.

"Oh, Malek," Sabine murmured, placing the box on the table. She picked up one with a leaf carving and ran her fingers along the sparkling green crystal. "They're exquisite. I've never seen ones with power crystals in them."

Rika's eyes widened. "They're so pretty."

Malek reached over and unscrewed the top of the hairpin, removing the leaf to expose hollow tubing. "They're designed to hold poison." He pointed at a small button that was barely noticeable on the side. "The poison dispenser is here."

Sabine stared at the pins, remembering when Dax had given her the set she'd lost. She'd been angry with him for intentionally manipulating another situation to his advantage. She'd stormed out of the tavern and hadn't spoken to him for days until Javyn brought the gift. Dax never apologized outright, and the gifts he had provided were a poor substitute. She usually relented, knowing it was his way of reaching out to her.

Emotion choked her, and she carefully returned the pin to its box before turning to face the man who had stolen her heart. She wrapped her arms around his neck and kissed him, sending a strong surge of magic over him. He pulled her closer, his hands running down her back in a gentle caress.

"They're beautiful, Malek," she whispered, looking up into his blue eyes. It was impossible to put into words how she felt about such a gift. There had been no anger, no other reason than he'd walked past a shop and thought about her.

Malek's gaze softened. "I noticed you weren't able to wear your weapons easily in this dress. It's not as effective as your knives and you'll need some poison, but I figured Blossom could help with that."

She swallowed, trying to control her emotions. Gods. How was she ever going to let this dragon go? Every time she turned around, he did or said something that made her fall even more in love with him. It would destroy something inside her to lose him, but she couldn't hold on to a dragon. If there was one thing that would divide her people and force them to unite against her, it would be taking a dragon for a consort.

"Hey," Malek murmured, lifting her chin to look into her eyes. "What's wrong?"

She shook her head, unable to speak the words that would fracture this moment. Bane's warning about keeping her distance flitted through her mind, but she pushed it aside. It was foolish, but she couldn't let Malek go yet. They wouldn't have forever, but she wasn't willing to tarnish the precious time they had left.

"It's a wonderful gift," she said, pressing her hands against his chest. She kissed him lightly. "And you are a wonderful man."

Footsteps approached, and Sabine turned and saw Dagmar entering the room with two of her cousins. Each carried a large tray filled with a selection of foods.

Dagmar grinned at them. "I hope you guys are ready for a feast!"

Sabine managed a smile, even if her heart was breaking inside. "It looks and smells wonderful."

Malek took her hand and lifted it, then pressed a kiss against her knuckles. "I have a feeling tomorrow's going to be a busy day. Why don't we table the more serious discussions until then? For now, let's eat and try to relax."

Sabine nodded. "I think that's a good plan."

Chapter Seventeen

Sabine opened her eyes and stared at the ceiling in the darkened room. She turned her head to find Malek sleeping peacefully beside her. A lock of inky dark hair fell over his face, marring his strong features and making them appear softer. Gods. He was beautiful. Unable to resist, she reached over and brushed his hair away from his face. She trailed her fingers across the rough stubble along his jaw, but he didn't stir.

A rustling sound caught her attention and she sat up. Sabine swept her gaze across the room, sensing something wasn't right. There was a heaviness in the air, a thick coating of some sort of magic she couldn't identify. She automatically reached for her knives on the small bedside table.

"Malek?" she whispered, but he didn't respond. He still hadn't moved, which wasn't like him. Malek was always on alert, quick to react to even the slightest hint of danger.

Sabine reached for him through their bond, but he was completely silent. He was still connected to her, but their bond had somehow been muted. She reached over and tried to jostle him awake, calling his name a little louder. He grunted and then resumed his deep breathing.

Her heart pounded in her chest, and she equipped her weapons by feel alone. Whatever magic was at work wanted him to remain sleeping. Sabine slid out of bed and reached for her robe. She quickly pulled it on and tied the sash around her waist. Faerie wouldn't have allowed anyone to enter without her permission unless they intended her no harm. But unfamiliar magic was always suspect, and she'd learned at an early age the most dangerous monsters didn't obey the rules.

Sliding one of the knives from its sheath, she crept toward the door. The faint sound of music reached her ears, coming from somewhere deeper in the embassy. Sabine pushed open the door, the lights automatically adjusting their intensity to account for her nighttime vision.

She moved down the hall, her bare footsteps completely silent on the tile. Pausing at Rika's door, Sabine listened but heard no sound from within. She cracked it open and found Rika sprawled on her stomach, her blankets askew and wings flattened against her back. Her eyes were closed and her breathing deep and regular, indicating the young seer was fast asleep. Blossom was nowhere to be seen. Sabine closed the door and continued to follow the sounds of the music.

It was growing louder now, and she could make out the clear tones of crystalline bells, a flute, and even a harp. The melody was familiar, perhaps something she'd heard played in the various Faerie courts of her youth. She rejected that thought almost immediately. It didn't feel right. She knew that song somehow, but the memory eluded her.

Sabine stopped outside a closed door, hearing the music playing from within. With a pounding heart, she tightened her grip on her knife and pushed open the door.

A cloaked figure was standing with his back toward her,

studying something on a table. A wave of power emanated from him, a harsh and bitter sort of magic almost too complex for her to comprehend. There were some similarities to her power, but she felt like an awkward and clumsy child beside a master.

"The Unseelie claim no masters," a harsh and brittle mental voice intoned.

Sabine's breath hitched, her palms growing damp as she lowered her knife. Of all the possibilities, she hadn't considered meeting him again—and especially not here.

"Huntsman," she said, naming him and watching as he turned around to regard her with glowing red eyes. His hands were skeletal in nature, as though the flesh had long since been seared from his hands. In his hands, she saw her fate. In his eyes, she saw her death.

"I seek not your death this night."

She didn't answer, unable to formulate a coherent thought. He wouldn't have come here unless he wanted something, and she had nothing to offer him except her life.

"I bring you a gift and a warning, Young Queen."

Sabine swallowed. Gifts were always suspect, but she chose to focus on the other part of his statement. "What warning?"

"The Wild Hunt waits for you beyond Razadon's gate. Step foot onto their mountain path, and your life shall be forfeit, whether it be a day, month, or century. Another seeks to claim your magic."

Sabine squeezed her eyes shut and took a steadying breath. If she couldn't walk along the mountain path, she would be forced to live out the rest of her days in Razadon. The Huntsman had offered an escape before, and she had to cling to hope of another possibility.

She opened her eyes and asked, "Will the Wild Hunt pursue me if I leave Razadon through other means?"

She sensed a flicker of approval from the Huntsman, but

he didn't respond to her question. Instead, he turned away and approached the wall on the far side of the room. With a wave of his skeletal hand, a portal similar to the one she'd used to traverse the in-between in Akros slid open. He couldn't be suggesting she follow him.

Sabine stared after him for a moment and then shook her head, rejecting the absurdity of the thought. A thousand unanswered questions flitted through her mind. Everyone feared the Huntsman and especially the Wild Hunt, including her. She knew how easily he could end her life, but he'd chosen to aid her three times now. She didn't understand why.

The Huntsman paused at the portal, turning to stare at her with his glowing red eyes. They seemed to gaze right through her, right down to the depths of her soul.

"In time, daughter." He touched his mind to hers, the fragile thought as fleeting as a spiderweb, and as easily broken.

A moment later, he stepped through the portal and was gone. The music began playing again, and Sabine turned to stare at a small music box on the table. Dagmar had stacked other gifts on the opposite side of the room, but this item had been placed separately for a reason.

She sheathed her knife, finding it pointless. The Huntsman didn't concern himself with mundane weapons, having given up his mortal existence thousands of years earlier.

Sabine walked to the music box and picked it up, staring at the emblem of a golden crown in wonder. Small sapphires had been affixed into it, each sparkling with their own light. They pulsed in time with the music, almost hypnotizing her.

"I don't understand," Sabine whispered, picking up the music box and cradling it in her hands. "Why did you come to me? Why would you give this to me?"

The music continued to play, but it didn't provide her

with any answers. The melody was strangely soothing, and she continued to stare at the twinkling gemstones, trying to remember how she knew its song.

"Sabine?" Malek asked from behind her.

Sabine turned and found him standing in the doorway, his expression concerned. He crossed the room toward her and asked, "Are you all right, sweetheart? I didn't hear you get up."

She nodded, not wanting to tell him he'd been in an enchanted slumber. It would only worry him, and it wasn't possible to prevent such a thing from happening again. She didn't need to give him more reasons to encourage her to join him in the Sky Cities.

Malek gestured at the music box. "That's pretty. What is it?"

"I believe it's a coronation gift," she said quietly, running her fingers along the gems. She closed the box, quieting the music, and placed it back on the table.

"Hey," Malek said, taking a step closer to her. "What's wrong?"

Sabine didn't answer right away. Part of her wanted to confide in him, but a tiny voice inside her warned she was becoming too dependent upon him. Her reaction to his gift earlier was proof enough.

There wasn't anyone else she could talk to about what had happened. Blossom hadn't yet returned, Rika was too young and inexperienced, Bane was locked up, Dax was trapped in the underworld, and Balkin was still in Faerie. Malek had proven himself dozens of times, but something still held her back. Perhaps it was Bane's earlier warning or the frightening realization she'd fallen in love with Malek.

Malek reached over and took her hand. "I won't push if you don't want to tell me, but I'd like to help."

Sabine took a shaky breath and decided to follow her

heart. Lifting her head to meet his gaze, she said, "The Huntsman came to see me."

Malek stared at her in shock. "The Wild Hunt was here? Tonight? Are you all right?"

"I'm fine. It was just the Huntsman, not the Hunt," Sabine said and gestured toward the music box. "He brought me a gift and a warning."

Malek's brow furrowed. He glanced at the music box before meeting her eyes again. "What was the warning?"

"If I step foot onto the mountain path outside of Razadon, my life will be forfeit."

Malek frowned. "We'd already assumed as much."

She nodded. "Yes, but he led me to believe he would look the other way if I left in another manner. Whatever agreement was forged between the Huntsman and the person who summoned him gave him another loophole to exploit."

Malek paused, considering her for a long time. "Then you're right about the Huntsman having some affection for you. Either that, or he isn't fond of whomever summoned him. What are you thinking?"

Sabine hesitated, her gaze drifting to the wall where the Huntsman had disappeared. "When I spoke with Bane earlier, he wanted me to locate one of the doorways to the underworld. He said I could use our bond to find it while he was still alive. If something happens to Bane and I can't save him in time, he wants me to go to Dax and bind him to me."

"You can't be serious," Malek said, gaping at her. He turned away and paced the length of the guest room. "If you go down there, you're going to be putting yourself at even more risk. At least you have potential allies in Razadon, even if they keep challenging you. The demons will continue to push until you break. You said your mother used to travel to Razadon somewhat frequently, but she only went to the underworld once a century. There's a reason for that, Sabine. Going there will change you."

"I can't stay here forever," Sabine said, curling her hands into fists in frustration. "Like it or not, the demons are Unseelie allies, and Dax is there. I'm not planning on staying in the underworld forever. There are exits all over the world through their tunnels. I simply can't step foot onto the mountain path, but I can walk out through any of their doorways."

"Do you know where these exits are? Do you have any allies in the underworld other than Dax?" Malek snapped, his eyes flashing with barely restrained emotion. "If he's being held down there in less-than-pleasant circumstances, he may not be able to help you. What then, Sabine? I'll be even more crippled down there than I am here. I won't be able to protect you. I can't fight hundreds of demons and keep you safe at the same time."

"I can stand on my own if I must," Sabine said, taking a step toward him. "I don't *need* you to protect me, Malek."

"Don't you?" he asked, arching his brow. "You almost passed out earlier and then succumbed to a demon's spell. Other than a human girl with negligible talent for seeing through glamour and a pixie who's more interested in playing with cave trolls, I don't see anyone else trying to help you survive, Sabine. Face it. You're alone in this world, and for some reason, you keep slapping away the one person who keeps holding out their hand to help you."

She turned away, the truth of his words cutting her to the quick. She wanted more than anything to fall into his arms and embrace the protection he offered, but she couldn't. If she was ever going to stand on her own, she needed to find her way without his help. "Maybe it would be better if you left."

Malek froze. "What?"

"It might be for the best if you left Razadon, Malek. I need to do this on my own, without your protection," Sabine said and turned away, her heart shattering into a million pieces with every step she took toward the door.

Malek reached for her hand, but she jerked away from him and backpedaled. If he touched her right now, her resistance would crumble.

Malek stared at her, his jaw hardening. He studied her for a long time and then a flash of surprise crossed his face. He shook his head and said, "You're scared. Not of the Wild Hunt, the demons, or even the dwarves. You're scared—of me. That's why you're trying to push me away."

Sabine stiffened, wishing she could lie or say anything to convince him he was wrong.

"I'm right, aren't I?" Malek demanded, taking a step toward her. "What the hell happened? Something changed in the last few hours."

Sabine looked away, trying desperately to blink back the tears that threatened. "It's better if you leave now, before this goes any further. You can probably catch Levin if you leave tonight."

"I'm not walking away from you, Sabine," Malek said, his tone gentle but unyielding. "I told you before, and I'll tell you again: I love you."

Sabine inhaled sharply at the sharp stab of pain that pierced her heart. Her eyes welled with tears, and she shook her head. "Don't."

Malek muttered a curse and approached her. He took her hand and pulled her gently into his arms. She stiffened against him, but he continued to hold her. "I'm not walking away from you, sweetheart. Even if I didn't love you, I still wouldn't leave you right now."

"I can't do this with you anymore, Malek," she whispered, a tear sliding down her cheek. "It'll only get harder."

"Talk to me," he said, tilting her chin up to look into her eyes. "I can't fix this if I don't know what's wrong or what started all of this."

"It was the hairpins," she said quietly, looking away again. "You keep giving me things or doing things without any expectations in return. There's no balance between us, Malek. I keep falling more into debt with you, and I don't know how to handle it."

Malek smiled and tucked her hair behind her ear. "I keep forgetting how little you know about dragons. We don't exactly have the same concept of balance as the Fae, but there are similarities. Giving gifts to someone we love is a bit different than offering them to a stranger or acquaintance."

She blinked up at him, confused by the concept. Humans gave gifts all the time without any regard for maintaining balance. They might have some slight pull toward reciprocity, but it didn't upset the balance of power between them. She'd assumed dragons were more like the Fae or other magical races in that regard.

Sabine shook her head. "I don't understand. I thought dragons hoard their treasures. You're saying giving gifts is a dragon trait?"

He chuckled. "Not exactly. We seek out beautiful, extraordinary, and priceless treasures for a reason. It fulfills something inside us, and collecting these items is more than a desire. It's a need, similar to your need to use your magic."

She frowned. If she didn't use her power regularly, her control would slip and her magic would burst like a dam holding too much water. That was a large part of the reason she'd formed an alliance with both Blossom's family and Bane, to help provide an outlet for her Seelie and Unseelie magic. If Malek had a similar need to acquire items, perhaps masquerading as a ship captain made more sense than she'd first thought.

"The trading and smuggling," she murmured, considering the possibility. "Is that why you've been so successful?"

"In part, yes," Malek replied, running his hand down her back. "Each trade increases the value of my hoard while also allowing me to try to locate the portal artifacts."

"I still don't understand how that ties into giving me gifts."

Malek took a deep breath and let out a slow exhale. "Technically, as long as I have you, I still have access to all those gifts. It's my hope you'll be mine completely one day. Then you'll be my greatest treasure."

Sabine started to pull away, but he held her even tighter. She frowned up at him and said, "I can't be yours, Malek."

He smiled and kissed her lightly. "You already are, even if you won't say the words."

"Stop it," she warned, narrowing her eyes on him. The idea she would ever agree to be part of a dragon's hoard was absurd.

He chuckled and kissed her again. "No. I love you, and I know how you feel about me."

Sabine scowled and glared up at him. "Are you purposely being obtuse?"

His smile deepened. "When you fell asleep tonight, you curled into me. Your eyes automatically find me whenever I'm in the room. You've shared things about your past that you haven't shared with Bane or Dax. You asked me to protect you in this city and keep your secrets. You've trusted me in ways you've never trusted anyone."

Sabine swallowed, knowing every word he spoke was true. "It doesn't change anything, Malek. The longer we allow this to go on between us, the harder it'll be when we need to walk away."

Malek cupped her face and said, "I meant what I said to you before. I would follow you to the ends of the world,

Sabin'theoria. I don't plan on ever letting you walk away from me, and I don't believe you want me to let you."

Sabine squeezed her eyes shut and pressed her forehead against his chest, breathing in the smell of burnt leaves that always surrounded him. Curling her fingers into his shirt, she whispered, "I won't say the words back to you, Malek. One day, this will end, no matter how I feel about you. Words have power for the Fae. It's why we can't lie. Opening myself up to you will only make it that much harder."

Malek made a noncommittal noise. "I suppose now might be a good time to tell you dragons always relish a challenge."

Despite herself, Sabine's mouth curved upward. She lifted her head and found his eyes dancing with amusement. "I'm beginning to understand why Elisa fell for your grandfather. If he had a fraction of your charm, her heart was lost the moment he set his sights on her."

Malek laughed. "Indeed. Elisa always said I took after him. I never fully appreciated the lengths he went to in order to capture her heart. I have a feeling you're going to give me even more of a challenge."

"Sabine!" a tiny voice shrieked. "The Huntsman's coming for you!"

Sabine turned to find Blossom barreling into the room, her dust tinged with red.

Sabine immediately held out her hand so Blossom could land. "Blossom? What in the world?"

Blossom crash-landed into her hand, slamming face first into her palm. She squeaked, giggled, and rolled over, blinking up at Sabine with a wonky grin.

"Walls keep moving," Blossom said and hiccupped. "Bad walls."

"You're drunk?" Sabine frowned, lifting her hand to study Blossom a little better. Her left wing was crooked, but

Blossom didn't appear to be suffering any permanent damage.

Blossom hiccupped and clamped her hand over her mouth. "Mom always said not to drink and fly."

Sabine sighed, doubting she'd get any coherent information out of the pixie. "There's a reason for those rules, Blossom. Your wing is bent. You're lucky the main vein didn't snap."

"Honeyed ale," Blossom said, her eyes fluttering shut. "So, so good. 'Twas worth it. Hadta get the cave trolls drunk. Right o' passage."

Sabine arched her brow and looked over at Malek. "Was she drunk when you saw her?"

Malek chuckled. "It's possible. She was riding one of the cave trolls like a thontin. Getting drunk with them might have been the quickest way to gain their trust. I've found it's pretty effective with the dwarves."

Blossom wrapped her arms around Sabine's thumb and started snoring.

Sabine sighed, shifting Blossom slightly so she didn't further damage her wing. "At least she's safe. I'll give her some magic when she wakes up so she can repair her wing. Unfortunately, we won't be able to find out what she's learned until she's sober."

Cradling Blossom in her hands, Sabine nodded toward the music box. "Would you mind bringing that? I'd rather not leave it in here."

Malek nodded and picked it up. Sabine turned and headed back down the hall toward the bedroom. A soft noise coming from Rika's room caught her attention, and she paused outside her door. It sounded like Rika was crying.

"I'll take Blossom if you want to check on Rika," Malek said quietly, gesturing toward the snoring pixie.

Sabine nodded. She carefully eased Blossom onto Malek's

outstretched palm before opening the door and stepping inside. Rika's room was mostly shrouded in darkness, except for the small dwarven crystal lamp glowing dimly in the corner. Rika was huddled in bed, her arms wrapped around her knees.

She sniffled and said, "I'm sorry for waking you, Sabine."

"Shh," Sabine said, crossing the room toward Rika. "I was already awake. Why don't you tell me what's wrong?"

"I don't know," she whispered, wiping her eyes. "I woke up because I thought I heard music. I tried to go back to sleep, but I can't stop thinking about everything. Everything's so different now. I miss my grandmother and my friends. It wasn't too bad at first, but now Blossom and Bane are gone too."

"Blossom came back a little while ago," Sabine said quietly. She'd been wondering when Rika would fall apart. It was a surprise she'd been strong for so long.

Sabine had done the same thing after being forced from her home. It had been easier to bury the pain rather than focus on it, but the suppressed emotion eventually had to come out. Sabine's reaction had been a little more volatile, thanks to her magic.

"I understand better than most what you're going through," Sabine said and sat on the edge of the bed beside Rika. "I went through something similar after I left Faerie. I was thrown into a new world that was far different from anything I'd experienced. My family and friends were gone, and I was left with strangers."

Rika rested her chin on her knees. "How did you deal with it?"

"Not as well as you," Sabine admitted with a trace of a smile. "I was angry, hurt, and scared. I lashed out at Bane and Dax quite a bit. Esmelle was the one who broke through and helped me realize things weren't as bad as I thought."

"How did she do that?"

Sabine smiled at the memory. "We'd been staying in a cottage outside of Akros. Bane and Dax had been trying to help me gain better control over hiding my magic so I could pass as a human. I had just finished a particularly difficult lesson with Dax. He did something that annoyed me, and I ended up throwing him through the living room wall."

Rika's eyes widened. "Dax is Bane's brother, right? You threw a demon through the wall?"

"Mmhmm," Sabine agreed, shifting so she could lounge against the headboard of Rika's bed. "I was so angry with him. I stormed out of the cottage and into the forest. Esmelle came after me. She'd been really patient with me up until that point, but I'd finally pushed her over the edge." She paused, her mouth quirking in a grin. "Dax landed in her garden and destroyed some of her plants."

Rika's mouth dropped open. "You messed up Esme's garden?"

Sabine laughed and nodded. "I did. She was furious. I think she yelled at me for twenty minutes and threatened to hand-deliver me back to the Fae if I ever touched her garden again."

"She wouldn't have really done that."

"No, but her reaction made me think about things differently," Sabine said, remembering how difficult those first few weeks had been. No one other than Sabine's mother or the Elders had ever spoken to her that way. "I left Faerie because I was in fear of my life, just like you were in danger back in Karga. I had trouble adjusting to living with Bane, Dax, and Esme, but it was then I decided to look at it as an opportunity."

"What do you mean?"

"Living with them gave me the chance to reinvent myself. I was no longer confined to the role I'd been forced into, and

I could be anyone or anything I wanted. The realization was liberating."

Rika picked at the threading on the blanket. "I don't know how I could be someone different. I can't change my appearance like you do."

Sabine smiled and lifted Rika's chin to meet her eyes. "No, but you've been living behind an illusion your entire life. You now have the opportunity to be the person you were always meant to be. You don't have to hide your abilities around us, Rika. You're a seer. You have the chance to discover what that means more than you ever could back in Karga. I believe that's part of the reason your grandmother wanted you taken out of the city."

Rika stared at Sabine, a tentative hope shining in her eyes. "Really?"

She nodded. "It's all right to be homesick, but you can't let your fears paralyze you. There's an entire world out there waiting for you. You just need to grasp ahold of it. We'll all help you."

Rika threw her arms around Sabine and hugged her. "I know I'm not supposed to thank you, but I can't help the way I feel. I'm really glad you came to Karga, Sabine."

"I am as well," Sabine murmured, returning the hug. She leaned back and brushed Rika's dark hair away from her face. "It's almost morning. Would you like to try to get some more sleep? Or we could work on trying to remove your wings. Blossom will probably sleep for another hour or two, but I'm sure she can help us after that."

Rika smiled. "I think I'll get up. Don't tell Blossom, but I don't like my wings much. They're not very comfortable for sleeping."

Sabine laughed. "I can see that. I'll let you get cleaned up and meet you in the common area in a bit."

Sabine stood and headed out of the room, closing the

door behind her. Malek was leaning against the wall, and he smiled at the sight of her.

She paused, arching her brow at him. "How long were you listening?"

"Long enough to know Rika's fortunate to have met you." He took her hand and brushed a kiss against her knuckles. "I'm feeling extremely fortunate as well."

Sabine allowed him to pull her into his arms. She leaned against his chest and listened to the beating of his heart. "Talking to Rika made me realize I'm the fortunate one. You're right that I've been trying to keep you at arm's length. I don't know what will happen in the future, but I would be foolish not to accept help when it's offered. I made that mistake at first with Dax and Bane simply because they were demons, but their differences helped make me stronger."

She lifted her head and cupped his face, looking up into the eyes of the dragon she loved. "I can't make any promises to you, Malek, but I do treasure each moment we spend together."

He smiled, leaned down, and kissed her. "Good. It's a start."

Chapter Eighteen

Sabine signed her name, rolled the parchment, and affixed her family's wax seal. After infusing it with a trace of magic to ensure it wouldn't be opened by anyone other than the intended recipient, she handed the missive to Dagmar. "Can you make sure this is delivered to Hargrim Icemail first thing this morning? I'll need his answer before the council meeting."

"Got it! I'll hand it off to our fastest runner. Hargrim doesn't usually get out of bed until after noon, but I'll make sure it's the first thing he sees," Dagmar said with a grin and headed for the door.

Malek lowered the steaming mug of tea he'd been drinking. "Exactly how much did you offer Hargrim for his vote?"

"An additional five percent on all trades between the Unseelie Fae and Razadon for the next five years," Sabine said with a sigh and sat back, rubbing her temples. "If he agrees, I'll send a note to Balkin to handle the details."

Malek let out a low whistle. "That's a pretty substantial amount. From what I've heard, your people do a significant amount of business with Razadon."

Sabine nodded. "He won't receive a better offer, and I don't have time to haggle with him. They'll execute Bane tomorrow if I can't secure the votes to get him released. Even if Hargrim agrees, we still need one more vote."

Malek handed her the parchment he'd been working on with Dagmar. "We have five other possibilities for votes: Rugara from the Stoneworker Guild, Raniel from the Archivist Guild, Hopper from the Brewmaster Guild, Dolan from the Weaponsmith Guild, and Gimly from the Steward Guild." He pointed at the last name. "It's unlikely you'll be able to secure Gimly's vote. Dagmar said his father was murdered by a demon. He thinks all demons should be eradicated."

Sabine frowned and took the list to scan it over. Gimly had been the only one she thought might be swayed, especially given Dagmar's relationship with him as the embassy's steward.

Tapping her finger on Raniel's name, Sabine said, "Raniel Lorekeeper from the Archivist Guild is probably our best bet. I might be able to offer her access to some of Faerie's archives to supplement Razadon's knowledge. It's a long shot, but I'm not sure who else we can convince in time."

Malek nodded and took a sip of his tea. "I was going to suggest her. Your Beastman gave me Raniel's name as a contact for the dwarven portal artifact. I don't know how well Balkin knows her, but any connection is better than going in blind."

Sabine looked up at him in surprise. "You believe Raniel has one of the artifacts used to seal the Dragon Portal?"

"It's possible," Malek said, putting his mug on the table. "Balkin told me it was entrusted to the Lorekeeper family. That's how they acquired their name. They've been keepers of knowledge here in Razadon for centuries."

Sabine picked up her mug and took a sip, wrinkling her

nose at the tepid tea. It had cooled while she'd been composing the request to Hargrim. Malek chuckled. He glanced around to make sure Dagmar was gone and then removed his warding medallion. He leaned over and blew on her cup until it steamed again. With a wink, he fastened the medallion around his neck once more.

Sabine laughed, amused by his antics. "That's a handy skill."

Rika's mouth dropped open. "I didn't know you could do that."

"One of the benefits in having a great deal of fire power at my disposal," he said, leaning against Sabine's writing desk.

Sabine looked at the list of names again. "When Dagmar gets back, I'll ask her to inquire about Raniel's schedule to set up a meeting. Even if she's not available until later, I'd like to visit the archives right away."

"How come?" Rika asked, lifting her head from the letters she'd been sorting. The stack of invitations for meetings and balls in her honor was higher than Sabine had expected. At least half of those invitations were from people likely working for her father. They either wanted to spy on her activities or stage an assassination attempt and secure her father's goodwill. Either way, they would all need to be dealt with.

"Bane suggested there might be something in the archives that could point to the source of the corruption and help prove he wasn't responsible," Sabine said, warming her hands with the heated mug. "I also want to see if there's any record of a magical transformation gone wrong. If Blossom can't give me more insight into what caused her illusion magic to backfire, the archives might point us in the right direction."

"Blossom's been sleeping a long time. You're sure she's okay?" Rika asked, looking at the small pot of flowers on Sabine's desk where Blossom was curled up and snoring. Her hand was flung over the side of the flowerpot, her wings twitching every so often when she had a particularly exciting dream.

"Mmhmm, but let's see if we can coax her awake. Dagmar should be back soon, and I'd like to spend as much time as possible in the archives before we have to attend the council meeting."

Reaching over, Sabine broke off a piece of her leftover breakfast honey cake and placed it next to Blossom's head. The pixie turned her nose toward the cake, sniffing the air, but her eyes didn't open.

Malek chuckled. "Must have been an exciting night last night. I've never seen her ignore a honey cake."

"Like the Fae, pixies can fall into a restorative slumber when they use too much magic. If she needed to hurry back here last night to warn me, she probably burnt through most of her power."

Sending a fortifying wave of magic over Blossom, Sabine teased, "It would be a shame if Blossom missed out on the last of the honey cake because she's sleeping."

"Honey cake? Where?" The pixie's eyes flew open, and she dove for the small piece of cake. She shoved the entire piece in her mouth and eagerly looked around the flowerpot for more. Sabine waited until she finished chewing before breaking off another piece. This one, she dipped into her herbal tea and then offered it to the small pixie.

Blossom snatched it out of her hand and shoved it into her mouth.

Sabine shook her head in exasperation and warned, "Pace yourself, Blossom. You're going to choke."

Rika giggled. "It looks like she's awake now."

"Mmhmm," Sabine agreed and gave Blossom a third smaller piece. "Once the honey hits her system, she'll be able to tell us what she learned last night."

"So, so good," Blossom said and licked her fingers. When she finished, she looked around again and picked up a few crumbs that had fallen. With a wide yawn, Blossom started to curl back up to go to sleep again, but Sabine quickly scooped her up.

"Oh, no you don't," Sabine said and sent another wave of magic over Blossom. "You bent your wing last night. You need to fix it and then we have work to do."

Blossom peered over her shoulder at her wing and squeaked. "Bumbling beetles! The wall must have jumped up and bit me!"

Sabine bit back a smile, watching as Blossom closed her eyes and formed tiny fists with her hands. She scrunched up her nose in concentration and said, "I'm ready! Hit me with whatever you've got!"

"She can heal herself?" Malek asked, leaning closer.

"Only for this type of injury," Sabine said and held her hand over Blossom's head. She sent a more substantial wave of magic over the pixie. Sabine might not be able to heal, but Blossom had the ability to repair her own minor damage—provided she had access to a strong source of magic.

Blossom's entire body glowed with a silver light. It became brighter, moving up and down her body before converging on her wings. Blossom fluttered her wings furiously, the glow becoming nearly blinding. A moment later, the light stopped abruptly and Blossom grinned.

"Good as new," she exclaimed and jumped to her feet, wiggling her wings with pride. She flew into the air and hovered in front of Sabine. "I met the cave trolls last night! They don't have wings, but they're pretty cool. Boy, they sure know how to party."

"I heard about your exploits near the market district," Sabine said, holding out her hand for Blossom to land. "Did you learn anything that might help us free Bane? Or who tried to kill us with the obelisk?"

Blossom's eyes widened, and she nodded eagerly. "Ohhh. There's a lot. I mean, all sorts of stuff is happening in Razadon. I tried to come back earlier, but Blueboy wanted to do sneak attacks on the goats. I hadn't heard of such a thing, so I naturally had to investigate."

"Naturally," Sabine said, her mouth twitching in a smile.

"The goats have been eating the plants on the mountainside, and we had to stop them because the plants have all gone wonky. But before we could do that, we found a cask of honey ale someone left in the archives. Bomblin wanted to play this drinking game that took four beetles from the archivist's laboratory—"

Sabine's brow furrowed, wondering if she'd given Blossom a little too much sugar. "What does any of this have to do with Bane?"

"It's all connected!" Blossom exclaimed, throwing her hands into the air.

Rika cocked her head and asked, "What's all connected?"

"The corruption!"

Sabine glanced up at Malek, but he appeared equally confused. "I think you need to explain."

Blossom flew down to the desk, her entire body vibrating with energy. "You know how Razadon closed their doors because of the corruption?"

When Sabine nodded, Blossom said, "We thought it was because people were dying and that's not good for business. But I heard a bunch of dwarves talking, and it sounded like it was the other way around."

Sabine regarded Blossom with surprise. "You're suggesting someone's trying to force the city leaders into sealing Razadon from outsiders? They're using the corruption to do it?"

Blossom nodded. "Yep. We didn't think about *why* the corruption happened. Bane said the dwarves were probably drunk. What if they weren't? What if it was on purpose?"

Rika stood and walked to stand next to Sabine. "Would the dwarves really do something so terrible?"

Malek muttered a curse and then said, "If it got them what they wanted, they absolutely would. I overheard a few conversations on my way back from meeting with Hargrim. People were talking about how Razadon should shut down trade permanently until they could renegotiate their place in the world. They don't believe dwarves are getting their proper due."

Rika's eyes widened. "I didn't think about it until now, but I heard similar talk when I was with the servants. Some of them weren't happy you were here, Sabine. A few others were upset because you had humans, pixies, and demons in your retinue but not dwarves. They think they're not good enough to travel the world with you."

Sabine frowned. "That's absurd. This trip wasn't planned, and I don't select my friends based on whether they're human or dwarves."

"They don't know that," Blossom said with a shrug. "Hey! I know what we should do. We should all go to the pub tonight and have some of that honey ale with Dagmar! Then they'll see you can party like the dwarves."

"Nice try, but I think you probably drank your fill last night," Sabine said. It was worrisome the dwarves felt as though others were receiving some sort of preferential treatment. If anything, she would have expected such complaints from the demons. The dwarves at least had ambassadors who frequently traveled to Faerie.

Sabine paused, glancing toward the door where Dagmar had disappeared. "I've been considering promoting Dagmar to a household management position here in the embassy. I could have Balkin arrange a tutor for her and Evelyn so they could become more familiar with Faerie politics. I'll need someone to let me know what's happening while I'm away from Razadon. I believe Dagmar can be trusted, provided she learns some discretion. Her family has worked closely with mine for centuries. They deserve to be rewarded."

"I think she'd like that," Rika said with a smile. "I talked to her a little bit about what it's like living in Razadon. She told me many dwarves don't like being trapped in their mountain, but she doesn't mind because she gets a taste of Faerie every time she comes to work. I think Blossom's right. A lot of the people here are unhappy."

Sabine drummed her fingers on the armchair, wondering how things could have degraded to such a degree. If the Seelie spies Astrid mentioned were as prolific as the councilwoman believed, they might be working to cause unrest in the city. Upsetting the trade empire between Razadon and the rest of the Unseelie would strike a critical blow to all of Sabine's people. She couldn't allow that to happen.

"Everyone has a place, but balance *must* be maintained," Sabine said, picking up her heated mug. "Only the dwarves can decide whether the sacrifice of their magic is worth the cost of so-called freedom. If they want things to change, there are proper channels for that. No one is forcing them to remain in this mountain, but this is their seat of power. They won't be as strong once they step outside. Those who live here have chosen power over freedom."

Malek considered her thoughtfully. "But what if those channels to promote change are shut down or aren't willing to cooperate? Your mother's been absent for a long time. With the gods not around to hear their plight either, what options do they have to push for a change?"

Sabine stared at Malek, not wanting to believe what he was suggesting. She wondered if this was part of the reason her mother had traveled to Razadon so frequently. "You're talking about a potential uprising. You believe we might be on the brink of an Unseelie civil war?"

"I think it's definitely possible," Malek said, picking up his tea again. "We saw the conflict between the merfolk. It could be happening here too. Ten years may be a long time without a queen, but it's been more than a thousand since the gods touched this world."

Sabine swallowed, trying to bury the worry gripping her. "Blossom, I'll need you to send word to your family and have them relay our suspicions to Balkin. He also needs to know what Astrid said about people being targeted near the Silver Forest. If my father's part of the reason this unrest is happening, I can't risk notifying Balkin through normal channels and have those messages intercepted."

Blossom nodded. "Okay. Do you want to know about the bad juju with the goats first?"

Malek frowned. "Goats? What in the world do goats have to do with anything?"

Blossom threw her hands in the air and exclaimed, "Patterns! There are patterns everywhere! Everything's connected to the corruption."

"All right. Tell us about the goats, Blossom," Sabine said, motioning for her to explain. "How is everything connected?"

Blossom nodded and started counting off her fingers. "One, Malek's ship got hit with bad magic and people died. Two, Bane went kooky because of the bad magic and people died. Three, Rika grew wings because I used flowers with bad magic and the flowers died. Four—"

Sabine held up her hand, startled by Blossom's comment. Pixies were masters when it came to keeping flowers and plants alive. "Wait a second. We knew Bane was acting out of character, but you're *sure* Rika's wings are tied into the corruption? The flowers you used to power the magical working died?"

Blossom nodded. "I thought maybe the crystals in Razadon messed up my magic. The sprigs in the mushrooms at Astrid's house had funny magic on them too. But when we went goat tipping, I checked out some flowers and realized it wasn't *my* magic that was the problem."

Malek choked on his tea. "Wait, what? Goat tipping?"

Blossom grinned. "Yep. If you scare a goat, they faint and fall over. You have to sneak up on them with heavy glamour, which is a lot harder because goats can see through it sometimes. That's part of the reason why the dwarves breed them on the mountain. They want to know if the Seelie are planning an attack."

"I wasn't aware of that," Sabine said and shook her head. She'd need to consider the potential implications later. "All right. Go back to the corrupted flowers."

Rika nodded. "I want to know what the flowers have to do with my wings."

Blossom flew to her flowerpot and sat on the edge. "The cave trolls were telling me they've been trying to keep the goats away from the bad plants. They were turning into zombie goats, which wasn't pretty. They would drool, chase their tails until they collapsed, and then they'd roll down the mountain and die."

Malek frowned. "I can see how that would be a problem if the goats are part of Razadon's defense."

Sabine shook her head. "That's what happened to your crew, Malek. They lost control of themselves and then died. That's probably why the merfolk warned us all living animals were fleeing the southern lands. Whatever they're doing affects anything alive. We might have escaped it because of my ties to the gods."

"Yep," Blossom said in agreement. "Since I'm an expert

when it comes to plants, I wanted to see if I could figure out why they were making the goats go crazy. That's when I realized the storm was raining bad magic on the plants. They were absorbing it."

Sabine sat back in stunned disbelief, wondering how she could have missed all of this. "When you pulled power through the flowers to change Rika's appearance, you used the corrupted magic, which made it a permanent transformation."

Blossom nodded, her wings twitching as she turned toward Rika with rounded eyes. "I'm sorry, Rika. I didn't know it would happen. Sabine managed to stop the corruption before. I bet she can do it again."

Sabine stood and paced, uncertain about anything. She needed to get to the heart of the corruption and remove it, just like she had back in Atlantia when the treeheart had been corrupted. The goddess had aided her back then, but she was reticent to call upon Lachlina unless absolutely necessary. Bane had warned her against it, and he didn't know everything that had transpired.

She paused, considering another possibility. "If Blossom's right, there's a good chance Bane was affected by the corrupted magic far more than I originally believed."

Malek set his mug aside. "What are you thinking?"

"Eshon, the rigger on board your ship who died," Sabine said, walking back toward him. "Bane took his life force after Eshon succumbed to the corruption. Bane would have tethered Eshon's life force into his essence to stabilize his ties to this realm."

Shock colored Malek's expression. "Shit. That's why Bane was having such a strong reaction to the corruption, more than any of us. If he'd already absorbed a substantial amount from Eshon, smaller amounts would have tipped him over the edge."

Rika's wings perked up. She looked back and forth between them and asked, "This means we can free him, right?"

Sabine hesitated and then shook her head. "Not without finding something in the archives to prove our theory. I think we're on the right track, but the dwarves seem eager to execute Bane for some reason. With everything you're telling me, I'm wondering if they might be trying to weaken my position here, and they're trying to use Bane to do it."

Malek's jaw clenched, and he turned back toward Blossom. "Did you discover anything about who pushed the obelisk that nearly killed Sabine?"

Blossom shook her head. "Nope. I think it was one of the cave trolls, but they were pretty hush-hush about everything. When I found their camp, one of the trolls was getting assigned cleaning duties near the demon caves for a whole week. Blueboy told me it was a terrible punishment because that's where the stinky magic came from."

Sabine straightened. "Wait. Stinky magic as in corrupted magic?"

Blossom shrugged. "Not sure. I couldn't go investigate without making the cave trolls suspicious. I think they know who's behind the corruption, but they're scared. They wouldn't tell me her name because they said she has magic that can listen in on them."

"She?" Sabine asked, reaching for the list of guild leaders Malek had given her. The person who was manipulating the cave trolls had to be someone in a position of power within Razadon. Cave trolls were similar to lesser Fae like Blossom, and only a Royal Fae could command a group of pixies. It stood to reason only a powerful dwarf could command the cave trolls.

Blossom nodded and flew to look at the paper in Sabine's hand. "Blueboy said she'd kill all of them if they didn't obey her. They have to use code names to talk about things so she can't hear them. They won't use her name, but I know they don't like her much."

Malek put down his mug of tea and said, "To my knowledge, dwarves don't have that sort of power to listen in on conversations."

Sabine considered that for a moment and then shook her head. "Not by themselves. Dwarves have very little of their own magic. If this person has the ability to listen in on conversations and is responsible for the corruption, power crystals *must* be involved. Someone would need quite a bit of access to them."

Running her finger down the list of names, Sabine named each woman who held a seat on the Council of Ten. "Astrid Onyxborne, Brigette Barrelblade, Raniel Lorekeeper, and Rugara Shadowborn are the only women on the council."

Rika's eyes widened. "Do you think Astrid's responsible?"

"I don't know," Sabine said, not wanting to believe her mother's friend could have done such a thing. "It may be a close ally or someone in her guild, but Astrid's anger was real. I'd like to give her the benefit of the doubt."

Sabine rolled the parchment containing the names and slid it into a drawer, then locked it with a trace of magic. "Before we go to the archives, I want to locate the place with stinky magic Blossom mentioned. If it's near the entrance to the demon's lair, Bane said I should be able to find it using his mark. Finding the actual source of corruption should be enough to prove Bane wasn't responsible for his actions."

"I can show you where the cave trolls live. I don't think it's far from their lair."

"Good idea," Sabine said to Blossom and stood, motioning for Rika to leave the rest of the letters for later.

Dagmar came running back in, practically out of breath.

Her eyes were wide with panic, and she darted her gaze around the room.

"They're calling the council meeting right now," Dagmar said, pressing her hand against the wall and panting for air. "I handed your message to our runner and ran into another who arrived with an urgent message from Astrid. There's also a bunch of guards outside the embassy demanding an audience. They have an official summons from the Council of Ten. They're here to escort you to the council chamber."

Malek frowned. "They never call the council meetings before noon. Half the councilors are either too hungover to function or still asleep. Something's not right."

Dagmar nodded. "It's bad news, whatever it is. They wouldn't tell me anything. They said I needed to find you and bring you out. You have your own guards sworn to serve you as part of the treaty. You shouldn't need others unless there's bad official business."

Blossom landed on Sabine's shoulder and said, "Don't go, Sabine. It's a trap."

"I must," Sabine said and took Astrid's message from Dagmar's outstretched hand. She broke the seal and scanned the document quickly.

It had been penned in a hasty script, telling Sabine she needed to speak with her before the council meeting. Astrid promised to find her in a small waiting area inside the council chamber. It didn't explain any reasons behind the sudden change, but the urgency of the message was worrisome.

If they were calling the meeting now, it would be impossible to secure the votes they needed to save Bane. Even if Hargrim received her message, they still needed one more vote. She couldn't help but think the timing was intentional. The presence of the armed escort made it even worse. If her father's spies were at work here, Blossom was probably right about it being a trap.

Malek placed his hand against Sabine's back and read the note over her shoulder. "I don't like this. Someone either really wants Bane dead or they're trying to goad you into action."

Sabine frowned and crumpled the note. "It looks like they're going to get their wish. Negotiation is apparently off the table."

"Let's do it!" Blossom exclaimed, flying to Sabine's shoulder. "I can dust them while you give them a magical whammy."

Malek studied Sabine in surprise. "You're going to force them into submission? Are you sure that's wise?"

She took a steadying breath and nodded. "I only need to force some of them. We've secured at least four votes, possibly five. The others can bend, or they can break. If they want to play games, I intend to win."

Malek and Rika exchanged a worried look. Without waiting for a response, Sabine headed for her bedroom. Footsteps sounded from behind her and followed her down the hall. Blossom flew ahead and darted into the bedroom just as Sabine crossed the threshold.

Sabine's hand hovered over the crystal panel by the door, waiting for Malek and Rika to enter. Dagmar was hovering just outside, appearing unsure whether she should be there. Sabine paused, remembering Rika's earlier comment about the dwarves feeling excluded.

Sabine waved her inside and said, "Dagmar, your family may have sworn allegiance to mine, but I know you have strong ties to Razadon. I won't ask you to do anything to harm your people, but I would like you to stand by my side during this meeting and act as my subject. Would you be willing to do that for me?"

Dagmar's brow furrowed, and she stepped into the room. "You're asking me? You're not telling me? You could always order me, you know. I'm oathbound to follow your orders."

Sabine shook her head. "No. I've seen the kind of person you are, and I won't force my will upon you. This needs to be your choice. I'm asking as a friend if you'd be willing to stand by my side and help me save the life of another friend. I believe if your people see all of us standing together—Fae, humans, pixies, demons, and dwarves, they'll understand my concerns that this corruption extends beyond any one group."

Dagmar's eyes rounded, and her mouth dropped open. "You want to be friends? With me? Are you sure? I mean, you're the queen. And a Fae. I mean, of course you have friends. I think they're your friends. Rika likes you a lot. And Malek does too." Her face flushed, and she lowered her head. "I mean, being a dwarf aside, I'm technically your servant. Are you sure you want me to go with you? It's a council meeting."

Sabine smiled and nodded. "Yes, I'm sure. I'd like you to be there with us."

Dagmar grinned widely. "I'd like to go. But, um…" Her smile faded. "Um, the council leaders are going to get mad, aren't they?"

Sabine hesitated, knowing this had the potential to go extremely bad. "I don't know why they've called this meeting so early, but I believe someone intends to do me or my friends harm. I can't make any promises since I don't know what will happen, but I've always done whatever's necessary to protect my friends, Dagmar. That's why I'm going to these lengths to save Bane. I would do the same for any of my companions."

Dagmar nodded, straightening her shoulders. "Then I'm in. I'll be your friend and help you."

Rika grinned and walked to Dagmar. She linked arms with the dwarf and whispered something in her ear. Dagmar grinned and nodded.

Sabine smiled at them and placed her hand on the crystal panel beside the door. She sent a mental request to Faerie to adjust everyone's attire. Illusion would be more important than ever to reinforce solidarity and indicate their support for Bane.

The room filled with a bright light, and the cloying scent of the forest filled the air. Underneath was a trace of sulfur as Faerie wound demonic magic into the fray. Sabine felt her clothing shift, the cut of the cloth becoming heavier as Faerie adorned her with garments suitable for a more formal setting. She looked down and found herself wearing a long red gown edged with black-and-silver trim—the colors most closely aligned with the demonic underworld. No one who saw her would doubt her intentions in saving Bane's life.

She turned around, looking everyone over. Their clothing was similar, and she took a moment to appreciate the way the bold colors made Malek's golden skin and dark hair even more striking. His mouth twitched in a smile, and his eyes warmed at her perusal.

Rika looked down and squealed. "I even have holes in the back of my dress for wings."

"Me too!" Blossom exclaimed and then shook her head, frowning at her red-and-black pixie dress. "Hey! Wait a minute. I look like an evil pixie. I don't think demons have pixies."

"They don't," Sabine said and walked to the box containing Kal'thorz's gift. She might not be fond of the demon who had offered it to her, but it made a powerful statement. She was attending this meeting to save a demon's life, and it was fitting she wear a gift forged from stones and magic acquired in the underworld.

Malek approached her and placed his hand over hers. "Let me help you."

She nodded, and he lifted her hair to fasten the elaborate choker around her neck. The silver links dangled past her collar bone, but they were surprisingly lightweight, even with the gemstones. Sabine slid on the wrist braces, which covered most of her forearms with intricate silver links matching the necklace.

"You look like your mom, Sabine," Blossom said, landing on her shoulder. "I've seen paintings of her, and she had that same serious look you do right now."

Sabine lifted her head and stared into the mirror, barely recognizing herself. It was almost as though her mother were looking back at her through the glass. Sabine swallowed, trying to quell her unease. She wasn't ready for this.

Blossom patted the silver links around Sabine's neck, making them jingle slightly. "You should take another sip of the Faerie wine. The goddess says you might need a power boost."

Recognizing the wisdom of Blossom's words, Sabine reached for the bottle of Faerie wine containing the essence of her family's power. It wasn't typical to imbibe this particular wine often, but necessity had changed the rules.

Sabine lifted the bottle and took a drink. Her eyes unwittingly fluttered closed as the power surged within her. Her ancestors touched her mind, lending their support to her cause. This time, there was no burning sensation in her wrist. It was almost as though Theoria knew why she needed the power and had offered her aid. Steadier than she had been, Sabine sealed the bottle and placed it back on the table.

Malek rested his hands on her shoulders. Leaning close, he whispered, "I've never seen a more beautiful queen, but I think I prefer you in your blues and silvers."

Sabine smiled at his reflection. She reached up to place

her hand over his and squeezed gently. "Will you get me the hairpins? I know they don't have any poison in them, but the crystals are beautiful. I'd like to have something of yours close to me."

"You'll have more than the hairpins. I won't leave your side," Malek promised and squeezed her shoulder before retrieving the box. Sabine watched him through the reflection, admiring the fine cut of his clothing and how it accentuated his physique.

Malek handed her the box with the hairpins, and Sabine selected several of them. Faerie had chosen to braid her hair in an elaborate fashion, coiling it around her head. Her crown was once more upon her head, but the stones were now blood red.

She slid the hairpins into her hair and turned to face the room. Smoothing out her dress, Sabine said, "Well, I suppose we're as ready as we can be. Let's do this."

Dagmar grinned and led the way out of the Faerie embassy. At the entrance, nearly twenty dwarven guards were waiting. Sabine's heart pounded in her chest. She hadn't been expecting so many of them. All of them jumped to attention at once, and the one closest to the front took a step toward Sabine.

He was heavily armored, and it wasn't simply ceremonial. It was well crafted and polished, but a few dents suggested it had been used often over the years. The dwarf had removed his helmet to reveal red hair braided tightly against his head. His beard wasn't nearly as long as others she'd seen, but it was tightly coiled in a manner to prevent it from being a liability in a fight.

He thumped his fist over his heart and bowed swiftly, the respectful gesture incongruent with the large force standing outside the door. Blossom flew off Sabine's shoulder and disappeared from sight.

"Greetings, Your Highness. My name is Avirin Brightblade, captain of the Warrior Guild. By order of the Council of Ten, we've been asked to escort you and your retinue to the council chamber. A meeting has been called, and your presence is requested."

Sabine paused, realizing these men reported to Brigette Barrelblade. The gesture of respect was likely because of her efforts in saving their guild leader's life the previous day. Sabine tilted her head in acknowledgment of his politeness. If he was grateful for the life of his commander, Sabine likely didn't have anything to fear from these men.

"Well met, Avirin. For what purpose is my presence requested?"

Avirin hesitated, glancing at Malek before turning back toward Sabine. "I'm afraid only the council may divulge their purposes. None among us are privy to what occurs behind council doors."

Sabine clasped her hands together, not buying his attempts at dodging the truth. He hadn't said outright he didn't know.

Her gaze swept over the other guards. Their posture was rigid, their eyes focused, but none of them had their hands anywhere near their weapons. Still, they were paying a great deal of attention to Malek, which was somewhat worrisome. If they suspected him of being a dragon, she would have expected a larger force.

No. They had to be here because of Bane. If they were trying to rush the official sentencing, every minute she stalled was more time the runner had to deliver her message to Hargrim. She'd bought some time with getting ready, but a few more minutes couldn't hurt. Even one vote might be the difference in her ability to turn the remaining dwarves to her side.

Sabine gave Avirin a knowing smile. "Perhaps you weren't

present, but I have no doubt Brigette Barrelblade shared her reasons for sending you to my doorstep."

"Aye," Avirin agreed with a quick grin. "I'd be remiss if I divulged my commander's orders without her leave. You understand, I'm sure."

Sabine smiled at the dwarf's charm and inclined her head. "Of course, but you also understand I'm under no obligation to accompany you without a reason."

Avirin blew out a breath. "Had a feeling this was going to be more challenging than I expected. Brigette's going to have my head."

Malek cleared his throat and said, "I'm sure Queen Sabin'theoria is willing to attend the council meeting, but we were under the impression it wasn't scheduled until later in the day. Can you tell us why the meeting time changed?"

Avirin considered Malek for a moment and then nodded. "Astrid Onyxborne called the original meeting, but some new information came to light last night. An emergency session has been called this morning to handle the situation. We've been dispatched to rouse everyone from their beds. The safety and security of all of Razadon is at stake."

Sabine frowned and motioned for Avirin to lead the way. Perhaps she'd been wrong, and something else had happened. "Very well. I'll accompany you."

Avirin called out orders for the guards to assume a protective stance around them. They snapped into action, and Sabine followed the captain away from the embassy.

Blossom landed on her shoulder. Leaning in close, she whispered, "They smell like sulfur, Sabine. I also saw a little bit of black blood on one of them."

"Bane?" Sabine asked in a low voice, careful not to be overheard.

"It smelled like his blood, but I couldn't get too close to the guard. He has one of those purple crystals on his weapon.

I think they put crystals on their armor that protects them from demon blood."

Sabine nodded toward Malek, indicating Blossom should share her information with him. Blossom flew to Malek's shoulder and whispered into his ear. His entire body tensed, and he glanced at Sabine. She caught his eye and shook her head. They wouldn't have executed Bane yet, but they might have been forced to subdue him if they tried to move him without her help.

They turned a corner, leading toward the government district of Razadon. Each guild had a designated meeting hall within the grand council building at the end of the street. It was a large structure, more like an arena, which towered upward several levels. This was where the council gathered, where laws were created, and where judgments were issued and executed.

Sabine took a steadying breath, lifted the hem of her heavy skirt, and climbed the stairs to the large double doors. They were made of stone and inlaid with crystals cascading outward in a starburst design. The guards at the door saluted her and stepped aside to allow her entry.

The foyer gleamed with polished marble and large statues of iconic dwarves. Murals of Lachlina, the crystal caverns, and dwarves battling dragons lined the walls. People were scattered throughout the area in small groups, talking in hushed voices. The overall feel was one of barely restrained fear and concern. A few of them turned wary or curious looks in Sabine's direction as her group moved through the room.

Astrid pushed her way forward and waved Avirin away. "Shoo. You've delivered her. Go maintain order somewhere else. I need a private word with the Unseelie queen."

Avirin scowled. "I'm under orders to escort the queen's entire party to the chamber."

"Then stand here until we're finished," Astrid snapped and motioned for Dagmar and Rika to wait there. Gesturing for Sabine to follow her, she said quietly, "We don't have much time. Keeping Dagmar and yer butterfly girl with him will appease him somewhat, but we need to hurry."

Sabine frowned, but she and Malek followed the dwarven councilwoman into a small alcove where Thetar was waiting. Astrid closed the curtain, concealing them from view, and asked, "You can give us some privacy, yeah?"

Sabine nodded and lifted her hand, surrounding them in a bubble that prevented anyone from listening. "We can still hear anyone approaching, but no sound can escape the shielding. What's going on?"

Astrid nodded and said, "Hopper Tapmaster was murdered last night."

Malek inhaled sharply. "The brewmaster?"

"Aye," Astrid agreed, her expression grim. "Two of our council leaders murdered in as many days. I'm afraid this doesn't bode well for you or yer demon. People are angry and demanding the culprits be brought to justice."

Malek frowned. "I've met him a few times. Hopper Tapmaster was a good man. I can understand why people are upset, but Bane didn't have anything to do with it."

"Bane's been in prison," Sabine reminded her. "Can you tell me what happened?"

"They can hold him responsible if he possessed someone. I'm afraid removing the demon's shackle yesterday was enough to cast new suspicion over him. Hopper's wife found his body in the pub's cellar late last night. He'd been decapitated with crystals shoved in his head. It looks like someone used his body to power some sort of spell."

Blossom squeaked, creeping closer to Sabine's neck. In a quiet voice, she whispered, "I told you! The bad magic came back. She's gonna be mad, Sabine. The goddess warned us."

"Then it's the same as Badac," Sabine murmured, her heart falling into her stomach.

Demonic possession was a convenient scapegoat. It was nearly impossible to prove someone was possessed unless you located the person while they were being actively controlled. She'd wrongly assumed the corruption Lachlina sensed yesterday had occurred outside of Razadon's gates. There had to be a link between these murders and the corruption.

"Do you know anything about this magical working? How bad is the situation?"

Astrid blew out a breath. "We've put a containment cage over his body until we can neutralize the threat. It looks like no one can discount your claims about magical corruption, but I'll be damned if I know how to fix it. They're still out for blood."

"I'll need to see the body once we're done here. I believe I can remove the corruption."

"We called in Raniel, our head archivist, to help figure out a solution. She said she'd check the archives, but who knows how long that'll take. If you can do something faster, your assistance will be welcome. I don't know if yer demon was responsible or not, but it's been centuries since our people were this riled. I'll be limited with any aid I can offer you. Stay on your guard once you enter the council chamber."

Thetar nodded and gestured at Malek. "Keep yer man close and his weapon closer."

Malek placed his hand against Sabine's back and asked, "Do you think they're trying to move up Bane's execution?"

Astrid nodded. "You still have the votes I promised you, but I'm not sure how much good they'll do. People are angry, and some of the councilors would rather be forsworn than risk a mutiny in their guilds." She paused, her brow furrowing. "Something else is going on I'm not privy to. Deals are being struck behind closed doors, and everyone's tight-lipped. I have my suspicions on the reasons, but no one's talking."

Sabine frowned. "Have you seen Hargrim Icemail?"

"Aye," Thetar said. "He stumbled in here hungover a few minutes ago."

A bell chimed loudly. Sabine paused, hearing a commotion outside.

Thetar muttered a curse and said, "First bell. We need to go before they begin."

Blossom patted Sabine's hair. "The cave trolls, Sabine. We need to know about the cave trolls."

Sabine nodded and turned back toward Astrid. "Of the three other women on the council, who has ties to the cave trolls?"

Astrid's brow furrowed. "The cave trolls? I haven't the foggiest idea. My guild uses them for polishing crystals."

"Raniel and Rugara use them too," Thetar said, naming the archivist and stoneworker from the council. "The cave trolls clean up the archives and also polish the gems and equipment. Most of us use them in some way."

The bell sounded a second time. Astrid glanced toward the heavy curtain and said, "I'll see you inside. Stay on your guard."

Astrid stepped out of the alcove with Thetar following her. Sabine blew out a breath. This situation had gone from bad to worse.

Malek stroked her back over the heavy material of her dress. "Astrid was shaken by Hopper's death, more so than when she had heard about Badac. We may need to have an exit plan if things go bad."

Blossom fluttered her wings. "I can ask the cave trolls where the exits are. They know the tunnels below the city better than anyone.

An idea formed in Sabine's mind. She held out her hand for Blossom to land, and the pixie immediately obeyed. "I need you to fly faster than you ever have before, Blossom. Can you do that for me?"

Blossom's eyes widened, and she nodded immediately. "I'd do anything for you, Sabine."

Malek arched his brow. "What are you thinking?"

"I want Blossom to find the cave trolls and broker a deal for us," Sabine said quietly. "I'll bring them under my protection if they swear fealty to me. In exchange, they'll report everything they know to me, including who is responsible for the corruption. We need to shift the blame off of us."

Sabine held out her hand and sent a wave of magic over Blossom, infusing the pixie with strength. Blossom sat up, her wings glowing with a silver light from the power surge.

She blinked up at Sabine and said, "But they're cave trolls, not pixies. They're not aligned with the Fae. You want them to turn against the dwarves and spy for you?"

Sabine's mouth turned downward. "They're Unseelie first, a fact most everyone here has forgotten. As queen, I'm going to assign them the task of spying for the Unseelie—for me. I'm willing to offer them protection against the person threatening them. We're putting a stop to this nonsense once and for all."

"Clever," Malek said, his eyes gleaming with approval. "This could work, if they agree to it."

Blossom nodded. "What do you want me to tell them?"

"I want at least one of your family members stationed here in Razadon. The cave trolls will report directly to them, and they can pass you messages through the in-between. If the cave trolls are worried about their safety, they can temporarily take up residence in the embassy until Balkin arranges more permanent protection. I'll leave it to you to oversee their spy network. Offer the cave trolls whatever you think is fair, but I need you to make it happen. Hurry. I need an answer before the meeting ends, or Bane will be executed."

"Okay!" Blossom agreed and lifted herself into the air. Malek pulled aside the curtain and the pixie took off, disappearing almost immediately.

Malek turned back to her and said, "There's no guarantee Blossom will get back in time. Tell me you have another plan."

"Not a very good one, but we're all out of options," Sabine admitted and smoothed her dress. So much depended on this moment, and she wasn't prepared for what she was about to attempt.

Malek tilted her head back and asked, "What are you thinking?"

Sabine took a deep breath and held his gaze. "I'm going to take Bane's suggestion and embrace my birthright. I'm going to become Razadon's queen."

Chapter Nineteen

Malek kept his hand on his weapon as they followed Avirin to the council chamber. If it came down to protecting Sabine with his sword, the dwarves would have the advantage in skill and numbers. He was struggling in trying to keep his draconian instincts in check, especially with the heightened danger to the woman he loved. He wasn't sure he'd be able to keep them suppressed during a battle.

"People keep staring at me," Rika said, her wings twitching slightly.

"They've never seen a human butterfly before," Dagmar said with a grin. "When we get inside, we're going directly to the Faerie alcove. We'll stand right next to Sabine while the meeting is being held. Everyone's going to be paying more attention to her."

Malek glanced at Sabine, but her face was carefully blank. She was the quintessential vision of Fae royalty. Her beauty was enough to steal his breath, but the aloof and cold demeanor she'd adopted was the image the Fae had carefully cultivated for thousands of years. It was nearly impossible to reconcile the warm and passionate woman he knew with the detached queen who walked beside him.

They approached the double doors leading to the council chamber, and Sabine reached out to brush her fingers against his. It was the slightest gesture, but it spoke volumes to him. She was nervous, and rightfully so. They were about to walk into the stronghold of the dwarves with little more than their ability to bluff. He'd witnessed Sabine's remarkable power, but it paled in comparison to the thousands of dwarves who might decide to turn on them.

It might be against protocol, but he wouldn't allow her to walk into that room without a reminder she had strong allies at her side. He captured her hand and quickly lifted it, then placed a kiss against her knuckles. Her eyes softened for a moment, and her mouth curved upward before the mask fell back in place.

Avirin nodded to the guards at the door. They pulled open the heavy wooden doors and stepped aside to allow them entry. Malek would be lying if he said he wasn't curious about the seat of Razadon's power. Even at the height of the war, no dragon had been able to penetrate Razadon's innermost depths. They'd laid waste to the land outside and waged a fierce battle over the mountainside, but the dwarves had been crafty and clever foes who had simply retreated deeper underground.

Sabine squared her shoulders and entered the council chamber. Her shoes were silent on the mosaic tile, but she didn't need to make any noise. Conversations halted abruptly, and every dwarf immediately turned their attention toward her. Malek tensed, sweeping his gaze around the room for potential threats.

A crier stepped forward and announced, "All hail Queen Sabin'theoria of the Unseelie, daughter and heir of Queen

Mali'theoria, and blood descendant of Lachlina, the One True Goddess, and Vestior, Harbinger of Nightmares."

A wave of cheers rose in the rafters as the new queen of the Unseelie made her appearance. Hundreds of dwarves had turned out for this meeting, and their feet pounded on the stone floor above them, causing the ground to rumble like thunder. Trumpets blared their calls, the cacophony of noise nearly deafening.

Dagmar let out a whoop behind them, and Malek turned and saw the dwarf grinning widely. She jiggled and danced behind them, her braids swinging as she lifted her hands in celebration. Rika laughed and joined her, emulating Dagmar's movements and cheering wildly.

Sabine glanced at him, her mouth curving in a hint of a smile. Malek relaxed slightly but not enough to release the grip he had on his weapon. The dwarves continued to cheer, calling out adulations and praises for Lachlina's blood relative. He hadn't realized how indebted the dwarves were to the goddess. Some might fear Sabine and what she represented, but she was also admired and even revered. He hoped it was enough to keep her safe.

The circular council chamber was larger than Malek had expected. He'd been expecting a building like others he'd seen in Razadon, but the chamber had been embedded directly into the side of the mountain. It made sense if the mountain itself was the seat of dwarven power.

From what he could tell with only a cursory inspection, it had been divided into different sections, one for each guild. He counted eleven different alcoves, each independent from the other with only one way in or out. It might make guarding each guild leader easier, but it also didn't allow for a quick exit.

Elaborate thrones had been installed in each alcove, each ornately decorated with carvings or in a style suited to their particular guild. Dozens of dwarves filled each alcove, most of them standing behind their guild leader in a show of support. They were all drinking and talking among one another, but their gazes were currently trained on Sabine and her companions.

Malek lifted his gaze upward, where the loudest cheers were coming from. An enormous balcony stood above the alcoves, with hundreds of curious onlookers watching the gathering on the main level. The masses were the ones cheering and calling out to Sabine, while the more stoic guild representatives watched silently from below them.

They crossed the room to the largest alcove, with Rika and Dagmar following two steps behind them. Gathering her skirt, Sabine climbed the shallow stairs up to the dais where a throne even more spectacular than the others awaited. It had been carved from the wood of a Silver tree, and the emblem of a crown rested on the top.

If the resemblance to the murals they'd seen was any indication, this was the same throne Lachlina had used when she taught the dwarves the secret of infusing power into their crystals. It was no small wonder they were cheering for Sabine. She was the living embodiment of the goddess who had gifted them with the knowledge of manipulating magic.

Sabine turned and took her seat, while Malek assumed a position immediately to her right. Dagmar and Rika settled in on the opposite side of her, both of them standing at attention. In accordance with Sabine's earlier instruction, Rika was standing closest to Sabine with her knife easily within reach. Six embassy guards stood at the entrance, their polished armor gleaming under the crystalline lanterns.

An attendant approached and placed refreshments for their group on a nearby table. Dagmar spoke to the young woman with a great deal of familiarity, which led Malek to believe it was another of Dagmar's many cousins who helped take care of the embassy. Rika went to the two dwarves to help lay out the dishes of food and pour wine for everyone.

The crier announced each of the other guild leaders as they arrived, including their detailed family history and feats of accomplishment. The crowd cheered with each name being called, but none of the introductions so far had the same impact as Sabine's entrance.

Malek leaned down and asked, "Are you all right?"

Sabine nodded. "Do you see Hargrim? I'm not sure if our messenger reached him in time."

Malek scanned each alcove for his friend, taking the opportunity to study the other guild leaders. Not all of them were Sabine's enemies, but some would be by the end of this meeting if the vote didn't go in her favor. She had scarce few allies, and it was impossible to know how the dwarves would react if she tried to force the objectors into submission.

Even without the crier's help, it was easy to identify each guild leader based on the emblems affixed over each alcove. Astrid's area was heavily inlaid with swirling power crystals, while Brigette Barrelblade of the Warrior Guild had murals depicting famous battles. All her companions were wearing full armor and weaponry, which was somewhat worrying.

Malek's eyes fell on the alcove decorated with vines and wooden casks. Carved grapes and hops lined the archway over the brewmaster's alcove. The group inside was more muted than the others, with a dour-faced man slumped in his chair and drinking from a mug. Malek frowned, suspecting the grieving guild leader was either Hopper's brother or some other close relative.

"I found him," Malek murmured, catching sight of Hargrim lounging on a throne inlaid with gold and heavy blue silk in the far corner of the chamber. He appeared to be drinking heavily, taking a sip often while chatting with a man standing nearby. A buxom woman beside Hargrim kept refilling his mug, the crystal bangles around her wrists catching the light every time she moved.

As though sensing Malek's eyes on him, the new leader of the Tradesmen Guild turned in their direction. Hargrim jerked his head toward Sabine, winked, and lifted his mug in salute. Malek grinned and inclined his head in understanding.

Leaning close to Sabine's ear, Malek whispered, "You were right about Hargrim wanting the request to come from you. He just gave me a sign he'll accept your terms. You have one more vote for Bane in exchange for the trade agreement you promised."

Sabine nodded but didn't reply. Her face was still expressionless, her nerves hidden behind a mask nearly as impenetrable as her glamour. If it weren't for the tension in her shoulders and the ironclad grip she had on the armrests of her chair, he might have thought her completely unaffected by the outcome of this meeting.

Hargrim's warning about Sabine's mother echoed in his thoughts. Hargrim had spoken of the former queen with obvious fondness and affection, but Malek couldn't forget the troubled look in the dwarf's eyes when he'd mentioned how she'd changed. He had no doubt Sabine was emulating her mother, but Malek wasn't sure that was the best tactic. It might endear her more to the dwarves if they could see another side of Sabine—the same side he'd fallen in love with.

Malek caught Dagmar's attention and motioned toward the wine. Dagmar nodded and brought a glass to Sabine, who accepted the wine with a polite smile. Her hand trembled slightly as she brought it to her lips and took a sip.

The crier was about to announce the last couple of guild leaders, so they had a few more minutes. If Malek was going to set her at ease, the time was now.

He leaned toward Sabine and whispered, "What's your favorite food?"

"What?" Sabine asked, her brows pinching together in confusion.

He smiled and placed his hand over hers, trailing his thumb along her soft skin. "Your favorite food. I'm just curious. Was it something you had back in Akros? Or maybe in Faerie?"

Sabine tilted her head and asked, "You're trying to distract me, aren't you?"

He grinned. "Is it working?"

Sabine's mouth curved upward, her eyes shining with appreciation. "When I was living in Akros, Martha made some wonderful dishes, but I think some of my favorite meals were back in Faerie."

"Was there one in particular you enjoyed?" he asked, noticing her shoulders had relaxed slightly with the trivial conversation. He gave her a devilish grin. "If you say you like forest foods like roots or grubs, I might have to rethink sharing future meals with you."

She laughed. "Not hardly. We had a cook who used to make a marvelous pastry filled with cream and fresh fruit. She would drizzle the top with honey. That was probably my favorite."

"You haven't had it since then?" Malek asked, pleased to find Sabine's hand had steadied while she'd been talking. Her laughter had caught the attention of some of the nearby dwarves, and they'd turned to watch the new Faerie queen.

"No, I haven't," Sabine admitted, taking another sip of her wine. "I thought about asking Martha to try recreating it, but I was concerned a dish from Faerie might draw too much attention. I didn't know if humans had something similar."

Rika took a step closer and said, "That sounds really good. We made something like that in Karga, but we put goat cheese inside the pastry instead of cream. The fruit is served on top."

"I wouldn't mind trying something like that," Dagmar said, placing the jug of wine back on the table.

The crier announced Rugara Shadowborn's name, and another cheer went up from the gallery. The Stoneworker Guild leader grinned and waved at the crowd while the crier went through the extensive list of her accomplishments and familial ties. Her dark hair had colorful stones braided into its locks, giving her the illusion of having multicolored hair that had been kissed by a rainbow.

"That's one of the guild leaders on your list," Malek said quietly, wondering if Rugara might be responsible for the corruption.

"Dagmar," Sabine said quietly, motioning for the dwarven steward to come closer. "How much interaction does Rugara have with the cave trolls?"

"A lot," Dagmar said, refilling Sabine's wine. "They're great at cleaning the dust off the carvings and equipment. They brush up against the stone, and the dust sticks to their fur. The stewards use them for cleaning hard-to-reach places too."

Sabine drummed her fingers on the armrest. "What about Raniel?"

Dagmar nodded. "She does too. You wouldn't believe how much dust can gather in the archives. The cave trolls help organize and catalogue the records too. If you want to see some cave trolls, we might have better luck going to the crystal caves where the temperature is colder. I think their nests are close to there."

The crier announced Raniel's name, and an even louder cheer went up. Malek lifted his gaze to the ceiling, hoping it didn't end up falling on their heads from the dwarves jumping up and down.

"She's popular, isn't she?" Malek asked, watching the crowd chant her name.

Rika clamped her hands over her ears and said, "I didn't think it would be so loud."

Dagmar grinned and nodded. "Raniel's from one of the oldest and grandest families in Razadon. If we had royalty like the Fae, I guess she'd be our queen." Dagmar winced and lowered her head. "Ah, er, sorry. Guess that didn't sound very good, especially since you're a real queen. I mean, if she were—"

Sabine held up her hand and smiled. "It's all right, Dagmar. I understand what you were trying to say."

Malek studied the dwarven woman as she stepped out of the archivist alcove. Unlike the previous guild leader, she didn't cater to the masses. Instead, she held her head high as she walked toward the front of the room where a podium had been set up. On top was a large crystal, which glowed with a soft yellow light.

The woman's golden hair had been parted severely, braided, and then coiled into buns on the sides of her head. Pointed crystals jutted out from their center, the smoky, swirling magic contained within them visible from across the room. Unlike some of the other dwarves who wore armor, she was dressed in a heavy formal gown similar to the style Sabine wore. In her hand, she held a large gavel of sorts with more power crystals affixed to the top and bottom.

Malek frowned, trying to get a better look at the object in Raniel's hand. "That item she's carrying, what is it?"

Dagmar squinted her eyes and said, "Oh, that's the Guardian Hammer. It's one of our items of power. Her family's kept it safe for centuries. Supposedly, it was given to us by Lachlina herself."

Sabine straightened. "Do you think that could be the artifact used to seal the portal?"

"I think it's a good possibility," Malek replied, watching Raniel speak with a group of warriors at the foot of the dais. They were too far away to be overheard, but their body language made it clear Raniel was arguing with the leader of the group. He wasn't happy with whatever Raniel was telling him.

"What's that big yellow crystal on the podium?" Rika asked, pointing at the small dais where Raniel was standing.

"Raniel Lorekeeper runs all the council meetings," Dagmar said. "Anyone who wishes to speak either needs to use the crystal sitting on the podium or try shouting, which happens a lot. If they get too unruly, Brigette Barrelblade keeps order with the warriors under her command."

"Interesting," Sabine murmured, leaning forward. "My people use their power to amplify their voices. I've never seen a crystal with the ability to project sound."

Dagmar nodded. "Our alarm crystals use the same kind of magic. It makes them really loud when they go off."

The dwarven warrior glared at Raniel and gave her a curt nod and then called out orders to his men. Half of them marched off the floor with their commander, while the rest fanned outward in a protective stance around Raniel.

"He doesn't look happy with her," Malek said in a low voice. "The rest of his men don't either."

"No, they don't," Sabine agreed with a frown.

Raniel approached the podium and rapped the gavel against it. "I hereby call this meeting to order. Silence! Everyone!"

Her voice projected loud enough to be heard in the farthest reaches of the council chamber. The large yellow crystal had pulsed slightly in reaction to Raniel's words.

Malek wondered if they were using bartered magic from Sabine's people to power the crystal. It was a strange contradiction for people who might want to shut down trade and force a renegotiation of their place in the world. Perhaps he and Sabine were wrong about why the corruption was happening.

Voices quieted as everyone in the room turned their attention to the dwarven councilwoman. She straightened to her full height and said, "Our first order of business is to welcome our newest visitor to our fair city. Once again, the Unseelie have sought refuge within the most powerful city in the world!"

Malek grimaced. It might have been the truth, but claiming Sabine was dependent upon Razadon's goodwill was a not-so-subtle jab at Faerie's queen.

Raniel turned her gaze on Sabine and said, "Welcome to Razadon, Sabin'theoria. It's our pleasure to host you here."

Another wave of cheers went up, and Sabine inclined her head in acknowledgement. It was impossible to miss Raniel's omission of Sabine's honorific title. If Sabine's rigid posture was any indication, she was more than a little annoyed. This didn't bode well for the tone of this meeting. If Raniel considered herself to be like a queen in Razadon, she might view Sabine's presence as competition. A few of the guild leaders were frowning and darting furtive glances toward Sabine.

"Uh oh," Rika muttered. "I don't think Raniel's happy you're here, Sabine."

"Are you going to challenge her?" Malek whispered.

"Not yet," Sabine said, drumming her fingers on the armrest again. "I'll allow her leeway up to a point, but I won't tolerate any further slights."

"Razadon has been plagued with tragedy over the past few days," Raniel said, her voice carrying to the farthest reaches of the chamber. "Both Badac Coinbasher and Hopper Tapmaster have returned to the stone's embrace far too soon. We shall remember them in the dust of our ancestors, and their bodies shall be returned to the stone to be born anew."

The dwarves in the gallery above them pounded their feet on the stone, causing the ground to rumble. Dust from the earthen ceiling floated downward, reminding Malek of the snowfall that had plagued his ship. The similarity was a little too unsettling.

Dagmar stomped her feet next to them and shouted over the noise, "We coat ourselves with the dust of our ancestors to honor the memory of those who are gone."

Rika copied Dagmar's actions. "Like this?"

Dagmar nodded. "Yep. We carry a piece of them with us."

Raniel held up her hand to stop the stomping. The dwarves slowly ceased their movement, the sound fading away as the dwarves took their seats again.

Once it was quiet, Raniel continued. "These men were taken from us far too soon. We have gathered today to witness the execution of not only the demon assassin, but the tool he likely used to commit atrocious deeds. We shall not suffer these demons in our city any longer! We will protect our people and enter a new dawn as the gods intended! We will no longer be shackled to this mountain!"

A resounding roar went up through the entire chamber, even louder than when Sabine had entered. The dwarves all leaped to their feet, cheering and chanting.

Shouts from the overhead gallery called, "Kill the demon!"

"Kill all of 'em!"

Soon, several others had taken up the cries for vengeance. Some of them were waving their weapons in the air, the mob growing frenzied in their thirst for justice.

Sabine tensed, her knuckles turning white from how hard she was gripping the armrests. "They can't mean to execute him here and now. There's always been a three-day grace period to reflect and pray to the gods."

Malek straightened in alarm, his hand going immediately to his weapon. "She's trying to bypass the vote, isn't she?"

Dagmar shook her head. "I don't know. I've never heard of anything like this happening before."

Not every guild leader appeared to be on board with this news. Astrid was yelling something at Thetar, while her guards armed themselves.

"If they're pulling weapons, we're doing the same," Malek said and unsheathed his sword. He ordered the embassy guards to ready themselves. They obeyed immediately, drawing their weapons and shifting their stance to one better suited to defend.

If things turned ugly, their options were limited. Sabine wouldn't sit by and allow them to execute Bane, but he wished they had more numbers than the few embassy guards sworn to protect her. Even Levin and some of his crew might have made a difference. He couldn't trust the skill level of the embassy guards, even if they were sworn to serve Sabine.

Sabine stood and said, "Keep your weapon ready, Dagmar. Rika, if you need to avoid danger, use your wings."

Rika nodded and gripped her knife, moving closer to Sabine as a group of warriors approached her throne. Malek recognized the one in front as the same warrior who had argued with Raniel minutes earlier.

The leader of the group scowled and tried to push past the embassy guards. "Move aside. We have official business here."

"Not another step closer," Malek said and moved forward, angling his body to better protect Sabine. "State your business and back off. No one needs to get hurt."

A tingle of magic filled the air. Thorned vines sprung from the wooden archway, forming a barrier to prevent anyone from passing. Either Sabine or Faerie had decided to ensure these trespassers wouldn't take one step into their alcove.

"You know the law, Brigby," one of the embassy guards said to the warriors standing on the opposite side of the thorny wall. "No one other than Faerie's attendants are allowed in."

Brigby, the warrior who led the group, swept his gaze over the magical wall. "We mean the queen no harm. You can stand down."

Sabine moved to stand beside Malek, placing her hand on his arm. "This alcove is part of Faerie's embassy. By what rights do you dare approach without my leave?"

Brigby bowed briefly to Sabine and said, "By order of the Council of Ten, we have been commanded to take Captain Malek Rish'dan into custody. We ask you to step aside and allow us entry, Your Highness."

Malek stilled. Of all the things he'd expected, that hadn't been one of them. If they knew his identity, they wouldn't be bothering with threats of an arrest. They'd be trying to fillet him with their swords.

Sabine's hand tightened on Malek's arm. She leveled Brigby and his men with a piercing gaze and demanded, "On what charges do you seek to strip me of my trusted bodyguard?"

The warrior grimaced and said, "My apologies, Your Highness. I will assign other warriors to your protection if you wish it. However, Captain Malek Rish'dan has been accused of being demon-possessed. You will need to surrender him into our custody for your own safety."

Malek nearly laughed at the absurdity of such a claim. "You can't be serious. You think a demon is possessing me?"

Sabine, on the other hand, appeared less than amused. Dim gold flickers of light shimmered from the goddess's mark on her wrist. Her lavender eyes narrowed on the dwarves, and Malek instinctively took a step toward her to hide the golden power. She needed to get control of her emotions, or Lachlina might emerge sooner than they'd anticipated.

"Sabine," he warned quietly, nodding toward her mark. She froze and then removed her hand from his arm before turning back toward the warriors.

"I have no intention of surrendering this man into your custody," she said to Brigby, pressing her wrist against her heavy gown to hide it from view.

"Who's accusing me of being possessed?" Malek asked the warrior, already guessing the answer.

Brigby met Malek's gaze. "Raniel Lorekeeper."

Dagmar sucked in air. "Not good. Really not good."

Rika frowned and moved closer to him. "Malek's not possessed."

Malek glanced toward the center of the room where Raniel was watching them. The gathered crowd had realized something was happening in Sabine's alcove and quieted down. Most of them were straining to get a glimpse behind the wall of thorns.

The warriors looked back and forth between themselves, clearly reluctant to have a showdown with the new Faerie queen. Brigby looked ready to give up on the whole endeavor, but he didn't move. Whatever Raniel had said to them made it clear failure wasn't an option.

"Your Highness, perhaps we can—"

Sabine held up her hand to cut him off. "Enough. I will hear these claims directly from the accuser."

Sabine had spoken in a normal voice, but Raniel must have guessed there was trouble. The archivist leaned over the podium and spoke into the crystal, addressing the entire room rather than Sabine.

It was another slight, and it wouldn't take much more to

push Sabine over the edge of civility. Malek didn't know what game the archivist was playing, but it wasn't going to end well. He'd be damned if he'd allow anyone to separate him from Sabine. He'd destroy this entire mountain before he allowed any harm to come to her.

Raniel gestured toward their alcove and said loudly, "Our guild leaders were not murdered until the captain's ship made landfall and a day-walking demon assassin was escorted to our shore. They might hope to hide behind the new Faerie queen's inexperience, but the demon and his minion must be destroyed to prevent more lives being taken from us. If Sabin'theoria is truly a queen, she will see justice at hand!"

Malek muttered a curse under his breath. As far as arguments went, it was a powerful one. Raniel had single-handedly not only struck a blow calling into doubt Sabine's ability to lead but also threatened to strip her of her closest allies.

Sabine narrowed her eyes and sent a pulse of power along her markings. Her skin glowed with a silver light.

Malek blew out a breath. Sabine was apparently done playing nice. He caught sight of Hargrim across the chamber who shook his head in warning. Malek frowned, understanding immediately what the dwarf was trying to tell him.

Leaning close to Sabine, Malek whispered, "Be careful. If you use your power against them too soon, you may alienate them even more. We have one shot at this. Hargrim wants you to keep trying to get them to see reason. I think we need to trust him."

She paused, darted a quick glance at him, and gave him a barely discernible nod before turning back to the crowd. In a voice infused with enough magic to be heard over the loudest shouting, Sabine said, "Justice will be met, but only if it is righteous and not idle speculation. Captain Malek

Rish'dan is not now, nor has he ever been, possessed by a demon."

Raniel clucked her tongue. "Now, child, you aren't the first Fae to be intrigued by a handsome face. But it's time to turn your human plaything over to those who are more accustomed to ruling."

Malek's hand reflexively tightened on the hilt of his sword at the insult. Both Rika and Dagmar gasped. Sniggering and nervous laughter filled the gallery above them. More than a few of the guild leaders appeared uneasy, and several of them were either leaving their alcoves to confer with one another or moving deeper into their small protective rooms.

Sabine's hands curled into fists, and Malek shook his head. He didn't know what Raniel was thinking in pushing Sabine or why Hargrim had encouraged restraint. Even if Blossom managed to get the cave trolls here in time, all of their hastily constructed plans had been shattered. Sabine couldn't allow these insults to continue without losing serious standing among the dwarves.

Sabine opened her mouth to speak but was interrupted by Hargrim storming out of his alcove and onto the main floor.

With a bellow loud enough to cut through the din, Hargrim shouted, "He ain't possessed, and you damn well know it!"

Malek turned and saw the dwarf making his way toward the podium. He pushed past the warriors surrounding Raniel and climbed up the dais. They were equal in height, but Hargrim had enough bulk to make Raniel seem like a wisp of a girl.

"Sit down and wait your turn, Hargrim," Raniel said, turning her nose up at him in disgust.

"Piss off, Rani," Hargrim retorted, loud enough for the

crystal to project his voice. "I've known Malek for years. He's no more possessed than I am."

"I'm not surprised to hear you claim responsibility for this outsider," Raniel snapped, glaring at him.

Raniel turned back toward the room, resting her hands against the podium. "My good people of Razadon, do not be swayed by these misguided claims. Hargrim Icemail means well, but we have seen the negative impact these humans have had upon our culture for centuries. Witnesses claim both Hargrim Icemail and Malek Rish'dan were present at Hopper's pub last night. They both disappeared into the back rooms of Tapmasters, and Hopper's body was found a short time later. Draw your own conclusions, but the evidence is damning."

Gasps of surprise and fearful whispers broke out, filling the air with a low hum.

"Are ye daft, woman?" Hargrim sputtered, shaking his head at Raniel. "I've been living in this city fer centuries. No way am I possessed and I wouldn't harm a hair on Hopper's beard, unless I caught him watering down my ale. We went into his back rooms to fetch an item I'd been keeping in storage fer Malia's daughter."

Sabine looked at Malek and asked quietly, "Did you see Hopper last night?"

"No," Malek said with a frown. "The last time I saw him was on my previous visit to Razadon."

Raniel leaned close enough to the crystal on the podium to ensure everyone could hear her. "Even if Hargrim is innocent of any wrongdoing, the evidence against Captain Malek Rish'dan cannot be denied. The demon prisoner is a known assassin and companion of his. Two of our people are dead, and more may follow if we don't stop them.

Hargrim crossed his arms over his chest. "Woman, yer

tugging on the wrong crystal here. Malek couldn't be possessed, even if he agreed to it."

Raniel scoffed. "I understand your need to defend him, but we all know how susceptible humans are when it comes to demonic influence. Malek Rish'dan has been present in every location where a body was discovered. He was also there when Astrid Onyxborne and Brigette Barrelblade were nearly crushed to death yesterday. Which of us will be next?"

Some of the dwarves in the galley leaped to their feet, calling out for the warriors to arrest Malek. Even more chanted for the demon to be executed.

Raniel turned her smug expression toward Malek and Sabine. With a wave of her hand, she ordered, "Captain Quartzblade, arrest that man at once!"

The captain muttered a curse under his breath. He lifted his axe and said, "Apologies, Your Highness. We need to take this human into custody until this is settled. Lower the wall and surrender your weapons, or we'll be forced to destroy any who stand in our way."

"You will do no such thing," Sabine said and waved her hand, sending a sharp blast of power outward. The warriors were expelled backward, scrambling to stay on their feet. The magical assault wasn't enough to seriously hurt them, but they'd have some bruises under their armor in the morning.

"Approach again, and I won't be so gentle," Sabine warned, glaring at them.

Malek nearly snorted. If his sister could see him in the middle of Razadon being defended by Faerie's newest queen, she'd likely laugh hard enough to burn their house to the ground by prematurely shifting.

Sabine turned back to address Raniel and the rest of the room. "Malek Rish'dan wears my mark, as does my demon protector, Bane'umbra Versed. Bane'umbra cannot possess someone without my leave, and I have not allowed him such rights. As far as Astrid Onyxborne and Brigette Barrelblade are concerned, they are both powerful and competent leaders. I'm sure they can make their own accusations if any such exist or are worth repeating."

Astrid's laugh rang out across the council room. She slapped her thigh and shouted, "Nay. That obelisk would have made me flatter than a stone paddy if it landed on my head. Queen Sabin'theoria was right next to me, as was her man. Don't think he was trying to do himself or his lady in. Such accusation is nothing but cave troll shit."

Brigette inclined her head. "I make no such accusation against Queen Sabin'theoria or her bodyguard."

Raniel scowled. She opened her mouth to speak, but another dwarf waddled forward. This one was also wearing a formal robe, rather than the armor many of the dwarves preferred. It only took a moment for Malek to recognize Gimly Grimston, the leader of the Steward Guild who had been introduced earlier by the crier.

Gimly clapped his hands and called, "I haven't yet had the pleasure of making his acquaintance, but my girl, Dagmar, has said good things about Malek. The demon is no doubt guilty of heinous acts, but I can't support any action taken against this human. We all know demonic possession comes with vacant stares, speaking in strange languages, and movement unnatural to humans. I've heard no such complaints."

Malek arched his brow at Dagmar. "You've been talking about me?"

Dagmar blushed, her face turning as red as her hair. "Maybe a little, but nothing bad. I promise."

"The human's possessed!" someone shouted from the gallery. "I saw him leap up on the ledge of the prison. No human could have done that!"

Another round of gasps and loud murmurs filled the room.

"Damn," Malek muttered, having forgotten to mask his abilities when he'd been attempting to locate the culprit.

Sabine reached over and placed her hand on his arm. He glanced at her, but she was focused on the people standing on the upper balcony.

In a loud voice, she said, "You're correct. Malek does not claim to be completely human. The feat you saw could have been accomplished by almost any person with mixed blood. You have my solemn oath he was not possessed by any demons."

Malek frowned. There were few races who could withstand demonic possession, and it wouldn't take much for people to draw dangerous conclusions.

Sabine's efforts to divert suspicion from his true heritage was clever, but having people believe he was human had always been the safer course of action. He'd found people tried to identify his origins when they thought he had mixed magical blood in his background.

"Careful they don't question too much," he warned, making sure to keep his voice low enough that no one other than Sabine could hear.

"You're not human?" Dagmar asked, her eyes wide in surprise. "Are you one of the shapeshifters like the kumili?"

Rika bit her lip and remained silent. She was one of the few people who knew his identity, but unlike Dagmar, Rika had been sworn to silence.

"We'll talk later," he whispered to Dagmar, not willing to divulge anything while surrounded by potential enemies. They'd eventually need to tell Dagmar the truth, especially if Sabine elevated her to more of a household management position. It would be impossible to hide his true nature forever, but they needed to survive the next few minutes first.

Raniel continued to glare at them, the fierce anger in her gaze somewhat surprising. Malek could have sworn he'd never met her during any of his previous visits, which made the vehemence of her claims troubling. Sabine must be the root cause, but he didn't know why.

"She hates you for some reason," he murmured quietly. "Have you ever met her before?"

"No," Sabine whispered, straightening her shoulders. "My mother never mentioned her either."

Raniel motioned to a nearby guard. The guard nodded and hastened away from the central dais, heading for a side door. The archivist turned back to the crystal on the podium and gave Sabine a smug smile.

"It's a shame when one of the Unseelie puts bed play over the wellbeing of an entire people. Fortunately, the dwarves have handled their own matters for a long time. The best way to rid ourselves of the problem is to eliminate the source of the threat. Bring out the prisoner, and let the execution begin. We shall purge each of our enemies from our mountain once and for all!"

The crowd cheered, but all Malek felt was dread.

Chapter Twenty

Sabine inhaled sharply at the sight of Bane being led across the far side of the room. The proud demon was bound, the heavy crystal restraints around his wrists and ankles rendering his abilities useless. The guards accompanying him shoved him forward and up onto the dais, angling their weapons in his direction.

Bane was wearing nothing more than a pair of ripped and torn breeches stained with blood. Even from this distance, she could see he had several more injuries and something was wrong with one of his horns.

Anger flared within her, her magic rising like a tidal wave and threatening to unleash its fury on those who had harmed him. This could have been avoided if the guards had called upon her for assistance. Sabine curled her hands into fists, trying to find a calm oasis in her mind. She wanted to run down to Bane and protect him from these dwarves who were determined to hurt him.

Rika let out a gasp and then whimpered, clamping her hand over her mouth. Dagmar whispered something to her, but Sabine couldn't afford to split her attention. For some reason, Raniel was doing her best to strip Sabine of her remaining allies. It could be something as simple as a power play, but this attack felt a little too personal. She had given Raniel more room for games than she intended, a slip she would not repeat.

Gathering her power, Sabine made a sharp gesture and shattered the crystalline restraints holding Bane. The demon roared, his eyes and horns turning pure silver, and the contrast against his midnight skin became even more striking than usual.

The dwarves nearby sucked in air and backpedaled, scrambling to get away from the enraged demon. Bane ignored them and instead launched himself at Sabine. Demons always went after the strongest threats first.

She lifted her fist, wrapping a magical band of energy around him and halting the demon in his tracks. With another wave of her hand, she retracted the thorny vines keeping their alcove separate from the rest of the chamber. She held Bane's gaze, mentally willing him to regain control of himself without forcing her to assert her dominance.

Bane dropped to his knees, his entire body trembling from the power she'd used to bind him. Intelligence and awareness still reflected at her in his silvered eyes. He wasn't quite in the throes of bloodlust, but he was teetering on the edge. It was only by sheer force of will that he'd resisted so long without her presence. Another wave of anger surged within her, and she had to force herself to breathe through the desire to strike Bane's oppressors down where they stood.

"Queen Sabin'theoria," Bane said, his voice gruff from disuse. "How may I serve you?"

"You will take your place," she replied in a carefully dispassionate tone, waving him to her side.

Bane rose, an imposing figure on the best of days but

nearly terrifying in his silvered state. Rika and Dagmar moved behind Sabine's throne, while Bane took the place immediately to her left. Several of the dwarves began talking among themselves, their voices a muffled roar of protest.

"Heal yourself," she murmured in a low voice, reaching over to brush her hand against Bane. She sent him a strong wave of power, and the worst of his injuries knit back together. He shuddered in response, and his eyes reverted to their normal amber color. It was enough to allow him some semblance of control, but she couldn't risk giving him more until they were out of danger.

"Glad to see you're back," Malek said to the demon.

"I doubt that," Bane muttered in response and then turned toward Sabine. "While your aid was well-timed, I'm afraid you've made a grievous error. Not the least of which is accepting my father's shackle around your neck."

Sabine tensed, barely resisting the urge to touch her necklace. She hadn't considered the jewelry to be anything more than a coronation gift. She should have known better, especially when it came to demons.

"Assuming we survive what's to come, we can deal with that later," Sabine said, taking stock of each guild leader's location. Her actions had temporarily thrown them into disarray, but she needed to conserve her remaining power. "We won't be safe until we're back in the embassy, but we can't leave until I determine who's responsible for the corruption. I need to put an end to it before Lachlina uses us to kill everyone."

Raniel was still standing at the podium, clearly incensed by the development. Sabine stared her down, mentally daring the archivist to make another move against her or any of Sabine's companions.

"The woman Raniel wants you under her thumb or

removed from power," Bane said with a growl. "You're a threat to her position here."

"I'd wondered if it might be something like that," Sabine said quietly, watching Raniel move away from the podium to speak with an armed stranger standing nearby. "My presence here upsets the hierarchy. Razadon has gone too long without a reminder of their oaths and obligations. I won't make that mistake again."

"Be careful, Sabine," Malek warned. "I think you have potential allies in Astrid and Hargrim, but the rest are either your enemies or waiting to see which side is stronger. Raniel is definitely on the enemy side."

"She's also the most likely culprit behind the corruption," Sabine said, studying the woman who was currently the most powerful dwarf in Razadon. "Rugara hasn't openly challenged me and appears more closely aligned with Astrid's allies. I need Blossom to bring me proof before I can accuse Raniel of anything."

Malek frowned, nodding toward a group of armed dwarves who were heading their way. "We're running out of time, Sabine. We need to end this before they unite against us. You may want to consider another power display."

Sabine nodded, knowing he was right. If the guild leaders combined forces, it would be impossible to stand against them. "I'll need to tap into the goddess's power. It's the only thing that might work."

Malek frowned. He took her hand in his and squeezed it gently. "Be careful, sweetheart."

She took a deep breath, preparing to embrace the goddess once again.

Rika inhaled sharply and said, "I just saw a cave troll, Sabine."

Sabine froze, hope unfurling inside her. She looked in the

direction Rika was staring but didn't see anything other than dwarves. "Are you sure? Where did you see it?"

"In the balcony area," Rika said and shook her head. "Something small and blue just ran through there with a spear in his hand, hopping up and down. The image shimmered like it does with glamour and then he was gone. I think he was looking for someone."

Malek frowned. "Could Blossom have instructed them to gather in a different location rather than coming directly to us? If they're afraid of someone, they could be worried about being spotted."

"Perhaps," Sabine murmured, but she had her doubts. Blossom would have returned immediately to share the outcome of her negotiation efforts unless something had happened. The weapon was a little strange. She knew pixies used them on occasion, but they were more formidable with their magic. It was possible the cave trolls were the same.

One of the dwarves, a squat little man who was nearly as wide as he was tall, hastened toward the podium with several guards in tow. His face was flushed red with a fine sheen of sweat glistening on his brow. Sabine suspected his decision to wear his heavy fur coat was to showcase his wealth rather than to encourage comfort. His beard had been braided with numerous crystals, but these were simply decorative and didn't contain power from what Sabine could tell.

Dagmar leaned close and whispered, "That's Dolan Ironside, leader of the Weaponsmith Guild. He's mostly bluster and hot air, but he's also Raniel's biggest supporter."

"What's the meaning of this?" Dolan shouted into the podium crystal, his face turning red. "That demon is our prisoner. You can't just come in here and free him without cause. You may be queen, but you're not our queen."

Sabine narrowed her eyes. With a wave of her hand, she sent a thin band of power outward. Using the strength of her will, she bound the dwarf tightly in her metaphysical grasp. He thrashed against her mental hold, his earthen power pummeling against her power. He was stronger than she'd expected, but as an individual, he wasn't a match for Sabine's command of the elements.

Cutting aside his resistance, she forced him to the ground in a position of obeisance. He collapsed, surrendering to her entirely. She sent a pulse of magic along her markings and took a step forward. She swept her gaze over the guild leaders, their attendants, and the dwarves watching from above. What she planned wouldn't work for all of them, but those with a weak disposition would embrace her strength.

Infusing her voice with enough power to bind the dwarves to her will and project her voice outward, she called, "I am Sabin'theoria of the Unseelie, blood descendant of the goddess Lachlina. I have been proclaimed ruler by Faerie herself and recognized by the Wild Hunt."

Reaching inward, she abandoned her reservations and grasped her ties to the goddess through the marks on her wrist. The first had been forged by blood and magic months earlier when she'd accepted the magic contained within the chalice. The second, a pearl gifted to the merfolk, was unfamiliar and alien to her nature but no less potent. All magic had a cost, and Lachlina's influence adorned her wrists like shackles. Yet, she would embrace their power if it saved the people she loved.

The goddess touched her mind, and Sabine allowed Lachlina's power to fill her like an empty vessel. *She* was the chalice. The magic of the gods flowed through her, both foreign and achingly familiar. Lachlina's thoughts intermingled with hers, and Sabine knew the goddess was once again present.

The markings on her skin glowed both silver and gold, the sign of the Fae and the gods intertwined as one. She took another step forward, standing at the entrance to the Faerie alcove and stared down those who would dare challenge her authority.

"You have forgotten yourselves, dwarves," Sabine shouted, channeling Lachlina's strength along with her own. "*You* are Unseelie, and I have been proclaimed their queen. If you reject me, you renounce your claim to this mountain and the magic that was gifted millennia ago."

Raising her hands, she sent out a piercing blast of magic that shot through every power crystal in the room. Each piece of jewelry, weapon, and lantern infused with dwarven magic glowed brightly, pulsing in time with her markings. The dwarves cried out in alarm, dropping to their knees at the realization the goddess walked among them.

In a voice loud enough to be heard throughout the room, Sabine said, "By rights of blood, your ability to manipulate the magic of this world begins and ends with me. Abandon the Unseelie, abandon your heritage, and you shall return to the dust from whence you came."

She sent another burst of power outward, causing dust to fall once again from the ceiling. Unlike the dwarves, she didn't need to stomp her feet to make the earth obey her will. She was Fae, one of the original guardians of this world, and it responded to her whims like a child reaching for its mother. Her skin pulsed even more brilliantly with its strange gold light as Lachlina's power surged even stronger than before.

Raniel pushed away from the podium, whispering something furtively to a sharp-eyed man standing to the side of the dais. He didn't have the appearance of a warrior but rather some sort of administrator. He ran toward the balcony stairs, likely to gather reinforcements, but Sabine had made her point. Lines would be drawn, but more than a few would align themselves with her.

She took a shaky breath, trying to pull back on Lachlina's

power before it consumed her. The goddess wanted to punish those who had corrupted her gift of magic, and she wasn't concerned about the potential collateral damage.

"Let it go, sweetheart," Malek said quietly, placing his hand on her lower back. The warmth of his touch helped center her thoughts, giving her a lifeline to find her way back to herself.

Lachlina didn't understand the tender feelings Sabine held for Malek nor the desire that surged within her every time he touched her. Using her growing feelings for the dragon at her side, she managed to drive a wedge between herself and the goddess. Sabine pushed away from Lachlina's hold, and after a moment, the goddess's power dissipated.

Sabine took an unsteady breath, shaken by the increasing control the goddess was demonstrating each time they shared power. It was becoming more difficult to tell where she began and Lachlina ended.

"Good people of Razadon," Raniel said loudly, commanding the attention of everyone in the room. "What you have just witnessed is one more example of the Fae and outsiders trying to dictate the path Razadon has chosen. While Sabin'theoria may hold remarkable power, she is not one of us. We are dwarves, masters of the stone and crystal. We need to embrace our heritage and hold on to that which makes us strong, or we shall be ground to dust under the chokehold of the Fae."

Rika leaned toward Sabine and whispered, "The crystals on Raniel's hammer flare whenever she talks. Could she be doing something to control the crowd? Sort of like what you do with your voice? I see magic coming from them."

Sabine frowned, trying to get a better look at Raniel standing on the dais. She relaxed her vision to see the flares of magic, surprised Rika had been able to detect them. Her seer abilities were growing stronger or she was finally embracing her gift.

The crystals on Raniel's hammer were glowing softly, but they brightened with every word the archivist spoke. It was possible Raniel had somehow infused them with the Fae ability of coercion. It was a subtle magical working, but trying to hold such power over a large audience was incredibly difficult.

"You may need to make an example of Raniel," Malek said quietly, moving up to stand beside her. "If the power you displayed already hasn't had an effect on her, nothing will. You run the risk of turning the city against you if you take action against her, but she's your strongest opposition. I believe the others will fall in line if you eliminate her."

"I'm starting to see the merits of dropping the damned mountain on their heads," Bane muttered. "I can assassinate her, but the dwarves already have a death threat hanging over my head. My interference will weaken your position. You'll need to handle her."

Dagmar's eyes widened. "You're going to kill her? But, but, she's Raniel! She's our archivist! She holds the memories of our people."

Sabine frowned, sensing the goddess was in agreement with both Bane and Malek. Taking a life wasn't something Sabine did lightly, even though she'd ended more than a few over the years. Turning toward Dagmar, Sabine said, "If I can avoid it, I will. But Malek and Bane are right. I can't allow her to sow dissent."

Dagmar's lower lip trembled, and she nodded. Rika patted her shoulder and spoke softly to the troubled dwarf. Sabine turned away, unable to offer her any reassurances. Instead, she focused on Hargrim and Raniel, who were still arguing on the dais. The dwarves in the balcony were straining to listen, but the guild leaders were speaking quietly enough that only those on the main floor could hear them.

Hargrim crossed his arms over his chest and tsked at Raniel like she were a naughty child. "Still goin' on with that ole argument, Rani? Thought you realized by now we need the Fae, just like they need us."

"We've never needed them, a fact you would do well to remember," Raniel snapped, glaring at Hargrim with contempt.

Hargrim sighed and shook his head. "Go on then. Renounce your ties to our mountain, but don't drag our people into yer madness. From what I've seen and heard, Malia's daughter's more like her mum than anyone expected. She'll turn you out if you keep spouting this nonsense."

Raniel scoffed. "She's a child playing at ruling. Look at how she's hiding from the Wild Hunt camped outside our gates. Even if I trusted the Fae, I wouldn't allow her inexperience to destroy our fair city. We have much to offer the world, but not as lesser citizens."

Sabine's hands curled into fists, but she didn't lash out. Everything Raniel had said was the truth, no matter how much Sabine might wish it otherwise. She was ill prepared to handle the responsibility of ruling, even if it was her birthright. No matter what doubts or insecurities plagued her, Sabine couldn't allow them to cripple her.

Raniel turned away from Hargrim and addressed the dwarves standing on the balcony. "I ask you all to stand with me now. Help us renegotiate our place in this world so our children might know the feel of the sun on their skin. We should not be forced underground like the unwanted children of the gods. Together, we can lead Razadon in a new direction. The power and knowledge to accomplish our goals is within our grasp!"

Some of the dwarves on the balcony cheered, while

others began talking among themselves. Sabine couldn't hear what they were saying, but she relaxed her vision enough to read their energies. The red, gold, and green hazes around them indicated many of them were responding favorably to Raniel's words.

The most curious thing was how their auras shared a similar resonance with the power crystals embedded on Raniel's hammer. Raniel might not have access to Sabine's full range of magic, but she was a powerful orator with an item of power in her hands.

Sabine stared up at the hundreds of faces she didn't know. Grasping the railing in front of her, Sabine tried to absorb some insight from the wood of the Silver tree under her fingertips. The dwarven culture had always been a fascination to her, but it was alien in many ways. She'd been in a similar situation when she'd been thrust into a human city, struggling to adapt and learn their ways. If it hadn't been for her friends, she never would have survived the human world.

The insight gave her pause. If she could find a way to bridge the chasm between their cultures, she might be able to pacify their concerns and make an even stronger alliance with them. The treaty and old ways had created the foundation, but someone needed to take the next step to unify all the Unseelie.

"People of Razadon," Sabine called, allowing her magic to unfurl within her once again. "I may be new to your city, but I grew up hearing about the wonders of Razadon. No other race has your level of skill when it comes to your craftsmanship in jewelcraft, armor, and weapons. Your power crystals, your stonework, and your engineering abilities are legendary. Even your warriors are renown for being among the fiercest in the world."

Each of the dwarves who belonged to the guilds she mentioned straightened, puffing their chests with pride. The whispered murmurs took on a more boastful tone, and Sabine watched as they elbowed one another and gestured in her direction.

"I may be new to ruling," Sabine said, sweeping her gaze over the watching dwarves. "But centuries of magic and memories run through my blood, renewed and reaffirmed with each generation since our inception. I have drunk of these memories, absorbing knowledge that belies my years. The one thing that's been made clear is how much I still have to learn."

Raniel narrowed her eyes, but Sabine ignored her and continued addressing the crowd.

"I have chosen to surround myself with advisors whose experiences far outweigh my own." She gestured toward Malek. "Captain Malek Rish'dan has traveled the world and learned more about it than most dwarves and Fae combined." She gestured at Bane. "Bane'umbra Versed grew up in the underworld but has lived among humans for years, learning their ways and how to adapt to different environments." She then motioned toward Rika, whose wings twitched in surprise. "Rika of Karga is a human seer, the first of her kind to embrace the Unseelie and work cooperatively with them. I count her a trusted friend and ally."

Gasps and surprised utterings floated down from the balcony. Raniel made a derisive remark too low to be heard clearly, but Sabine ignored her. If she wanted a true alliance with the dwarves, she needed to win them over on her own merit, not because they were frightened of her.

"Before traveling to Razadon, I met with several of the merfolk. I have formed a new alliance with them and reopened the once-abandoned trading city of Atlantia. The location of this city shall be shared with Hargrim Icemail as leader of the Tradesmen Guild, so he might bring further bounty to Razadon."

Hargrim gave her a salute and called, "Trading with the merfolk has always been rewarding. Razadon will surely prosper with yer good will, Your Highness."

Sabine tilted her head in acknowledgement of Hargrim's words. "It's my hope Razadon will prosper even more in the centuries to come. To that end, and to ensure I understand the concerns of everyone who aligns themselves with the Unseelie, I will install Dagmar Frostfall as household manager of my estate here."

Dagmar squeaked, her eyes wide at the sudden promotion. She grinned and bounced on her toes, causing her red braids to swing wildly.

Sabine gave her a warm smile and then turned back toward the council chamber. "Dagmar will be granted certain rights and duties far beyond those normally given to anyone who is not Fae. I believe this will help us grow closer as a people. We are all Unseelie, and I intend to shatter any preconceived notions that suggest otherwise."

"Dagmar doesn't have any experience," someone shouted from the balcony. A few others began protesting, but Sabine held up her hand.

"Like myself, Dagmar is young. But I believe she will provide me with valuable insight. I also intend to select a new Unseelie ambassador from among your ranks, with consideration given to each of your guild leader's recommendations. This person will listen to your concerns and work directly with me to resolve issues. Razadon will still maintain its autonomy, but you *will* have my ear. We will work together as one people and find a new way forward."

The crowd cheered, chanting her name with barely restrained frenzy. Malek gave her a warm smile, his eyes filled with admiration and approval.

Bane frowned. "It won't work, little one. The dwarves will

pit themselves against one another to win your favor, and you'll have a whole new host of problems."

She nodded, having already considered the possibility. "Perhaps, but I'm hoping this might buy us enough time until Balkin's people arrive. He'll likely send someone better accustomed to handling Razadon's politics."

Rika pointed up at the balcony. "Look, Sabine! It's back. The cave troll is sitting on that dwarf's head. I think the dwarf has something in his hand—"

Sabine started to turn in the direction she indicated, but Rika's face paled.

The seer screamed, "Sabine, look out! He's got a crossbow!"

Too stunned to react, Sabine caught sight of the crossbow bolt hurtling through the air in her direction. Malek grabbed her around the waist and dove toward the ground. She slammed against the tile floor, pain searing through her shoulder. Sabine screamed, agony racing through her body from where the crossbolt had struck her. Her fingers curled into Malek's shirt as ice penetrated deep into her soul, freezing her magic and shattering her thoughts.

Malek shouted to the embassy guards, "Stand ready and don't allow anyone to pass."

The guards nodded and assumed a defensive position. Malek stared at Sabine's shoulder, the look of rage on his face promising vengeance against her attacker.

She gritted her teeth, perspiration running down her face. It was poison. It had to be. Nothing else could cause her to feel this way. Her insides were slowly turning to ice while her skin was boiling. She couldn't even form the words to tell them what was happening. They had to get it out before it killed her.

Sabine reached for the bolt embedded in her shoulder,

the movement causing her eyes to water. A sudden wave of nausea ripped through her, and she gasped, struggling for air.

Rika's eyes filled with tears. "We have to do something! Don't they have healers here?"

Dagmar nodded. "I'll find someone. Hold on, Sabine."

"No dwarves," Bane snapped and grabbed Rika's dagger from her belt. He gripped the crossbow bolt with his free hand and angled the knife toward Sabine. "All of you need to hold her still. If it's barbed, it'll cause more damage when I pull it out. We can't wait to numb it."

"Breathe, Sabine," Malek urged and grabbed her arms, pressing her to the ground. Rika and Dagmar knelt by her feet, placing their hands on Sabine's ankles.

Bane met her gaze and said, "Brace yourself, little one."

Sabine managed to nod, but panic was setting in. Her fingers and toes were going numb. She couldn't respond or even take a full breath. They needed to just rip it out, no matter the damage it might cause. She had only minutes before she succumbed to whatever poison had been used.

Bane dug the knife into her skin, cutting through sinew and muscle. Sabine screamed in pain, but it came out as a strangled gasp. Another wave of nausea rose to meet her, and she inwardly begged herself to lose consciousness. It was too much. Tears sprung to her eyes. She couldn't bear much more.

Malek used the bulk of his bodyweight to keep her pinned to the ground. "Dammit, Bane. Hurry already. She's losing too much blood."

Bane growled, his eyes flashing silver as he continued to work. After what felt like an eternity, Bane pulled on the bolt, yanking it out of her shoulder. She gulped air, but it was tainted with the metallic taste of blood. Her blood was wrong somehow. Whatever they'd done had changed her.

She whimpered in pain, darkness edging in on her vision

and offering a release from the agony. Sabine tried to resist, knowing if she closed her eyes, she'd never open them again.

Bane sliced the dagger across his hand and slapped it against her injury. Power surged into her, his demonic magic forcing the muscle and tendon back together. Sabine cried out again, thrashing to get away from him as his poisoned blood soaked into her wound. Bane pressed his arm across her, holding her in place.

"Stop fighting me, Sabine," Bane ordered, pushing harder against her wound. "I don't have enough magic to heal you properly."

Sabine shook her head and whispered, "P-p-poison."

Rika gasped. "They poisoned you?"

Bane scowled. "Dammit. We need to send a runner to fetch Esme."

"She's gone," Rika said, her face turning pale. "Malek ordered the ship to depart. The corruption came back, and the crew was in danger."

"Iron," Malek whispered, staring in shocked horror at the crossbow bolt on the ground. He picked it up, his skin glowing softly. The warding medallion around his neck flared red as he curled his fingers around the shaft. "The bastards poisoned her with an iron bolt. I'll kill every last one of them."

Dagmar paled. "That's impossible. The only one who has access to our iron stores are the archivists so they can test it. Raniel wouldn't have—"

Malek tossed down the bolt and ripped off his warding medallion. Draconic magic and power surged outward, filling the room with its heat. Malek roared, his skin glowing bright enough to blind anyone who tried to stare directly at him.

Sabine turned away and gritted her teeth from the relentless pain coursing through her. Iron was lethal to the Fae.

The dragons had used it for centuries during the war to drive her people close to extinction. Bane might be able to repair the physical damage from the crossbow wound, but he couldn't repair the effects of iron poisoning.

Screams filled the air, and Sabine opened her eyes. Bane was still hovering over her, his midnight skin turned blue from the demonic power he was channeling into her. His eyes had shifted to silver, and even his horns had become nearly iridescent. Bane dug his nails into her skin, sending more of his demonic energy toward her. Sabine reached up and grasped his wrist, shaking her head at the fruitlessness.

"M-Malek," she managed to say, struggling to take a full breath. She tried to sit up, but it was too late. Malek had shifted into his dragon form, his tremendous size taking up the majority of the council area. His dark scales glittered in the crystalline light, giving the illusion of fiery stars dancing upon the night's sky. His beauty was almost cruel in the face of the destruction he promised.

Dwarves screamed and ran in all directions. Malek flicked his tail against one of the stone supports. A deafening crack resounded throughout the chamber as part of the balcony collapsed. Dwarves spilled onto the ground, along with dust and debris.

Malek ignored all of them, except for one. With his clawed talons, he tossed a man from the crowd up into the air. The crossbow he'd been holding fell to the ground with a clatter.

Malek's jaw clamped shut, and the gruesome noise of crunching bones filled the air accompanied by more screams as people sought to escape. Dagmar clamped her hands over her ears and squeezed her eyes shut, huddling in the corner. Tears streaked down Rika's face as she stared in shocked horror at the scene in front of them.

Several warriors had grabbed their weapons and were

rushing toward Malek. He swiped outward with his tail, knocking the dwarves back and slamming them into a column. The column teetered and then crashed to the ground in a pile of rubble, dangerously close to them.

"Get back!" Bane shouted at Rika and Dagmar. He grabbed Sabine and pulled her to the far side of the alcove with Rika and Dagmar scrambling after him. More warriors were beginning a second offensive, circling Malek's large form.

Bane tore off a strip of Sabine's dress to bind her shoulder. "That dragon is a damn fine sight. Maybe he'll take out a bit more of your opposition."

Rika scooted toward Bane and asked, "How bad is it?"

"Bad," Bane replied, his face grim. "She'll be dead in less than an hour unless we can stop the poison."

Sabine tried to swallow, her throat impossibly dry. She rubbed her neck and whispered, "D-drink."

Rika lifted her head and said, "Dagmar! The refreshments! Quick!"

Dagmar nodded and ran to fill a goblet. She brought it over and held it out with shaking hands. Bane took it from her and held it to Sabine's lips, but it turned to ice the moment she touched it.

Bane scowled and snatched the cup away, squeezing it tightly. The water began to boil, and he quickly offered it to Sabine again. She took a sip, managing to swallow before it froze again. Only one person might know how to save her from the otherworldly metal that was killing her.

"Malek's grandmother was Fae," she whispered, her throat closing again. Sabine tried to reach for her connection to Malek, but it had frozen over.

Rika's brow furrowed. "I don't understand. Why is that important?"

Understanding dawned in Bane's eyes. "She was a

captive who had been injured by an iron weapon. Malek's grandfather saved her, which means Malek might know how to eliminate the effects." He scowled and stared up at Malek. "We just need to get the giant lizard to change back."

"We won't be able to get close to him," Rika said, her face pale.

"I'll go," Bane said and started to pull away from her.

Sabine grabbed his hand and shook her head. Her strength was continuing to fail, but Bane's ties to the underworld and his body heat were slowing the progression of the ice stealing her magic. There had to be a way to get Malek's attention without endangering anyone. She had to believe some other sort of bond connected them, beyond the one they'd created simply to share power.

Smoke spiraled from Malek's nostrils as he peered through the crowd of running dwarves. He swiped his tail again, spilling another set of dwarves across the floor. His efforts at keeping them off balance had been effective so far, but they were becoming more organized.

Groups of dwarves had gathered, trying to flank Malek with their extended spears. Malek reared up, his scaled head hitting the ceiling of the chamber and sending small dust and rocks flying everywhere.

A dwarven warrior tried to jab him with a spear, but Malek knocked it aside. He turned quickly, his tail slamming into the side of the mountain with enough force to rip a hole through the earth. Sunlight streamed into the chamber, dirt and rocks crumbling downward from the opening in the mountainside.

The sound of screams filled the air, combined with terrified sobs and prayers to the absent gods. The sunlight dimmed suddenly, dark clouds stealing the daylight. A cold wind kicked up, sweeping through the council chamber.

Sabine shivered, unable to feel her fingers as the chill penetrated to her soul.

Black smoke poured inside the hole, and lightning struck the ground below it. Sabine's markings began to glow on her skin again, pulsing in time with the lightning flashes. Sabine took a ragged breath, knowing what was coming.

One of the Wild Hunt's riders emerged from the smoke, riding atop his midnight steed. He landed hard on the council chamber floor, the sound akin to thunder. The cloaked rider dismounted, turning his glowing red eyes on Sabine. The world slowed with every step of his approach. None of the dwarves in the council chamber appeared aware of the Huntsman's presence or his approach to the Faerie alcove.

Bane angled his body protectively in front of Sabine and growled, "You cannot have her."

The Huntsman lifted his gloved hand, sending Bane upward and suspending him in midair. The demon's eyes flashed silver, and he struggled against the Huntsman's hold.

The Huntsman ignored his futile efforts and approached Sabine. His cloak shifted slightly, and she caught sight of his skeletal form. His image wavered, shifting slightly until she could see the impression of a face. It increasingly overlapped the longer she gazed at him.

She blinked, trying to focus on the changing image and understand what she was seeing. The Huntsman leaned down and pressed a kiss to her forehead. She gasped, her back bowing from the darkness unfurling inside her. His touch was the kiss of death, cold enough to burn, but something else was happening inside her. She could still feel the iron consuming the magic within her, but it had been somehow temporarily suppressed.

She stared up at him in disbelief and whispered, "What did you do? I feel stronger."

His mind reached out and brushed against hers. "*A reprieve. Nothing more. All magic has a cost, and the debt is yours to pay.*"

The Huntsman held out his skeletal hand, offering it to her. Sabine swallowed, the heavy weight of the debt hanging over her head. If Death was willing to offer her a chance, she'd be a fool not to take it. She just hoped it wasn't her last payment.

Chapter Twenty-One

Sabine took the Huntsman's hand, and he pulled her upright. She blinked up at him, surprised by the change in his appearance. He was no longer skeletal but instead possessed a youthfulness in his face. His hair was longer than she'd expected and silvery white like hers. He regarded her with eyes that were the deepest shade of blue she'd ever seen. Something about him was strangely familiar, but she could have sworn she'd never seen him in this form.

"Am I dead?" she asked, trying to focus on the chaos surrounding them. Everything and everyone were moving in slow motion, and her vision was hazy. It was almost as though the Huntsman had displaced them in space and time.

Her body was still on the ground, her gown stained with blood. Rika sobbed into her hands, kneeling beside her, while Dagmar stood a few steps back with tears streaming down her cheeks.

Bane was trying to shake Sabine's body awake, shouting something she couldn't understand. Sabine struggled to make out individual words. His voice was long and drawn out. It was almost as though she were listening to someone shout underwater. If this was the afterlife, it wasn't what she'd been expecting.

"You have not fully left your realm," the Huntsman replied, his baritone voice wrapping around her and leaving her strangely disconcerted. It shouldn't be possible. The Huntsman had always spoken to her using his mental speech. Whatever he'd done to her had changed all the normal rules.

He arched his brow. "I am not bound by the same rules in this realm as I am in yours."

Sabine started. "You can still hear my thoughts?"

He laughed. The rich sound was infused with enough power to leave her trembling from the onslaught of his magic. She automatically stepped back, needing some distance from him. He must have been one of the most powerful Fae alive before he'd agreed to become the Huntsman.

The Huntsman considered her for a long time. His bearing was regal, with a careless arrogance many of the Fae possessed. She couldn't even begin to imagine how much magic he had at his disposal. She'd never heard of anyone with the ability to pull people in and out of reality.

His blue eyes filled with amusement. "While I am no small power, I cannot keep you here without consequences. You have a choice to make, Sabin'theoria."

She frowned. "What choice?"

The Huntsman led her away from her body and onto the council chamber floor. She darted a glance back at her body, reluctant to go too far for some reason. She could feel some sort of tether tying her to her physical form, and it pulled taut the farther away she moved.

The Huntsman stopped in front of the center dais and said, "You may choose to return your mortal body for a price, knowing it is beyond my arts to save. I cannot return that which was stolen."

"My magic, you mean," she murmured, turning back to stare at her motionless body on the cold ground. She'd felt a great deal of her magic leave when the iron bolt had been pulled out of her. The effects of the poison were slowly freezing the rest of her power. Without access to her magic, she would surely die.

"Indeed," the Huntsman replied and gestured toward the hole Malek had created in the side of the mountain. "Or you may give yourself over to the Wild Hunt and accept a new path. You will be free to take to the skies with us and walk in between life and death."

Sabine stared at him in shock. Join the Wild Hunt or die? Those were her options? Sabine swallowed and shook her head. She'd heard about people being given the opportunity to join the Wild Hunt, but she'd never expected to receive such an offer, especially not without her magic to barter. Like most Fae, she understood very little about what motivated the Wild Hunt. They were a separate entity from Faerie, operating by their own rules and mores.

A suspicion crept over her. If the Huntsman couldn't reclaim her frozen and poisoned magic, he must want something else in return.

Sabine hesitated and then asked, "What's the price for returning me to my body and realm?"

"A life debt is due."

Sabine blew out a breath, realizing she was trapped. By pulling her into this place, the Huntsman had navigated her into a corner. If she insisted on being returned to her body, she needed to offer him a life in exchange.

Her gaze drifted back to her body, unsure of the Huntsman's motivations. The likelihood of dying from iron poisoning was almost guaranteed unless she could find a way to reclaim her magic. Assuming she traded a life, she'd be taking a huge chance by returning to her realm. Like the crystal in the ritual proclaiming her queen, she needed to make a choice: embrace a new reality or potentially die.

"Few are given this choice," the Huntsman said in a dispassionate voice. He honestly didn't seem to care whether she accepted his offer or not.

"There has to be another way," Sabine whispered, desperate for an alternative. She wasn't ready to die, especially not when she'd barely begun to live. There was a whole world to explore, a pixie to play with, demons to rescue, a young seer to teach, and a dragon to love.

Thoughts of Malek made her heart ache. She'd promised to help him find the artifacts needed to close the portal. If she abandoned him and the rest of her companions, what would happen to everyone when the war began again? Thousands of innocents would die, not just her friends.

Her hands curled into fists, resolve strengthening her. As long as she was able, she needed to keep fighting. She wasn't willing to give up on life.

"A life is due, Sabin'theoria," the Huntsman said, and Sabine caught a glimpse of compassion in his gaze. It caught her off guard, and she frowned.

She hesitated, studying him thoughtfully. The last time he'd looked at her like that, he'd offered her a loophole to escape her fate. Was it too much to hope he was offering her another?

"Perhaps you would rather barter another life to save your own?" he asked, gesturing toward Bane, who was still kneeling beside her body, trying to rouse her. Bane had to believe she could still be saved, or he would have given up already.

"The demon has already offered his life to protect you, Sabin'theoria. Will you trade his for your own?"

Sabine jerked back. She vehemently shook her head. No. Bane had already done so much for her. She couldn't allow him to sacrifice more. If it hadn't been for him, she never would have survived the past ten years. He could be gruff and difficult at times, but there were softer aspects he kept hidden from the world. Sabine hadn't missed the secret weapon training he'd begun with Rika or how he'd taken to growling at any of Malek's crew who gave her a hard time.

"I see," the Huntsman murmured. "You are thinking of the young seer. Her kind have made the Fae vulnerable for centuries. Will you trade her life for yours?"

"No," Sabine said immediately, staring at the dark-haired girl who reminded her so much of herself. She might have only known Rika for a short time, but she'd already become part of their makeshift family. Rika would live, learn her gifts, and have a chance to become one of the most skilled seers in the world. Sabine would make sure of it.

A noise caught Sabine's attention, and she turned and saw a herd of cave trolls dart onto the council floor in slow motion. Unlike the rest of the people in the council chamber, their images weren't hazy. Their forms were clear and crisp, but their sounds were still muted. They stood no taller than her knees, their tufts of blue fur sticking out in all directions. They were unusual-looking creatures, but it was the pixie riding on the one in front that caught her attention.

Blossom was grinning widely, gripping the fur on a cave troll's head while her wings fluttered behind her. Sabine couldn't help but smile at the sheer delight on Blossom's face as she embraced the frenzied chaos surrounding them.

"The pixie? They are not equal to the Fae in terms of power, but you have placed a great deal of trust in that one. I will accept her life and those of her clan. Will you make the trade?"

Sabine stared at the Huntsman in shocked horror and shook her head. "No. I won't trade her life or her family's lives. They've served me honorably, and Blossom is one of my dearest friends. I've never met a more valiant and honorable individual."

"The dragon then," the Huntsman murmured with a nod of approval. "He will be a suitable sacrifice. With his power, I would be able to give you at least another few months of life."

Sabine's heart clenched at the thought of a world without Malek in it. No matter what happened to her or however long she had left, she could never hurt him. He might be a dragon, but he possessed one of the most beautiful hearts and minds she'd ever encountered.

"Not Malek. Never Malek," Sabine whispered, staring up at the fearsome dragon who had captured her heart. "Even if I can't be with him, I would never trade his life for mine."

"Do you have any other life debts you can call upon?" the Huntsman asked, his eyes calculating.

Sabine managed to tear her gaze away from Malek's hazy image and focus again on the Huntsman. A headache was forming behind her eyes. It was becoming more difficult to see the real world the longer she remained in this one.

"I will not sacrifice anyone I care about," she said firmly. "If they are my debts, I will be the one to pay the cost."

"I shall ask you one last time: If you do not wish to join the Hunt, what life will you give me to return you to your true form?"

She paused, considering the Huntsman's question carefully. Dealing with any of the older Fae could be tricky, a lesson she'd learned well as a child. He'd now asked her several times about who would pay a life debt on her behalf. There had to be a reason.

As the Huntsman had indicated, the bonds she'd formed with her friends were the most obvious. Blood ties drew each of them together, and they would be the easiest to manipulate and surrender. Easy was convenient, but the hardest path was usually the right one.

Sabine tapped her fingers against her thigh. Another sort of life debt could be incurred if a task of equal measure had been performed, such as saving her life.

"Or if someone tried to take it," she murmured, straightening as the realization struck her. Malek and Rika had been the ones who thwarted the assassin's attempts. Because they were bonded to Sabine, she was within her rights to claim vengeance or blood rights against the one who orchestrated the attack. Malek had already killed the dwarf wielding the crossbow but not the person who had issued the order. As long as she could keep him from killing the other culprit, she might have a chance to survive.

Sabine scanned the crowd, trying to identify the dwarves who were running back and forth trying to get out of Malek's way. It was more difficult to make out individual features with every second that passed. She needed help, but only one person might be able to aid her while she was in the in-between.

Sabine walked away from the Huntsman, feeling the strange pull again toward her body as the tether stretched. Several dwarves darted through her corporeal form, and she froze at the sense of wrongness that filled her. She shivered and rubbed her arms, trying to alleviate the sensation.

Blossom was still riding the cave troll, running circles around Malek's large legs while he pushed back the advancing dwarves. The pixie seemed completely unaware what was happening to Sabine's body on the other side of the room. Since she hadn't truly died and was still in a place

Blossom could reach her, the pixie probably hadn't yet realized anything was wrong.

"Blossom," Sabine called, and Blossom whipped her head in Sabine's direction.

Sabine called her name even louder. "Blossom, can you hear me? I need you!"

Blossom flew off the cave troll, looking around in alarm. "Sabine? Where are you? It feels like you're right in front of me, but I don't see you. Are you glamoured?"

"Your time is almost up, Sabin'theoria," the Huntsman said, walking toward her. "You can remain here only another few minutes before your choice will be made for you. I have slowed the progression of time to give us time to speak, but the cold iron continues to ravage your magic."

Sabine tried to clamp down on her panic as she shouted, "Blossom, I'm dying! I need a source of power in exchange for mine. I can't leave the in-between and return to my body without it!"

Blossom's eyes widened. "You're in the in-between? Take my power, Sabine! I'll save you!"

Sabine stilled, overcome with emotion by Blossom's fierce courage. She blinked back the moisture gathering in her eyes. There had been no hesitation or resistance in Blossom's offer. Like Sabine, Blossom would die without her magic, yet she was willing to make the sacrifice.

"No, my dearest friend. I need you to locate Raniel for me and stop Malek from killing her. I believe she arranged for the assassin. If I'm right, her life is a suitable exchange for mine. The Huntsman *must* be the one to claim her life."

Blossom's dust turned red in agitation, and she saluted Sabine. "I'm on it. One dwarf coming up and hand-delivered to the Wild Hunt to make dead."

She flew away, raced back to the cave troll, and whispered furtively in his ear. A high-pitched trilling noise filled the air, and all the cave trolls joined in the song. They made a beeline to the far side of the council chamber where a group of dwarves were hiding behind a column and out of Malek's line of sight.

Sabine turned toward the Huntsman who was watching the cave trolls. If he'd been surprised by Blossom's offer, he showed no sign of it. "What do I need to do to return to my body?"

The Huntsman fixed his deep-blue eyes on her, the mysteries in their depths making her feel like a child barely able to comprehend the world around her. "If this is your desire, you will be returned to your body. You will have but minutes before you succumb to the effects of the iron and the loss of your magic."

Sabine swallowed. "Will I regain consciousness?"

He inclined his head. "It's within my power to grant you such a gift for a short time."

Sabine turned her gaze toward her body, hoping she was making the right choice. Iron might be fatal to the Fae, but she had ties to a dragon. Cold iron had been brought to the world by the dragons, and if anyone knew anything about how to circumvent their effects, it was Malek. She had to believe he would find a way to save her. His grandfather had saved the Fae woman he'd loved. Maybe it wasn't too much to hope Malek could do the same.

"A gamble?" the Huntsman asked, a flicker of interest in his gaze.

Sabine managed a weak smile. "Life is a gamble, and so is love. I have to believe Malek will find a way to save me." She lifted her gaze to stare at the hazy image of the dragon once again. "He loves me enough to risk his life seeking vengeance on my behalf, and I love him too much to leave him. Isn't love a gamble of sorts?"

He held out his hand and said, "Surrender your will to

mine. I will return you to your body, but I will leave you with a warning before you depart."

Sabine placed her hand in his, the Huntsman's cool fingers gripping her tightly. He trapped her in his gaze, sending a shiver through her body as he said, "Be wary of anything done in the name of love, Sabin'theoria. Few intentions are rarely as honorable as we might imagine. I was once different than what you see before you, but betrayal has made me both prisoner and warden."

Sabine's brow furrowed, confused by his words. She'd always thought the Huntsman had chosen to give up his magic to help create the Wild Hunt. If he was suggesting he had been deceived, that was a perversion of the highest order.

If he heard her thoughts, the Huntsman gave no indication. He led her back toward her body and said, "The Fae cannot survive without magic, and yours has been stolen by the iron. I will accept the iron bolt in your name and take the life force of the one who ordered it crafted. It is a suitable trade."

A strong band of magic wrapped around Sabine's chest, making it difficult to breathe. Whatever power he'd woven into his words had changed the fabric of the universe in some small way. She just wasn't sure whether she'd made the correct choice.

The Huntsman turned toward her again. "Should you find a way to survive, your life shall be forfeit once you step upon the mountain path. Those who seek your death have become clever with their summoning, and I am bound to obey as long as the price is paid. Such is the agreement that was struck long ago."

Sabine nodded, unsure why the Huntsman had gone out of his way to protect her. She searched his expression but couldn't find any clue to his motivations. Something about him was so familiar, but she wasn't quite sure how or why. She sifted through her memories, straightening when the realization slammed into her.

"The music box," she whispered in surprise. "I remember you playing that song for me when I was a child. You came to see me when I was still in Faerie."

The Huntsman didn't answer. Sabine started to take a step closer but then stopped short. She couldn't afford to forget his true identity. No matter what kindnesses he'd afforded her, he was still one of the deadliest and most fearsome individuals in the world.

The Huntsman lifted her hand and kissed it, sending a rush of ice through her body. She gasped, trying to breathe as pain and cold slammed into her. She blinked open her eyes to stare up into Bane's amber gaze. The Huntsman she knew was gone, and only his cloaked skeletal form remained. He turned away from her and headed toward the center of the council room. Sabine struggled to sit up, hoping Blossom had managed to locate Raniel. If Sabine was wrong about Raniel ordering the attack, the Huntsman would be within his rights to claim any of her friends' lives as his due.

"Dammit, Sabine," Bane said with a growl. "I thought we'd lost you for a minute. Your heart was beating, but you weren't moving or responding."

Sabine didn't answer, her body weakening by the second. She grabbed Bane's arm and said, "I'm dying, Bane. I need Malek. He's the only one who might be able to stop the iron from killing me. I only have a few minutes."

Bane's eyes flared to silver, and he leaped to his feet. Without stopping to question how she knew this information, he raced toward the edge of the Faerie alcove and bellowed, "Change back and get your lizard ass over here. Sabine needs you!"

Malek swiped out with his tail again, sending another

group of warriors flying through the air. He turned in Bane's direction and moved toward him.

Sabine scanned the room, catching sight of Blossom and dozens of cave trolls. They'd discovered Raniel and were running in circles around the terrified archivist. Even from here, Sabine could see the magical working holding Raniel captive.

They ran faster and faster while the Huntsman walked toward them. Sabine saw him lift his hand, shadows emerging from around him like thousands of snakes. Raniel screamed, her voice louder than any other in the council chamber. It was the same scream Sabine had made when she'd been forced to sacrifice her magic to evade the Wild Hunt. She knew that agony, that weakness, that brush with death when all hope was threatened.

Raniel collapsed, her magical hammer falling to the ground with a clatter. The image of the Huntsman appeared briefly, his skeletal visage sending a new wave of terror through everyone. The warriors abandoned their efforts to attack Malek and raced away from the Huntsman.

"We need to activate the protections of the alcove once Malek enters," Sabine said, hoping it would buy them time before the warriors regrouped. "Faerie will need to shield us for a few minutes."

"I'll do it," Dagmar said, running toward the entrance of their alcove.

Sabine motioned toward the iron crossbow bolt still on the ground. "Rika, take the bolt and guard it well. I've promised it to the Huntsman. He won't harm you when he collects it."

Rika immediately went over and collected it. Her eyes were full of fear, but she held it tightly against her chest. "Can I do anything else?"

Sabine shook her head, watching as Malek's entire body

began to glow once again. With a sharp flash of light, he transformed back into his human form and knelt by her side a moment later.

"Talk to me, sweetheart," he said, taking her hand.

"The iron bolt stole most of my magic when it was ripped out of me. The effects have been slowed, but I don't have much time before it kills me. Can you reverse it the same way your grandfather saved your grandmother?"

Malek's brow furrowed. "It took my grandfather more than a year to heal Elisa. How much time do we have?"

"Only a few minutes," Sabine whispered, hope slowly dying within her. She could already feel the chill deepening around her, and it was becoming more difficult to breathe.

Malek's hand tightened around hers, and his eyes searched her face. "There's only one way I know. I need the words, Sabine."

"What?" she whispered, confused why he would be demanding this from her now.

"It took more than a year because Elisa didn't love or trust my grandfather. We have a deeper bond than they did when she was injured, but this isn't something I can do alone. I need you to open yourself to me completely, or my efforts may end up killing you faster than the iron."

Sabine swallowed, her mouth going dry. The words shouldn't be so hard to say, but admitting such a thing out loud would shatter the remaining barriers between them. She'd never be able to let him go, and her people would never accept her while Malek remained by her side. Even if she survived the iron poisoning, she wasn't sure she'd survive the assassination attempts once she bound her heart to a dragon.

Admitting her feelings would put him equally at risk. He wouldn't leave her if he knew how deeply she'd grown to care for him. Now that the dwarves knew his secret, it was only a matter of time before whispers spread upon the wind. He would be in danger every moment he remained at her side.

When she didn't respond right away, Malek cupped her face and urged, "Please, sweetheart. I know you feel it in your heart. I can't lose you, not like this. Not because you won't say the words. I'm asking you to trust me."

Sabine took a shaky breath, knowing this would be the last chance to say it. Even if Malek's efforts in saving her didn't work, she didn't want to leave this world without telling him how she felt. There were no guarantees in life, and he'd asked for her trust. With everything they'd been through together, she needed to take this chance—even if it were her last.

"I love you, Malek Rish'dan," Sabine whispered, her eyes filling with moisture as the bond connecting them tightened around her heart.

Malek squeezed his eyes shut, his shoulders slumping with relief. "Hold your emotions close to your heart, Sabin'theoria," he murmured, pressing his forehead against hers. "Open our bond fully and embrace everything I am."

Sabine lowered her inhibitions, opening her heart and mind completely to the dragon she loved. Her heartbeat slowed, and she could sense Malek's heart beating in time with hers. His magic surrounded her in a protective shield, and he lowered his head to kiss her.

Dragonfire surged within her, and her back bowed from the sudden rush of power. He held her still, pouring his searing heat into her. She whimpered against his mouth, her body jerking as the dragonfire warred against the icy chill from the iron. Her fingers curled into his shirt, trusting him to burn away the iron without destroying her in the process.

This was why he'd needed her to say the words. If she hadn't, the iron would have remained lurking within those hidden places in her heart she'd kept locked away. Its poison would have stolen every last trace of her magic, killing her without qualm.

Sabine forced herself to relax against Malek's chest, giving herself over to him completely. She ran her hands through his hair, accepting his offering and recognizing the sacrifice he was making in return. His dragonfire was different in its intent, hotter and more focused somehow. He was giving her part of his essence, an ability to withstand the worst effects of iron—something no Fae should ever possess. The realization left her strangely disconcerted, and it was humbling to know how much he trusted her.

When the last of the chill had dissipated, he eased away. His gaze roamed over her face, his eyes filled with concern. "How do you feel?"

Sabine was lightheaded, barely able to move, but she was able to take a full breath for the first time since the bolt had struck her. She lifted her hand and ran her fingertips along his strong jaw.

"I can breathe again."

Malek pressed his forehead against hers. "The iron's not gone completely, but I've given you enough dragonfire to help withstand the worst of the effects. Over the next several weeks, I'll need to give you more until it's fully eliminated."

Bane knelt beside her and sliced open his hand. "Drink, Sabine. The dragon's got you so hyped on light magic, I can barely sense your Unseelie side."

Sabine blinked at Bane and sat up. Demonic blood was lethal to the touch for most people, but drinking it was even worse. It wasn't an appealing thought, especially on the heels of an assassination attempt, but she needed to reinforce her Unseelie magic. Telling Malek how she felt about him would likely have long-lasting repercussions when it came to her Seelie side, but it was impossible to regret it. He'd saved her life and given her something impossibly precious to keep fighting for, no matter the consequences.

Malek grabbed Bane's wrist. "Your blood could kill her. She's still weakened from the effects of the iron. She needs a few days at least."

"We don't have days," Bane snapped and then turned back toward her. "The dwarves will try to break through the barriers at any moment. If they succeed, they'll kill you along with your dragon. You must restore yourself, and I don't have enough of your magic to return to you."

"He's right, Malek," Sabine whispered, cradling Bane's clawed hand in hers. This was their only option, and Bane would never have made this offer if the situation wasn't dire. Demons never sacrificed their blood without good reason.

She leaned down and tasted the sharp, bitter flavor of Bane's power on her tongue. It slammed into her, squelching the lingering flames of Malek's dragonfire. She started to shake, a wave of nausea rushing through her at the warring powers. Life and death battled together, both heated magics but vastly different. She forced herself to continue drinking, unwilling to allow her Seelie power to overtake her Unseelie side.

"Enough," Malek said with a growl, yanking her to her feet and away from Bane.

The demon's eyes flashed silver. He growled and took a threatening step toward them. Malek pulled Sabine tight against him and shot his hand outward, sending Bane hurtling against the wall.

Sabine pressed her hand against Malek's chest. "I'm all right. Weak, but I'll live. Bane's only trying to protect me."

Malek relaxed his arms slightly, but he didn't release her. "You can barely stand, Sabine. You shouldn't try to do much more. The effects of the dragonfire take time. It's still inside, trying to remove any trace of the iron within you. If Bane's power negates too much, the iron will still kill you."

A mental voice touched her mind. "*The dragon is correct.*"

Her gaze whipped toward the entrance where the Huntsman approached. The magical barrier protecting the Faerie alcove collapsed the moment he passed through, and the dwarven warriors all stumbled back at the sight of the Huntsman. They dropped to their knees, either throwing their bodies into a position of obeisance or collapsing from sheer terror at what the cloaked skeletal figure represented.

Malek's arms tightened around her again. She pressed her hand against his chest and said, "It's all right."

Motioning toward Rika, Sabine said, "The Huntsman has come to claim the crossbow bolt."

Rika held out a shaking hand, her entire body and wings trembling hard enough to lift her feet off the ground. Dagmar scrambled forward, grabbed Rika around the waist, and hauled her back down. Rika squeaked and then offered the Huntsman the iron bolt. He held his hand over it, not touching it or Rika. Sabine felt more than saw her magic rush out of it and into the Huntsman. His form solidified even more for a moment, and Sabine caught a glimpse of the same visage she'd witnessed while they'd been in between life and death. The bolt turned to dust a moment later in Rika's outstretched hand.

Sabine stared in stunned disbelief at the Huntsman. He turned toward Sabine, his eyes glowing red. Their striking deep-blue color was nothing more than a memory, along with his true face.

He studied her for a long time and then turned away, walking out of the alcove and back toward the center of the council chamber. Once he was in the middle of the room, he fanned out his cape and made a sweeping bow in her direction. In the next instant, he vanished.

The dwarves throughout the chamber began talking in low, frightened murmurs, darting furtive and wary glances in Sabine's direction.

Malek leaned in close and asked, "What was that about?"

"I think he's trying to protect me," Sabine whispered, shocked by the Huntsman's actions. The dwarves were all watching Sabine with the same fear and reverence they'd shown the Huntsman moments before. By all rights, he wasn't beholden to any of the Faerie courts. His gesture was the equivalent of announcing she was allied with the most feared nightmares in the world.

"I don't think we have to worry about the dwarves trying to kill you or the dragon right now," Bane said quietly. "They're all trying to figure out what the hell to do. About time these shorties decided to show some respect."

Sabine shivered from her close brush with death. She had no idea why the Huntsman was showing such interest in her, but she wasn't sure it was a good thing. At least they'd managed to survive this latest encounter.

Blossom came flying toward Sabine. She hovered in midair and threw her hands in the air. "You're alive! I knew you could do it. I've never met anyone who went to the in-between with the Huntsman. What was it like? Did you see the gardens? I heard there are gardens in the in-between, but they're near his palace. I've never been there. Pixies aren't allowed."

Sabine held out a hand, offering Blossom a place to land. "I'm fine, and I don't know anything about a palace. We didn't leave this room."

Blossom's wings drooped. "Drat. I wanted a flower from there." She perked up again and pointed at the large group of blue cave trolls standing outside the alcove. "I want you to meet my friends. They accepted your agreement, and they'll work for you. Hey, Blueboy, come meet Sabine."

The largest of the cave trolls waved his spindly arm in her direction but didn't approach. Blossom giggled and said, "He's shy. The dwarves don't talk to them like you talk to me. I told them you're different, not as stuffy."

Sabine smiled at the cave trolls. "Well met, Blueboy and everyone else. I'm honored to meet such brave and valiant individuals. Your assistance has been invaluable today, and I will see each of you suitably rewarded."

Blueboy trilled out a melodic song and then lowered himself to the ground in a strange sort of bow. The other cave trolls followed suit before backing away.

Dagmar's eyes widened. "I've never seen them do that before. They really want us to talk to them?"

Blossom nodded. "It makes them sad you don't include them in stuff. Sabine takes me everywhere and gives me lots of important jobs. The cave trolls want to do that kind of stuff too. Just because we're little doesn't mean we're not important."

Sabine gave Blossom a warm smile. "You're more than important to me, Blossom. If it weren't for your efforts in subduing Raniel, I wouldn't have been able to return from the in-between." She turned toward Rika and said, "And without your ability to see through glamour and offer a warning, the crossbow bolt would have killed me outright instead of just wounding me."

Rika's face flushed at the praise, but she stood a little taller. "I'm glad I could help."

Sabine looked at Bane and reached her hand toward him. "I'm glad you're back with me, my protector. Without your healing and offer of power, I wouldn't have survived either."

Bane grunted, but he appeared pleased with the praise. Sabine turned back toward Malek and gazed up at the dragon she loved.

Before she could speak, Malek kissed her lightly and said,

"You've already given me the words I've been wanting from you, sweetheart. You don't need to say anything else."

Sabine swallowed and nodded, but she still wasn't sure how to reconcile her feelings for Malek with the obligations and duty to her people. In the days ahead, they'd both need to make some hard choices. But for now, she was content to live in the moment and in the relative safety of the dragon who'd claimed her heart.

Chapter Twenty-Two

Astrid and Hargrim climbed the steps to the Faerie alcove. One of the embassy guards turned toward Sabine, and she nodded to indicate they could approach. As one, the guards stepped aside, allowing the guild leaders to enter. Astrid and Hargrim stepped forward and knelt in front of Sabine.

Astrid lifted her head and said, "Queen Sabin'theoria, this lot of fools has asked me to represent the Council of Ten. We're all downright pissed over Raniel's actions. I hope you won't hold it against all of us."

Sabine motioned for Astrid and Hargrim to rise. She swept her gaze over the rest of the dwarves watching silently from the main chamber area. They'd likely selected Astrid based on her relationship with Sabine's mother. She wasn't sure why Hargrim had accompanied her, except he had ties to Malek and Sabine's mother too.

Recognizing she needed to make sure all potential troublemakers were handled, Sabine asked, "Was anyone else responsible for the actions Raniel took today?"

Astrid and Hargrim exchanged a look before turning back to her.

"Can't say," Hargrim said with a shrug. "At first glance, she acted alone, but there might be more in her guild who had a hand in the treachery."

Sabine nodded. Malek had spoken highly of Hargrim, but she was reassured by the dwarf's frankness. "I'll leave it to you both to ferret out any accomplices."

These two would be able to conduct a more thorough investigation than she could. It would also be a good exercise for the newly conscripted cave trolls. If they wanted an important job, this was a great opportunity to see how well they could work with Blossom.

Hargrim took a step toward Sabine and held out Raniel's hammer. "Given everything that's happened, we thought it might be best to give this to you. Raniel always conducted these meetings with it, rapping it on that damned podium when things got a bit noisy. Since you've decided to be our queen in truth, we figured you should be the one to rap heads with it."

Sabine had to force herself not to react. Taking a deep breath, she accepted the golden hammer. It was heavier than she expected, with the metal being surprisingly warm to the touch. But it was the crystal points affixed to the bottom and top of the handle that caught her attention. Dusky smoke moved within them, flashing periodically with traces of red and blue.

Her brow furrowed as she studied the swirling magic. Some innate part of her warned something was wrong. She lifted it to her nose and sniffed, catching a trace of demonic power and merfolk magic surrounding it.

Blossom flew off her shoulder and said, "Hey! That's got bad magic in it!"

One of the cave trolls twittered at Blossom, and the

pixie's eyes widened. "Uh oh. Blueboy said Raniel used it to kill Badac and Hopper."

"What's this about Badac and Hopper?" Hargrim demanded.

The cave troll continued chattering at Blossom in their strange language. After several minutes, Blossom said, "Okay. I think I've got the story. It sounds like Raniel found something in the archives that made her think she could duplicate the magic of the gods."

Astrid gaped at Blossom. "Was she daft? Such a thing isn't possible."

Sabine frowned but didn't comment. She didn't know if it was possible to recreate their magic, but the touch of the goddess reminded her of the crystal she'd used to proclaim herself queen. She had some suspicions, but these things were better not discussed openly.

Malek placed his hand against her back, and she glanced up at him. His jaw was hard, and his eyes had turned cold. Sabine could understand his anger. If the dwarves figured out a way to duplicate the power of the gods, everything they'd worked toward in sealing the portal would be for naught.

"What else did Blueboy say?" Sabine asked.

Blossom fluttered her wings. "Raniel wanted the dwarves to have powers and abilities like the Fae or the gods themselves. She started mixing magics, but she needed a really large sacrifice from a dwarf to bind the powers together."

"As an Elder, Badac would have been one of thc most powerful sources of magic in Razadon," Sabine muttered, shaking her head in disgust. The murder of an Elder was one of the most heinous crimes possible. Magic grew and blossomed with age, and Elders had access to the strongest source of power available.

"True, but few would cry over his loss," Hargrim muttered, crossing his arms over his chest.

Astrid elbowed him in the gut.

He grunted and rubbed his belly, giving Astrid a dark look. "I'm just saying what everyone's thinking. Why do you think no one spent much time looking for the culprit? The man was kin, but he was also an ass."

Dagmar took a step toward them and asked, "But what about Hopper? Everyone loved him. Why did she kill him?"

Blossom nodded. "Blueboy said Hopper was suspicious about the experiments Raniel was conducting. The corrupted magic affected the hops he'd been growing, and he was really mad. Raniel went to his pub yesterday to talk to him, and he confronted her about it. They got into a big argument, and he threatened to tell everyone what she was doing. She killed him with the hammer."

Astrid put her hands on her hips and scowled. "That's why the corruption was different on Hopper. It wasn't planned. If she wasn't dead already, I'd kill her a second time. Hopper was a good man. He didn't deserve such an end."

Blueboy made a few more noises, and Blossom's eyes widened. She turned back toward Sabine and pointed at the hammer. "That's the source of your corruption, Sabine. She used that to pound the power crystals into Badac's head. She used Elder blood to bind the magics together."

Sabine stared at the hammer in her hand with shock and horror. The crystals swirled with different colors from multiple sources of magic. If the hammer itself had been a gift from Lachlina, Raniel must have thought she could harness the goddess's power to combine the magics.

Rika's wings twitched, and she asked, "Can we destroy it?"

Sabine frowned, studying the hammer. If this was truly an item of power and a portal artifact, she knew what needed to be done. She would have to accept the power of the hammer and take it into herself.

She hesitated. If the magic was corrupted, the results could be disastrous. With traces of iron still in her body, she wasn't sure she was strong enough to survive the effects of twisted magic.

The goddess's mark on her wrist warmed, and Sabine glanced down and saw the golden glow encompass her skin. Blossom landed on her shoulder and said, "She wants you to use it, Sabine. She said she'll help you. Malek can help too."

Malek's brow furrowed. "How?"

Blossom shook her head and shrugged. "I'm not sure. She said you'll know."

Bane scowled. "No. Sabine, it's too risky. You should wait until we can fully test the hammer and you have time to heal completely."

Malek ran his hand down her back. "I'm inclined to agree with him, Sabine. There's nothing to be gained by doing this right now."

Sabine nodded, knowing they were right. "I'll keep it with me for now. I may be able to remove the corruption around Hopper's body so he can be properly returned to the stone's embrace."

Astrid placed her closed fist over her heart. "His clan and guild would welcome your assistance."

"Uh oh," Blossom said with a squeak. She flew off Sabine's shoulder and said, "Not my fault! She said she warned you!"

The goddess's mark on Sabine's wrist glowed even brighter. It flared outward, creeping into her hand—the same holding the hammer. Malek reached toward it, but the goddess rose inside her. Sabine jerked away from him and said, "No. Don't touch the hammer. I don't know what she'll do to you."

Malek froze. "Fight her, Sabine. You're stronger than her."

Sabine inhaled sharply, trying to regain control of herself. The goddess's power rushed along her skin and down into her hand. It encompassed the hammer, its light making the golden metal shine even more brilliantly. It touched the crystals, shattering them in an instant. The sharp pungent aroma of raw sewage filled the air as the oily corruption splashed against her skin. The contact stung like a thousand knives.

Rika stumbled away, gagging on the foul scent. Her wings glowed, pulsing in time with the marking on Sabine's wrist.

Sabine cried out and crumpled to the ground, still clutching the hammer. She tried to release it, but the goddess was holding her fast. At least she'd managed to stop her from taking control completely. The corruption was moving outward across her skin and dampening the glow from her power.

"Sabine!" Malek shouted, kneeling beside her. "You have to drop the hammer."

Lachlina's voice sounded in her mind. *"Daughter. Accept this gift."*

"This is *not* a gift," Sabine managed to say, her hand shaking from the battle waging within her. "It'll kill me if I accept it."

"Cut the mark off your skin," Bane said, sliding his knife in her direction.

Sabine tried to reach for it, but the goddess sent a blast of power outward, pushing the weapon away. Sabine gritted her teeth, trying to stop the corrupted magic from spreading inside her.

Bane dove for the knife. He leaped to his feet and stalked back. "The hammer's trying to steal her life force. I'll cut off the damn mark myself."

"Wait," Malek urged, grabbing Bane's wrist before he could get close to Sabine. "That's it. This is exactly like what happened with the chalice. Sabine, you need to stop fighting. It'll kill you, but only if you don't embrace it."

Sabine's eyes widened. He was right. The attack was similar, the magic incompatible with her own. This power had been gifted to the dwarves for a reason. It needed to determine her worthiness to receive such a gift. The hammer itself was trying to destroy her, not the corruption.

Sabine opened her mind to the magic contained within the hammer. The attack ceased abruptly, its power surging through her and tasting her magic. It stopped at the mark of the goddess, surrounding Sabine with a warmth that was uncomfortable but not scalding.

"Cut my hand," Sabine said, holding out her free hand toward Bane.

He frowned but nicked her skin and allowed her blood to well to the surface. She smeared it against the hammer's head, reciting the words Lachlina whispered in her mind.

"I claim you, by blood and magic. In tribute to the gods and the last sacrifice of the goddess Lachlina, I swear by all I am and the last of this world's magic to uphold my family's oath in defense against those who would see this land destroyed."

The hammer glowed brighter and sharper until it became nearly blinding. It lifted from her hand and hovered in the air overhead. The sound of drums pounded in her temples, beating a staccato rhythm in time with her heartbeat. The world slowed, similar to the way it had when she'd stepped through to the in-between.

As I will it, the pact is sealed.

Light and magic exploded from the hammer, sending an intense shockwave outward, dropping everyone to their knees. The power from the hammer settled over her like a thick blanket. It raced up her arms and down the rest of her body, the marks on her skin glowing and pulsing in time with her heartbeat and the drums.

In the distance, she heard other instruments. A flute and a stringed instrument of some sort played an accompaniment to the drums. The melody was strangely familiar. She gasped as realization slammed into her. It was the same song from the music box.

The strong scent of dust, rock, and earth filled her nostrils. This magic was as hard and unyielding as the strongest of metals. It was rough, like uncut stone. It held similarities to the magic of the Fae, but it was coarser somehow.

Pain lanced into her skin from the hammer's magic, and she cried out. It was even worse than when she'd accepted the chalice's power. In addition to the hammer's magic, the corruption slithered through and embedded itself into the marks on her skin. Months of pain she'd endured, accepting the Elder's etchings of power, became new once again. The corruption burned like an abrasive salt scoring each injury. Tears sprung to her eyes, and she gritted her teeth, trying to breathe through the worst of it.

"I accept this," she whispered, squeezing her eyes shut. "I accept all of this."

Dark spots danced in her vision, the world going hazy. A tight band wrapped around her chest, reminiscent of how she'd felt when the iron had tried to steal her magic. That was it. If the iron could consume her magic, it could also feed upon the corruption. Sabine turned her focus inward, pushing the corruption to the surface of her skin and making it an easier target for the iron to embrace.

She sent her awareness outward, reaching through the confines of the dwarven city and beyond. She called to all the corrupted magic Raniel had unleashed. It immediately responded, recognizing her familiarity from the power she'd already accepted.

It came in a rush, and her body jerked when it slammed into her. It was too much, the poison threatening to destroy her from within.

Sabine mentally reached for Malek and found him almost instantly. His mind touched hers, and a moment later, he was there. His arms slid around her waist, pulling her against him while his power surrounded her in a protective cocoon. She opened her eyes and met his worried gaze.

"The dragonfire," she urged, curling her fingers into his shirt. "Now, Malek. Hurry!"

He lowered his head and pressed his lips against hers, breathing the dragonfire into her once again. She welcomed it and him, allowing his heated magic to fill her and burn away all traces of the iron. When it was finally gone and he broke their kiss, she slumped against him, her energy spent.

Malek ran a hand against her hair, holding her tightly. He pressed a kiss on her temple and murmured, "Are you all right?"

She nodded, unable to form words just yet.

Rika gasped and said, "My wings are gone! You got rid of them!"

Blossom grinned and landed on Sabine's lap. "You did it, Sabine! The goddess said the corruption is gone. Everything's back to normal."

Sabine glanced at her wrist at the new mark that had formed. An image of a hammer had formed beside the chalice and the pearl—three different sets of power, two of which had never been held by a Fae. She lifted her head, hearing something like music. She listened closely, hearing the song of the stone throughout the mountain. It was beautiful yet foreign and alien.

Everything was different. Her vision was sharper, and she

could see more nuances to the décor and artistry crafted by the dwarves. It was almost as though she'd been blind for her entire life up until that moment. A whole new world had opened up for her.

Blueboy, the cave troll who had befriended Blossom, peeked around the corner at Sabine. "You can hear us now?"

Sabine smiled and then nodded. "Yes, I can hear you."

The cave troll slowly approached her, a third lid sliding over his eyes as he blinked up at her. He held out a spindly arm and brushed against her skin, his touch featherlight. He gave her a shy smile and said, "We will serve you well, Queen Sabin'theoria. You are the first true queen we've had in thousands of years. We will punish the one who helped cause you injury and ensure such a thing never comes to pass again."

Overcome with emotion, Sabine watched as he crept backward and disappeared around the corner. She could feel them in the same way she sensed Blossom.

Malek cupped her face, searching her expression. "Sweetheart? Are you all right?"

Sabine nodded. "I'm better than all right. It's going to take some time to adjust to these new abilities, but I believe the iron is completely gone."

"It bound itself to the corruption, didn't it?" Malek asked and stood.

"Yes," Sabine said, allowing him to help her to her feet. "I believe it's why the goddess thought you could help me. She knew it would make the traces of iron large enough for you to eradicate completely."

"I still think you should cut off that damn mark," Bane muttered.

Sabine made a noncommittal noise. Part of her was tempted, but this new power was a gift of sorts. She had the feeling she'd need every ounce of strength in the days to come.

Astrid and Hargrim were both staring at her in shock and wonder. Many other dwarves had recovered from the magical explosion and were standing just outside the Faerie alcove.

Sabine looked upward at the hole Malek had ripped in the side of the mountain. Lifting her hands, she allowed the power of the land and stone to fill her. The ground shook, and Sabine continued to raise her hands upward as she sealed the wall of the council chamber shut once more. A loud cheer went up, the dwarves celebrating the repair of their home.

Sabine turned to face them and said loudly, "The corruption is gone, and Razadon is once more entrusted to the dwarves for its safekeeping. Under the terms of the treaty, each one of you has a duty and a responsibility to ensure the abilities gifted to your people are protected and safeguarded."

She glanced at Malek and took his hand before facing the crowd again. "Our differences make us stronger than if we stand alone. I've chosen to surround myself with individuals who all work together to accomplish their goals. The dragon at my side was once a hated enemy, but he's now one of my most trusted friends and allies." She gestured toward Rika. "Rika is a human seer. Her kind were once considered enemies of the Fae, but she was among the first to try to warn me of the assassination attempt."

She turned toward Bane and smiled at her demon protector. "Bane'umbra is a fierce warrior, and he stood by my side today and protected me when it was my duty to protect him. Demon or not, I trust him with my life and value him deeply as a friend."

Sabine's gaze fell on Dagmar, whose green eyes were shining with emotion. "Dagmar Frostfall is one of you, yet she chose to stand by my side even at great risk to herself.

She is proof of the remarkable valor and heroism of the dwarves, and I name her friend and ally."

Dagmar's face turned bright red, and the crowd cheered loudly. Sabine swallowed and turned to face Blossom who was sitting on Rika's shoulder. "The most valiant of all were the smallest warriors—one in particular—and her companions, the cave trolls. Blossom, you were willing to sacrifice your life to save me. What reward can I offer you, my dearest friend?"

Blossom's eyes widened, and she lifted herself into the air. "Oooh! I know! Mushrooms!"

Hargrim let out a booming laugh. "Aye. I'll make sure a case is delivered to the Faerie embassy within the hour."

Sabine smiled. "Will that work for you, Blossom?"

Blossom nodded, a wide grin on her face. "Absolutely! But there's one important question I want to ask Malek."

Malek frowned, his gaze wary. "What is it?"

Blossom gave him a mischievous smile. She landed on his shoulder and whispered, "What did that dwarf taste like when you decided to turn him into a snack?"

Malek grimaced. "Some things are better left unsaid."

"Drat," Blossom said, crossing her arms over her chest in a pout. "Hey, Sabine? Next time I save your life, can you turn me into a dragon? I want to eat a dwarf."

Sabine blew out a breath. "Come on. I think it's time we headed back to the embassy. I don't know about anyone else, but I could use a bath and strong drink."

Malek lifted her hand and brushed a soft kiss on the back of it. "I'd follow you to the ends of the world and back."

Sabine smiled up at him. "I'd do the same for you, Malek Rish'dan. In some ways, I already have."

Chapter Twenty-Three

Malek pulled a blanket over Sabine and reached down to brush her hair away from her face. When he thought about how close he'd come to losing her today, another wave of panic rushed through him. He trailed the backs of his fingers along her cheek, marveling at the softness of her skin. She murmured something unintelligible and burrowed deeper under the blanket.

He needed to tell her everything about the portal and soon. Esme and Levin's departure had bought him a brief reprieve, but he needed to find the right time and circumstances to share his intentions. If he could convince Sabine to travel to the Sky Cities with him, she could see for herself how his people had been affected. Sabine had a compassionate heart, and Malek doubted she'd allow anyone to suffer once she learned the truth.

Malek reluctantly stepped away from the woman he loved, knowing she needed rest to fully regain her strength. He headed out of the bedroom, closing the door softly behind him.

He moved down the hall and stopped outside Rika's door,

but no sound reached his ears. The young seer had gone to bed a short time earlier, and thankfully, her dreams were so far undisturbed. Her help earlier had been invaluable, and Malek owed her a debt he could never repay. Without her warning, the assassin's aim would have been true.

He continued walking down the hall and into the main seating area. Bane didn't look up from the large power crystal he was studying, but the rigidity in his shoulders indicated he was aware of Malek's presence.

"She's asleep?"

"Yes," Malek said, walking to the table and pouring himself an ale from the cask the dwarves had delivered. "What did you want to discuss with me?"

Bane turned around, the light from the crystalline lanterns almost seeming to avoid touching his midnight skin. "I once believed your presence endangered Sabine. You've proven yourself several times. You protected her when I wasn't able to, and for that, it would seem I'm indebted to you."

Malek didn't bother masking his surprise. "Does this mean you actually trust me?"

"To a point," Bane admitted, crossing his arms over his chest. "Enough to warn you about what needs to be done."

Malek frowned and took a sip. "I'm listening."

"I'm sure Sabine has shared her intentions to travel through the tunnels beneath Razadon to reach the underworld. She's concerned about Dax, but more importantly, she needs additional allies to secure her position. Now that Sabine's announced her claim to the Unseelie throne, she has only three lunar cycles to perform the ritual there."

"I've suggested she wait a few weeks," Malek said, taking another drink. Sabine was safe enough in Razadon for the time being, and the additional time would give her a chance to fully recover from everything that had happened.

"She can't afford to wait," Bane said, his jaw hard. "I recognized the necklace she was wearing during the council meeting. She believes it was a gift from my father."

Malek lowered his glass. "That's what the note suggested. You're saying it wasn't?"

"Demons don't give altruistic gifts," Bane said in disgust. "Such a concept is for sentimental fools, a fact Sabine would do well to remember. Those stones are among the rarest in the world, forged in lava and cooled in the ancient springs below the world. He's planning something, and Sabine is ill prepared to handle his treachery."

Malek frowned. "All the more reason she should wait."

Bane scowled. "Not when dealing with Kal'thorz. The more time she gives him to plot, the less likely she'll be able to escape whatever he's planning. We must leave as soon as possible, and you must not leave her side while we're there."

"What aren't you telling me?" Malek asked, abandoning his ale.

Bane pushed away from the table to pace. "I may be blood-bonded to Sabine's service, but my father shares my blood in ways you cannot understand. Neither Dax nor myself ever intended to return to the underworld until Sabine was powerful enough to withstand his threat." He paused, turning to pin Malek with his amber gaze. "In the underworld, my father is Lord of Darkness. *Everyone* who enters is subject to his will, including me. Sabine will be the one exception, and she won't have any allies there, except for you, a seer with little control over her abilities, and a pixie likely to get eaten within the first five minutes."

"You won't be able to protect any of them," Malek guessed aloud, his misgivings growing. Both he and Sabine had wrongly assumed Bane would be able to help her navigate whatever they faced in the underworld.

"Not completely." Bane's jaw hardened, and he stared at

the wall. "I don't know what we'll face once we're in his dominion. If we had any other option, I would take it. Given everything I know about my father, we need to head there immediately and leave just as fast. He will likely take great pains to keep Sabine there as long as possible."

"When we arrived here, one of the dwarves mentioned Dax was in trouble. Do you know what that's about?"

Bane didn't answer right away. "I cannot say for certain, but I suspect Kal'thorz learned about Dax's ties to Sabine and her… affection for my brother. He's likely spent the last several months interrogating Dax to learn everything possible about Sabine."

Malek narrowed his eyes. "To what end?"

Bane snorted. "An untried, young, and powerful Faerie queen has just inherited the Unseelie throne. She would be a prize for anyone to claim, but especially for a demon king who needs an agent of the light to bring him and his people out of the underworld."

A raging fury brewed within Malek. His hands curled into fists, and his draconic power flared to the surface. "Over my dead body."

"It may come to that," Bane replied without a trace of humor. "Regardless of my issues with you or the effect you've had on Sabine's magic, you've been good for her. You've protected her when neither Dax nor myself were able to do the same."

"Then let's make sure she continues to stay protected." Malek walked to the desk and grabbed a stack of parchment Dagmar had been using to make notes on dwarven politics. "Grab yourself a drink. We have a lot of our own plans to make and only a short time to do it."

Bane's lips curved upward, and he inclined his head. "I was hoping you'd say that."

ABOUT THE AUTHOR

Jamie A. Waters is an award-winning writer of science fiction and fantasy romance. Her first novel, Beneath the Fallen City, was a winner of the Readers' Favorite Award in Science Fiction/Fantasy Romance and the CIPA EVVY Award in Science Fiction.

Jamie currently resides in Florida with a murder of crows in her backyard and two neurotic dogs who enjoy stealing socks. When she's not pursuing her passion of writing, she's usually trying to learn new and interesting random things (like how to pick locks or use the self-cleaning feature of the oven without setting off the fire alarm). In her downtime, she enjoys reading, playing computer games, painting, or acting as a referee between the dragons and fairies currently at war inside the closet. Learn more about her at: jamieawaters.com.

Printed in Great Britain
by Amazon